THE MAN WHO CRIED

Catherine Cookson

CORGI BOOKS

THE MAN WHO CRIED
A CORGI BOOK : 0 552 14831 8

Originally published in Great Britain by
William Heinemann Ltd

PRINTING HISTORY
Heinemann edition published 1979
Corgi edition published 1980

13 15 17 19 20 18 16 14

This book is set in 11/13pt Sabon by
Phoenix Typeseting, Ilkley, West Yokshire.

Corgi Books are published by Transworld Publishers
61–63 Uxbridge Road, London W5 5SA,
a division of The Random House Group Ltd,
in Australia by Random House Australia (Pty) Ltd,
20 Alfred Street, Milsons Point, Sydney, NSW 2061, Australia,
in New Zealand by Random House New Zealand Ltd,
18 Poland Road, Glenfield, Auckland 10, New Zealand
and in South Africa by Random House (Pty) Ltd,
Endulini, 5a Jubilee Road, Parktown 2193, South Africa.

The Random House Group Limited supports The Forest Stewardship
Council® (FSC®), the leading international forest-certification organisation.
Our books carrying the FSC label are printed on FSC®-certified paper.
FSC is the only forest-certification scheme supported by the leading
environmental organisations, including Greenpeace. Our
paper procurement policy can be found at
www.randomhouse.co.uk/environment

Printed and bound in Great Britain by Clays Ltd, St Ives plc

Contents

The man who cried

I stood and watched the man who cried,
His face awash, his mouth wide,
His head beating against the tree,
His shoulders heaving like hills set free
From the body of the earth;
And I felt his anguish take birth in my being,
And there I knew it would abide
And eat into my days
And guide my ways
And be the judge of my mortal sins.
My father's tears were a key
Which opened the world to me,
Its ecstasy, and its misery.

C.C.

PART ONE

The Journey 1931

1

'If you go to that funeral you won't live long to dwell on your sorrow, I promise you that. They haven't got wind as to the man yet, but by God! they will do if you show your face at that funeral. And when those men of Hastings Old Town finish with you, you won't have much face left to speak of, I know that.'

Across the small space of the cottage, Abel Mason stared at his wife. The tanned skin of his face looked taut as if it had been set in glue; the wide, thin lips lay one on top of the other, not pressed tight, just resting together as if under the influence of gentle sleep. It was only the eyes that showed any sign of awareness and their expression made up in full for the immobility of the face. But what that expression was it was hard to define, no one emotion could describe it, for the brown depths of his eyes burnt not only loathing, but the contradictory emotion of pity.

It was this last that came through to his wife, and it now brought her screaming, 'You dirty, whoring sod you!' and on the last word she picked up a jug of milk from the table and threw it at him.

The contact of the jug against his forehead and

the milk spraying over his mop of fair hair, down his face, and under the collarless shirt on to his chest, brought him springing forward, his fist upraised, only to bring it down on to the corner of the table with a bang as a falsetto voice cried from the corner of the room, 'Dad! Oh Dad!'

His fist still tight on the table, he bent his body over it, and the milk that dropped on to it now was tinted pink.

It was some seconds before he straightened his back; but with his head still bent he made for the stairs at the far end of the room which rose steeply, almost like a ladder, to the floor above.

His wife watched him until his legs disappeared from view; then, her face working as if with a tic, she went into the scullery and returned with a dish-cloth, and with great wide sweeps of her arm she dragged the cloth from one end of the wooden table to the other. When she came to the corner where the milk was stained with blood she went at it madly as if by obliterating the stain she would wipe out the source from where it came.

Thrusting her hand towards her seven-year-old son, she ordered, 'Pick those bits up!' and the boy, after a moment's hesitation, bent down and gathered up the pieces of broken crockery, and as he left the room with them and went through the scullery towards the back door, his mother came behind him and her fingers prodded his shoulder giving emphasis to each word as she said, 'If he thinks he's gettin' out of this house the day he's got another think comin' to him.' Then gripping the boy's collar and swinging him round towards her, she bent down until her face was on a level with his and, her eyes like circles of grey steel, she glared at him as she said, 'Look, boy; you tell me what you know 'cos if you don't I'll make it worse for him. He's got you on his side, he's turned you agen me, but afore you're much older you'll know which side your bread's buttered. Where did he meet her? Tell me that. Tell me!' She now shook him and when the pieces of broken jug fell from his hands her own hand came out and caught him a resounding slap across the ear; and now she cried at him, 'Tell him I hit you again. Aye, go on, when he comes down, tell him I hit you again.'

As he ran for the door, his hand pressed tight over his ear, he moaned aloud because of the pain which was like a needle going through the centre of his head into the back of his nose and down into his throat, making it impossible for him to swallow.

Outside he ran through the hens that were scratching in the yard and round by the little pond where the two families of ducks were busy washing themselves, and so down to the copse that led him into the woods. Here, sitting on the ground, he rocked himself as he held his head.

When the pain subsided he leant back against the bole of a sappling and he muttered half aloud, 'I'm glad me dad didn't see her do it,' and there was that element of pity for her in his thinking too.

His dad had warned her if she just once again boxed his ears he would do the same to her, and he had. It was the first time he had lifted his hand to her, and he had knocked her flying into the corner where she had lain holding her head very like he himself did every time she hit him, which was always after there had been a row.

Inside he felt sad. The feeling went to such a depth that he imagined it must encompass the whole world, his known world where it stretched from Rye, which lay along the coast to the left beyond Winchelsea, to the right to Fairlight and the coves and glens, right to Hastings.

It was to the coves and the glens that his mind turned now and he doubted if his father would ever take him that way again.

When had he first taken him into Fairlight Glen? Oh, it was a long, long time ago. Had he been four or five? He didn't know, only that it was a long time ago. But he could remember the day distinctly when he first met Mrs Alice in Ecclesbourne Glen.

He always thought of her as Mrs Alice, not Mrs Lovina, because his father called her Alice. Of course, he couldn't and so he called her Mrs Alice. She used to laugh when he said Mrs Alice. She had a lovely laugh; it made you smile, then spread your mouth and laugh with her.

It was on a Sunday his father first spoke to her. There were lots of other people walking about the glen that day because it was fine and the sun was warm. People were picnicking and children were jumping among the rocks leading to the sea. His father had told him to take his shoes and socks off and to go and play with the other children. And he had done so. But every now and again he had stopped and looked up towards where his father sat on a dry rock talking to . . . the lady. Yet he had known from the first that she wasn't a real lady, not like the ones who lived in Winchelsea, particularly the one who had a long drive to her house and for whom his father had worked since coming back from the war . . . Well, not really the war . . . There was a pocket of his mind that held something shameful concerning his father and the war.

No, Mrs Alice wasn't a lady, in fact she was like his mother in that she talked like her, using the same words, except that her voice wasn't harsh and bawling. When was it he had begun to wish that Mrs Alice was his mother? That was a long, long time ago too, weeks, months.

The following Sunday, too, they had gone to the glen, even though the weather had changed and there was drizzly rain. And Mrs Alice was there. But on that day they all three sat under the cliffs and his father broke a bar of Fry's chocolate, and they all had a piece; he had always associated Fry's chocolate with the glen after that.

It was winter before he again accompanied his father to the glen. On that particular day his mother had demanded to know where his father was going and when he said, 'For a walk,' she had wanted to know why he had taken to going alone and not taking him along. On that day his father had said, 'Get your coat on; wrap up well.'

They had been gone from the house more than five minutes when his father whispered, 'Don't look back, your mother's behind. Don't look back.' And on that day his father took a different direction and they came out on the road that led to Fairlight church, where his father, having hoisted him up on top of a high wall, had himself leant against the wall and lit a cigarette, which he puffed at slowly, not looking to right or left. They seemed to have stayed there for an eternity, until quite suddenly his father lifted him from the wall, saying, 'Come on,' and he had run him through fields, over stiles and, for some distance, right along the cliff top.

When at last, panting and puffing, they came to the glen it was raining heavily and a wind was blowing. But there was Mrs Alice waiting in the shelter of some trees, and before they reached her his father let go of his hand and ran towards her, then put his arms about her. It seemed on that day his father forgot all about him.

After a while his father had taken his hand again and the three of them walked on, up through the trees to a jutting rock, and his father, pushing him round into the shelter of one side, said, 'Sit there a minute, Dickie, just a minute. I'll . . . I'll be around the corner here.'

What was a minute? Was it a short time or a long time? He had felt very alone, quite lost sitting there waiting a minute. He became frightened thinking his father had gone off and left him as he often threatened to do to his mother when there were rows in the house, and so he had run out of the shelter and into the wind and as he rounded the rock he stopped suddenly. His father was kneeling on the ground; and Mrs Alice was kneeling too; and his father was holding Mrs Alice's face between his hands and he was saying to her, 'Don't say that. Don't say that. You're the best thing that's happened to me in my life. You're the only good thing I've ever known. Look; bring Florrie, and I'll bring Dickie, and we'll go off away from this cursed place, because for all its beauty the whole area has always been a cursed place to me. Will you? Will you, Alice?'

He watched Mrs Alice stare into his father's face and he was always to remember the tone of her voice as she said, 'Oh, Abel! Abel! if only I could . . . Oh, Abel, if only I could.'

'But you can,' his father said; 'you've only got to make up your mind. Just walk out.'

'You don't know Florrie. She's twelve, and all she thinks about, all she talks about, is her dad. And he, well, as he said, if I ever left him or brought shame on him in any way he would do for me. If it took him his lifetime, he'd do for me.'

'That's just talk, big talk. Sailors always come out with the same jargon. We could be across the country before he gets home. And then I've been thinking, there's Canada. The . . . the world is open to us, Alice . . . Oh, Alice, say you will. We've both had enough of hell to deserve a glimpse of heaven. Say you will . . . Say you will.'

'The boy!' She had turned her head to the side, and his father put out his hand and beckoned him forward, and he never moved from his knees when he put his arm around his shoulders and said, 'The boy's for us. He's been through it too, he's been made older than his years. His life's a misery. He's torn between the two of us, but yet he's for me, aren't you?' His father pressed him tight against his side and he looked up at him and moved his head once and his father said, 'There. There now, Alice.'

He watched Mrs Alice's face. She was gupping in her throat, the rain dripping down from the brim of her hat on to their joined hands, and it seemed another eternity before she said, 'Yes, yes, Abel, I'll do it . . .'

When had that happened? It seemed another long, long time ago, and yet it was only two weeks or perhaps three. He couldn't pin-point the time but he remembered his father saying, 'We'll make it next Sunday. I'll walk out, him with me, just as if it was our usual stroll; and you do the same. Oh, Alice! Alice! . . .'

He started, his back springing from the tree as he heard his mother's voice yelling again. At the same time there came to him deep thuds as if someone was battering a door down, and he rose quickly to his feet and threaded his way through the copse until he came in sight of the cottage; and there was his mother standing in the open yard that gave on to the field, and she was crying, 'I said you're not goin', and you're not goin'. She'll be where she should have been his long while, well under the clay, afore I let you out of there.'

When the thuds came again he knew it was his father's boot kicking at the lock.

Of a sudden the thudding stopped and there came a silence all around him. He could hear the birds singing, a wood pigeon coo-cooed above his head; a cheeky rabbit scurried across the opening between the copse and the duck-pond. He heard in the distance the clear sound of a train whistle, which clearness his father always said forecast bad weather. He pictured the train choo . . . chooing from Hastings, through Ore on to Doleham Halt, and all the way to Rye.

His mind was jerked from thoughts of the train by the sound of breaking glass. There was a great crash at first then tinkling sounds like notes being struck on a piano.

When he saw his father come head first through the kitchen window and drop on to his hands on the flags that surrounded the cottage he wondered why he hadn't just opened the window instead of smashing it. Then he remembered the tapping sound he had heard earlier on like a woodpecker on a tree bole. His mother must have nailed up the window.

He held his breath as he watched his father dusting himself down, with his mother standing like a ramrod not three yards from him. He saw his father turn his back on her and reach back through the broken pane. When he withdrew his hand he was holding his trilby in it.

He watched him bang it twice against his coat sleeve, then press the dent further into the crown, put it on and pull the peak down over his brow before slowly walking away. But he hadn't reached the bridle path before his mother was screaming again.

'You're not a man, you're spineless! A conchie! A conchie! Objectin' 'cos of your principles? Bloody liar! Objectin' 'cos you were a stinkin' coward. Decent lads bein' killed, slaughtered while you hoed tatties. You spineless, spunkless nowt you!'

Dick put his hands tightly over his ears, but his eyes remained fixed on his father as he watched him getting smaller and smaller the further he went along the path, until he looked minute as he jumped the stile; and then he was gone.

And now the world was empty, terrifyingly empty. What if he never came back? What if he went to Mrs Alice's funeral and then kept walking on right back to that far place called the North? The place he was always talking about, the place where he had been born, the place where people were kind and open-handed and didn't fight all the livelong day! . . . But his mother was from there too and she fought all the livelong day.

He would die if his dad didn't come back . . . No, he wouldn't; he would set out and look for him, and he'd walk and walk until he found him . . .

He sat down where he was on the dried leaves and from the distance he watched his mother sweep up the broken glass, then trim the broken remnants from the window sash. She did this with the hammer, bashing at the framework as if she'd knock it out. Every now and again she would stop and look about her and say something out loud.

When he first started school he used to grumble to himself about the long walk over the fields to the main road where he caught the bus, but whenever his mother yelled he was glad they lived so far away from everybody for otherwise he knew the boys at school would have taunted him, as they did Jackie Benton because his father was in prison for stealing.

After what seemed almost a whole day he rose from the ground and began to walk back through the copse and into the hazel wood. His father called it the dirty wood because the trees were thin and jammed together. If the place was his, he'd said, he'd have all these trees down and decent ones planted. But there were decent ones in the big wood which was separated from the hazelnut grove by a right of way that led from well inland through two farms until it came out on the cliff top.

He stood on the path and looked upwards. The sun was directly overhead, which meant that his father had been gone over two hours. And yet he had imagined it to be much longer. It would be dinner time, but he didn't feel hungry and he should do because he hadn't eaten any breakfast. Twice he had heard his mother calling him but he had taken no notice. He wasn't going to go back into the house until his father returned; that's if he returned, for although he had gone to the main road to catch the bus into Hastings he had the feeling that he wouldn't come back that way but would return through the glens, and if he did, this would be the path along which he would come from the top of the cliffs.

He didn't know how long he wandered about, sat, lay on the grass both on his back and his face, he was only aware that he was tired of waiting; and he was frightened because he knew he couldn't follow his father as he didn't know which way he had gone; and he was frightened too because he must now return home to his mother and her yelling and her talking at him, her face close to his, her mouth opening and shutting and her grey-coated tongue wobbling about in it, and her hand coming across his ear, and the pain going through his nose and into his throat.

He had actually turned towards home when he saw away along at the far end of the path, where it turned round Farmer Wilkie's yard, the figure of a man, but it was so far away that at first he couldn't make out whether or not it was his father. It might be just one of those hikers, or a man on the road begging. There were lots of men on the road begging, but not many came this way, it was too far off the beaten track.

His heart leapt when he recognised his father while still some long way off. He was walking with his head down. Slowly now he went towards him, but stopped of a sudden when he saw him turn abruptly off the path and run into the wood. He stood still, his head moving in perplexity. Why had he gone into the wood like that? Did he want to go somewhere, the lavatory? Well he wouldn't have run like that, would he?

Jumping a narrow ditch, he, too, went into the wood. The trees were large here, oak and beech, but there was a lot of scrub that had been allowed to grow in between them, mostly brambles and young struggling oaks that had no hope of reaching maturity.

He made his way in the direction his father had taken and after a while came on him; but he heard him before he saw him and the sound brought his eyes wide, his lips apart and his fingers pressing on them. Carefully he moved in the direction from which the sound was coming, and then he saw him. He had his arms halfway around the bole of an oak tree and he was beating his head against the trunk while he cried aloud.

The sight and sound was something so painful it was not to be borne; he wanted to turn and run from it but all he could do was bow his head on his chest and stand as if he, like the saplings, had taken root in the earth.

His father was moaning now, saying over and over again, 'Oh, Alice! Alice! . . . Oh, Alice! Alice!'

From beneath his lowered lids he watched his father cling helplessly to the tree now as if he were drunk, then slowly turn around and lean his back against it. The bark of the tree had opened the small cut the jug had made above his eyebrow and the blood was trickling over his eye and down his cheek, but he made no attempt to wipe it away; he just stood there, his shoulders against the tree, his head moving slowly from side to side, his features no longer expressionless but contorted and so twisted that he appeared at this moment like a very old man.

Slowly lifting each foot well from the ground, he walked towards his father – he did not want to startle him – but when he reached his side, his father looked at him with no surprise. It was as if he expected him to be there and now he groaned, 'Oh, Dickie! Dickie!' then dropping on to the ground, he put his arms around him; and the boy hugged his face to his own, and as his father's tears and blood spread over him there opened in him an awareness of anguish and compassion that should not have been tapped until he had tasted wonder and joy, the natural ingredients of childhood and youth.

'Oh, Dad! Dad!'

'It's all right, boy. It's all right. Here, dry your face.'

Abel used his handkerchief to staunch the blood, and asked in a broken voice, 'Been waiting long?'

'Yes, Dad; all the time.'

Abel nodded slowly; then taking the boy's hand, he rose to his feet and stood looking about him for a moment before he spoke again; and then it was not to his son but more to himself that he said, 'It's over, finished. Come.'

Dick didn't speak, not even to ask one question, on the journey back to the house. He knew that something was going to happen, that his father was going to make something happen, and from his silence he knew it would be something big.

The kitchen door was open. Abel pushed the boy before him and into the room where his wife was sitting at the far end of the bare table. It was as if he had left her presence only two minutes earlier for she started immediately: 'So you went then? Lot of good I hope it did you. You should be ashamed of yourself. If I was to tell Lady Parker the truth you'd be out of a job tomorrow, she would throw you out on your neck.' She paused; then her eyes narrowed before she shouted on a laugh. 'My God! you've been cryin'.'

As if to protect him, Dick pushed his hand back until it touched the front of his father's thigh and he felt a tremor running through the leg as his mother added now in deep bitterness, 'You wouldn't shed tears over me but over that whore . . .'

'Shut your mouth!'

'What did you say?' She was on her feet.

'I said shut your mouth. If you don't I'll shut it for you.'

'You and who else? I told you what would happen if you ever attempted to lift your hand to me again.'

'Perhaps if I lift my hand to you this time, Lena, it'll be final. I was a conscientious objector in the war, I went to prison because I didn't believe in killing, but now I've changed me mind, in fact I changed it some time ago.'

During the silence that followed Dick saw fear on his mother's face for the first time. It caused her to move back a step until she was leaning against the small sideboard, and when his father moved forward one step he grabbed hold of his hand and pressed his nails into his palm. The action seemed to check his father's movement but his voice went on, and the words coming slow and flat were more frightening than if he too had shouted.

'You know how he killed her, but did you know he did it slowly? He must have thought it all out for he peppered her feet first with shot, and when her brother from next door tried to get in he found the whole place barred. The police even couldn't get in, for between times he had the gun levelled at them, and he told them what he was going to do to her bit by bit. He next shot her in the stomach.' There was a break in Abel's voice now, and his lower lip trembled before he went on, 'I don't know whether she was dead or alive when he emptied the gun into her face. And he did all that, Lena, because of you. Do you realise that? Because of you.' There was a long pause, so quiet that their breathing could be heard; and then he said. 'You were very clever, very thorough, you didn't send your letters to the house, you sent them to the shipping company. You did your work well. The only thing you didn't do was to mention my name. Why? Because if you had, as you said, those blokes down in the Old Town would have finished me off, an' you didn't want that, did you? No, you wanted to blackmail me for the rest of me life. Well, it's not going to work, Lena. No, it's not going to work. And don't worry' – he put out his hand palm upwards towards her – 'I don't intend to murder you; what I intend to do you'll see in a minute.'

At this he turned about and pushed Dick before him towards the stairs, and when they were on the landing he said hastily, 'Get your things together, boots, clothes. Roll them up as tight as you can into a bundle.' Then going into the bedroom he took down from a peg in the makeshift wardrobe his working clothes, then from a drawer he took underwear and socks and two working shirts, and from under the bed he pulled out a rucksack, and after stuffing the clothes into it he gripped it by the straps and went out on to the landing and into the tiny boxroom that served as a bedroom for his son, and without a word he grabbed up the two sets of underclothes, the two pullovers, socks and shirts that were in neat array on the bed and, stuffing them unceremoniously into the top of the rucksack, he said harshly now, 'Don't waste time, come on.'

Dick paused and looked towards the narrow window-sill on which was standing an array of clay birds and animals. Swiftly now his hand went out and grabbed up two ducks, one which was standing on one leg while its other webbed foot scratched its wing, and the second one a smaller model of the same bird, its legs out behind it, its neck craned forward, caught for ever as it would appear while swimming. As he stuffed these one into each pocket of his breeches his father said nothing, but he whipped from the back of the door a small topcoat. Then they were going downstairs again.

'What you up to? What do you think you're up to? You're not goin' anywhere, an' you're not takin' him with you.'

'No? And who's gona stop me?'

'I'll have the polis on you.'

'You do that.'

'You can't leave me, not out here on me own.' She was moving sideways towards the door now, blocking his way. 'You know I can't work.'

'You can't work because you're lazy.'

'I'm not lazy. Look how clean I keep this place.'

'A child of five could do the work of this place in half an hour. Lady Parker's been wanting help in the house for years. The kitchen maid's post is open, she'll take you on. When you go after the job tell her I've left; he owes me three days' pay.'

'Damn and blast you! I'll be no kitchen maid.'

'Then you'll have to starve.'

'I won't starve. By God! I won't starve. You're me husband, you've got to support me.'

'I've done supporting you.' His voice was coming from the scullery now amidst the rattle of pans.

'I'll get you for abducting him.'

'I can counter that with the fact that I'm savin' him from being knocked stone deaf by you. You've never wanted him and you've showed it from the day he was born.'

He was in the kitchen again staring at her where she was standing in the doorway, and as he looked at her he was seeing her as she had looked ten years ago when at twenty-four she had appeared years younger. She had always managed to look pathetic.

As a boy he had warned himself not to be taken in by his overwhelming feeling of compassion. He had warned himself that compassion was only safe to be bestowed on animals; yet the devious Lena had recognised his weakness and used it. By God! how she had used it. She had aligned herself with his principles of nonaggression, she had made him feel the big man, the wise man. His disillusion had come so quickly it had been sickening, so much so that for a time he had lost his self-respect and seen himself as a big, gullible fool. Even now the cock in the yard was likely to find itself knocked flying when in the process of treading the hens. All she ever wanted from life was ease, someone to work for her; respectability, oh yes, the respectability of being called missis, this desire having grown in her as the result of her having been born on the wrong side of the blanket.

And because of her birth and her early environment, at the beginning he had made allowances for her peculiarities, but no amount of talking or reasoning could get it into her head that the sex act was anything but dirty. How he had ever managed to give her a child he didn't know.

'Get out of me way!'

'I'll follow you. I'll find you. I know where you're goin'; you're heading North, back to the scum there.'

'That's the last place I'll go. Try Canada or Australia or America . . . Out of me way!'

When she didn't move his hand came out like an uncoiling whip and, catching her round the neck, flung her to the side, where she fell into a heap on the floor.

He stood looking at her for a moment; and now his voice trembling, he said with deep bitterness, 'When you're lying alone up there at nights think of what it would be like to have your body sprayed with buckshot until you died, just think on't and know that it wasn't him who did it, but you. You killed them both . . .'

His father had already lifted him over the stile when they heard her voice again and Dick knew that if they were to continue straight on towards the road she would catch up with them. The same thought must have been in his father's mind because, gripping his hand now, he pulled him to the right and so across a stubbled field, then into the hazel wood and on into the big wood; but not straight through it. Twisting and turning and out of breath, they came to a by-road, and here Abel paused a moment and, sitting down on the grass verge, he said, 'I'll have to spread this load out.'

When he opened his rucksack the boy saw the pan and kettle and the two tin mugs that had been kept under the sink in the scullery. Presently his father paused in his arranging and looked at him and asked quietly, 'You wanted to come, didn't you?'

'Oh, yes, Dad, yes. Oh yes, I want to be with you.'

'Good.' He nodded at him, then added, 'I'll get you a smaller rucksack somewhere along the road and then we'll be fitted up for tramping, eh?'

'Yes, Dad . . . Where we goin', Dad?'

Abel rose to his feet, swung the rucksack up and thrust his arms into the straps before saying, 'At the present minute you know as much as I do about that, lad, but wherever we're going we'll arrive safe, you'll see.'

2

Four days later they took the ferry from Gravesend to Tilbury. They had walked through Sussex into Kent and were now about to enter Essex. Dick was so fascinated by the docks, the ships, the cranes, that momentarily he forgot about his skinned heels, his chaffed toes, and his tired legs.

For three nights they had slept out. It was June and the weather was warm. His father had told him last night they were, after all, going to make for the North because *she* wouldn't believe they would go there now. But they weren't going too far north, not to the Tyne, which was a river and the place where his grandfather had been born. Somewhere in the country, his father had said, where they'd find a farm. He would like that wouldn't he? He had said he would.

But he hoped it wasn't a long way to walk because his feet were so sore. He hadn't told his father about the blisters, not the first day, because he was afraid that if he did they might go back. Then again, he realised that was silly, his father would never go back.

After getting off the ferry, Tilbury proved disappointing, flat, dirty. There were a few shops.

They went into a café and had a cup of tea and Abel bought some food, sausages, bacon, lard, potatoes, sugar, tea, and a big loaf of bread. Once clear of the town, Abel picked a place where he could make a fire and brew up, and then fry sausages and bacon. They ate their fill. And when the meal was finished and the utensils had been cleaned with newspaper and stowed away in the rucksacks Abel sat down on the grass and, taking his son's hands in his, he said, 'We've crossed the river, we're never going back. It's going to be a new life for you and me, Dickie. You understand?'

The boy nodded at him, then asked a question that had been in his mind for the last day or two. 'Will I ever go to school again, Dad?'

'Why, of course you will. Once we get settled you'll go to school, boy; and you'll learn. You'll learn quick; you'll make up for lost time because you've got it up top, not like me, my brains are in my hands.' He unloosened his grasp and looked at his hands, turning them first one way and then another. Then as if to himself, he said, 'I could have done things with them, with training I could, carved things, got somewhere.'

'You make lovely animals, Dad. Look at me ducks.' He now reached over into his rucksack and, unfolding a small cotton vest, he revealed the two ducks lying as if in a nest, and his father, lifting the tiny model of the scratching duck on to his palm, nodded at it as he said. 'It's got life but it's only in clay, ordinary river clay. It was never fired; it's a wonder it's stood up to your handling all this time.'

He smiled at his son, then handed him back the model and, getting to his feet, said, 'Well, let's see this fire is well and truly out, and then on our way again. Your feet feel any better?'

'Yes, Dad, a bit.'

'Don't worry, they'll harden; the more you walk the easier it'll be. And we won't be walking all the time; I'll get work on the way and you'll be able to take it easy.'

'How long will it take us to get there, to the North, Dad?'

'Oh, it all depends on what jobs I get on the way. A month, two; but we'll be settled before the winter sets in, don't worry. Come on.'

As they entered Brentwood it began to drizzle and they took shelter in a church porch. There Abel took out a tattered map and having studied it, looked down at Dick and said, 'We'll make for Cambridge.'

'How far is that, Dad? How many days?' It was important to know the number of days it would take from place to place for then he knew how long his feet would pain.

'Oh, between forty-five and fifty miles. If the weather holds we'll do it in three days or so. But don't worry' – he patted his son's head – 'it'll be all right; I'm going to buy some cotton wool and bandages and when we settle in for the night I'll fix your feet.'

'Will we ever be able to sleep in a boarding-house, like the holidaymakers did in Hastings, Dad?'

Abel's lips moved into a wry smile as he said, 'Not as I stand at present. Once I get fixed up with a job then we'll see. But we've been lucky so far, haven't we?'

'Yes, Dad.'

'Well, let's brave the elements and see if we can be lucky again.'

And they were lucky. Two miles out of Brentwood they came to open pasture land and having espied what looked like an old barn in the corner of a field some distance from the road, Abel made for it. On entering, he found it wasn't as dilapidated as it looked; more than half of it was dry and there was evidence of a fire having been recently lit in one corner.

'Good . . . good. Aren't we lucky? Rake round for some twigs, we'll soon have a fire going and I'll see to your feet.'

The fire going, the tin can of water bubbling on the sticks – he made sure always to carry a bottle of water with him – he was about to unwrap the bacon left over from their breakfast when a shadow appeared in the doorway of the barn and a voice said, 'Don't you know you're on private land?'

Abel rose from his hunkers and faced the squat tweed-coated, brown-breeched man and his voice was civil as he said, 'No, sir. Well, I knew it would belong to somebody, but we're doing no harm.'

'Doing no harm? Tramping my fields, stealing the beet or anything else you can get your hands on!'

Abel's face was grim and his voice equally so as he said, 'I'm not in the habit of stealing, sir.'

'Oh; then you're an exception.' The man stepped further into the barn and, looking towards Dick, said, 'You're on the road with that child?'

There was a pause before Abel replied, 'We're on our way North.'

'Evidently you're on your way somewhere, but I should have thought . . .'

'He's my son and it's my business.'

'Yes, yes, it is your business; and it's my business to see you don't destroy my property, so get out.'

Before his father turned towards the fire, Dick was already packing up their belongings.

A few minutes later they were outside the barn where the man was standing with one hand in his breeches pocket while with the other he was swiping the fairy clocks from the tops of the dandelion stalks.

'I hope you're never in want, sir,' Abel said as he passed the farmer; then glancing down to where the seed heads of the dandelions were spraying into the wind, he added, 'And your weeds grow plentiful.'

The stick stopped flaying and the man, now red in the face, said, 'You'd better get a move on before I put this stick to a different use.'

'Yes . . . well, I'd get rid of that idea, sir.' They stared at each other for a moment before Abel, hitching the pack up on to his back, turned away, pushing Dick before him.

They had almost skirted the field when a voice coming from out of a ditch startled them. 'He havin' a go at you?'

Abel looked down on to what appeared to be a bundle of rags with a face in the middle of it. 'Don't want to take no notice of him; wait till's dark. Bloody upstart him. You're new on this game, eh? Never seen you afore. Where you bound for?'

Abel answered the last question briefly. 'The North.'

'Oh aye. Funny going that way. Not expectin' to find work there are ya? The whole place is emptying itself over to this end, Scots, Geordies, Welshmen, the lot. Got a tab on ya?'

'No.' Abel shook his head.

'Wouldn't give me one if ya had, is that it? Aw well, might do the same for you some day.'

'I don't happen to have a tab on me.'

'OK, I believe you. Broke are ya?'

Abel smiled wryly to himself. The old fellow was amusing. But was he old? He couldn't tell what age he was, dressed in that bundle of old clothes.

'You know summat?'

'What's that?'

'Ya'll lose that pack afore ya get North.'

Abel hitched the rucksack further up on his shoulders. 'They'll have to take me along with it then.'

'Aw, there's ways and means. Ya've got to sleep. It looks too new an' too full; you look wealthy, man. Want my advice? Get an old coat, raggy, stick your things under it an' scratch a bit . . . like this' – he now demonstrated – 'an' they won't come near you.' He laughed now, a deep, chuckling laugh. 'They're all new 'uns at the game. Me, I've been at it these thirty years. Do me round once a year. Ask if I can do a job; they gi'me somethin' to get rid of me. You, ya look naked, sittin' pigeon y'are. Still soles on yer boots an' the kid with ya . . . Hope to start a racket with him?'

'What do you mean?'

'Well, sympathy, 'cos of the kid. Ya won't get it, more like police after ya if ya try to take him into a grubber.'

'He's got to come with me.'

Even as he spoke Abel wondered why he was standing there, why he didn't get on his way? And he scorned himself because he had the urge to sit down in the ditch and let this fellow go on talking and to listen, and learn, because he knew what he was saying was true.

As if the man had read his mind, he said, 'Stick along of me if ya like . . . show ya the ropes.'

Abel hesitated for a second, then said, 'Thanks all the same; I'll learn as I go. Nevertheless, I'm grateful for your advice.'

'Here! have a tab.'

He watched the dirty hand diving into a pocket, then the packet of Woodbines was being held up to him.

'Go on, take one. They're clean; I bought them just a little way back. A fresh packet; look, still five in.'

Abel reached out and took one of the cigarettes, then said, 'Thanks very much.'

' . . .Goodbye.'

He had turned away before the man in the ditch

answered, 'So long. Look out for yer bits and pieces.'

He turned his head on his shoulder. 'I will, I will.'

'Funny man, Dad, isn't he?' Dick half turned round and smiled, and when the man waved he lifted his hand tentatively and waved back; then on a laugh, he said, 'He waved to me, Dad. He is funny; makes you want to laugh.'

'Yes, I suppose he is funny. He's an old stager and he's wise in the ways of the road. It looks as if we've got a lot to learn, doesn't it?'

They exchanged glances, then walked on in silence until Dick spoke, and then the question he asked was a personal one. 'How much money have you got, Dad?' he said.

'At the last count, twelve and threepence.'

'That seems a lot.'

'It'll do until we get more.'

But from where was he going to get more? He wouldn't admit to himself he was worried. From now on he must look for work, any kind of work as long as it provided them with food.

It was odd but this necessity to get food was in some measure obliterating the ache and pain which had consumed him during the past days. The times were now fewer when all he wanted to do was to throw himself on the ground and to beat it with his fists, and to cry, cry, and cry. He was ashamed of his weakness and he managed to throttle it during the day, but at night whenever he woke himself up calling 'Alice! Alice!' his face was always wet with tears.

3

During the three days it took them to reach Cambridge the professional tramp's words had been proved true more than once. First, there wasn't any work to be had even of the meanest kind; and secondly, his pack had acted as a form of temptation to others not so well off as himself.

He had once before many years ago visited Cambridge, and so he remembered the layout of the town, where the colleges were, the Backs, the river . . . and the station. It was towards the station he made his way now, and when his step quickened Dick said to him, 'Where we going, Dad?'

'To the station.'

'Going to get on a train, Dad?'

'No, no.' He gave a short laugh. 'No; going to meet those coming off the trains. There must be a lot of people come here even now for holidays and to do trips on the river; they'll want their bags carrying. When we get there I want you to sit on the rucksacks tight and don't leave them, not for anything. Understand?'

'Yes, Dad.'

'Good.'

At the station Abel saw that Dick wouldn't be

needed to sit on his rucksack because for every passenger coming off a train, if a porter was not already carrying his luggage there were half a dozen men waiting to oblige.

'Come.' More slowly now they walked back through the side streets towards the river, and there they sat on a green bank and watched the swans. Away to the right of them along the bank a fleet of hired boats were berthed. That was the boatyard; he remembered the name, Banham's. Saturday was the usual day that the land-locked sailors took the boats out. Would it be any use going along there and having a try? No, no. He shook his head to himself; and again he said, 'Come on.'

They had crossed the river and were about to take the road that would eventually lead them to Huntingdon when Abel slowed his step and, drawing Dick back into line with him, looked down at him and nodding his head, said, 'I wonder, eh? I wonder.'

Dick looked ahead of them. Two young women were each carrying two suitcases and finding the job heavy going. He grinned up at his father, saying, 'You could try, Dad. But you've got your own pack.'

'But me arms are still loose, aren't they? Here goes.'

'Can I help you carry your cases, miss?'

The two young women stopped simultaneously and one of them gasped, 'Oh! if you would I'd be ever so obliged. Wouldn't we, Mary?'

'Oh, yes. Aye. Me arms are snappin', we didn't

think it was this far from the station.'

'Where you bound for?'

'The boatyard, Banham's boatyard; it's some-where round here. The man said it was just along this road and down the second turning on the right.'

'You've come a long way round, you know. Well, I can manage two of them. Give them here.' He picked the two largest cases and while he strode ahead, with Dick having to run now by his side, the girls walked along behind, giggling and talking.

'We've never been on a boat before and we didn't want to waste money on a cab because they said it wasn't very far from the station.'

'Where you from?'

'Manchester.'

'Manchester!'

'Yes, we've been looking forward to this for months. Do you think it's going to keep fine?'

'Oh yes, I should say so.'

'It was pouring when we left . . . Flaming June!' They giggled and Dick turned and looked at them; and now they said, 'You on a hike . . .?'

'Sort of.'

When ten minutes later they entered the boat-yard it was to a scene of almost gay activity. Holidaymakers were stowing their belongings on board their particular craft; others were carrying boxes of groceries from a side shed; workmen were cleaning some boats while others were explaining the simple mechanism of the steering to the amateur sailors. There was laughter and chatter and an air of bustle everywhere.

'Will you wait here until we see which boat we've got?'

The taller of the two girls now brought her companion's attention away from Abel, saying, 'Don't be silly! we know what boat we've got. It's the *Firefly*. We've just got to pay our bill.' They were giggling again as they went towards the office.

Abel stood looking about him, and when one of the boatmen passed him, he touched the man's arm lightly and said, 'Excuse me, but is there any chance of being set on, I mean temporary like for an hour or two?'

The man looked at him somewhat sadly before saying, 'Sorry, mate, not a hope.'

'Thanks.'

On their return the girls were accompanied by one of the workmen. He was leading the way to the quay, and the girls as they passed grabbed up their smaller cases and followed him, and indicated by their laughter and nods that Abel should bring up the other cases.

The *Firefly* was a two-berther; next to it was a larger cruiser, and sitting on top of the cabin was a woman dressed in a short skirt and white sweater. Glancing at her, Abel noted the look of disdain on her face as she watched the antics of the new arrivals.

The workman now took the cases from Abel and disappeared into the cabin, and the girls, looking up at Abel, said almost simultaneously, 'Ta. Thanks.'

He stared at them, and as he did so the smiles slipped from their faces and one of them nudged the other. Going down into the cabin, she hissed to her companion, who was still standing open-mouthed in the cockpit, 'He wants a tip.'

'Oh!' There followed a rummaging in a handbag, then a coin was handed up to him; and he left it on his open palm as he looked at it. It was a penny. Slowly he picked it up between his first finger and thumb and, handing it down to the girl again, he said, 'You'll need that likely before I do, miss.'

As he walked away, his hand on Dick's shoulder, the words, 'Well, I never! Did you see that! What did he expect? He asked to carry them, didn't he? The cheek!' followed him.

Some of the humiliation his father was feeling seeped into Dick as they walked along the towpath by the side of the river. A penny was nothing and his father had carried those cases a long way. Why, his father never used to give him less than three-pence a week pocket money. Things weren't going right; he was worried . . .

It was quite some time later when they stopped by a lock. It was the boy who drew his father to a halt, saying, 'The boats look bonny, don't they, Dad, all lined up. What they waitin' for?'

'To get through the lock.'

'Oh.' He didn't know what a lock was and from his father's tone he knew that it wasn't the time to ask. His father had hardly spoken a word since they left the boatyard.

'Can we stay a little while and watch them, Dad?'

'I suppose so.'

He watched his father slip the rucksack from his

back; then he did the same with his own small one; and then they sat down side by side on the bank beyond the towpath.

There was a boat coming down the river and they watched it make for the bank. A young girl was standing in the bows with a rope in her hand, and a woman was at the wheel. The wind that was blowing off shore and the current running over the weir to the side of the lock were giving her trouble, and twice she had to go out into mid-stream before she could eventually turn the bows straight towards the bank.

When the girl jumped off the boat on to the bank and pulled on the rope the wind took the stern and slew it round.

Dick felt his father hesitate for a moment before getting to his feet; then going to the girl, he took the rope from her and pulled the bows into the bank and pushed against them, and when the woman on board quickly thrust a boat hook towards him he slipped it into a cleat and gradually brought the boat alongside.

He was holding the boat steady when the woman, leaning now into full view over the side of the cockpit, said, 'Thanks. Thanks very much.'

'You're welcome.'

'I . . . I saw you down in the boatyard, didn't I?'

He had taken his eyes from her. Now he looked at her briefly again as he said, 'Yes. Yes, I was down there.'

There was a pause before she said, 'It'll be a time

before we get through, do you think we should anchor?'

'I don't know, that's up to you.'

'I think we should. Would you knock the rond anchor in for me? Here Daphne, hand the gentleman the rond anchor.'

Dick felt an easing of the tension in him. She had called his father a gentleman. She was a nice lady.

He watched his father take first an iron hook, then a wooden hammer and with it bang the hook into the ground. When he had done this the young girl tied the rope through the loop in the piece of iron.

When the same thing had been repeated at the other end, the boat rested quietly against the side of the bank; then the lady stepped from the boat and approached his father. She stared at him for seemingly a long time before saying quietly, 'Could I ask you to see us through the lock? I'm not quite up to handling a boat on my own. The last time I was on the river was some years ago with . . . with my husband.'

It seemed another long moment before his father answered, 'What am I expected to do?'

'Oh, just hang on to the ropes and keep her steady while the lock is being emptied.'

'Very well.'

'Perhaps your son would like to come aboard?'

When she turned towards Dick his face lighted up and he looked from her to his father and said, 'Oh, can I, Dad?'

Again there was a pause, then his father said, 'How's he going to get off?'

'Oh, we can drop him off at the bank beyond the lock; and you too. You could step aboard from the top of the lock and we could put you off wherever you wanted.'

Dick found his father's eyes tight on him, and he knew that it was touch and go about his decision; but then he said, 'I can see no harm in that.'

It was lovely, exciting standing in the cockpit of the boat, and yet at the same time a little frightening. The girl stood by the wheel but she didn't speak to him, and his dad and the lady stood on the bank and they didn't speak to each other, until all of a sudden the lady became excited and cried, 'Look!' – she was pointing towards the lock – 'that lot's gone through and we'll be able to get in with these two smaller craft ahead; we'd better take up the anchors and get ready. Put your baggage . . . luggage aboard.'

When he saw his father, grim faced, pull the pieces of bent iron from out of the grassy bank he felt uneasy; but when Abel, holding the two ropes in his hands now, nodded to him and smiled, a spurt of happiness shot through him. It was the first time in weeks he had seen his father smile like that.

The woman and girl were already aboard, and now the woman, looking up at his father, cried, 'I won't start the engine, I'll leave things to you; as soon as the gates open pull her along.' But his father didn't answer, he was looking towards the lock.

Now the girl spoke to him for the first time. 'Come to the front,' she said; 'you can stand and look over the top.'

He followed her down steep steps and into a cabin, with padded seats along each side, then up through a hole in the roof; and there he was standing at the front of the boat.

'Do you want to sit on top of the cabin?'

He shook his head and clung to the handrail.

'How old are you?'

'Seven.'

'What's your name?'

'Dickie.'

'Seven.' He watched her turn her head away and look across the river, then add under her breath, 'You would be.' Looking at him again she said, 'I'm nearly fifteen.'

He did not know what to say to this, but he felt she was blaming him in some strange way for being only seven.

When the boat began to move slowly away from the bank he shivered with excitement and looked at her and smiled, and she said, 'Is it your first trip on a boat?'

'Yes . . . no; I once went on a boat trip from the beach at Hastings, but I was sick although we weren't out very long. But . . . but this is different, it's smooth. I wouldn't mind being on this boat and goin' a long trip.'

He watched her jerk her chin upwards now and look towards his father who was pulling the boat into the lock, and what she said was, 'Don't worry,

45

you will'; and on this she scrambled through the hole and disappeared.

He was so puzzled by her remark that he only vaguely took in the actions of the man now pushing against a great black wooden lever, and not until well after the lock gates had clanged did he bring his full attention back to the boat and the fact that it was sinking. Startled, he jumped down through the hole and scrambled through the cabin and he went on hands and knees up the further steps into the cockpit, and there was surprised to see the lady and the girl standing quite calmly looking upwards to where his father was disappearing.

'It's all right; don't look so scared.' The lady patted his head.

'How . . . how will he get in?'

'He'll jump on to the roof.'

'He'll be drowned.'

'No, no, he won't.' Again she patted his head.

He looked in horror at the green slime dripping down the black walls and he had the desire to shout for help when he saw his father throw the ropes down, then lower himself over the wall and drop on to the cabin top with only a slight thud.

'There! he didn't even have any need to jump, did he, because he's so tall.' The lady was at the wheel now and she didn't speak again until she had steered the boat through the open lock gates, and when he saw the flat stretch of water ahead and the treelined banks he turned, a wide smile lighting up his face, and looked to where his father was standing now at the other side of the cockpit, and he said, 'Isn't it bonny, Dad?'

'Yes, very bonny.'

'It's a beautiful stretch of the river this. Have you ever been to Cambridge before?'

His father didn't look at the lady as he said, 'Yes, many years ago, but I've never been on the river.'

'Do you like boats?'

'I've yet to find that out.' He kept his gaze fixed ahead.

'Put the kettle on, Daphne.'

'You can make tea here?'

The lady laughed. 'Yes, dear, we can make tea and have a roast dinner or anything you like. Go and look at the galley.' She nodded to where another set of steps led downwards and after glancing at his father he went down them and his mouth fell into a gape, and his eyes widened as he saw the neat stove and the sink.

'Eeh! it's nice, like a real kitchen.'

When the kettle whistled he hunched his shoulders and laughed aloud, and for the first time the girl smiled at him and said, 'You're a funny kid. Here; take this tin of biscuits up aloft.'

He had a job to manage the stairs with the biscuit tin held in the curve of one arm and when he emerged from the galley on all fours the lady was saying, 'Surely if you were making for Huntingdon, following the river would have taken you the long way round?'

'I didn't intend to follow the river, I lost my

bearings back there and a bit of me temper besides.'

The lady laughed before she said, 'Through the generosity of those girls?'

'Aye, yes, you could say that.'

'Are you in a hurry?'

'In one way, yes, I'm in a hurry to find work.'

'I've engaged this boat for a fortnight, I . . . I could employ you for that time.'

Dick rose from his knees and he was holding the biscuit tin in both hands now as he stared from his father to the lady, then back to his father again. The lady was offering him a job and he wasn't jumping at it, he was looking straight ahead. When his father spoke his voice sounded tight. 'You don't need a crew on a boat like this.'

'Oh yes, I do.' She had turned and looked at him. 'There are a number of locks between here and Huntingdon and some are dreadful to get through, it's a man's work. I . . . I felt a bit nervous about taking the boat out at all but Daphne wanted to come.' Her voice now had almost sunk to a whisper as she went on, 'I can give you three pounds a week and your food and . . . and I'm sure the child would love it. Has . . . has his mother been long dead?' Her head swung quickly round now as she added, 'That's silly of me; I'm assuming that she is . . .'

'Here, take this tray, will you?'

Dick watched his father bend down and take the tray of tea from the girl's hand but as she was about to step on to the deck her mother said to her, 'Bring the fruit cake up too, Daphne, I'm feeling peckish.'

The girl had hardly disappeared before the lady

turned to his father again and said, 'Well, what about it?'

'I'll go as far as Huntingdon with you; you can pay me what you think I'm worth by then.'

'Fair enough.' She pursed her lips slightly, then smiled at him. 'What's your name?'

'Abel Mason.'

'Abel. Old-fashioned name that, isn't it?'

'I'm an old-fashioned man.'

'Oh!'

Dick watched the lady swing the wheel right round as they turned a bend in the river, and she swung it back again before she again said, 'Oh.' Then when her daughter appeared on deck and put a plate holding a fruit loaf none too gently down on the seat, her mother spoke to her without looking at her. 'Mr Mason is going to crew for us as far as Huntingdon,' she said.

The girl stood for a moment looking over the side of the boat; then crossing the cockpit she pushed past Dick and went down into the saloon, and her muttered words came up to him as she said, 'That doesn't surprise me in the least.'

4

This was the third night out, their progress had been very slow. The lady, Dick felt, hadn't been in a hurry to get anywhere. He sensed she was happy just lying on top of the boat with hardly any clothes on. He also sensed an unease in his father. Last night they had been berthed in a little bay near a public house and the lady had done her best to persuade him to go for a drink, but he wouldn't, and so she had gone by herself, leaving them alone with Daphne.

He liked Daphne; she was different when her mother wasn't there. He thought she didn't like her mother, and he could understand that for he knew how it felt not to like your mother.

They were all in bed now, and it was very dark in their cabin, and stuffy. The two bunks on which he and his father lay formed a V in the bows of the boat, and his father had to lie with his knees up because his bunk wasn't long enough for him. And he was muttering again in his sleep. Twice last night he had shouted out Mrs Alice's name, then had sat up with a start and bumped his head. After that he had got out of his bunk and sat on the edge of it, and although he couldn't see his father he knew that he was leaning forward with his head in his hands because of the short muffled cough he gave.

It was very hot. He wished he could get to sleep but he couldn't because he was worried. He couldn't put his finger on exactly what was worrying him except that it was to do with the lady and his father.

He was on the verge of dropping into sleep when he was made vitally aware of two things. The first startled him, it was his father's voice calling louder than usual 'Alice! Oh Alice! Alice! Your poor face, Alice. Alice! Alice!' The second thing he became aware of was that the door had opened and the lady had entered the cabin. If he hadn't heard her he would have smelt her for she seemed to him always to be wrapped round in a mist of scent.

'Wake up! Wake up!'

'Wha'! What! . . . What do you want? What's the matter?'

'Nothing, nothing. I . . . I heard you crying out in your sleep.'

In the short silence that followed, Dick remained still and taut. How could she have heard his dad call out in his sleep? She slept at the other end of the boat and she had come in almost at the same time as he had cried out.

'I'm sorry if I disturbed you. There's nothing to worry about.' His voice was low and throaty.

'But I am worried about you. You are very troubled, aren't you? I've heard you each night since you came aboard. You must have cared for your wife very much.'

There was silence. Then her voice began again, very low now, hardly audible. 'I know how you feel; I felt the same after losing my husband, but ... but life must go on.'

'Don't-sit-down-there.' The muffled words were strung together.

'Don't be silly.'

'Get by ... get out!'

'You're being stuffy.'

'You're aware there's a child in that bunk, aren't you?'

His father's voice was merely a hissing whisper and hers too was a whisper as she replied, 'Children sleep through anything, especially on this river.'

'Go on, leave me for a minute, I'll come outside. There's something I want to say and it's better said now.'

There was another moment's silence before he heard her leave the cabin; then he knew that his father was scrambling into his clothes.

When a few minutes later he was alone he sat up in the bunk. It seemed to him the two of them were still in the cabin, so clearly could he hear them speaking; but this, he realised, was because they weren't whispering so low now. It was the lady talking and rapidly, 'You're looking a gift horse in the mouth, do you know that? We could get along well together, I've ... I've grown fond of you. Yes, yes, I have in this very short time. You're the kind of man I suppose any woman would grow fond of.'

'Stop it, will you? Please.'

'No, no I won't. You wanted to talk, so do I, and

I'll have my say first. So it's like this. I'm not rich but I've got enough to be independent – he left me comfortable. I could set you up in anything you like. You should think of this. And the boy there. What life is it for a child of that age tramping the roads? And only a fool would be going northwards looking for work. By your own admission you're not going to relatives or anyone who could help you, so, Abel, what about it? . . . No, no, don't say anything, not yet; just let's try it out, eh? You're lonely, so am I, we can help each other. I could make you forget. Oh yes. Yes, I'm sure of that; I could make you forget your wife, or whoever she was. One doesn't usually go on about a wife, you know, as you've done about this Alice. And the boy. Well, when I asked him if his mother was dead he couldn't answer me. But I don't mind; I don't mind in the least; your past means nothing to me but your future does . . . Oh Abel!'

'Take your hand off me!'

'Don't speak to me like that. I'm offering you . . .'

'I know what you're offering me, and I say thank you very much, but no!'

'You're a fool!'

'Maybe; it's how you look at it. I'm going back to bed now and I'll leave first thing in the morning.'

'No! No! You said you'd go on to Huntingdon with me.'

'Yes, that was when you wanted a crew not a fancy man. I am to be nobody's kept man, missis.'

As the door opened the woman's voice, louder now, spat out words that seemed to bounce around the small cabin. 'You're a common thankless clod, that's what you are. You've got the makings of a tramp, I saw that too at first. What do you think you are anyway? And don't imagine I'll pay you. We agreed on Huntingdon; if you want your wages you'll stay till then, if not you'll get nothing. Do you hear? Nothing . . .'

'Mother! Mother! Listen . . . listen to me. Come away.'

The cabin door was closed. His father had switched on the light and he was sitting on the side of the bunk, and they looked at each other, then he started, and his father did too as the woman's voice screamed, 'Leave go of me!'

'I won't until you stop making a fool of yourself.'

When the sound of a ringing slap came to them, Dick watched his father's eyes close tightly.

Following this there was silence.

For the next fifteen minutes he watched the shadows leaping around the small cabin as his father packed the rucksack. He didn't seem to hurry, but did everything in a tired sort of way. When the packing was completed he turned to him and pressed him down into the pillows, saying, 'Try to get some sleep, and we'll leave at first light.'

He made no answer but watched the light being switched out, then lay staring into the darkness.

Why was it women wanted his father? His mother, Mrs Alice, and now the lady.

He was trying to sort out the reason when he fell asleep . . .

He seemed to have been asleep for two or three

minutes only when his father's voice came from a distance, saying to him, 'Come along, Dickie. Come along, get up.'

He blinked, sniffed, and was about to say, 'Will I go and get a wash in the sink, Dad?' when, as if reading his thoughts, his father said, 'Leave your wash; we'll have a sluice down along the bank somewhere.'

He noted that his father was already dressed and ready for the road, and he himself had just got into his clothes when his father switched off the light and caused him to exclaim, 'It's still dark, Dad.'

'No, the light's breaking, it'll be quite clear when we get outside. Come on. Go quietly now.'

On tiptoe he followed his father into the cabin, through the galley, and up the steps on to the small deck, and to his surprise he found it was already light enough to see; but the bank and the fields ahead were covered in mist and he shivered.

As his father hoisted him and his rucksack over the side the boat rocked slightly. Everything was very quiet, very still. He couldn't see his feet for the mist, he couldn't see the water for the mist; everything seemed buried in mist.

They hadn't gone more than a hundred yards along the bank when his father stopped abruptly and turned about. He himself hadn't heard anyone coming, having been too concerned about where he was placing his feet.

As Daphne approached she appeared legless. She was wearing an outsize woollen sweater and she kept pulling the sleeves up around her elbows as she talked. 'I just want to say goodbye. I'm sorry to see you go, you've been the best of the bunch. She's man mad; she can't help it and it isn't only since my father died. He's only been gone six months; she always says it's a year.' She held out her hand, not to shake but proffering something.

Abel looked down at the pound note for a moment and then into the face of the young girl and he said softly, 'Thanks, my dear; but I don't want anything. I've had bed and board for the both of us.'

'Take it, you've earned it and she's got plenty, we've both got plenty. It's nothing, only a pound. I'll . . . I'll be upset if you don't.'

Dick watched his father hesitate for a moment, then take the note, saying, 'Thanks'; then pause before adding, 'I wish things could have ended differently for your sake anyway.'

'You don't wish that more than I do. You know what I thought when I first saw you? Well, I mean what I wished when you first came aboard? I knew she was gone on you, and I thought that if only Dick had been a little bit older we could have made a double. I . . . I would have liked that.'

As she gave a soft chuckle Dick looked at his father. His head was bent, his face looked red against the greyness of the mist, and his voice was soft as he said, 'You're a nice girl, Daphne. Look after her, she needs someone. I'm sorry it can't be me.'

'So am I . . . I hope you find work.'

'I shall. Thanks again for this.' He flapped the pound note gently. 'Goodbye.'

'Goodbye, Abel. Goodbye.'

They had turned from her and gone a few yards when her words came to them softly as if she had laid them on the mist and blown them forward. 'I'll always remember you,' they said, 'as the man who had little to say, but looked a lot.'

It was some seconds later when Abel turned and glanced back, but she was no longer there.

'Don't cry.'

'I'm not, Dad, I'm not.'

He didn't know why he was denying it for he could hear himself crying. He was crying because of the great sadness that was choking him. He was cold, he wished he was back in the bunk, he wished his dad could have liked the lady. He had liked Daphne, they had laughed together.

As the sky lightened he saw the day stretching away into eternity and during it he knew he would be hungry and tired, his legs would ache and he would have more blisters on his feet. Why couldn't his dad have liked the lady?

It took them twelve days to reach the outskirts of Leeds. For most of the way they had kept to the Great North Road, diverting from it only at night to find some place to shelter.

Dick didn't chatter on the journeys now; although he didn't feel so tired at the end of the day and his legs had stopped paining there was one blister on his foot that refused to heal, and he wished, oh how he wished, that they didn't have to walk any more, and that the men, particularly the young ones, they met up with on the road would stop calling out such things as, 'You're goin' the wrong way, mate.'

He didn't want to go back to his mother but he wished he could go back home and sleep in a bed . . .

Abel was well aware of what was going on in the boy's mind and within himself a feeling of desperation was growing rapidly. He was down to his last sixpence. The past three days they had eaten sparingly, even after standing from five o'clock that morning in a baker's shop queue to get a share of the stale bread and cakes that were sold off cheaply, and then stuffing themselves with the dry buns and broken pastry, they were still hungry.

Yesterday he had so pleaded with a farmer for a job that the man, becoming irritated, had sworn at him. One thing was certain, tonight he had to make for the nearest workhouse if only to give the child a meal and a night's rest in a bed of sorts.

Earlier in the day he had decided to leave the main road and its vicinity, hoping that in the villages further away from the traffic there would be more chance of something turning up. That was the phrase that was on the lips of every man he had spoken to on this journey. They were hoping for something to turn up.

He had drawn out a rough map of the road he must take but as he sat looking at it now he realised that he had wandered someway off it because a signpost a dozen yards away stated: Leeds 5 miles. And he had imagined he had glimpsed it from the last rise. Well, perhaps he had, distance was deceptive. Nevertheless, they were both too tired to waste their steps, and so he must make sure of where he was.

'Sit there a minute,' he said in a soothing tone; 'I'm just goin' up that bank to have a look round.'

At one time the boy would have cried, 'I'll come along with you, Dad,' but not now; whenever he had the chance to sit, he sat.

From the top of the rise Abel again viewed through the smoky haze the blurred horizon of a straggling town, but much nearer he could see a huddle of roofs, indicating a quite large village, and nearer still, not more than half a mile away, over two stubby fields was a house, a large house, and near it a range of buildings.

He had already decided it wasn't a farm, then he noticed some animals moving about in a field beyond the house. He screwed up his eyes against the light and muttered to himself, 'Pigs.' He had never liked pigs. Sheep, cows, horses, any other animals could draw his hand to them but not pigs. But who knew, this might be the one place where he would be lucky. He went down the bank and had swung the rucksack on to his shoulders before he said, 'Come on; there's a place down there that looks likely. They keep pigs.'

Dick was trailing some yards behind him when he came to the gate leading to the yard and the house, and he stood waiting leaning against it taking in what was before him. It was evident that the house, a large sprawling one and stone built, had never seen paint for years, and what he could see of the yard showed him that it was no farmyard, it was more like the courtyard at Lady Parker's with half a dozen horse boxes going off one side of it, with the doors on the other side, he surmised, leading to harness rooms and storerooms. What he could see from where he stood, and close to the house, were two great open doors leading into a barn.

He could offer the owner his labour in exchange for sleeping dry in there tonight at any rate, and by the look of things at first glance the place was in need of labour. In any case, if he were to reach the workhouse in Leeds he'd have to pay hard with a full day's work tomorrow for their night's stay: nobody gave you anything for nothing. No, no; they didn't.

He was about to open the gate when a chorus of squeals and screams came to him from somewhere beyond the house and he reckoned those pigs in that field were getting some slop.

The place looked deserted but if he were right in his reckoning the owner would be seeing to his animals, and so he decided to go round the back of the house. But first he took off his pack and, laying it on the ground, said to Dick, 'Sit on it; I'm going to see if I can find somebody.'

When the boy again made no reply, Abel gazed at him sadly for a moment, then gulped deeply in his throat before walking slowly along what had once been a short drive but which was now hardly discernible for the matted grass covering it.

As he passed the front door of the house he looked towards it. It was obviously made of solid oak but was now weather-beaten to a whitish grey.

Before rounding the side of the house he cast a glance towards the barn-like building. Just inside he could make out two stalls divided by stout pillars and there was a quantity of loose straw in one of them.

He was just turning the corner at the back of the house when he started visibly as he almost ran into the apparition, because that's how he viewed her from the beginning. What age she was he couldn't make out. She was a tall woman, and wisps of hair from under the battered trilby hat showed her to be fair, or was she white? Her face was long, lean, and weather-beaten, yet his first impression was of a delicate etherealness. Even under the bulky, old army topcoat she was wearing he could sense her thinness, and the oddness of her was made clear by the long mud-stained flowery dress that fell to the top of her boots, men's boots, again which had an army flavour about them and in which he guessed her feet could float, so big were they.

He was the first to speak. 'I'm sorry, ma'am; I was looking for the owner.'

When she put out her hand and her fingers gently touched his arm he felt inclined to spring back, but restrained himself. She couldn't possibly be the owner, yet he told himself as he stared at her that her appearance linked her with the place. He almost stammered as he said, 'I . . . I was wondering if you would allow us, my son and me, to sleep in your barn tonight? I'd do any odd job you wanted in payment.'

He now watched her draw in a breath that seemed to make her even taller and when she spoke he was amazed at the sound of her voice, for it had a high cultured tone. He recalled his late employer; she too had spoken like this, only not so high.

'Who sent you?'

'Nobody, ma'am . . . I mean, we are making our way North, we were goin' on to Leeds, but it's coming on to drizzle and my son is very tired.'

'Who sent you?'

He shook his head. 'I told you, ma'am, nobody.'

'Oh, yes they did. God sent you. I knew He would.'

When he half turned away and looked to the side, her voice and manner changed completely, so much so that he was startled again. Her tone, still high, was brisk now, even businesslike as she cried, 'Yes, yes, of course you may stay the night, and . . . and I'd be glad of your help. Oh yes, I'd be glad of your help; although mind it isn't everyone I take on. Come. Come, I'll show you. You can sleep in the barn. Are you hungry?'

She had walked on in front of him and now she paused and looked over her shoulder, and again that strange ethereal quality forced an impression on him, causing him to blink twice wondering whether or not he were dreaming. Then he answered her, saying hesitantly, 'Well, yes; you could say we are a bit hungry, ma'am.'

'I thought you would be, they're all hungry; and that makes them weak, you know, and so they can't work. The old men just want to be fed, while the young ones just want money. This is the barn, you may sleep in there. There aren't any rats, the cats see to them. I have fourteen cats. I don't like dogs; fawning creatures, dogs; cats run their own lives, I run my own life.' She turned on him suddenly now, saying, 'You're not to come to the house for anything, I'll bring your food here. You understand?'

'Yes, yes, I understand.'

She walked to the front of the barn now where she stopped and looked towards the gate, then asked slowly, 'Is that your boy?'

'Yes.'

'I don't like children but I'll put up with him if you work well. You'd better get bedded down because I expect you up at five in the morning, mind, not later.' She was wagging her finger at him now, and when she turned away and walked towards the back of the house he stared after her for a moment before going slowly to the gate and saying quietly to Dick, 'Come on.'

They had scarcely got the rucksack unpacked and their bedding out when the high voice came to them from the open doorway. 'There it is! Five o'clock mind, not later.'

He had no time to answer before she disappeared and he was about to go forward when Dick spoke for the first time in hours, saying in an awe-filled voice, 'Who's that, Dad?'

'She's the wom . . . the lady who owns this place.'

'She looks funny.'

'Funny or not, she's given us the chance of a good night's rest.'

When he reached the barn door he looked at the tray. It had on it a mug of steaming cocoa, a small loaf of apparently home-made bread, a hunk of cheese, a piece of belly pork, and a slab of butter. Well – he nodded to himself – however odd she may appear she kept her larder well stocked. Apparently she knew how to bake, too, unless she had someone in the house doing it for her.

As he laid the tray on the straw he glanced up at his son as he said. 'What about that?'

'Oh! Dad, it looks good.'

'It'll taste better. Come on, let's tuck in. Here, take a drink of this hot cocoa for a start.'

For the first time in days Abel saw the boy smile as he wiped the thick cocoa from his mouth, and he wished it was in himself to smile too, but he felt uneasy: she was queer that woman, odd. It wasn't only the way she dressed and the state of the place, it wasn't only the things she said, it was how she said them. There was something uncanny about her.

He slept well, and he aroused himself quietly at first light so as not to disturb the boy, and was in the yard at five minutes to five. But she was there before him, and immediately she gave him his orders. He had to clean out the pigsties, then take the slops to the pigs; afterwards, he had to set about clearing up the yard.

She didn't allot any jobs to the boy, Abel noticed. She seemed bent on ignoring him completely; he couldn't be there for all the notice she took of him.

The one mug of cocoa last night had been a pointer.

It was well past eight o'clock before Dick made his appearance. He came on Abel at a run and leant against the wall of the pigsties gasping, 'I couldn't find you, Dad, an' there's nobody about.' Then after another gasp he added, 'Do we get any breakfast, Dad?'

'There's no sign of it yet, but I'll be finished here in a minute and then we'll go looking.'

'This place stinks.'

'Yes, it stinks.'

'It looks as if it's been a long time since they were cleaned out. Have you dug all that mound out this mornin', Dad?'

Dick pointed to a large heap of manure some distance from the sties.

'Yes, I have,' Abel said; 'an' me back's letting me know it.' He gave a slight smile. 'That's what comes of being lazy for days.'

'Your boots are all messed up.'

'They'll clean.'

'It's a good job you turned your trousers up . . .'

'You there!' The voice came from the direction of the yard and they both turned quickly and looked towards the woman, and she pointed back to the barn, saying, 'Your breakfast's there.'

'Thank you.' Abel nodded; then throwing the shovel aside he walked towards her, saying, 'Where can we clean up?'

'There's a pump round the corner of the yard. What's your name?'

'Abel Mason.'

She nodded three times, then said, 'Abel. Abel. Hah! I thought you were sent by God, and your name proves it. Now after you've eaten you'll start on the yard. Get all the grass up between the slabs. I should think that will take you up till this evening; then tomorrow you can continue down the drive. I have five acres of land here, that's all, just five acres.' She shook her head. 'Can you believe that, just five acres? It used to be five hundred, and before that a thousand. But we'll clear those five acres, you and me. Yes, we will.'

As she took two steps nearer to him her features spread into a smile and at the sight he felt himself once again recoiling from her. His jaw tightened for a moment; then he asked a question. 'What wages are you offering, ma'am?'

She seemed surprised and she repeated, 'Wages? Oh, wages. Well, you'll get your food and your bed and . . . and a pound a week. A pound' – she was nodding again – 'that should be enough for your requirements. Money isn't everything. Money is a curse, do you know that? If you have money everybody wants it; you have no friends if you have money. The only true friend one has is God and' – she was smiling again – 'He has answered my prayers. At last He has answered my prayer.'

After three more nods of her head towards him, she turned about and stalked, which was the only word that could describe her walk . . . towards the house.

In the barn, Abel looked down on the large tray which held a teapot, a jug of milk, one mug, one plate, a knife and fork, another small loaf of bread, and a covered dish. When he lifted the lid of the dish and saw two fried eggs flanked by two thick slices of ham he heaved a deep sigh, then turning to Dick, he said, 'Fetch your plate and mug.'

When the boy returned with the plate he said quietly, 'She didn't mean me to have any, did she, Dad? She never looks at me or speaks to me.'

Abel didn't answer him, but set about dividing the food; then they both sat down on a wooden plank that ran alongside the stalls and they ate in silence.

Abel was just about to say, 'We're leaving here, son,' when a sudden shower of rain hitting the roof of the barn brought his eyes upwards. Since dawn the sky had promised rain and now it had come, and it was heavy, and he couldn't, he decided, take the boy out in it.

They had hardly finished their meal when the woman appeared at the door of the barn again, saying and without any preamble now, 'The rain needn't stop you working, there're sacks in the corner there to put over you.'

He made no reply, he just sat and stared at her, and she, too, stared back at him for a moment before turning away and disappearing from his view.

He had seen some weird creatures in his time but this one, he told himself, took the cake.

'Will I come out and help you, Dad?'

'No, no, you won't!' His voice was harsh. 'You stay where you are in the dry.'

'All day?'

'Yes, all day if it comes to that . . .'

And it was all day. For most of the time Dick stood within the door of the barn and watched his father, who looked like a giant hunchback under the pointed sack covering his head and shoulders and part of his back, scrape out the long grass from between the stones of the yard. At intervals he would come into the barn and change the sack for a dry one, but he didn't speak to him; and something about his father's face warned the boy to be quiet.

The dinner-time meal was again pork, and when around four o'clock Abel walked slowly into the barn and, having divested himself of the sack and his wet coat, slumped down on to the plank of wood and after wiping his face on the towel that Dick had taken out of the rucksack he looked at his son and said, 'Rain, snow, or hail, we go in the morning.' The words and the tone in which they were said were as if the boy had been protesting at the prospect of leaving.

'Will she pay you for the day, Dad?'

'That I'll have to find out . . .'

And he found out an hour later when she came scurrying into the barn carrying another tray. Under other circumstances he would have said, 'I'll come and fetch the tray, ma'am;' but not with this one.

What she said to him right away was, 'You finished early.'

'I don't suppose it escaped your notice, ma'am, that it's pouring with rain and it has been all day and I'm wet through.'

'Rain won't do you any harm, and you don't look a weakling. No, no, you certainly don't look a weakling. It's God's rain, pure water ... You didn't finish the yard. Well, there's another day tomorrow; you can do it first thing and ...'

'I'll be leaving in the morning, ma'am.'

He watched her body droop slightly to the side, her ear cocked towards the ground as if she were straining to hear what he had said, and her words actually were, 'What did you say?'

'I'm leaving in the morning. My son and I' – he stressed the word son – 'we'll be on our way.'

'You said you would stay for a pound a week.'

'I did nothing of the sort, ma'am. I asked what you were offering in the way of wages. It was you who said a pound a week, but I think the amount of work I've done today is worth five shillings.'

She screwed up her face now until her eyes were almost lost in their deep sockets and she peered at him for a full minute, an embarrassing minute, before she said, 'You can't go, not you. I told you you were the answer to my prayer.'

'I'm sorry, ma'am.'

'I'll give you an extra meal, supper, and two pounds a week; yes, yes, I'll give you two pounds a week.' Her head was bobbing again.

'It's kind of you, ma'am, but ... but I've ... I've been promised a position in the North.'

Again she was staring at him; and then quietly she said, 'Eat your tea,' and turning about, walked slowly away.

For a moment he felt sorry for her; she was a pitiful creature. But she was weird, slightly mad, and he wouldn't know a moment's ease of mind until he had left her and this place well behind him.

As if he had agreed to her new proposal she brought him a jug of cocoa around seven o'clock, but she had nothing to say to him. She didn't bring a tray this time, just a jug and a china mug; and she didn't even look at him as she placed them on the plank of wood before turning and going out.

'This cocoa's bitter, Dad.'

'Yes' – Abel nodded at the boy – 'it's too strong but drink it, it'll keep you warm inside.'

Dick tried to drink the remainder of the cocoa, but after another mouthful he said, 'It would make me sick, Dad.'

'All right, all right; leave it alone and get yourself down to sleep.'

They were both lying in the straw when Dick asked, 'What time are we leaving in the mornin', Dad?'

'First light; if not afore.'

'But will she be up to pay you?'

He paused a moment before answering, 'Well, if she isn't we'll have to go without.'

The boy realised that his father must want to get away very badly if he was thinking of going without his pay because they hadn't any money. He felt very sleepy, heavy. 'Good night, Dad,' he said; but there was no answer, Abel was already asleep.

When the dream began he didn't know, he only knew when it ended. It started with Alice; she had come again to him not as she did most nights running down the glen and into his outstretched arms, but had appeared from nowhere. He couldn't see her face, but he knew she was behind him and she was carrying him. His mind told him it wasn't right that a woman should be carrying him and he struggled, but she held him tight; her arms were like thin cables, different from usual, and her voice was different. She kept talking at him. He tried in vain to turn round and look at her. Then a wave of nausea attacked him; he felt he was about to retch but told himself he mustn't because if he dirtied his blanket he wouldn't be able to get it washed again.

When he heard himself yell, almost scream, he knew that he was awake yet he couldn't believe it, and he wanted to close his eyes again and tell himself that he was in a nightmare, but his eyes were riveted on his left hand and left ankle around each of which was an inch-wide iron-band with a chain attached. His eyes now followed the chains up to where they were linked into a hook at the top of the post that supported the stall.

From the hook his gaze now travelled to the lantern that was set on the floor near the feet of the woman who was sitting on an upturned box.

He opened his mouth to yell again but the cry was strangled in his throat by blind, fear-filled panic. He was chained up. She had chained him up. She was mad, a lunatic! Nobody knew that they were here . . . Dick. Where was Dick? Dick. The name came like a whimper from between his lips; then as he brought himself to his feet he swung round, grabbing at the stanchion for support, and when he saw the boy lying still fast asleep in the straw he lay back against the thick wooden partition, closed his eyes and drew in a deep breath. She hadn't touched him, and this very fact added to her weirdness; she might never have seen him, so completely was she ignoring him.

Now he turned towards her and, gathering the spittle into his mouth, he said, 'You can't do this. Unloose me, do you hear! Unloose me!' Even to himself his words sounded weak and inane and he knew that they would have as much effect on her as a stick would have on an incoming wave.

'You brought it on yourself.'

'You can't keep me here.'

'Oh, yes I can. God has pointed the way with this.' She stooped to the side and picked the book off the floor, and when she held it out towards him he recognised it as a Bible. 'You swear on this that you'll not leave me. Take a deep solemn oath on it telling God that evil will befall you should you break your word. Then I will release you, and I promise I'll look after you well, I'll even let you into the house. Now that is something, that is really something when I say I'll let you into my house, because it was all prepared for Arthur.'

She paused now as if waiting for him to ask her

a question, but he didn't speak or move, he just stood leaning against the partition, and she went on. 'You see, Arthur was in the war, he was a hero. They objected to us marrying. They said he wasn't my class but that didn't matter, we loved each other and we were to be married. I had everything ready, they're still ready, all lying in the drawer. They said he was missing. Missing, they said, but I know right in here' – she beat twice on her chest with her fist before going on – 'he'll come back. Loss of memory, that's what happened to him. So you see' – she now nodded towards him – 'until he does, I must have help. I must get the land tidied up; the inside is ready but I can't do the outside alone. And so I prayed to God. I've prayed for such a long time; and when you came in the gate and said your name was Abel I knew He had answered my prayers . . . now you understand? . . . see' – she again held out the book to him, open now – 'Luke, Chapter Eleven, verse nine. "And I say unto you, Ask, and it shall be given you; seek, and ye shall find; knock, and it shall be opened unto you.

"For every one that asketh receiveth; and he that seeketh findeth; and to him that knocketh it shall be opened."

'You see I knocked on God's door and He opened it to me and listened to my prayer. Now I'm going to give you time to think. I'm going to get you some breakfast and when I come back you will do as I ask, won't you?'

Do as she asked? He'd swear anything to get out of this, anything.

As she stared at him he made a downward movement with his head and she said, 'Very well'; then picking up the lantern she went out.

He waited until he heard her steps fading away across the yard before he turned and cried under his breath, 'Dick! Dick! do you hear me? Get up! Get up! Do you hear?'

When there was no movement or sound from the straw he reached out towards it but his hand fell short by a yard of the boy's feet.

Stooping down, he gathered up some loose straw from the floor and swiftly kneaded it into a ball, then threw it full at his son's face.

'Oh! Oh! Dad! Dad! Something . . . something hit me. Oh!'

'Wake up! Do you hear me? Wake up! Get on your feet, quickly!'

'Where are you, Dad? It's dark!'

'I'm here.'

'What's the matter? Are you bad?'

'Listen, son. Here, let me shake you awake.' He took the boy by the shoulders and shook him vigorously, then said, 'Did you hear that clanging?'

'Aye. Yes, Dad. What is it?'

'She's got me chained up.'

'Wh . . . wh. . .what?'

'She's clean mad, she's a lunatic. Now do as I tell you. Get out of here. Go as hard as your legs can carry you back to the main road, stop the first person you see and tell him. Better still, if there's somebody in a car or a cart get him to go to the nearest village and bring the polis. You understand?'

'Yes, Dad.'

'Go on then. The light's breaking; you'll see your way once you're outside.' He pushed Dick and when the chain clanged again he screwed up his face against the sound.

Once more he was leaning back against the partition. How had he got into this? In the name of God, what was happening to him? All he had ever wanted to do was lead a quiet, decent life. It didn't matter about being happy. He had never been happy – not until he met Alice. Yet it was since meeting Alice that evil seemed to have befallen him. This latest business, this was evil at its worst.

He was brought abruptly from his thinking by the sound of hurrying footsteps, then the light flooding the barn again, and there she was, lantern in one hand and Dick held by the collar in the other.

Stopping a few yards from him, she pushed the boy forward and he fell on his knees on to the stone floor, and she stared down on him for a moment before turning her attention to Abel, saying, 'You're stupid, you know that? I expected that's what you'd do. I'm up to any trick you can think of, just remember that. Now if you tell him to go out of this barn again I'll lock him up in the house.'

As she stared at him through the lantern light he had the impression that at this moment she was perfectly sane. Her voice was full of authority, her manner was brisk, and so he appealed to her as if she were sane, saying now, 'Look; let's get this straight. Unloosen me and we'll talk. I'll talk to you; I'll meet your demands. I promise I'll stay for a week

75

or so until your place is straight. I promise.'

She now put her head on one side as she gazed at him before saying, 'Well, that's more like it. You've come to your senses. We'll talk again after breakfast, or perhaps after dinner; or again it might be good for you to taste restriction for a day or so. We'll see about it. I'm going to give you plenty of time to think before you swear your oath, because once your oath is sworn *it . . . is . . . sworn*.'

The sweat was dripping from his chin as he stared back into her long white face and the panic that was already in him was increasing with a swiftness that was threatening to choke him. She could keep him here for days . . . for weeks! She needn't let anyone past that gate. Oh my God! He moved his head as if looking for some implement on which to lay his hands; but there was nothing on the floor except straw and the sacks he had discarded yesterday and their rucksacks lying against the far wall.

His lips moving soundlessly, he stared at her again, and she turned from him and went hastily out through the barn door.

He started when Dick, coming from behind, touched him on the hip and in a voice that was a whimper, said, 'Oh, Dad!'

Taking hold of the boy's hand he gripped it and, his own voice trembling, he said now, 'Don't be frightened; it'll only be for a short time. Something will happen, someone will come. Someone's got to come.'

'Dad.'

'Yes?'

'If . . . if I had a stick I could hit her from behind.'

Abel peered downwards into his son's face which he could just make out now against the coming dawn and he said, his words almost tumbling over each other, 'L . . . Look around, yon end of the barn, everywhere. See . . . see if you can find a stick or . . . or a piece of wood. Go on. Go on, look around.' He had hold of Dick's shoulder and went to push him forward, but stopped, saying, 'I know it's not light enough to see properly yet, but grope. Go on grope.' And he gave the boy such a push he almost fell on to his face.

After some minutes of listening to the boy moving about he hissed impatiently, 'Haven't you found anything yet?'

'No, Dad.'

'Oh my God! If only—' He tugged viciously at the chains; then stopped as Dick's voice came to him, saying, 'I've got this, Dad.'

'What is it?'

Dick was standing close to him now holding out a three foot rusted iron rod with three hooks on one end.

'It's a scraper. Good boy. Good boy.'

'What are you going to do with it, Dad?'

'I don't know . . . Yes, I do. I'm going to use it on her. I'll lash out at her legs. Now listen. When . . . when she brings the food in I'll reach out with it and swing it like this.' He demonstrated. 'Now if I miss her, I'll throw it to you. You'll likely have time to pick it up because she'll be staggered for a minute or so, and then you hit out at her legs with it. Just

77

hit out at her legs, mind. Bring her down. Then it will all depend on where she falls and how bad she is. But you might have to drag her towards me so I can search for the keys. Now stand over there near that stanchion. Be on the alert; keep your wits about you. Do you think you can do it?'

The boy swallowed, blinked, swallowed again, then said, 'Aye, Dad, aye. If you don't manage to hit her I've got to hit her across the legs.'

'Aye; just hit her across the legs . . .'

The light lifted and they could see about them now, but for the most part they kept their eyes on the open barn door; and the minutes seemed to stretch into hours as they waited.

When eventually Abel heard her footsteps on the cobbles his own knees became weak and his hands trembled. He knew that when he flung this iron rod at her and it made contact it would injure her badly; but it was either them or her and, as he kept telling himself, he was dealing with a mad woman.

The tray still held only breakfast for one, and he also noted something else. Her face had altered, it was full of suspicion, it was as if she was aware of the rod gripped in his fist, for she put the tray down on the ground quite some distance from him and, motioning towards Dick, said without looking at him, 'Come and take the tray.'

When the boy neither moved nor spoke, she said, 'You heard what I said, boy. Come and take the tray and put it where your father can reach it.'

'No!'

'What did you say?' She now looked directly at him.

'No . . . o!' Even the syllable was split with his fear.

'Well then, it'll have to remain where it is.' Yet as she spoke she pushed the tray a foot or so nearer towards Abel, and he, reaching out with his manacled hand as if to touch it, suddenly brought his other arm forward and threw the rod in a swirling movement full at her.

Her unearthly scream filled the barn and when her whole body left the ground and seemed to hover in mid-air for a moment, Dick joined his voice to hers. It wasn't until she lay twisted and silent on the stones that Abel could find his voice and yell at his son, 'Shut up! Shut up! will you?'

In the silence that followed he had no power left in him to direct the boy, it was as if the iron rod had stunned him too. Then he was brought to his senses by something that went beyond the suggestion of her being stunned when Dick whimpered, 'Is . . . is she d . . . dead, Dad?'

He gazed towards her. Dear God in heaven! she looked it. But the rod had only caught her on the arm; she'd likely hit her head when she fell. His own voice now came out on a stammer. 'Go o . . . o . . . over to her and l . . . look in her pockets for the key.'

When Dick hesitated he exploded. His voice high, almost reaching a scream, he cried, 'Go on, do as you're told!'

As Dick approached the twisted form he fully

expected her to spring from the ground and grab him by the throat, and his fingers tentatively touched her coat three times before he could put his hand into the pocket of it.

When he found the pocket empty he hastily withdrew his hand as if it had been bitten and, turning towards his father, he muttered, 'There's nothin' in it, Dad.'

'Try the other one.'

'She's . . . she's lying on it.'

'Well, turn her over!' Again Abel's voice came as a shout. 'Straighten her legs and . . . and she'll roll on to her back.'

Fearfully the child pulled one heavy booted leg straight, then the other, and when the body seemed to become alive as she rolled on to her back, he sprang away, crying, 'Oh, Dad! Dad!'

'Boy, listen to me.' Abel's voice was very low now, but it held more command than when he had bawled. 'If you don't find the key that will unloosen these locks she might well die, an' me with her. You understand?'

Dick understood nothing at this moment only his own fear, but he whimpered, 'What'll I do then, Dad?'

'Open her coat and look inside for a pocket in her skirt.'

It was a full minute later when the boy, as if he had found a treasure, cried, 'I've found them, Dad! I've found them, the keys.'

'Fetch them here, quick.'

Abel looked at the keys in the palm of his hand.

There were four on a ring and one by itself. He tried that first. Fumbling, he inserted it into the lock of the iron bracelet, then paused for a split second before turning it, and when it moved with ease as if it had been newly oiled and the two half circles fell apart, he slowly slid to the floor and for a full minute he stayed down there as if he were about to go to sleep while the boy stood looking at him open-mouthed.

When he did move it was almost with a spring, then he was on his feet, and with both hands he tore at the shackle around his ankle.

Now he was standing over her, and as he gazed down on her a new fear enveloped him. She looked dead; there was blood running down the side of her face from her hair. Oh my God! He put his hand tightly across his mouth, then turned his head slowly towards Dick as the boy said, 'She's bleedin', Dad. She's bleedin'.'

Reluctantly, he lowered himself down on to his knees beside her on the stone floor but he had to force his hand out to take hold of her wrist. When a pulse beat came to him he closed his eyes and drew in a long breath. With more courage now, he took her by the shoulder and called to her as if she were at a distance, 'Wake up! Come on, wake up!' But the only movement she made, and that an involuntary one, was when her head fell to one side and the flow of blood oozing through her hair increased.

He pulled himself to his feet and stood rubbing his chaffed wrist as he looked down on her. It could be just a surface scrape . . . But what if there was a gash there and she bled to death? He stepped back. Well, whatever happened to her he wasn't staying to find out. He'd had enough, more than enough. Staggering now as if slightly drunk, he said, 'Come on, get your pack, we're going.'

Dick obeyed him immediately by grabbing up his rucksack and ramming his blanket into it; then he ran to the opening of the barn and there he waited, his body half turned as if on the point of a run.

When Abel reached the barn door, his rucksack hitched high on his shoulders, he turned and gave one last look towards the figure lying now like a dead animal waiting to be carted away; then turning swiftly, his hand on the boy's shoulder, he propelled him across the yard at a run. But having passed through the gate, he stopped. He did not look back but stared ahead. What if she didn't recover and lay there all day, perhaps into the night and died of exposure? They could have him up.

Don't be silly. He shook his head at himself. Nobody knew he had been here; it could be days before anyone looked in again . . . Aye, it could, and she'd certainly be dead by then.

If was as if the words had been spoken by somebody else and they brought his chin in to his chest, and when the boy's hand gripped his and the small voice said, 'What's the matter, Dad?' he took no notice but continued to stand, his head bent, until, giving another hitch to the rucksack, he walked on.

Five minutes later he was standing on top of the hill looking into the distance down on to the cluster of houses he had noticed the night before last and to the left where lay a narrow strip of road leading to them. And now, so quickly did he go down the hill that the boy had to run to keep up with him.

The first cottage they came to was actually some three hundred yards from the village itself, and as he passed the gate the door opened and a man came out, evidently a farm worker. He stood on the step for a moment and gazed at the pair before saying, 'Mornin'.'

'Good mornin'.' Abel stopped and waited for the man to come to the gate and he definitely surprised the man by saying abruptly, 'Is there a doctor in that village, or . . . or a polis . . . policeman?'

'Aye, there's one but not t'other. Polis is a good two miles away but Doc Armstrong, he's in the first house.' The man nodded along the road.

'Thanks, thanks.' Abel was about to hurry away when the man added, 'But you won't find him there this mornin', he's over at young Phil Gallespie's; his wife's havin' her first, an' hard goin' with her it is they say. Saw doc goin' along there past the gate here with his buggy close on ten last night, hasn't come back yet, else wife would have heard him. Light sleeper she is, wake half the night, sleeps half the day. You feelin' bad or summat?'

'No, no.' Abel shook his head. 'It's . . . it's the lady over . . . over at the pig farm; she's had an accident.'

'Ah, Miss Tilda.' The man smiled broadly now. 'What's happened to Tilly-the-touched now?'

Abel paused before answering. Tilly-the-touched,

he had called her; it must be common knowledge that she was barmy. 'She . . . she had a fall.'

'Well, I shouldn't worry about her, the doc will see to her when he gets back. Related he is to her, half-cousin he is; the only one that bothers about her . . . 'cos he's the only one she'll allow to bother about her. Barmy, barmy for years. She should be locked up, everybody says so . . . Speak of the devil, there, look! there's the buggy. That's the doc comin' back. See, round the end of the road there. You'd better go and tell him, although he won't thank you 'cos he'll be wantin' his bed.'

Abel nodded, then hurried along the road with Dick following him towards the advancing trap, and just before coming abreast of the horse he hailed the driver and, looking up at the man sitting on the leather-covered seat, he said, 'Excuse me, sir.'

The doctor drew the trap to a stop and, gazing wearily down at Abel, asked, 'Yes, what is it?'

'It's . . . it's the lady over at the pig farm.' He didn't say your relative. 'There's something I must tell you.'

He watched the doctor ease his soft trilby from off his brow and push his fingers through his hair, then almost sigh, 'What's happened now?'

'Well, sir, I stopped there the night before last and asked if we could sleep in the barn, my son and I' – he nodded towards Dick – 'an' she said, yes, if . . . if I worked for a night's rest and some food. This I did all day yesterday. Then she got it into her head that she wanted me to stay on. She . . . she tried to make me promise and I said I couldn't, we . . . we were leaving in the morning. You see I am making me way North. Well . . . well—' He shook his head as if he couldn't believe the substance of what he was about to say and he brought the words out at a rush; 'Believe it or not, sir, she had me chained up. When I woke up I found meself chained both by the ankle and the wrist.' He held up his hand to show the chaffed skin. 'She must have put something in the cocoa she brought last night because I remember nothing until, as I said, I woke up. Then she kept at me to swear by the Bible. I would have sworn on anything to get loose, but when I promised she just left. Well' – he again shook his head – 'to cut it short, sir, I got my boy to look for a piece of wood or anything with which I could hit out at her. He found an iron rod and . . . and I used it on her, but only on her arm. As she fell she must have struck her head against the stone floor for it split open somewhere at the back. I tried to get her round, but I couldn't. Anyway, all I wanted was to get away from that place but . . . but I thought . . . well, she might peg out lying there. I'm sorry. I . . . I didn't mean to hurt her but to find meself chained up, well, I nearly went mad, I . . .'

'It's all right, it's all right, don't harass yourself.' The doctor sighed. 'But I think you'd better come back with me.'

'Back there?' Abel stepped on to the grass verge in protest saying, 'Oh no! sir. I don't want to go back there ever; I don't want to see that place again.'

'Well, from what you've told me I'm afraid I'll have to insist. What if she's dead? Come on, don't worry, get the boy up, the sooner we get there the sooner we'll see what damage has been done.'

Abel hesitated for a moment before swinging Dick up into the back of the trap; then pulling himself up, he sat in the corner of the seat, his body bent forward, his hands hanging between his knees, the rucksack still on his back . . .

It seemed to him it was only seconds later when there he was again standing in that awful barn looking down on the woman while the doctor examined her.

'Well, she's not dead. It'll take more than a fall I'm afraid to kill Matilda, but she's got a nasty gash in the back of her head and I'm afraid you've managed to break her arm. Now we've got to get her into the house. Give me a hand. There's nothing of her, she's as light as a feather.'

And Abel found she was indeed as light as a feather, he could have carried her himself, all her weight seemed to be in her clothes.

'We won't get in the front door, we'll have to go round the back.'

Having pushed their way through the back door, then through a large kitchen, a hall and now into a sitting-room, Abel's mouth almost fell into a gape with surprise, because the contrast between the inside and outside of the house was amazing. Everything here was shining; the furniture and the floors were polished to a high intensity, the curtains were white; there were even flowers in the vase on the table.

'Just lay her on the couch here.'

'I can't believe it.'

'What?' The doctor looked to where Abel was standing gazing round the room, then said, 'Oh, the spruceness. Oh, that's all part of Tilda . . . ah, she's coming round. Look, help me to get these coats off her before she becomes fully conscious else I'll never get them off. I'd better give her a jab; then set her arm too, for they won't have her in the hospital, they'll send her over to the asylum and if she goes in this time she'll never come out again. Poor Tilda.'

Abel stood back from the couch. The woman had opened her eyes and though they were levelled on him they seemed expressionless, until their gaze took in the doctor; then there came into them a look of bright eagerness and she made to raise herself, saying as she did so, 'Oh, John! John!'

'It's all right, Matilda, it's all right. You've just had a fall.'

'John, make him stay.' Now she was clinging on to the doctor and gabbling, 'He was sent by God to see to things and get the place ready for Arthur coming back, but . . . but he wouldn't stay. He wouldn't stay, John. M . . . make him stay, John. Make him stay.'

'All right, my dear, all right. Now just you lie back; you've hurt your arm and your head. I'm just going to give you a little jab and you'll go to sleep, and when you wake up Molly will be here

87

to see you. You don't mind Molly, do you?'

'I want him to stay, John. I want him to stay.'

'There you are. There you are.'

When she closed her eyes and her body went limp the doctor turned to Abel and said, 'You certainly made an impression on her. Now let's get her fixed up. Just hold her arm, so . . .'

It was not until half an hour later, in the kitchen, that the doctor, having poured out three cups of tea, was handing one to Abel and another to Dick, asked, 'Where do you hail from?'

'Sussex.'

'Oh, Sussex. Nice county Sussex. I know it well. Which part?'

Abel hesitated a moment before saying, 'Hastings.'

'Oh, Hastings. I know Hastings and roundabout. What's your name? In all the excitement I've forgotten to ask.'

Abel hesitated. He had said that he came from Hastings and the man had said he knew Hastings and roundabout. Perhaps that was why in the next fleeting second he decided to give a false name. Well, it wasn't exactly false, he told himself, for it was his mother's maiden name. 'Gray,' he said. 'Abel Gray.'

As the doctor turned again towards the teapot, nodding as he said, 'Gray. Oh, Gray,' Abel glanced swiftly at Dick and with an almost imperceptible shake of his head warned him to silence.

'I knew some Grays; they lived in Rye. Have you any relations there?'

'No, sir.'

'Well, now, Mr Gray, what am I going to say to you for all the trouble Matilda has put you through? I can understand it was a very frightening experience.'

'It was that. Yes, it was that.'

'You're not going to make anything of it, report her or anything?'

'Oh, no, no, sir. All I want to do is to be on my way.'

'That's good of you. She's to be pitied you know; she's had a very sad life. We are related way back. Her mother and my father were second cousins. But there's been insanity all along the line on her mother's side. The poor woman ended up in the asylum and Matilda was left to bring herself up. All this business of the shining house, the waiting, goes back to a hand they had here. She fell in love with him and the young swine he was, he would have married her just to get the place and the money, only he got one of the village girls into trouble and so that put paid to the romance. Then he went to France and she's still waiting for him coming back.'

'Yes, she told me; she said he was missing.'

'Missing!' The doctor laughed. 'It would be better for his wife if he was; she's just given birth to her eleventh.'

'He certainly came back then.' There was a suspicion of a chuckle in Abel's voice and the doctor laughed outright as he said, 'Oh yes, he certainly came back.' Then his laughter trailed away and he added sadly, 'But poor Tilda, she has this house all spruced up. Morning, noon and night she's cleaning it; everything ready for his return. And so it'll go on till the end . . . Well now, you'll want to get on your way, and if you'll do me one last favour you'll knock on the door of the cottage where you met old Harry this morning and ask his wife to come up here as soon as she can. Will you do that for me?'

'Yes, gladly.'

'Now about money. What does she owe you?'

'Well, she offered to give me a pound a week, but I wouldn't have stayed, not if it had been ten. I worked a full day yesterday. Still, I got my meals.'

'And a big shock along with them.'

'You're right there. Yes, you're right there, sir.'

'Well now—' The doctor went to the dresser at the far side of the kitchen and, opening a drawer, he took out a cash box and from it extracted two one-pound notes and, handing them to Abel, said, 'Will that do?'

'Oh, more than enough. But I won't refuse it, thank you all the same.'

'And here.' Again the doctor was dipping into the cash box, and now taking out half a crown he handed it to Dick, saying, 'I'm sure you could make use of that.'

'Oh ta. Thank you, sir. Thank you.'

The doctor patted his head; then nodded towards the kitchen door and said, 'Go and get your pack,' and as Dick obeyed him the doctor put his hand gently on Abel's arm restraining him for a moment, and when the boy was out of earshot, he said, 'Are you aiming to settle somewhere before the winter?'

'Oh, yes, certainly, sir.'

'Good, good. The child doesn't look over robust, and he's small for his age. You said he was what, seven?'

'Yes, coming up eight. But he's never ailed anything, he's wiry.'

'Yes, well, in the long run it's the wiry ones who turn out to be the toughest, but I'd get shelter if I were you before the bad weather sets in.'

'I mean to do that, sir, definitely.'

'Goodbye then, and good luck. And thank you for being such a help back there.' He nodded towards the sitting-room.

'Thank you, sir, I never thought it would end so . . . so peaceably . . .'

They were once more walking out of the gate and as they strode the same path along which he had scudded in fear only an hour or so earlier he thought to himself, By! it's a strange world. There was one thing to be said about the road, you did see life. But then he wouldn't choose to see too much of the life he had seen in the last few days.

Dick now broke into his thoughts saying, 'Why did you say our name was Gray, Dad?'

Abel looked down on the boy and paused before he answered, 'Well, I said I was from Hastings and he said he knew it well, so what was to stop him from enquiring about me should he ever go back there? It's a small world, you know, and news could just seep through to her . . . your mother. It might sound improbable like but such things do happen . . . You don't want to go back, do you?'

'Oh no! Dad. And Gray's a nice name.'

'It was your grandma's maiden name.'

'Was it?'

'Yes.'

'Oh.'

The knowledge seemed to please the boy and, looking up at Abel, he now said, 'He gave me a full half-crown, Dad. But I won't spend it, I'll save it.'

Abel looked down on his son steadily for a moment, thinking, he could have added, 'for a rainy day', and the doctor's words came back to him 'He doesn't look over robust and he's small for his age. Get into some place for the winter.' . . . Get them into some place before the winter? But what if he couldn't? What then, the workhouse?

He shook his head at the thought and his step quickened.

What did one do under circumstances like these? Pray? Pray that something might turn up? Everybody on the road was praying for something to turn up; he would have to aim his prayer higher and ask for a miracle.

PART TWO

The Miracle

1

Another eleven days had passed since they left Leeds and for the last five it had rained almost incessantly. They had been soaked to the skin and for three nights had slept wet. Abel was experiencing a new misery, one that was now bordering on despair. There were two avenues open to him; the first, to go into the workhouse and stay there for the winter. Were he to do so he knew he would be separated from the boy, but the child would be assured of shelter and of some form of education. The alternative was to make for North Shields where lived his half-cousin, John Pratt. The snag here was that Lena also had relatives living there, and once she knew of his presence there she would come scurrying across country and, to put it in her own words, claim her rights as a wife, which simply meant someone to work for her.

Well, were he to choose the latter course he might as well have not left the South at all; and so it was Hexham and the workhouse. Hexham he reckoned was far enough away from North Shields to preclude any fears of his being recognised.

He knew that the country they were passing through would have appeared beautiful had the weather been different. It was odd the effect the weather had on people, but they certainly seemed less inclined to be kind when it was wet. He'd had to knock on the back door of four houses in Piercebridge before he was given a can of boiling water to make some tea. Yet in the fourth house the woman had given him not only hot water but also a couple of meat sandwiches, half a loaf, and a dab of butter. And in the village of West Auckland they had been given a bowl of broth each and tuppence. He was glad of that tuppence and he had thanked the woman warmly, at the same time remembering how scornfully he had handed the penny back to the girl on the boat.

But now they were into the heart of the country, walking through great lonely stretches, hills with their summits lost in the rain clouds, everything under foot sodden, and where the fields ran level they were entirely covered with water.

They had just passed Scales Cross and were making for Riding Mill. How far Hexham lay from there he wasn't quite sure, eight, ten miles; well, however long or short they wouldn't make it today for within another couple of hours it would be dark and he'd have to find an outhouse or a byre of some kind in which to bed down, for the boy was on his last legs. After leaving Leeds the lad had perked up considerably, mostly from relief at being rid of the mad woman, he thought, but for days now he had spoken only occasionally, and his silences told Abel of his feelings more plainly than if he had whined all the way.

The squelching of his feet inside his boots seemed to get louder with each step, and when he espied a piece of woodland lying to the right ahead of him he looked back at the boy who was some steps behind him and said, 'We'll go in yonder and have a rest, eh?'

Dick did not say, as he had done confidently during the first days of the adventure, 'Yes, Dad,' he merely made a small downward motion with his head, so slight that it couldn't be called a nod.

As they neared the belt of trees Abel peered through the rain towards a dark object standing by the side of the road. Rubbing the water from his eyes he made it out to be a motor-car, a black motor-car. That was why at first he hadn't been able to distinguish what it was. When they came abreast of the car he turned his glance towards it and saw a man sitting in the driving seat. He was leaning back as if resting, and when he lifted his hand as if in salute, after a moment's hesitation, Abel returned the salute with the same gesture.

They were past the car when the man's voice stopped them and Abel turned round and looked to where the driver was hanging out of the window seemingly gasping for breath, and what he was saying again and again was, 'Help! Help! Help!'

When Abel reached him he bent down and said, 'Are you all right, sir?'

'Ill.' The man closed his eyes and gasped and again repeated, 'Ill.' And now his doubled fist was pressed against the front of his jacket.

Abel looked up and down the road helplessly,

then said, 'Can . . . can I help you? What is it?'

'Drive? You drive?'

'Not . . . not a motor-car, sir, not like this. Driven a tractor and a lorry, but . . . but a long time ago.'

'Please. Please drive.'

'But, sir.'

'Get . . . get me home, please.'

'Where do you live, sir?'

'Fell . . . Fellburn.'

'Fellburn?' He screwed up his face. Fellburn was miles away, near Gateshead. 'I . . . I could go and find a farm and get you help, sir.'

The man shook his head.

Abel looked down at Dick in bewilderment. Then as if coming to a sudden decision he reached out, opened the back door of the car, then stooped and lifted the boy bodily in. Pulling off his own rucksack that was dripping with water, he flung it on to the floor, banged the door, then opened the driver's door. Gently, he eased the man from his seat and helped, almost carried him round the bonnet and put him in the front passenger seat, then took his own seat behind the wheel.

The man was lying back, his eyes closed, his fist pressed again tight into his chest and he seemed to be fighting for every breath.

Abel bit on his lip. How in heavens did he start the thing? Of course, the handle. There it was lying between the two seats. He jumped out of the car again, went to the bonnet, plugged in the starting handle, and swung it a number of times but with no positive result. He seemed to have no strength in his arms, yet two months ago he could have felled a sapling with a couple of blows. Now as if he was attacking an enemy he gripped the handle again and, putting all his strength behind it, he forced it round, and when the car shuddered into action he, too, was gasping for breath.

The man looked at him as he entered the car again, and pointing to the gear box he said, 'Start her. Start her.'

There was a grinding sound and the car seemed to jump off the verge right into the middle of the road, and then was moving down it, dead centre.

It took them ten minutes to reach Riding Mill and as they entered the village Abel shouted to the man without taking his eyes off the road, 'Wouldn't it be better if I stopped, sir, and you saw a doctor?'

'No, just . . . just drive on.'

'But . . . but which way? I don't know the road.'

'Turn . . . turn right next corner and . . . and make for Newcastle. I'll . . . I'll tell you when . . . when to turn off . . . Go through Whickham and skirt Gateshead.'

There was very little traffic on the road. He passed a few vehicles, or at least they passed him: a few buses, three vans, and not more than half a dozen motor-cars. It was as if the rain was keeping indoors all the vehicles too, and for this he was mighty thankful. Yet as he sat behind the wheel, his hands gripping it, his body tense, he could not help but think how fantastic it was: he had been making for the workhouse and now here he was driving in this car. A touch of wry humour came into his thinking. It would be odd, he thought, if, after depositing the owner at his home, they were, by way of thanks, driven to the workhouse, Gateshead workhouse now, in a motor-car.

Having by-passed Gateshead and Low Fell without incident, they were leaving the countryside and entering the outskirts of Fellburn when he spoke again. 'Is it right in the town . . . your house, sir?'

'No, quite near. Past . . . past next house, open yard.'

Abel drove slowly past what looked from a sharp glance to the left of him like a big house standing in the middle of a large garden, then a narrow strip of paddock, and here was the yard as the man had said, an open yard. There was an iron framework all of ten feet high and fifteen feet wide and, swinging from the top bar, was a board on which was written: 'Cycles bought, sold, repaired, and for hire. Proprietor, Peter Maxwell.'

Not previously having had to stop he now fumbled at the gears and was able to bring the car to a halt only a yard from the house wall. As he lay back for a second and drew in a deep breath the back door of the house was opened and a young woman ran into the yard and, coming to the car, she looked in and exclaimed in some amazement, 'Oh, my goodness!'

'He . . . he had a bad turn, miss. He . . . he asked me to bring him home.'

'Very good. Very good of him . . . Very good.' The man now leaned forward in an attempt to get out of the car, and the young woman said, 'Help me with him, will you?'

Abel hurried from his seat and round to the other side, and there he said, 'Leave him to me; I'll get him in.'

The man was small, thin, and his body was light. Abel could, if he had been up to his usual strength, have carried him in. And he almost did. Pulling the man's right arm round his neck and with his left forearm under the man's left oxter, he half carried him.

'Bring him in here. Lay him on the couch.'

When the man was lying stretched out on the couch the young woman rushed out of the room, only to return within a minute, a glass of water in one hand and two pills on the palm of the other.

'Here, take these.' She half turned to Abel. 'Will you raise his head, please?'

As Abel raised the man's head and shoulders she said, 'Here now, get these down you. I told you you should never have gone all that way. If they wanted to sell it so badly they should have taken it themselves.'

'Ssh! Ssh!' The man closed his eyes wearily; then opened them again almost immediately and, turning his head slowly, he looked at Abel, saying, 'You were very good, very . . . very good. Kind . . . samaritan, yes indeed.'

'Don't talk; rest for a moment and then we'll get you upstairs.' She again turned to Abel, saying, 'Will you stay and give me a hand?'

'Yes, yes, of course. But first may I bring my

boy out of the car, he's very wet?'

'Oh!' She blinked and looked surprised, then said, 'Yes, yes, of course. Bring him inside.'

Abel went hastily out of the sitting-room, across a hallway, and into the kitchen, noticing as he did so the extreme neatness everywhere but mostly the warm, almost faint-making smell of food cooking. It came from the direction of a shining black-leaded oven at the far end of the room.

A few minutes later while pressing Dick down into a chair near the open fire, he realised the effect of the smell on the boy and he whispered, 'Sit there and get dry; you'll likely get a drink of something in a minute. All right?'

The boy nodded at him with more emphasis now and gazed round the room as if he had suddenly been dropped into some heavenly place.

When Abel re-entered the sitting-room again the man was saying, 'Now don't worry, don't worry; there's never a good but there's a better. Haven't I always told you God provides? Didn't He send me help in my hour of need?'

The words, Oh my God! almost escaped through Abel's own lips. Not another of them surely! He'd had enough of religious maniacs to last him a lifetime. Yet this man appeared normal . . . as yet; and what he said next seemed to substantiate the fact.

'I'm all right, Hilda. Just leave me quiet, then I'll get upstairs. What . . . what you can do is . . . is give this good man and his boy a hot drink. And . . . and let them dry their clothes.'

The young woman turned a sharp glance on Abel

before looking at the man again and saying, 'I'll see to that once you're settled, not until.'

'Oh, Hilda! Hilda! Child! Well . . . well, let's get it over with.'

Again Abel had his arms about the man and this time he actually did carry him up the stairs and on to a square landing.

'In here.' The young woman had preceded them into a bedroom and had swiftly turned down the quilt on a large mahogany-framed bed, and when Abel had laid the man on it she dismissed him rather peremptorily, saying, 'I can see to him now. Please wait downstairs.'

Abel made no reply but turned and went out of the room, closing the door behind him. On the landing, he took stock of the place, telling himself it was a fine house, one of the old sort. There were closed doors on three sides, the fourth side being railed with a mahogany balustrade except where the stairs led down into the hall.

As he stepped into the hall he had come to the conclusion that no longer were houses like this one built; here, there was a substantial feeling about the place. A warm and a homely one, too.

When he entered the kitchen Dick was still sitting where he had left him. The steam was rising from him as if he were being simmered and his face looked small, white, and weary, the eyes too big for him.

He went to the boy's side and, dropping on to his hunkers, he held his hands out to the blaze of the fire, saying, 'Nice kitchen, eh?'

'Yes. Dad.'

He turned and looked at the boy and there came a restriction in his chest and a tightness to his throat, and a break in his voice as he muttered, 'Don't worry, son. We'll . . . we'll have a kitchen like this one day. Yes, we will; I promise you.'

The boy didn't reply but bent his head forward and rubbed his sweating palms together.

Getting swiftly to his feet, Abel now went towards the table that was placed under one of the two windows in the room. There was on it a green chenille cloth bordered with tasselled braid and, as if he were in his own house, he grabbed a handful of the tassels and began to twist them between his two hands. But realising what he was doing, his hands sprang apart and with his fingers he hastily began to smooth the tassels out again.

He went to the window and stood looking out. The rain had eased to a mere drizzle. He looked at the flagged yard. It was so well paved there were no puddles on it. To the right was a row of what appeared to be workshops. The double doors of one were open and he glimpsed dismembered bicycles hanging on nails from the wall, and part of a bench. The buildings on the other side of the yard looked like garages. There were four of them, double-storeyed, having lofts or storerooms above them. The bicycle business looked to be thriving.

'He's settled, he'll go to sleep now.'

He started and swung round; he hadn't heard her come into the kitchen. He looked at her fully for the first time. She was what he would call comely;

she was of medium height, slightly on the plump side, her skin was fresh and her eyes clear, and her hair an abundant brown. Her mouth was small, her lips full. Altogether she seemed like the house in that she gave off an assurance, sort of God's in his heaven, all's right with the world. Good Lord! there was he spouting now. It was catching.

'What . . . what is the trouble with your father?' It was a polite enquiry, but when the answer came, 'He's not my father, he's my husband,' he felt the colour sweep over him and he almost stammered, 'I'm sorry, miss . . . ma'am.'

She stared at him for a moment, her head wagging slightly, then she smiled as she said, 'Oh, it's understandable; it's a mistake many people make.' Then she turned from him to the boy, and her voice took on a high-pitched note as she cried, 'Oh my goodness! child, you're steaming like a pudding. Get that coat off! You'll catch your death. Whatever made you sit before the fire with that on?'

As she pulled Dick from the chair none too gently, and tugged the coat from him, Abel said, 'It's my fault; I thought he would dry out before we went on again.'

'On again?' She turned her head towards him. She was holding the coat between her fingers and thumb as if it were lice-ridden; then she thrust it over the brass rod running under the mantelshelf and the length of the fireplace.

'Yes, we're . . . we're on the road I'm afraid. I've . . . I've been looking for work, but . . . but unsuccessfully.'

'With the child?'

'Yes.' He lowered his lids. 'I . . . I had to bring him; circumstances were such . . . well, I had to bring him.'

'Oh! Oh, I'm sorry.' Her voice dropped and she spoke in an aside as if the boy wouldn't be able to hear. 'His mother, is she . . . ?'

The question caused Abel to turn his head away from her. What did one say? What could one say? I've walked out on my wife and brought the boy with me and we've been on the road for weeks and another one will finish him and when that happens that'll be the finish of me too . . .

'Oh, I'm sorry, I understand.' From being low, her tone now rose sharply as she leant towards Dick, smiling now and saying, 'Do you like shepherd's pie?'

'Yes, ma'am.'

'Well, Mr Maxwell won't be eating any tonight and so you can have his share.' She was still smiling when she turned and looked at Abel, and he said, 'Thank you, ma'am. Thank you very much . . .'

It was a great effort to eat normally and not to shovel the hot appetising food into his mouth, and he knew that the boy was having the same trouble. The shepherd's pie was followed by a plateful of creamy rice pudding, and this by a mug of tea and a buttered teacake, a whole one each. Never before and never again was a meal to taste quite like this one.

Immediately they were finished he rose from the table, saying, 'I'll wash the dishes up, ma'am.'

'Oh no, no' – she shook her head – 'I'll see to those. Thanks all the same.'

He remained standing, looking at her now as she bustled around the table, and when she went to remove Dick's plate, Abel reached out and pulled the boy to his feet, and she said, 'It's all right, it's all right. Leave him be.'

'Ma'am.'

'Yes?' She stopped and looked at him.

'Could I ask a favour of you?'

'Well' – her face became straight – 'it all depends what it is.'

'Would you allow us to sleep in one of your outhouses tonight?'

'Sleep in one of the outhouses?' She looked down on Dick, then back up to him, and moving her head slowly, she said, 'I . . . I imagined you were on your way somewhere. You mean you have nowhere to sleep?'

'That's it, ma'am.'

'Well, where did you expect to sleep tonight . . . and with him?' She was again looking at the boy.

'We . . . we were originally making for Hexham and . . . and the workhouse. I felt I must get him into somewhere, he's had more than enough on the road.'

'Yes, yes, I should say so.' She nodded her head. 'Yes, of course you may sleep outside. There's rooms above the garage. They're in a bit of a mess; I haven't been up there since Jimmy went, I haven't had time. Jimmy, by the way was our hand, he helped Mr Maxwell, he died a fortnight ago. He . . .

he suffered from gas from the war, but he was a good worker. We miss him.'

During the time she had been talking she had cleared the table, put the dishes in the sink, washed out milk bottles, and put the rice pudding dishes and the shepherd's pie dish in to soak. Then walking towards the door and without looking at him, she said, 'Come along and I'll show you the room.'

They mounted a dark stairway set between two garages, and followed her through a door at the stairhead, where she switched on a light to reveal what apparently was a living-room. In it was an old couch, two armchairs, a bookcase, and two tables, one in the middle of the room, the other standing under a dormer window, and on this one was a gas ring and some cooking utensils.

'It's in a mess, he was never very tidy, and he couldn't cook for himself. He had his main meal with us, but made his tea and odds and ends on there.' She pointed to the table under the window. 'There's no heating except from the oil stove.' She again pointed, to the corner of the room now. 'But he didn't mind that; when he wasn't working he was mostly out at nights.' She gave a jerk to her head, then added quickly, 'But he was a good worker, none better. This is the bedroom. I'm afraid to look at it, the mess it'll be in.' She thrust open a door and showed a dishevelled bed, and equally cluttered wash-hand stand, and a chest of drawers. 'The other room is just full of his junk.' She pointed to another door, then added, 'He died in hospital.

He had no people . . . Well, if you can put up with this—' She turned and faced him.

He smiled quietly down on her as he said, 'At the moment, ma'am, it has the appearance of a palace to me.'

'Tut . . . tut.' She clicked her tongue, then added, 'Well, bring your things up. But first sort out what is wet and leave them in the kitchen, they'll be dry in the morning.'

'Thank you, ma'am. Thank you very much indeed.'

He watched her go towards the door. All her movements were quick, brisk like her voice. She looked so young and very much alive and she was married to that man! He must be fifty if he was a day. Anyway, they had been the means of providing them with a night's shelter, and for the time being that was all that mattered. He looked at Dick and smiled as he said, 'We'll be all right here, eh?'

'Yes, Dad.' Dick nodded, then said slowly, 'The house was nice, wasn't it, Dad?'

Abel turned away from the look on the pale thin face and from the eyes that held such weariness, and he answered flatly, 'Yes, very nice.'

'The kitchen was lovely and warm, wasn't it? I've never seen such a big kitchen. An' the young lady, she's nice an' all, isn't she?'

Abel bit on his lip, then turned and went into the bedroom. Here, flinging back the rumpled covers from the bed, he looked at the sheets. They were clean, comparatively so anyway. He put his hand on them. At least they were dry.

'It would make a nice house this, wouldn't it, Dad?'

He was still leaning over the bed – he hadn't heard the boy come into the room – and he remained so, his hand flat on the sheet as he said slowly, 'We're only here for the night; make the best of it, but don't start dreaming.' Raising himself slowly, he looked down on the boy, and the pain in the wide brown eyes stabbed at him with their misery. Turning abruptly from him, he said, 'Come on, let's get our things up.'

2

Strange, the bed had been comfortable. After having eaten another meal which she had called a bite, his belly had felt comfortably full too, and although every bone in his body had ached with tiredness, he hadn't been able to get to sleep for hours, and so when through a daze he heard the knocking on the door he imagined he had just dropped off.

Sitting up abruptly, he held his head in his hands for a moment, then pressed his thumbs against his eyeballs before swinging his legs out of the bed. After pulling on his trousers he made towards the door and when he opened it and saw her standing with her back to him placing a tray on the table he muttered, 'Oh . . . oh I'm sorry. I must have slept in.'

'It's all right. There's a jug of tea. Come down when you're ready and have something to eat.'

'Thank you. Thank you, ma'am.'

He went back to the bed and shook Dick gently by the shoulder, saying, 'Come on. Come on, it's time to get up.'

The boy hardly moved, and he had to shake him

again and pull him from his side on to his back before he could get him awake.

'Yes, Dad. Aye, Dad.'

'There's some nice hot tea here. Come on. Just put your jacket around you.'

'What time is it, Dad?'

'Nigh on eight. We slept in.'

It was a quarter past eight when Abel knocked on the kitchen door and her voice came to them immediately, saying, 'Come on. Come on in.'

They stepped into the kitchen and both stopped. Everything looked bright, sunlit; the sun was shining outside but in this room the light seemed intensified. The table was set for breakfast on a blue bordered cloth; the china, blue willow patterned, looked thick, chubby. The walls of the kitchen, Abel noticed, were painted yellow and the curtains were blue. They were what he termed to himself airy-fairy curtains for they were wafting in the breeze from the doorway. The floor was stone, made up of great slate coloured slabs but their dullness was relieved by coloured rugs; they weren't clippy mats like he remembered from the northern kitchens of years ago, these were real rugs.

'Sit yourself down. I hope you like porridge.'

'Anything, ma'am.' His voice sounded hoarse.

'And how are we this morning?' She was smiling down on Dick.

'All right, ma'am.'

She laughed outright at him and when he smiled back at her she said, 'That's better.'

'Now there you are, tuck in, and I'm sure you

won't say no to some bacon and eggs.'

Abel could make no reply. Picking up his spoon, he began slowly to eat the porridge, but before he could swallow it he had to force each mouthful over a lump in his throat. For a moment his mind seemed to go hysterical and he yelled at himself, My God! don't do that. He was on the point of crying. Why, he couldn't exactly say. He had never felt like this since the day he had run into the wood and beaten his head against that tree.

When he turned his head to the side and blew his nose, she said, 'What is it? Don't you like porridge?'

'Oh. Oh yes, ma'am, yes.' He kept his head down. 'I've got a bit of a cold, that's all.'

'Oh, and no wonder. Wet through as you were, as both of you were, it's a wonder you haven't caught pneumonia. By the way, when you've finished your meal, Mr Maxwell would like to have a word with you. He's much better this morning.'

'Oh, I'm glad to hear that, ma'am.'

'It was a very bad turn he had. He tells me it was a lonely road and he could have been left out there all night if you hadn't happened by, and . . . and that would surely have been the end of him. I've rung for the doctor. I don't always because I'm used to his turns, but he was in a bad way last night and he won't rest for me, it's only the doctor that can make him stay in bed for a few days.'

'What . . . what is his trouble, ma'am?'

'Mostly bronchial asthma, but . . . well, of late years his heart's turned on him. That's what I'm afraid he had yesterday, a heart attack. He said it wasn't, it was just the asthma. By the way, what is your name?'

'Er . . . Gray. Gray, ma'am, Abel Gray. And my boy is called Dick.'

'Oh.' She nodded from one to the other; then pointing to a shelf above the oven she said, 'When you're ready your breakfast is there; I'll be upstairs. When you've finished make your way up.'

'Yes, ma'am.'

The room to themselves, they looked at each other across the table and Dick said in a small voice, 'It's a lovely breakfast, isn't it, Dad?'

'Yes, yes, it is, so make the best of it, eat your fill.'

'You haven't eaten all your porridge, Dad.'

'No, but I'm going to, I'll get through it. You carry on.'

The bacon and egg and fried bread was delicious but he had to force himself to eat it. In panic, he wondered if he were sickening for something.

The meal over, he went to the sink and washed his hands, wet his comb under the tap, and combed his hair back, pulled his jacket straight at the back and the front, then saying to the boy, 'Sit there until I come back,' he went out of the kitchen and into the hall and slowly mounted the stairs, and when he was outside the bedroom door he paused for a moment before knocking.

'Come in. Come in.'

When he entered the room he saw the man sitting in bed propped up with pillows. He looked older, if anything, this morning, his age seeming to be emphasised by the youthfulness of his wife.

'Good morning, sir. I hope you're feeling better.'

'Aw yes, I'm feeling fine, thanks be to God . . . and to you.' He smiled slowly; then nodding his head, he added, 'For a man who said he didn't know anything about cars you did very well.'

'Thank you, sir.'

'My wife says your name is Gray, Mr Abel Gray.'

'Yes, sir.'

'Well, Abel, I'm going to ask you some questions and I want truthful answers. A lot will depend on them, you understand?'

'Yes, sir.'

'You are on the road, that is evident, but that's no disgrace these days except that you are trailing a young child with you. Now why is that?'

Abel looked down unblinking into the man's eyes now. He had asked for the truth and what would be the result if he were to tell him the truth: within the next five minutes he'd be going out under that gateway. If he told a lie, it was possible that tonight he'd be sleeping up above the garages again, but more important, the boy would be sleeping up above those garages again. He still hadn't blinked when he said. 'I suffered an emotional loss, sir.' That sounded good to his ears and it was true. Oh yes, it was true. Alice, dear, dear Alice had been an emotional loss.

'Well . . . yes, we thought it might be that.' The man turned and looked at his wife. 'Well now, have you ever been in trouble . . . prison?'

'No, sir, no, never.' It was the second lie, but his denial was emphatic because he didn't consider his term in the army prison the result of an offence on his part.

'Do you drink?'

'I . . . I used to have a glass of beer when I could afford it but I've never tasted it for the last two months or more.'

'Good, good. How long have you been on the road, just the two months?'

'Yes, sir, just about that.'

'Well now, my first question is, do you think you could do without drink altogether?'

'I'm sure I could, sir; it isn't important to me.'

'Good, good. Now one more question, what is your religion?'

Abel did blink now; he hadn't any religion, he didn't even believe in a god. He'd had doubts before he was dragged into the war but that massacre, in which he would take no part and was therefore branded, had eliminated from his mind once and for all any idea of a benevolent deity. The same question had been asked of him when he was conscripted, and when he had answered, 'None,' they had put him down as C. of E.

Again he was seeing the rooms above the garages but now he was there, shaking Dick out of a deep sleep, a warm deep sleep, a deep sleep that had taken place in a bed, and so his voice was low and his words hesitant as he said, 'I suppose you could say I'm Church of England, sir.'

'I suppose I could say . . . that means you've never kept it up?'

'That's right, sir, I've never kept it up.'

'Well, you're honest about it so there's hope for you yet.' The man was smiling now, then he went on, 'Now more questions, but technical this time. You said you hadn't driven a car but that you had driven tractors if I remember rightly?'

'Yes, sir; and a lorry during the war.'

'Are you mechanically minded?'

'Well, I had to maintain the lorry and the tractor, but they're different from the motor-cars of today. I'm speaking of fifteen years ago, sir.'

'Would you like to deal with cars, I mean maintain them?'

Abel swallowed deeply; then quietly and with great feeling, he said, 'Sir, I'd like to deal with anything that would provide us with shelter, my boy and me.'

'Well, that's what I'm offering you. But not only shelter, I'm offering you good employment if you are suitable. We'll take each other on trust for a month and see what transpires.'

'Oh, thank you, sir. Thank you from the bottom of my heart. And I promise you . . .'

'Ah! Ah! Now never make a promise that you don't think you can keep.'

'Sir, I can promise you I'll keep this one, and that is I'll give you of my best any hour of the day and night that you need me.'

The man now turned and looked at his young wife, saying, 'I didn't think I was mistaken, Hilda. I very rarely am, am I?'

'No, you're very rarely mistaken, Peter.'

'Sir.'

'Yes?'

'I notice that you deal in bicycles too; well, I know quite a bit about bicycles, I can take one to pieces and put it together again and . . .'

'And so can Benny Laton.' The man took in a deep breath, then said, 'I must put you in the picture about Benny, he's a boy I've had here since he was fourteen. He's a genius with bikes but' – he now tapped his head – 'God has destined that the poor lad cannot use his mind, he is backward there. But you or nobody else could beat Benny at mending a bike. God taketh away but He also giveth and He has given that boy a unique ability. No, from now on it's the car side of the business I want you for, and when I get on my feet, which will be tomorrow or the next day, we will get down to work together. In the meantime I'll give you the next two days to get those rooms cleaned out, for my wife tells me they are in a bit of a state, so get yourself settled in because once I get on my feet you'll have no time for housekeeping.' He pressed his lips tightly together as he smiled, and, turning to his wife, he asked, 'Isn't that so, Hilda?'

'Yes, yes, it is, Peter.'

Abel stood for a moment longer; then nodding first to one and then to the other he turned about and went quickly out of the room; and when he reached the head of the stairs he had the desire to leap down. He had said it would need a miracle and the miracle had come about.

At the foot of the stairs he stopped and looked back up towards the landing. Funny that he should ask for a miracle and it had to be given to him by one of the heavy religious sort. But then it could have been offered to him by the devil and he would have danced to his tune. There was only one thing he must do now, to tell the boy, or to put it plainer, to prime the boy.

He went into the kitchen and, grabbing Dick by the hand, he pulled the astonished boy from the seat out into the yard, up the stairs, and into the cluttered sitting-room, and there, dropping down on to the couch, he drew him towards him to stand between his knees and, gripping his hand, he said, 'What would you say if I told you you could stay here . . . we could stay here?'

Dick opened his mouth and closed it twice before he said, 'Oh! Dad, I would shout, I would shout. And then I would—' His voice trailed away and he muttered again, 'Oh! Dad. Dad!'

'Don't cry, son. Don't cry. There! There!' He drew the boy into his arms and hugged him tight; then he screwed up his own eyes and sucked his lips in between his teeth in an effort to stop the tears falling, but even so they spread over his face and on to the boy's hair.

After a moment he hastily rubbed his face with the back of his hand and, pressing the boy from him, said, 'But there's one snag . . . You know what a snag means?' He waited, and when Dick gave him no answer, he said, 'In this case it's something that can send us tramping on the road again in the wet with no place to sleep. That's what I mean by a snag. Understand? Well, it's like this. You know I told you that your name from now on is Gray not Mason, didn't I?'

Dick nodded slowly at him.

'Well now, if these people knew that . . . that I had taken you away from your mother and made you tramp the road with me and through this awful weather, they would have nothing to do with me; we . . . we would be out as I said. And so your mother is dead, you understand? You understand?' He shook Dick gently. 'If anybody asks you about your mother, she's dead, and that's why we left Hastings and came North. Now you understand, Dick, don't you? Tell me you understand.'

The boy stared at his father for a long moment before he said, 'I've got to say me mam's dead?'

'Yes, always remember that. She's not back there in the cottage, she's dead. That's the only way we can stay here. If you ever say your mother's alive, then . . . Well I don't have to repeat it again, do I?'

'No, Dad.'

'You want to stay here, don't you?'

'Oh yes, Dad, yes. And the lady's nice.'

Abel turned his head to the side. All the ladies had been nice to the boy, except the mad woman. He knew the symptom, the need for mother love, and this latest one was to him likely the nicest of all. And for himself, too, oh aye. And the safest, because she was married. And with both her and him being religious, there'd be no hanky-panky here as on the boat or with that maniac. No, if he worked for them as he would work, he could be set for years ahead.

The boy would have schooling and he perhaps would have peace of mind in time when Alice sank below the pain in his heart.

'You understand? Now tell me you understand.'

'Yes, Dad, I understand.'

3

Abel had been working for Peter Maxwell now for six months and to him it seemed like six years, six pleasant years, six pleasant life-times. He did a six-day week, often twelve hours each day. On Sunday he rested as they all did. No-one worked in Mr Maxwell's establishment on a Sunday; even the meals were cooked on a Saturday and eaten cold on the day of the Lord, as Mr Maxwell was apt to describe it.

Abel knew he had found favour in his boss's eyes where his work was concerned, and with his sober manner of living too. There was only one snag, as both Mr Maxwell and Mrs Maxwell and Abel himself saw it, he wouldn't attend, and they wouldn't get him to attend, church on a Sunday.

With tongue in cheek he had tried to tell them that in his view he could be as near God while walking on a hillside as he could within four walls, for wasn't God said to be everywhere? Yes, they admitted, but He touched man personally within the precincts of four sanctified walls.

As for Dick, the boy bore no resemblance to the white, wet, pasty-faced child who had come to this house those months ago. His cheeks were rosy, he had put on flesh, and he had grown a little, but above all he was happy: he was happy in his school, he was happy up in the rooms above the garage, but he was happiest, Abel realised, when he was in that kitchen.

They had their main meal in the kitchen at dinner time with Mr and Mrs Maxwell, and sometimes on baking day they were invited to tea. At other times, such as breakfast and a late snack, Abel saw to these up in the rooms.

And Abel was happy that the boy had made two friends, diverse in mentality but nevertheless close. The first one was the retarded Benny Laton. Benny was no longer a boy, at least he didn't look a boy, he was a man of twenty-two, but he talked and acted like a backward ten-year-old. But right from the first day he had taken to Dick, and Dick to him, and whenever possible the boy would be at Benny's side handing him tools, purposely the wrong ones to hear him laugh as he shouted, 'Why! man, you're daft; that ain't a spanner!' or 'that be a hammer not a nail.'

The other friend was a twelve-year-old girl who, as though in reverse from Benny, was being made into a woman before her time. She was the neighbour's daughter, the neighbour being a Mrs Esther Quinton Burrows who lived in the big house separated from the Maxwells by the strip of paddock and the garden.

Molly was Esther Burrows's only daughter, and since four years ago when her mother decided, on the death of her husband, to become an invalid, she had been used as nurse, companion, and house-keeper. The latter position she continually assumed when the maid would decide, on the spur of the moment, she couldn't stand the whims and demands of her mistress any longer and would walk out, which emphasised that the pressures imposed by Mrs Burrows were indeed great because work was as scarce for women as it was for men.

But when the young girl could escape from the house and her mother she would run over the pad-dock, stoop under the wire, skirt the Maxwells's vegetable garden and so come into the yard where she would invariably bring her running to a halt and look about her in order to find out where Dick might be.

On this particular day it happened to be baking day and tea time when she arrived.

Seeing no-one about, she hesitated in the middle of the yard; then looking towards the kitchen window and realising they were all at their tea, she was about to turn away when the door opened and Hilda Maxwell called, 'Come away in, Molly! We're just on finishing.' Then as the girl came shyly into the room Hilda turned towards the table and, wagging her finger towards Dick, cried, 'And don't gobble your last mouthful.' It was as if she were talking to her own child, but when she addressed Molly it was as she would a visitor saying, 'Sit your-self down, Molly. Now would you like a cup of tea and a teacake?'

'Oh yes, Mrs Maxwell. Oh, thank you.'

A few minutes later Molly was eating the freshly

baked teacake and sipping at her tea while the four at the table who had evidently finished the meal sat waiting.

The silence could have proved awkward but Abel was used to it by now: no-one started the meal at this table or left it without a blessing being asked, so he looked at Molly and smiled quietly at her. She was a nice little lass; he had grown very fond of her over the past months. He had never seen her mother but from what he had heard of her he imagined she was a lady born not to dirty her hands. The trouble was she had been brought up without having to dirty them in the very house where she now lay on a couch most of the day. He supposed her complaint was what in the last century would have been called the vapours, which was another name for laziness or escape from life.

'There now, you've finished.' It was Peter Maxwell speaking, and having done so he looked around the table, then bent his head and said, 'Lord, for what you have been gracious enough to provide us with this day I thank you on behalf of all here present. Amen.'

'Amen. Amen. Amen.'

'There now.' His voice altering, Peter Maxwell rose from the table and, bending towards Molly, said, 'I suppose you've come over here, young lady, to waste my third assistant's time?' He pulled a mock, stern face at the girl, and she, her eyes twinkling, said, 'Yes, I suppose you could say that, Mr Maxwell.'

The reply sent Peter Maxwell's head back and he

let out a roar of laughter, and Hilda Maxwell, as her husband had done, also pulled a mock prim face as she said, 'There's a saucy miss for you, straight to the point.' And she nodded from one to the other, lastly towards Abel, who nodded back at her as he grinned widely. But then the grin was swept suddenly from his face and the laughter in the room died as if it had been cut off by a knife for Peter Maxwell was now bent over double and was groaning aloud as he hugged his chest.

'Oh my goodness! my goodness!' Hilda was holding on to him at one side and Abel at the other. 'Get him down, on to the mat.'

'Peter! Peter! are you all right?' She went to straighten the huddled form lying on the rug now, but Abel said quickly, 'Don't touch him, get the doctor.'

'I can ring for him.' Molly was going towards the door. 'I know the number; it's the same doctor as ours, isn't it?'

Hilda turned towards her, saying, 'Yes, yes. Tell him . . . tell him Mr Maxwell has collapsed. It's . . . it's serious, tell him.'

'Get a blanket to put over him.'

She looked at Abel, then nodded before springing to her feet.

A minute later as Abel was helping to tuck the blanket around the prostrate man he felt a change in the man's body and his groaning stopped. He looked in apprehension down on to the drawn face, which was no longer twisted, and the lines seemed to have disappeared from it, leaving the skin smooth.

He raised his head and met Hilda's eyes, and she whimpered, 'Oh no, no! It can't be. He's . . . he's had them before. Oh no! No! No! No! He's not, is he?' She was appealing to Abel now and he said, 'I . . . I don't know, I don't think so, his pulse is very weak.' He was holding Peter Maxwell's wrist and his fingers could feel no beat under them, but he couldn't say to her, 'He's dead.' He couldn't even say that to himself, it had all happened so suddenly. He had died on a laugh. Yes, he had died on a laugh, he had died laughing. This religious man . . . this good, really good religious man had died laughing. It was a good way to go.

It was nine o'clock. Peter Maxwell was laid out in the sitting-room. They had brought a single bed downstairs. The undertaker's man having helped with this task, it was Mrs Maxwell herself, the young girl, as Abel still thought of her, who saw to the undressing and last dressing of him. And now here she was sitting at the kitchen table, her joined hands resting upon it, her eyes, quite dry for as yet she had not shed a tear, looking straight at him as she said, 'My father will have to be told, I suppose, and our Florrie.'

From his seat at the other side of the table, Abel blinked but said nothing. He had never before heard her mention her father or her sister; but then why should she? He knew nothing really about her except that she was Mrs Maxwell and efficient in all she did, and kind. Then his surprise was registered openly on his face when she said, 'Would you mind going and telling them?'

'What! . . . You mean they're hereabouts?'

'Very much so.' There was a note of bitterness in her voice now. 'I've never seen them for more than two years; he was . . . he was against me marrying Mr Maxwell.' She always referred to her husband as Mr Maxwell. She now unclasped her hands and, putting one to her cheek, she rubbed it up and down before saying, 'I . . . I could see his point because Mr Maxwell was older than my father by three years, being sixty-two. But . . . but I tried to tell him it wasn't what he thought, I mean our association . . . I mean—' She looked towards the fire now, then said under her breath. 'He wouldn't listen, he wouldn't listen to my reasons.'

Abel remained silent, thinking he could understand her father's attitude in not wanting to listen to the reasons why a girl like her was marrying a man of sixty-two. Yet Peter Maxwell hadn't looked anything near that, fiftyish yes, but not sixty-two. And that was over two years ago, so she said. Well! well!

'And then there's our Florrie.' She was looking at him again. 'I don't want to tell her anything but I suppose I'll have to. If I don't he will . . . Father, they're as thick as thieves and of like minds, godless both of them.' Her full-lipped mouth puckered itself, expressing how she felt about her godless relations.

She had risen to her feet now and gone to a

drawer in the dresser from which she took out a cloth and, with a sweeping movement of her arms, spread it over the table. The routine of setting the breakfast followed, and as she worked she talked as if to herself, yet all the while addressing him. 'I'll be surprised if you find her in, off jaunting likely. But if she is in she won't be alone, you can bet your bottom dollar on that. Oh no; not our Florrie. He'll be there. If not him, somebody else. Yet knowing what was afoot my father took her part. Can't believe it when you think of it.'

Abel looked at the table and noticed with surprise that it wasn't for one, for herself alone now, but for three. She stopped in her bustling, her glance following his, and without any preamble she said, 'I can't bear eating on my own, you and Dick can come over for breakfast. Anyway for the time being. And I'll have to keep busy to stop myself thinking. If you don't feel like going round and telling them tonight, tomorrow morning first thing will do; but . . . but' – now her fingers were clasping and unclasping themselves – 'I don't want to be left alone here the night, and . . . and if she's got any decency in her she'll offer to stay.'

'I'll go at once.' He was on his feet. 'Just tell me the names and addresses.'

'Well, our Florrie's not hard to find. She lives on Brampton Hill. Yes' – she nodded at him – 'not ten minutes' walk away. I . . . I think it's forty-six. Anyway, it's a big house, one of those that's been turned into flats. It's the only one with big iron gates on that side of the road. I don't know which flat she lives in; there'll likely be names on the doors. But my father . . . well, you'll have to go further afield. He's' – she turned her head now to the side as if about to admit something shameful as she added – 'in Bog's End, 109 Temple Street. My father's name is Donnelly, and hers is the same.'

As he made for the door she turned to him again, saying softly, even sadly, 'When you see 109 you'll understand why I'm here in this house.' She pointed her forefinger towards the floor. 'But makes no matter, tell them that Mr Maxwell's dead. He . . . my father will likely go out and drink to it, but our Florrie, well, her reactions remain to be seen.'

He paused and looked hard at her, then said, 'I'll . . . I'll bring the boy down to keep you company, he won't be in bed, he won't go until I go, and I'll be as quick as I can.'

When she nodded at him he turned from her and went out, closing the door quietly after him. In the yard he stopped for a minute and looked up into the dark starlit night. She was a funny lass, so young in some ways yet as old as the hills in others. She seemed to be a girl who had never experienced youth.

Abel had knocked on 109 Temple Street and before the door was opened Hilda Maxwell's last words were making sense to him. Even in the darkness he guessed that Temple Street was one of the poorer streets of Bog's End, and that was saying something.

'Well! who are you?'

'Mr Donnelly?'

'Aye, that's me.'

'I'm . . . I'm Abel Gray.'

'Aye, well, so what? What you after?'

Abel looked down on the thin, undersized man with the out-size voice and he had the odd desire to laugh. Anyone so different from Hilda Maxwell he couldn't imagine. That this little fellow could ever have fathered Mrs Hilda Maxwell appeared ridiculous. This raucous unshaven little chap belonged to another world altogether from 3 Newton Road which was in reality in the Brampton Hill area and Brampton Hill was Fellburn at its highest.

'I've come with a message from your daughter . . . Hilda.' He felt he had to add the Christian name and it sounded strange on his tongue. It was the first time he had said it aloud, and it seemed to have no connection with the person it represented.

'Hilda? Wor Hilda? What's up with her? Bad is she an' on her death bed that she sends for me?'

'No, she . . . she herself is all right but her husband died suddenly tonight.'

In the light from the dimly lit passage Abel saw the old man's expression changing. He watched the man's mouth open, then close; he watched his hand rasping across his unshaven chin; he watched him consider a moment before saying in a more moderate voice now, 'You'd better come away in.'

Taking off his cap as he passed the old man, Abel went into a room which he saw at once was used as a kitchen, sitting-room, and bedroom combined. The place looked as if it hadn't been cleaned for some long time, and yet it had two homely touches, a large battered, once red leather armchair drawn up before a blazing fire, and a couple of whippets sitting on a clippie mat; and they must have been so comfortable they didn't even bother to rise up and sniff him.

'Sit yoursel' down.' Mr Donnelly pointed to a wooden chair near a square kitchen table on which were a number of dirty dishes.

After Abel had seated himself the small man did not take his place in the leather chair but stood confronting him, asking now, 'When did this happen?'

'Around five this evening.'

'Expected was it?'

'No, no; he had just finished a meal when he collapsed.'

'Well—' He now turned from Abel and went to the fire, having to bend over the dogs to spit into it, then turned back to him and continued, 'She shouldn't have been surprised at that, he's been shaky on his legs for years that 'un. Yet it's always the creakin' doors that last out the longest. Well—' His features moved into what could be called a grin now and he nodded his head slowly at Abel, saying, 'She's got what she went for quicker than she expected, hasn't she now?'

'I don't follow you.'

'No, you wouldn't, you've only been there a few months. Oh, I know all about you. I know all about everything. I'm stuck at this end and she's stuck at that end but I know her every move. You were on the road weren't you, you an' your lad, and you helped old Maxwell when he had a turn? Oh, you see there's nothin' I don't know. Well, all I can say now is I hope she lives long enough to enjoy the fruits of her two and a half years' labour, 'cos my God! it must've been hard labour ... An' don't you say, mister' – his arm was thrust out to its entire length now, pointing straight at Abel like a gun – 'don't you say you can understand her makin' the move; this hole in the ground mightn't be everybody's choice but her and Florrie never wanted for nowt. Sent her to typing school I did, same as Florrie. Florrie made a go of it but she didn't. She didn't want to work in an office. No, she didn't want to be a secretary; she wanted to start at the top, a house and business all ready made for her. But there were no young lads around here with houses and businesses to bestow on her. She turned her nose up at every male in Bog's End. She even left the Chapel that she'd been to since a bairn and went to St Michael's, 'cos why?' He poked his small head forward and now his voice changed into refined mimicry. 'They were nice people who went to St Michael's, refined. There was nobody out of work that went to St Michael's. The men usually wore gloves and carried walking sticks who went to St Michael's, and the women always wore hats when they went shoppin', not head scarves, no, and they got up coffee mornin's for charity, an' at Christmas at the masons' dinner they vied with each other who could throw in the most to help the poor starving buggers of Bog's End.'

'Oh! Oh!' He now flapped his hands at Abel as if to silence him and went on, 'She had her eye to business had our Hilda, but she didn't find her path a smooth one there either because mothers of sons are not bloody fools, not the likes of them that go to St Michael's, they didn't want to be landed with a daughter-in-law from Bog's End. No. No. Well, when she couldn't get into that high-rachy, she had to do the next best thing, she took old Maxwell. Pillar of the church old Maxwell. Hadn't been married in his life and he didn't want her as a wife she said. What did he want her for then, eh? Dirty old sod.'

Mr Donnelly now paused for breath; then quickly turning, he again spat into the fire, after which he stood looking down towards it and, his voice quiet, even sad, he said, 'Well, she's got what she wanted, she's got a start, big house an' a business that's goin' places. I should be glad. Aye, I should be glad for her.' He turned now and looked at Abel, adding, 'I thought the world of her you know, always have done. From when she came I took very little notice of Florrie, put her aside sort of, hurt Florrie. Aye, I did. Yet Florrie's worth twenty of her. Still, you can't direct your feelin's can you?' He raised his eyes and stared up at Abel, and Abel, remembering Alice, moved his head slowly from side to side and answered, 'No, you're right there, you can't direct your feelings.'

Mr Donnelly now walked to the table, saying on a different note now, 'I can't offer you anything, haven't a drop in the house, only tea.'

'That's all right; I've got to get back, at least after I've been to your other daughter.'

'Oh' – there was surprise in his voice – 'she's sending to Florrie is she, not leavin' it to me?'

'Yes, she asked me to call and tell her. She . . . she needs company tonight I think, a woman's company.'

'Oh aye, aye, this is the time for company. You can't be alone with the dead no matter what you thought of them. Well, it's nice of you to come, mister. What did you say your name was?'

'Abel Gray.'

'Oh aye, Abel Gray. Well, I suppose we'll meet again. Not that I'll ever be a regular visitor, she'll have to ask me first, but to show me respects I'll turn up at the funeral. Then again' – he turned his head to one side – 'I'll feel a bloody hypocrite after all I've said about 'im. Still, if I don't go she'll bear that against me an' all. Well, I'll be seein' you.'

'Yes, yes. Good night then, Mr Donnelly.'

'Me name's Fred.'

'Good night, Fred.'

'Good night to you an' all.'

The door closed behind him. He walked for some distance down the street, then paused and once again he looked up into the sky. Amazing . . . amazing, people's lives, the things that went on. He thought his own was strange enough yet there appeared to be something strange in every life he touched on.

46 Brampton Hill he found was as different again from 109 Temple Street as it was from 3 Newton

Road. It looked the kind of house that had once been an industrialist's mansion. Now there were ten nameplates inserted in a mahogany frame on the left-hand side wall of the tiled lobby. They were set out in sections of three three's with a single name at the bottom. The nameplates were grouped in floors, ground floor at bottom he presumed. Starting from the top he looked for the name Donnelly, but he didn't come to it until he reached the bottom where it said, 'Miss F. Donnelly, Garden Flat.'

He looked about him. Where would he find the garden flat? Outside he supposed. As he turned towards the main door again the hall door opened and a man came through.

'Excuse me' – Abel turned to him – 'could you tell me how to get to the garden flat?'

'Oh yes, yes. But you needn't go outside, it's rather misleading. You go into the main hall, turn right along the corridor; it's the door at the end.'

'Thank you.'

'You're welcome.'

He went into the hall now and stood gazing about him for a moment. It looked vast; big enough, he thought, to make three flats. The floor of the hall and the circular staircase leading upwards were bare of carpet, but as he remarked to himself who would want to cover wood like that. He turned to the right and went along a corridor. There was a blank wall on one side and a row of curtainless, deep-bayed windows on the other and there at the end was the door to the so-called garden flat.

He hesitated a moment before ringing the bell. Of

one thing he felt sure, anyone who could choose to live in a place like this wouldn't be likely to show much connection with Mr Fred Donnelly.

When there was no answer to his ring he pressed the bell again, holding his finger on it for some seconds now, and as he did so he hoped there would be no response to it, for somehow he didn't want to meet this sister. The whole situation was too complex, he didn't want any more surprises tonight.

'Yes, what is it?'

He was now weighed down with surprise. The door was open and he was being confronted by a woman who appeared almost as tall as himself. She was wearing a white woolly dressing-gown, and her hands were extended above her head as she continued to pin her hair up.

Again she said, 'Well?'

'I'm . . . I've come from your sister Mrs Maxwell, I'm the hand there, Abel Gray. She . . . she sent me with a message.'

In the silent seconds that followed she had arranged her hair in a rough position on top of her head, then said, 'Oh!' then again, 'Oh!' but she now added, 'Well, come in.'

As she closed the door on him she laughed, saying, 'I didn't expect anyone at this time, I've been drying my hair. They don't like doing it at the hairdresser's, it takes too long, to dry I mean. It's my only concession to the idea of the old-fashioned girl. Come in. Sit down.' She had gone before him through a hallway that was as big as his

137

sitting-room above the stables and his moving glance took in the pieces of furniture standing against the wall. No modern stuff here, antiques if he knew anything about them, pieces like Lady Parker used to have in her drawing-room.

And now they were in the sitting-room; or was it a drawing-room? Whatever one had a mind to call it, it was an amazing room; even in the subdued light the colours flowed over you. French grey walls dotted with broad gold-framed pictures; a deep cherry-coloured carpet and on it and flanking a white marble fireplace, two deep couches upholstered in warm brown velvet.

When she motioned him to sit on one of the couches he sank into the down cushions, and even when she was seated opposite to him waiting for him to speak his mind was so taken up with the room that she had to prompt him again. 'You said you had a message from Hilda?'

'Yes.' He smiled at her now and nodded, adding, 'I'm . . . I'm sorry if I seem to be wool-gathering but . . . but it's an unusual room, very beautiful.'

'Thank you. But it's easy to make a room beautiful when the proportions are right; with the skirting boards and ceilings this high' – she waved her hand upwards – 'you can't go wrong.'

'Oh, I wouldn't agree with you there.'

'No? Well, perhaps not.' She returned his smile, then sat waiting, and his face becoming straight and a conventional tone in his voice, he said, 'It's rather sad news that I bring, Mr Maxwell died this evening.'

'*What*!'

With a quick jerk of her body she had pulled herself to the edge of the couch, and there she seemed to hover for a moment before saying, 'No!'

'I'm afraid so.'

'How did it happen?'

In a few words he told her how it happened and when he was finished she sat back once more and, her head dropping back now on to the cushion, she made a sound between a laugh and a huh. Then bringing her head forward again, she stared at him as she said slowly, 'And now she wants me round there?' Her tone had altered, it was now on the defensive. 'You mean off her own bat she's asking me to go round there?'

He returned her stare. The voice she was using now was different from the one with which she had greeted him and had carried on the introductory conversation. That voice had been the voice of an educated person, the tone of this voice could be linked with 109 Temple Street, Bog's End; he wouldn't have imagined that she had ever lived there, or that she had been bred by that particular old man.

He continued to stare at her, taking in her face. She was a beautiful woman. Well no, not beautiful, her nose was too big for beauty, her mouth too wide. Her eyes, too, although dark brown and deep-lashed should also have been wide in order to qualify for beauty; instead they were round. And yet they looked widely spaced; but that was the effect of her eyebrows which curved well beyond the bone formation of the eye sockets. Her skin was pale and in this light appeared colourless; but her hair, her hair was another thing, that was beautiful. It wasn't blonde or flaxen or light brown. What colour was it? A bit of all three, and she had plenty of it. He just couldn't place her as that old man's daughter or as Hilda Maxwell's sister. Oh, no, not as Hilda's sister. Not only was there no resemblance in the faces, their figures denied any family connection whatever. Hilda was short and plump, seeming still clothed in her puppy fat although she was well past twenty. Homely had been his first impression of her; it still was. But this woman, she didn't appear to have any shape to her body: her chest was as flat as a boy's underneath that garment, and her ankles and slippered feet looked bony, yet her thinness suggested elegance. She looked a woman. She was a woman; he doubted if she would see thirty again.

'I suppose you know all about me?'

'*What!*'

'I said I suppose you know all about me?' Her words were spaced.

'No, I can assure you I know nothing about you. I didn't know of your existence until tonight, just over an hour ago to be exact; nor of your father's either.'

'My father? Oh.' She put her hand across her mouth in order to still her laughter and she almost spluttered as she said, 'You . . . you haven't . . . you haven't, have you?'

'Yes.' He was smiling broadly at her.

140

'You mean you've been along to see my father?'

'Yes; I've just come from there.'

'Oh! Oh, my goodness! . . . Did he throw anything at you?'

'Only words.'

'I bet.'

She got to her feet now, looked down at him for a moment, bit on her lip, then crossing her arms, she pressed both hands under her oxters and walked twice up and down the rug that lay between the couches before she stopped and looked at him again, saying slowly now, 'She must be feeling low to send for us, particularly me dad . . . I say particularly him, but I am as bad. Oh no, worse; in her eyes I'm a bad woman.' She bent down towards him now nodding her head at him. 'Do you know that? I'm a bad woman.'

'No, I didn't.' A corner of his lips was pulled up in a one-sided smile.

'Well, it's a wonder she didn't warn you before sending you out on this errand. But don't worry, now she's brought me into the open you'll hear the whole tale. Oh dear me!' She straightened up, bit tight on her lip, put her head back and looked towards the high ceiling as she ended on a note that sounded like compassion in her voice, 'Poor Hilda!' Then swinging round from him with the agility that put him in mind of the flicking end of a whip, she was across the room and at the far door, having said as she went, 'I'll be ready in two or three minutes.'

He was looking towards what was apparently the open bedroom door when she appeared again, saying, 'In that cabinet behind you you'll find some drink, help yourself.'

He was on the point of saying 'I'm on the waggon, I've had to be,' instead, remaining quiet he pulled himself upwards from the couch and went towards the cabinet. Here, opening the doors, he displayed a double row of bottles and a whisky decanter three-quarters full. His hand on the decanter he looked over his shoulder, saying, 'I'll . . . I'll have a whisky; shall I pour you something?'

'Same as you.' The voice was muffled and he gathered she was getting into some garment or other.

He had poured the whiskies and brought them to a small table at the head of the couch on which he had been sitting when she came into the room again. She was wearing what appeared to be a shapeless blue woollen dress. It hardly reached her calves and was clinging to her body like a skin. She had a pair of high-heeled shoes in one hand and a dark blue coat over her arm. Sitting down she threw off her slippers, then pulled on the shoes, and when she stood up to take the drink from his hand their eyes were on a level.

The first swallow of whisky hit the back of his throat and as he bent forward and coughed she said, 'You definitely want·more water with it.'

Still coughing and patting his mouth with his handkerchief, he said, 'I'm not used to it, I've been on the waggon.'

'Oh I can quite believe that. 3 Newton Road's a T.T. citadel. It had to be with Mr Maxwell, and, of course, **Hilda** wouldn't have had it otherwise. Oh no; not our Hilda . . . I sound spiteful, don't I?'

'You must have your reasons.'

'Oh, I've got my reasons all right. But on the other hand so has she, and we both think they're good ones. Anyway, let's get going.'

As she went to get into her coat he quickly put down his glass and assisted her and she looked over her shoulder and stared into his eyes for a moment before saying, 'You don't look the kind of fellow somehow to stand a set-up like that.'

He stepped back from her, on the defensive for the moment as he replied, 'I was more than glad to accept what they had to offer six months ago, I was out of work, had a young boy to see to.'

'Yes, so I heard. Well, the saying is, beggars can't be choosers . . . and I know something about that an' all.' She did not elaborate on this but went from him now and switched off the table lamp, saying as she made her way towards the french window, 'We'll go out this way, it cuts off about a quarter of a mile and that's something to consider when you're walking in high heels . . .'

'I've . . . I've got a car outside.'

'Oh. Oh.' She made a deep obeisance with her head. 'The car. Well! well! that's different. But we can still go out this way.' She switched on an outside light, then pulled back a pair of velvet curtains, unlocked a french window, and when they were outside again, she relocked it before saying, 'Round this way. I'll leave the light on until I get back.'

She was seated in the car and he was about to

143

close her door when she said softly, 'God! but I'm as nervous as a kitten.'

It was such a change of front that it was a moment before he leaned down towards her and said, 'Nervous? Why?'

'Of . . . of meeting our Hilda.' There was that ordinary tone of voice again, the voice that was wavering between Bog's End and Brampton Hill.

'Why should you be nervous of meeting her? I should have imagined the boot would be on the other foot.'

'Oh no.' She gave a tight laugh. 'Our Hilda's the kind of person who can enlarge your sins without saying a word, she's just got to look at you. Even as a child she was the same. Good people are like that and she's good at bottom; you haven't got to believe all that Dad says about her. He'd give you the impression that she just took Maxwell because of his business and his house. But I don't believe that, well, not all of it. Naturally there was an attraction in that quarter, and I don't blame her for that. Oh no, it's no use the kettle calling the frying-pan black. No, I think she's one of those people who really tries to be good, but . . . well' – she gave another small laugh – 'they sort of make you uncomfortable doing it. You know what I mean?'

He answered her laugh with a quiet chuckle as he said, 'Yes, yes, indeed, I know what you mean. But I can only repeat I can't see you've got anything to worry about.'

'Aw, lad' – she was laughing aloud now – 'you know nothing, nothing at all about our set-up.'

He started the car. In some strange way there was rising in him a kind of happiness, it was just a tinge, a tiny, tiny candle flame in the universe of sorrow that had been weighing him down for months. Buried under the gratitude he owed the Maxwells and under the new security and happiness that Dick had found had remained the ache left by Alice. Now, for the first time a corner of the pall was being lifted. He didn't ask himself how or why.

4

There was a large turn-out at Peter Maxwell's funeral. As the vicar remarked to Hilda, it was very gratifying, not only from her point of view but from dear Mr Maxwell's, for it showed how highly respected he had been among the parishioners, a good man, in all ways a good man.

Later that evening, when the last well-fed mourners had left and there remained in the sitting-room only her father and sister and Abel, Hilda repeated the vicar's words from where she was sitting on the edge of an armchair. She looked from the small man seated in the chair opposite, to the tall, lithe figure on the couch, but her accusing glance did not take in Abel as she said, 'He was a good man. Say what you like, he was a good man.'

'I'm sayin' nowt against him, lass. He's gone an' he's where the good God pleases at this minute. Let the dead bury the dead so to speak, that's my opinion.'

'You never had a good word for him when he was alive, either of you.' She was still looking at her father.

'What's past is past.'

'It isn't in my mind.'

'Aw well—' Fred now wriggled himself up out of the chair, saying in a voice that was much more natural to him, 'If you're gonna start on that track I'll make meself scarce 'cos I don't want to bandy words with you the night of all nights. If you want me you know where I am, I'll come if you call, but I'm not stickin' me neb in now, no more than I did afore.'

Hilda had risen to her feet and now she looked towards where Florrie was also making to rise and with a tremble in her voice, she said, 'I suppose you're going too?'

Florrie became still and, looking straight at Hilda, said in a quiet voice, 'Not if you want me to stay.'

'Please yourself.' As Hilda swung round and went to precede her father out of the room, she looked full at Abel, who had not spoken since he had entered the sitting-room ten minutes before, and she seemed to bring him into the orbit of her small family as she said, 'It's always the same, always.'

He made no remark whatever because he couldn't see how her statement refuted anything that had been said. It was as if she was expecting him to know the ins and outs of some past family situation.

When he was alone in the room with Florrie he looked towards her. She was sitting well back in the couch, her eyes were cast downwards looking to where she was slowly moving the diamond-studded ring round and round the third finger of her left hand.

He walked quietly towards the fire and stood with his back to it for some seconds before he said, 'She's upset. It's natural.'

She raised her eyes to his. 'Yes, it's natural.'

'Will you stay the night with her?'

'Yes, if she wants me to. But it'll only be for the night . . . I mean she'll only need me tonight, she'll be in control of herself tomorrow.'

'You think so?' There was a note of surprise in his voice.

'Oh yes, yes.' She nodded slowly at him. 'I know so. Huh!' It was that small imitation of a laugh he had heard her use before. 'I always think that sounds so silly, I know so, yet from time to time I hear myself saying it. It sounds so pompous, so God-inspired, and I haven't much time for God . . . are you like—' She now waved her hand towards the door before adding, 'I mean, do you keep up a religion?'

'No.'

'Didn't they manage to convert you?'

'No.'

'You must be a strong character.'

'Just stubborn.'

The door opened and Hilda came in the room again and she began to talk immediately with the same defensive ring in her tone. 'He doesn't change, not in any way. You would have thought he would have bought a new suit, but no, he had to be himself and come in that old grey thing.'

'He's not flush, you know that.'

'I would have given it to him if he had asked me.'

'Oh, Hilda!'

Now Abel saw a startling change in the tall, elegantly dressed Florrie. Using the same movement that had caught his attention in her own room, she swung herself up from the couch and seemed to tower over her sister as she said, 'Ask you for it! You know he's never asked either of us for anything, and under the circumstances he would have died rather than ask you for money for a suit to go to your husband's funeral in. Talk sense.'

'That's it. That's it, start! There's a pair of you. Everything I do is wrong in your eyes, always has been.'

'There you're wrong.' Florrie's voice held a note of deep bitterness now. 'There's not a pair of us, there's a pair of you, because he spoilt you from the beginning, but since you were able to step out on your own, you've treated him like dirt, muck beneath your feet. Anyway, look; I'm going, you don't need me. If I stayed it would only end up in one holy row, and this is not the night for it.' Florrie's voice now dropped to an even note as she added, 'Good night. Like Dad said, if you want me I'll be there.'

As she walked towards the door leading into the hall, Abel had the desire to catch hold of her and say, 'Stay. Don't go. Stay.' But then he warned himself it wasn't his business. This was a family, this was their war, and by the sound of it, it had been going on for some time, and what he mustn't do in this war either was to enlist in it. Oh no! Oh no! he mustn't get entangled in this war; as he was in the other, so in this he must also be a conscientious objector.

It was with the sound of the outer door closing that Hilda went to pieces, and in consternation Abel now watched her drop on to the couch, turn her head into the wing of it, and begin to cry.

Embarrassed, he moved from the fireplace and stood near the head of the couch looking down on her, but he did not touch her.

For almost five minutes she cried, not an anguished crying, just a quiet sobbing, and when eventually she lifted her head she blinked up to him through her tears and said, 'I'm . . . I'm sorry.'

'Oh, it's the best thing; it'll do you the world of good. There's nothing like a good cry for easing pain – special pain.'

'I feel so lost, so alone.'

'That's natural; it's early days yet.'

She took her handkerchief and blew her nose, swept her hair back from her brow, pulled her skirt well down to the sides of her calves, then said, 'Our Florrie's hard. They both are.'

'I wouldn't say that.'

'You don't know them.' Her rounded chin jerked upwards. 'They don't care how they show you up, either of them; him like a tramp, and her with the life she leads.'

'We're all individuals. There's something in us that makes us take different roads.' His voice was very low now; in contrast, hers was high as she put in aggressively, 'But there are values to be considered. If you want to live a decent life you've got to live among decent people and stick to the rules, the laws, the laws of the church and—' Her voice now lowered as she stated, 'You're on their side, aren't you? Because you don't believe in religion of any kind, do you?'

'No, not really. But I'm on nobody's side, because it isn't any of my business.'

She stared at him for a full moment before asking quietly, and with some amazement in her tone, 'Don't you believe that . . . that you suffer in an afterlife for the sins you commit in this one?'

He allowed himself to smile, then preceded his answer with a light 'Huh!' before he said, 'I'm afraid I don't. What I do believe is that we punish ourselves for our misdeeds here. It's circumstances and environment that make people do all kinds of things. What I do believe is that the mind, or the conscience, whatever you like to call it, has its own way of extracting payment.'

'Oh, that's ridiculous!' Her indignation brought her to her feet. 'What about murderers and people like that?'

'Well, if society doesn't extract payment by hanging them or incarcerating them for life, the thing I was just talking about does the rest.'

'But how do you know? How do you know that anyone is ever sorry for the terrible things he does?'

'I don't; but then again how can you tell what's going on in my mind and how can I tell what's going on in yours? Nobody really knows what lies behind all the small talk and chatter. Nobody really knows what goes on in a man's or woman's mind in the small hours of the mornin' when thought goes wild and the filth and beastliness of ages erupts and the . . .'

He stopped suddenly. Her eyes were wide, there was even a slight look of fear on her face. He said hastily, 'I'm sorry; it's a deep subject. As you know I don't do much talking but when I once start—' He smiled tentatively at her before ending, 'I'd better get to the youngster up aloft. I told him to go upstairs once Benny left the workshop' – he glanced at his watch – 'and that must have been all of two hours ago . . . Will you be all right tonight?'

'I'll be all right.' Her voice was low, wary.

'It's a pity your sister didn't stay.'

'Oh' – she shook her head – 'it's just as well. We've never hit it off together. And anyway, I've got to get used to being on my own. But' – she paused a moment – 'I must admit I feel safer knowing you're out there because there's so many people on the road now. You never know—' She closed her eyes tightly and bowed her head, then gave it an impatient toss as she said, 'Oh, I'm sorry.'

'Oh, you needn't be sorry.' His tone was light. 'It's as you say, you never know. I was a traveller for only a few weeks, but it was an education on the best way to keep your skin on your body because some of them would have even taken that if you hadn't slept with one eye open.'

She smiled weakly at him now; then leading the way into the kitchen, she said, 'Will you want anything before you go over?'

'Oh no, not after that meal, thank you very much.'

'What . . . what about Dick?'

'Not for him either. If he isn't sick tonight I'll be surprised. Good night now. Try not to worry. Have a hot drink and go to sleep.'

'Thank you, Abel; you've . . . you've been a great help to me, and I must say it, you've . . . you've given me more comfort than my own folk. I don't know what I would have done if you hadn't been there.'

'Oh' – he nodded at her – 'somebody else would have turned up. You know what you're always saying' – he now poked his head down towards her as if he were talking to a child – 'God provides.'

Her face serious, she looked back into his eyes as she said, 'Yes, Abel, I know that, God provides.'

5

'Dad.'

'Yes, what is it?'

'Benny's actin' funny these days.'

'Benny acts funny every day, you know that.'

'But this is a different kind of funny, Dad. Before it was a nice funny, you know, you could laugh at him, but yesterday he was nasty and he said he was going to tell Mrs Maxwell that I had dodged Sunday school.'

'How did he know that if you didn't tell him?'

'I didn't tell him; but he must have heard Molly going for me because I wouldn't go with her. And then today he said a funny thing, not laughin' funny.'

'Well, what was it that was not laughin' funny?'

Dick screwed up his face as if thinking. 'Well, he said his mother said that I was aiming to sleep over in the house, an' if I did she would come and do me one.'

Abel straightened himself from where he had been looking into the little dressing-table mirror to adjust his tie and, pulling at the knot, he turned and looked down on Dick as he said, 'Have you ever told him you wanted to sleep over in the house?'

'Why no, Dad, 'cos I never thought about sleepin' in the house; I like it here. I wouldn't ever want to sleep anywhere else.'

Abel turned to the mirror again. He, too, had noticed a change in Benny over the past few months, ever since Mr Maxwell died. He had put it down to a bit of boyish jealousy of himself because now not only did he do the car repairs, but ran the whole yard with a hired man under him, at least the practical side of it, because Mrs Maxwell . . . Hilda saw to all the paper work, as she had done all along. Perhaps too he was jealous of the fact that she had allowed him to start doing pottery up here in his spare time.

During the past six months he had been attending night school twice a week in order to use the kiln. He wasn't interested in the wheel for the turning out of pots and vases and such like but he had delved wholeheartedly into his one-time hobby of modelling animals, and some of his efforts after painting and glazing had turned out so good that he was hoping she might allow him to set up a separate workshop in the yard where her customers could see his efforts. But as yet, he had told himself, he should bide his time and wait for the right moment; she was very touchy about some things, time for instance. She didn't like it to be wasted, not when she was paying him four pounds a week and a mechanic two pounds ten; even Benny's fifteen shillings had to be accounted for by his time spent entirely on the bikes.

Today there was on him the desire to be away

from the place when she came back from her weekly visit to the cemetery, because she was nearly sure to ask him in for a cup of tea, and over it the talk would revolve around the business of the past week and the business of the forthcoming one. It wasn't that he didn't like discussing business or that he wanted to shun her company but of late he had become uneasy in her presence . . . And he was well aware of the reason for it.

He had also become uneasy in Florrie's presence and he knew the reason for that too. He liked Florrie, but in a different way altogether from the way he liked Hilda. His feeling for Hilda was threaded with gratitude and a sort of compassion because he felt that behind her tight façade she was, as she herself had said on the night of the funeral, lonely and lost.

Florrie had a different effect on him altogether. Florrie's presence excited him; he thought of her when lying awake at night. She could in a way have been Alice; they were so different in all ways, yet so alike in their effect on him. She had called a few times during the past month, and each time had stopped and had a word with him in the yard. Only once since the night of the funeral had he been in her company inside the house. She had happened to call on a Saturday dinner time for the purpose of telling Hilda that their father was ill and didn't she think she should go and see him. How she was received whenever he wasn't present he didn't know, but it was evident to him that Hilda didn't welcome her sister's appearance on that particular occasion. He thought she would have been invited to have a bite to eat, or at least to take a seat, but Hilda proffered neither; what she did do was to turn to him and, using the manner of a boss, practically dismiss him. 'If you've finished, Abel,' she had said, 'see to Benny. If you don't make him go he'll be there all afternoon and his mother will complain that he doesn't get any time off.'

He hadn't really finished his pudding but on Florrie's entry he had already risen to his feet. It was a little trick of courtesy that had taken his fancy many years ago, for it seemed to place a man, if not in the class of a gentleman, at least among those who knew their manners when a woman came into a room. He recalled that he had glanced downwards but not at the remains of his pudding, and as he went to leave the room he kept his eyes averted from Hilda but had looked at Florrie, and she at him, and their exchanged glance had understanding in it.

The result of that incident made him determine to keep his place in the future, and the attitude he adopted from then on he knew hadn't been lost on Hilda because during the days that followed she had gone out of her way to be especially friendly to him, and almost broke her neck in her efforts of kindness towards Dick.

He looked towards the boy now, saying, 'Do you want to come for a walk?'

'Yes, Dad.'

Abel smiled. 'But you'd rather go over to Molly's, wouldn't you?'

'No, Dad.'

'Don't tell fibs.'

Dick hung his head and laughed sheepishly now as he said, 'Well, she's teaching me to play chess and she can't get out because of her mother . . . her mother's a right old . . .'

'Now! now!'

'Well, she is, Dad. She puts on airs and graces, an' as soon as Molly sits down she rings the bell. It's like as if she were a servant, like Lady Parker had.'

'All right, get yourself away. I'm going for a walk; if I'm not back by six you come over here and read or something, but don't go troubling Mrs Maxwell.'

'No, I won't, Dad. But she might want me to go into tea.'

'Well, if she asks you, that's different.'

'Where are you goin' walkin', Dad?'

'I don't know yet, perhaps up into the country.'

'You'll get blown away with this wind.'

'Aye, well, I've got a lot of cobwebs I want to get rid of.' He was about to add, 'It would do you good to come along, better than playing chess,' but checked himself. The boy hated walking; those weeks on the road with blistered heels and weeping toes had turned him against walking for life. It was a pity; he was going to lose a lot. Only last week when he had received Dick's school report, which had been very good, he had said to him, 'What do you fancy doing when you grow up?' and the boy had turned his head and looked thoughtfully away before adding on a laugh, 'Something that I can do sittin' down, Dad,' and they had both laughed.

'I'm off then, Dad.'

'All right, behave yourself . . . Here! wait a minute.' He went to a cupboard and, taking from the top shelf a bag of toffees, he said, 'Give them to Molly. Tell her they're from me, mind.' He poked his face down to his son and, pushing him in the shoulder, said, 'And don't you eat any of 'em unless she presses you.' And Dick laughed and said, 'Ta, Dad, thanks. I'll just eat one when she does.'

Abel stood still as he watched the boy running from the room. He had never seen him so happy in his life before, it was the happiness of security and contentment. The lad imagined he was set here for life. Well, why not . . . ? He turned, and the words became an audible mutter now as repeated, 'Why not? With what's looming up, why not?' He wasn't blind, he wasn't a fool of a man. No? Wasn't he? Why not indeed? There was just one reason why not and he knew it only too well, as he also knew he'd better get rid of any thoughts regarding an alternative, because Mrs Hilda Maxwell wasn't that kind of a woman. Now if it had been Florrie . . .

He dragged on his overcoat, picked up his soft felt hat, and went downstairs. As he opened the bottom door the wind wrenched it from his hand and as he went to grab it with one hand he flung out his other arm and caught hold of Florrie, where she was staggering back from the impact of the door. Only in time he caught her and prevented her from falling, and as he held her he shouted above the wind. 'I'm sorry; the door sprang out of my hand.'

'It's all right. It's all right' – she was laughing as she pulled her hat straight on her head – 'it was my fault; I was hugging the wall.'

He was still steadying her when he shouted, 'She's out . . . Hilda. She's at the cemetery. But let yourself in. She leaves the key on top of the wooden stanchion of the door.' He pointed, then added on a laugh. 'First place a burglar would look.'

He didn't loosen his hold on her but led her towards the door, and it was he who took the key from its hiding place and opened the door, and not until he was inside and the door closed did his hand leave her arm.

Both hands free now, she lifted them upwards and took off her hat, saying, 'I must look a right mess. And trust me to wear a hat with a brim as big as this, on a day like this an' all.' She fluttered the hat in her hand as she added, 'But it goes with the suit.'

He stood a little way back from her now and looked her up and down before saying, 'It's a lovely suit, a lovely rig-out altogether. With your taste you couldn't have gone in for anything else but clothes; no, you couldn't.'

He had discovered some weeks ago that she dealt in clothes, and not just ordinary clothes, club clothes, or those to be found hanging in lines in the big stores. Hers were the exclusive Yvonne models, sold in a small exclusive shop in a side street at the bottom of Brampton Hill.

He was taking a short cut one day when bringing in a car for repairs and he had drawn the car up sharply on the sight of her locking the shop door – it was natural to offer her a lift home – and when she was seated beside him he said, 'So you work there?'

'Yes, you could say that.'

'That sounds like a yes and no answer.'

'Well, I do work there, but it's my shop.'

'Yours!'

'Yes. Look where you're going!' she had said quickly as he turned towards her. 'Why be so surprised? Why shouldn't I have a shop like that?'

'No . . . no reason whatever I suppose, only I've heard it referred to as the most exclusive shop in Fellburn. I've often wondered how it kept going, who the people are who have the money to buy . . . well, your kind of clothes.'

'You'd be surprised.'

'Yes, I suppose I would.'

He said now, 'What is the material, corduroy?'

'Corduroy velvet.'

'It's beautiful.'

He was looking into her face. She was beautiful too. He had imagined her face as being just interesting but now it was beautiful; her skin had picked up a glow from the reddish brown of the material.

He blinked rapidly now as he asked, 'How is your father getting along?'

'Oh, he's much better. He's on his feet again and bawling like a bull, so he's all right. I got him into a new suit yesterday. Aw' – she turned her head to the side – 'Aw, you never saw anything like it. The poor man in the shop, it's a good job he knew me else he would have thrown him out. Dad said he'd come round here with me today just to show Hilda.' She poked her head forward and made a moue with her lips. 'You know what he yelled out in the shop?'

He shook his head as he smiled widely at her.

'"The next bloody thing you'll have me in is nancy knickers, bloody plus-fours." I know I have a tough hide but oh, was I glad when I got him outside.' She was bending towards him now, her hand on her mouth as she laughed and his laugh was joining hers, deep and free, as he pictured the old fellow being true to type, when the door burst open, seemingly they thought with the wind, because they both turned swiftly and their shoulders touched; but there, her face expressing her feelings, stood Hilda.

'How did you get in here?' She was leaning against the door now staring at her sister, but it was Abel who answered her, saying quickly, 'I told her where the key was, I opened the door.'

'Then you had no right to. What right have you anyway to come in here when I'm not about? And you!' She pulled herself from the door and it looked for a moment as if she were going to extend her arm either to strike or to punch Florrie, but instead she pointed at her. 'You know I go to the cemetery every Sunday. You picked your time, didn't you? Oh, I know what you're after.'

Florrie didn't answer, but for a moment she seemed to grow taller; her face from being pink-hued was now deathly white; and it was she who thrust out her arm now and, pushing her sister from the door, opened it and walked slowly out.

As Abel stood looking down into Hilda's tight-drawn face he thought for a moment he was in the cottage facing Lena again in the throes of one of their frequent battles, and his voice sounded as if he was really dealing with his wife when he cried, 'You want to be careful, you can go so far . . .'

'Don't tell me how far I can go, Mr Gray.' She walked round him, then sidewards to the table, keeping her eyes on him all the time, and there she tore off her black velour hat and flung it on to a chair as she used his very words: '*You* want to be careful, *you'll* go too far.' Then leaning across the table towards him, she cried, 'You know nothing about it; you know nothing about her. She's bad, she's man mad. Always has been. She breaks up homes. You think she's nice, funny, amusing to be with; the wives of the men she takes don't think that, let me tell you. The one who's running her now is married with four children, and he's lasted the longest, six years. Just think, Mr Gray, just think what the wives must feel. And you say *I* go too far. Oh, I know what she's up to, and if you had any sense you'd see it an' all. Oooh!' She let out a long-drawn sigh and her fury seemed to seep away with her escaping breath as she sank down into a chair and dropped her head into her hand. She was quiet for a moment; then more to herself than to him she said, 'All my life I've been plagued with her, plagued that's the word, and he's taken her part against me.

But then, of course, he would, she's a kept woman and she keeps him mostly out of it, so of course he would take her part. It's natural, isn't it?'

She seemed to have forgotten his presence until he said quietly, 'I'm going for a walk.' He had opened the door and had got one foot in the yard when she called softly, 'Abel. Abel, don't go.'

He took no heed of the plea in her voice but closed the door before going quickly across the yard, out into the road, past the gates, and into the open country.

He must have walked for two hours, by which time he had circled the outskirts of the town, come through Bog's End, through the deserted market place, up by the equally deserted park, and was now approaching Brampton Hill itself.

As he struggled up the incline, the force of the wind caused him to lower his head into his chest. If anything, the wind had increased and he knew it wouldn't let up until the rain started, and the low, dark sky promised this at any moment. He was within ten minutes' walk of the house but he didn't want to go back there, at least not until there was a chance of his getting up to his rooms without her spotting him, and the light was good for another hour yet.

When he came to a stop at the big iron gates of number 46 he questioned himself if it had been his intention from the beginning to make for here, and the answer gabbled in his mind, God no! for he'd had enough for one day. He didn't want to hear anything more from either of them.

Why did he get himself entangled in these situations? Ever since first setting out on the road it had been the same. No, no; he had to be honest about it, the entanglement had started with Alice; before that he had been just a married man, a bored, frustrated, unhappy man. But he was still a married man, he must remember that, the only difference now was he was no longer bored or frustrated . . . Aw, hold your hand a minute. He jerked his shoulders and nodded his head at the thought that had taken on shape, and he answered it, If I'm not frustrated then what is it that's eating me? Why am I here? Come on, why am I here? The reply was a little while in coming, it came as he was walking along the gravel drive: If she's had so many one more won't make much difference.

As he walked around the side of the house towards the french windows the wind met him with renewed force and, as he approached the windows, it seemed to be filled with voices. It was these voices which brought him to a stop before he actually reached the door. The drawing-room he saw was lighted and she was standing with her back to him; and not a yard from the door and to the side, holding on to one of the partially open french windows with both hands, was her father, and he was yelling at her, 'You tell her an' as God's me judge I'll never speak to you again as long as I live. Do you hear? I'll never open me lips to you. You breathe one word of it, one word . . . I'm warnin' you!'

'You can warn me all you like' – Florrie's voice was as high as his now – 'you can threaten all you like. You've done it since I can remember anything. Well, I'm telling you, Dad, and I mean it, just one more insulting remark from her and she'll get it, in one mouthful she'll get it. You're a bastard! I'll say. In every sense of the word you're a bastard.'

There was a pause during which only the voice of the gusting wind came to him; then he could just make out Mr Donnelly's words as he said, 'You wouldn't, Florrie, you wouldn't do that.'

'I would, Dad. Get this into your head, I would, and I will. I've stood enough. You've always said yourself there's nobody either black or white, but all shades of grey. Well, she's made me out to be deep black, pitch black. She tells people I'm bad, rotten. I know what I am, nobody better, but I'm not what she makes me out to be. And that man today was given the impression I was the lowest of the low. And you know why?'

He saw her now thrust her hand out and place it above her father's and bang the door closed, and he strained his ears to listen but no sound came from the room. He could see her face now, her profile contorted with anger; and her father's face, his eyebrows raised, his hand flapping as if dismissing what she was saying.

He was actually hesitating whether to step forward or to go back when the decision was made for him by a slate hurtling down from the roof and missing him by inches before crashing on to the terrace to the side of him.

The french window was now open; Fred Donnelly was standing on the step looking at him and shouting, 'What the hell do you want here?'

'Nothing.' The answer sounded inane even to himself.

'Well, I hope you bloody well find it. It's a pity it missed you,' he said, looking down on the splintered slate; then he marched away along by the side of the house.

'Come in; I want to close the door.' She was gasping as if she had been fighting against the wind.

He paused a moment before stepping into the room, and when she closed the doors behind her the peace, the warmth and the silence enveloped him so quickly and to such an extent that for the moment he felt weak and slightly stupid as if the tile actually had hit him.

That was until she demanded, 'How long have you been standing there?'

She turned from him, then put her doubled fist to her mouth and closed her eyes before walking towards the fire. There she thrust out her hands towards it as if she were seeking warmth, and now she asked flatly, 'Why had you to come here at this time?'

'I don't know.'

She swung round and faced him, shouting at him now, 'Don't say that! That's what they . . .' She stopped abruptly and once more her doubled fist was pressed against her mouth. Nor did he move from where he was as he said, 'Why don't you finish, that's what they all say?'

But his face screwed up in protest as she screamed at him. 'Yes! that's what they all say, all three of them.'

Her voice had been so loud and so high that he looked quickly towards the door, then upwards. 'Don't worry,' she cried; 'this is an old house, the walls are thick, and this flat is detached, there's only a cellar below. I can shout as much as I like. In any case if we were right in the middle of the hall I'd still shout. And now I'm going to tell you something so we can get it straight. I am thirty-two years old; there have been three men in my life; the last one has lasted for six years. *I am not a prostitute.*'

'I never thought you were.'

'Don't lie, that's why you came here. I know. Oh, I know.' She flapped her hand disdainfully at him. 'I know the impression she's given you. And, of course, she's laid it on blacker because she wants you, she wants to marry you . . . and don't look so surprised, you can't be that blind. Anyway, it's the best thing you could do.'

She turned from him and went slowly towards the couch and sat down; then looking up at him, and her voice quiet now, she said, 'Don't let what you heard stand in your way, she's not to blame for that, and I won't tell her. I said I would, but with her kind of temperament she wouldn't be able to stand it. As far as she's concerned, illegitimacy is a sin, she wouldn't only blame those responsible she would take the sin on to her own shoulders, being made as she is.'

He walked forward now and took a seat opposite to her asking quietly, 'You're half-sisters then?'

'No, no.' She shook her head. 'No relation whatever.'

'What! . . . you mean?'

'What I mean is, Dad's not her father and my mother wasn't her mother.'

'She was adopted?'

'Well, in a way you could say so. Funny.' She turned her head to the side and shook it slowly before looking at him again and saying, 'You've seen my dad, haven't you? A scruffly little man, five foot three inches tall . . . I take after my mother' – she accompanied this statement with a movement of her hand that started at her head and finished pointing to her feet – 'although I am much taller than even she was. But can you see my dad, looking at him now, consumed with fires of love? Well, he was. He was one of twins. His brother Len inherited both looks and height. They must have looked opposites. But they both fell in love with Annie the girl next door, not exactly next door but along the street, and, of course, she chose Len. Well, as I understand it from my mother who actually did live next door to them, he took himself off and nobody saw anything of him for five years, but when he came back he picked up with my mother. As she said herself, she had always liked him – she never used the word love. She was a shy woman was my mother, but kindness itself, and he on the long rebound needed kindness so he married her.

'In the meantime, so the tale goes, Len and Annie who had moved from the town came back, and from the minute they arrived Dad was never away from them. Even the night I was born he was along there; he didn't see me until I was some hours old. This situation went on for five years; then my Uncle Len died in a pit accident – both he and Dad worked down the pit. My mother waited for the worst to happen, that is my Dad to walk out and go to Annie's, because he had seen to everything, the funeral and all its details, and he was never away from her, at least for a fortnight after my Uncle Len died. Then, so my mother told me, he came in one day almost demented. She had gone, just walked out, left him a note to say that she was fed up with Doncaster . . . that's where we lived, and she was going to London. You know' – she now rose from the couch and went again to the fireplace and, again extending her hands towards the flame, she rubbed them together, talking all the while – 'I'm amazed at the things women do for men and at what men expect women to do for them; even today.' Her head snapped round towards him. 'Nothing's altered in the last thirty years. The vote? Huh! makes you laugh, that. You know what?' She turned fully round now and looked down on him. 'He expected my mother to sympathise with him, he even cried, for the first time in his life my mother said she saw him cry. He hadn't cried when his brother died, nor yet when his mother and father died. Can you understand it? Anyway—' She now took the seat opposite to him again and, leaning back in it, resumed quietly, 'Eighteen months passed, then one day who should turn up on the doorstep but dear Annie, pregnant to the hilt, and I mean to the hilt for the child was born only forty-eight hours after she stepped into the house, and as she brought it into life she went out of it.'

She paused, sighed, and then said, 'Now I can take up the story because I can remember seeing the newborn baby lying across the foot of the bed and Mrs Williams from up the street and my mother trying to bring back life into Annie. Later I can see myself sitting by the kitchen fire looking into the washbasket where the baby was, and I can see me dad sprawled half across the kitchen table, his head buried in his arms.

'Well, the next picture I have of all this is our furniture being packed into a little van, and then Dad carrying the baby and my mother with me by the hand boarding a train. We moved straight into 109 Temple Street. Dad had come up here and rented the house; he had arranged everything. To all intents and purposes Hilda was his daughter and my mother was to be known as her mother. In that quarter the obvious situation was accepted. There you have the full story; except for one thing, which is ironic when you think about it, all the love that he deprived my mother of and bestowed first on his twin's wife and then on her illegitimate child, because he never learned who the father was, was wasted because Hilda grew up almost disliking him. He knows this and it has turned his feelings into a love-hate relationship with her. He deprived my mother of love, even of consideration, and he certainly deprived me of the affection due from a father because before Hilda came on the scene he hadn't much use for me, but from the moment she appeared all I was good for in his eyes was seeing that no harm came to his little dear.'

She leant towards him again and there was a wry smile on her lips as she said, 'Can you imagine how he felt when she married Peter Maxwell, a man older than himself, because if anyone was in love with his daughter, who wasn't his daughter, he was . . . Don't look so shocked.'

'What makes you think I'm shocked?'

'For a moment you looked it.'

'Well, I can only say that my looks belie my feelings.'

'Anyway, that's that and I've no need to ask you never to breathe a word of it, have I?'

'No, you have no need.'

'Her birth certificate doesn't give her away either . . . Do you like her?'

Again there was a pause as if he were considering, and then he said emphatically, 'Yes; yes, I like her.'

'You could do worse than marry her.'

'I'm . . . I'm not that way inclined.'

'Oh, well' – she laughed gently now – 'you'd better make up your mind one way or the other because you won't be able to stay there if you don't. Well, you won't, will you?'

'Why shouldn't I?' His tone was on the defensive now.

'Can you imagine her consenting to having an affair with you?'

'Who's talking about affairs? I wouldn't dream

about suggesting such a thing to her with her religious outlook.'

'That's just it, that's just it.' Her head was bouncing towards him. 'Life would become unbearable for both of you, she'd make it so. She's young, she's been married to an old man, can't you see you'll soon be called upon to make a choice? It won't be any use thinking you can't be done without, she can get a manager in there any day.'

'I wasn't under the impression that I could be done without and I'm well aware she can replace me tomorrow.' He felt annoyed, angry at her. Now he could in a way understand why Hilda lost her temper with her, her bluntness was disconcerting. He knew that his face was flushed, he wanted to get up and walk out. And he was on the point of doing just that when she asked quietly, 'Did you love your wife?' and his voice was loud in contrast as he answered briefly, 'No.'

'Never?'

'A little at first; it didn't last.'

'Have you ever loved a woman?'

He stared at her, watching her face change into Alice's. He saw her flat body take on a fleshy bust, her hips swell into comfortable mounds, her long thin fingers with their painted nails become blunt and roughened, and he answered on a long drawn-out breath, 'Yes, I once loved a woman.'

'Very much?'

He didn't know whether it was she who had asked the question or if he had asked it of himself, so soft was it, but he answered, 'Yes, very much, very much.'

'Do you think it would have lasted?'

'Yes, I think it would.'

'I don't think love ever lasts, not that kind of love, not the consuming kind, the kind that's half pain. It isn't fair really; anything so short-lived should be wonderful. But real love doesn't work out like that. All the time you're in it it's playing hell with you, you're full of fear in case it isn't going to last. You're jealous in case you're going to lose it to someone else. The whole damn thing is an operation without anaesthetic.'

'Apparently you've had the operation?'

She looked up at him, then turned her gaze away and nodded as if to herself as she said, 'Yes, I've had the operation; but only the once, not the three times I've mentioned. I was near eighteen, it was my first job after leaving the typing school and within six months I'd worked my way up from the pool into the manager's office. Boy! that was something to be proud of.' She shook her head again, and now she nodded towards him as she said, 'You can bring your eyebrows down and take that grin off your face because I didn't fall for the manager. He had ginger hair and he sniffed; all the time he was dictating he sniffed.' She laughed outright now. 'No, I fell, like the fool I was, for an Adonis on the shop floor. I wouldn't believe that he had worked his way through most of the female staff because I reasoned one of them would surely have caught him before this time, him being thirty. You know I went with him two and a half years. We were courting, as the saying goes, and I became estranged from every girl in those offices; they all wanted to be my friend and tell me I was being duped. But I knew they were just jealous, for didn't I see my bold bohemian boy every night, up till ten o'clock that is? That was the time I had to be in or me dad locked the door. Can you imagine how I felt when I finally learned that the minute he left me he made straight for his young widow woman, who had four kids. I learned the truth from my boss – he was a nice man in spite of his sniff. He told me quite gently that my dear Fred had sent him notice and taken the widow and her brood to Doncaster. Huh! of all places, Doncaster, from where me dad had flown with the remnants of his love.

'You know something?' She leant forward again and, placing her hands on her knees, she patted them as she said in a tone that was full of soft bitterness, 'There wasn't one person in that factory who didn't believe that I knew about his capers; in some quarters they even said I had prevented him from marrying the poor widow woman and giving the bairns a much needed father. In other quarters it was said I deserved all I got and that I tried to keep him by buying him presents. It was true about the presents.' Her head moved slowly up and down. 'I spent every penny I had on him after paying my board. Anyway, I know what it's like to be in love . . . Was it anything like that with you?'

'No, with me it was a beautiful thing on both sides.'

'What happened?'

'She died.'

'Oh . . . oh, I'm sorry. Would . . . would you like a cup of coffee?'

'I wouldn't mind.'

Left alone in the room, he lay back on the couch and slowly he began to move his hand first across his chin, then up and down each cheek. It was a sure sign that he was agitated, and recognising it, he stopped the motion abruptly and joined his hands tightly in front of him.

Whether he liked it or not he was becoming involved in this family; but how deep it would go was another question. Suddenly, he asked himself how much money he had and gave himself the known answer, seventy-two pounds. It was quite a sum – he had never had that much in his life before – but even so it wasn't enough to set up a business. As things stood now he was on to a good thing: Hilda had refused to take payment for their midday meal and he was living rent free, so out of his four pounds a week all he had to do was to provide for the odd meals and to clothe them both. The latter he had done to excess with Dick. But if he were to strike out on his own he would have to rent a shop and find some place for them both to live, and with the particular business he had in mind, which would come under the heading of fancy goods, it would take some long time to become established. As a side line he could see it doing well, but to make a real living out of, no, it wasn't possible.

What he would do if he were faced with the alternative Florrie had suggested he didn't know, except he would tell Hilda the truth. And what would be the result of that? He could even now see the look in her eyes and hear her voice saying, 'You mean to say you walked out just like that and left your wife simply because she objected to your affair with another woman?' Now if it had been Florrie here to whom he had to speak the truth there would be no fear of her disdain; but then Florrie, by her own words, was used to men and their ways . . . Only three of them though, so she had said, and the first one had been a right rotter by the sound of it.

As she entered the room, he rose quickly to his feet and went towards her and, taking the tray from her, he placed it on the side table, and a few minutes later they were both sitting facing each other again sipping at the coffee now.

When she said abruptly, 'Do you want to hear about number two?' he gulped on a mouthful of the hot liquid, spluttered, then placed his cup on the table to his side and wiped his mouth, saying, 'Not if it hurts.'

'Oh, it doesn't hurt, not number two. Makes me a bit wild at times when I think about it, angry, mad at myself mostly for being such a damned fool as to be caught a second time. I'd left the factory office – I wasn't up to standing the comments, the hidden laughter and sneers – and having developed over the years a taste for dress, few and good is my motto in that line, I became an assistant in a big store in Newcastle and within a couple of years I was buying for my own department. But that came about through dead men's shoes, or dead women's in this case, for the buyer had a heart attack and I took over first on a temporary basis and did so well that I was offered the post. It was through this that I met William; not Bill or Billy, but William.' She began to laugh now, saying, 'I should have known from the beginning that anyone who demanded to be called William all the time, even by his girl friend, had something missing in his make-up, namely a sense of humour. Anyway, he was a traveller and to use his own words he caught on to me from the minute he clapped eyes on me. His work took him all over the North, so we didn't see each other as often as we might. We had known each other a year when the question of marriage came up. But that was difficult because, you see, William had a widowed mother and two young sisters to support. He lived in Leeds, by the way. Twice I was invited to spend the weekend at his home, only for something to happen. The first time, his mother took ill; the second, he was called away on business. I forgot to tell you that I wasn't living at home at this time, I had taken a little flat, and so William saved on hotel bills whenever he was in this part of the country by receiving bed and breakfast.'

At this point she stared unblinking at him, and in the same manner he returned her stare; but when she resumed talking her eyelids blinked rapidly and she threw out both hands as if in a final gesture when she said, 'Oh, let's make it short. Something cropped up that made me say to myself, no, not again, not again; lightening doesn't strike twice in the same place. And so I took a train to Leeds and found out the address that dear William had given me was an office. However, they supplied his private address, and when I knocked on the door I was confronted by his dear mother who was obviously his wife, and his two little sisters who happened to be his children. I made some excuse about calling at the wrong house, came back to Newcastle, waited for dear William to arrive the following week, then gave him the best pasting he's ever had in his life. I used pans, vases and everything I could get my hands on. How he explained the loss of two teeth and a black eye and bruised shins to his wife I don't know. That night I said to myself, no more; after this, I'm doing the choosing, I'm calling the tune, and it's me who's going to be paid by whoever plays it. And so I looked around . . . Another cup of coffee?'

'No, thanks.'

'Well, I need one.' She poured herself out another cup and sipped at it, and he waited without making any comment until she said briskly, 'Newcastle is a big place and in spite of the poverty of the North it's a rich city; there are a lot of wealthy men in it, and in the course of staff entertainment I came in contact with a number of them, and so I made my choice . . . I think we made it simultaneously, he and I. I knew he was married and that he had four children; I knew that his wife came out of a top drawer of society in this quarter of the globe, and I also guessed in a very short time that like all married men with four children and a wife he had become

used to, he wasn't happy. No married man is happy'
– she moved her head slowly, weighing each word
with cynicism – 'all the married men I have met and
who have, may I say with some pride, wanted to
make me comfortable, have all been unhappy with
their wives. And they have all told me that I was the
one they should have married in the first place and
if they had they would never have been in the
emotional predicament in which I found them.
Anyway, here I am.' She spread her arms wide now.
'This flat is mine, I don't rent it; the business is mine,
all signed and sealed in my name; and there you
have it, three men in my life and I still don't consider
myself a prostitute. What do you think of that?'

'I think you're a very honest woman . . . Do you
love this man?'

'No, not as I understand love. My idea of love, as
I've said, is an emotion made up of pain, fear, jealousy, the lot. No, I like Charles, I like him very
much. You could say we are, at the least, very good
friends.' She gave a self-conscious laugh here. 'And
now I have to force myself to be honest. We were
up to a year ago, when his wife got wind of me and
the screws began to turn. There was no talk of him
having a divorce. Anyway, he didn't want it, and I
didn't want it. But when I didn't see him for three
months life became rather empty; and now when I
haven't seen him for almost six months life is very
empty. But as they say, that's life, isn't it? . . . You
shocked?'

'Why do you keep thinking you're shocking me?'

'I don't really know. Something about you, the

way you look at me while I'm talking. It's funny, but if I didn't know you weren't of a religious turn of mind I could imagine you were condemning me on those lines.'

'Good God!' He laughed as he turned his chin slowly from one shoulder to the other; then looking at her again, he said, 'It shows how little you know of me.'

'That's true. But then, nobody seems to know very much about you. You're a secret sort of fellow, aren't you?'

From the heat creeping up from his neck he knew that his face was now red, and when he made no answer to her statement she said quietly, 'I'm sorry; I didn't mean it rudely and I wasn't prying. It doesn't matter to me. If nothing else, the experience I've had has taught me everybody's life is their own to do with as it suits them if that's at all possible, and if it is, then they've got to stand the consequences. After saying all that I'm still not being nosey, and yet I'm wondering why you came round here the night?'

What should he say to that? That he came to take her down? that he thought she would hardly notice, simply look on him as one in the line of her suitors? What he said was, 'I don't know.'

'I do. Shall I tell you?'

'I'd rather you didn't.'

'Well, it's to your credit. You saw that I was upset, hurt by what Hilda said. You don't like people getting hurt . . . Were you in the war?'

'Yes, and no.'

'Yes and no? That's a funny way of putting it. What were you?'

'A conscientious objector.'

'Good God!'

He watched her mouth widen to a broad smile, he watched her flat chest heave as she began to laugh, and he said, 'What's so amusing about it?'

'I don't know. I don't know why I'm laughing; it . . . it was such a surprise, and the way you said it.' The smile sliding from her face now, she said thoughtfully, 'You must have been a pretty brave man. I could never understand why people thought the objectors were cowards. I knew one when I was a child, at least I knew where he lived. The women roundabout couldn't take it out of him because he was locked up, but they took it out of his wife and bairn, broke their windows, the lot. You know something? The poor are very ignorant.'

'They haven't got the monopoly.'

'No, perhaps not; but it seemed to me even in those far off days that few of them ever thought for themselves, they let themselves be led. You know something else? I hated living in Bog's End among the poor, even more than Hilda did. I hate going down there now. I hate small rooms, dull streets, sharing a backyard. All along Temple Street they're still carrying the water upstairs.'

'Well, you don't have to worry about that any more, do you?'

'No, I don't.'

They looked at each other now in what could have been hostile silence. It was as if he were defending the way of life she despised.

But when they smiled and were both about to speak simultaneously a sound brought their heads around towards the door leading from the room into the hall. The sound was the turning of a key in a lock followed by a door opening and closing.

Before the sitting-room door was opened Florrie was already on her feet looking towards it; and now slowly Abel drew himself upwards and he, too, looked towards the unexpected visitor standing there, one hand on the door.

The man was as tall as himself but slim. He had thick fair hair and every feature of his face could be described as handsome. Over one arm he carried an overcoat and in the same hand he held a soft felt hat. Everything about him spoke of the well-dressed gentleman, and this was given the stamp of genuineness by the timbre of his voice when he said, 'I . . . I hope I'm not intruding.'

'Oh no, no.' Florrie went slowly towards him, smiling now, and having taken his hat and coat, she laid them over a chair; then extending her hand backwards without turning her head in Abel's direction, she said, 'This is Mr Gray. He's . . . he's Hilda's manager. He just called to give me a message from her.'

She did not give the man's name to Abel and the two men looked at each other and inclined their heads.

'Come and sit down; it's frightfully windy out. Have you had a meal?'

Abel watched the man coming towards him. He

watched him pass between the couches, go to the fire, and hold his hands out towards it, and he thought, Six months, she said, since she's set eyes on him; it could be six hours and he's just returned from the office.

'I'll have to be going.' He was moving towards the door now, not the french windows but the door leading into the hall, and she looked at him and smiled. It was a warm smile, a smile that was thanking him for his tactfulness.

'I'll tell Mrs Maxwell that it's all right, you'll be calling?'

'Yes, tell her that.'

He turned towards the man who was seated now in a corner of the couch. 'Good night,' he said, and the man who was looking towards the fire and who seemed to have forgotten his presence screwed round and answered, 'Oh! Oh, good night. Good night.'

As she let him out of the door into the passage which led into the main hall she said softly now, 'Good night,' and he answered her as softly, 'Good night.'

He walked down the drive, through the gates, and on to the road, and there he stopped. He had the strangest feeling on him; it was as if he had just sustained a loss. But if you never had anything to lose how could you feel you had lost it? He couldn't have been in love with her. Oh no! He had loved Alice and only Alice. Then why was he feeling as if the bottom had dropped out of his world, his new secure world? . . . *Secure world?* What was he yammering on about? If he didn't marry Hilda security was going to be short-lived, and he couldn't marry Hilda, so what was the alternative? The road again? Oh no! By God! not with the boy. Oh no! he couldn't subject him to that again. Well what then?

He was still asking the question when he made his way up to the room and found Dick, his eyes wide with a new fear as he stammered, 'Eeh! Dad, I thought you had gone and left me. An' Mrs Maxwell was in a bad temper. She pushed me out when I went into the kitchen and said I'd better go to Miss Florrie's for me tea. Why would she say that, Dad, 'cos I've never been to Miss Florrie's place? Eeh! Dad, I was frightened. Eeh! I was frightened 'cos I thought I'd have to go back and live with me mam.'

It was the first time the boy had mentioned his mother since he had been told to think of her as dead, but the fact that his fear had brought her to mind again proved that he must still think of her.

As he held his son tightly to his side he knew that the future did not lie in his own hands but in those of the boy, and that in order to provide him with security he'd have to do a great deal of work on him. But how did one go about obliterating a mother, a live mother, from a child's mind? The only way he could see was by offering him a choice, a choice of a comfortable bed and a full stomach or the road again.

And he knew what choice the boy would make because he couldn't fully understand what the choice implied, he was too young. But he wouldn't remain young; and what then? Would he be able to make a young man believe that all he had done was for his sake? If he had to impose the choice on him his young mind would be burdened with a load of guilt, guilt that of its very essence would build up a sly evasiveness in the boy's nature.

Aw! He could worry no more – sufficient unto the day . . . and the night. And this night Florrie had her man with her again, her fancy man. His lip curled even as the thought came to him: God! if only he was in his place, fancy or not, for there was in him a need that was burning him up. It had no connection with love, it was just a need, and at this moment if he could have torn it out of himself, thereby depriving himself of the resulting experience of any similar need still to come, he would have done so.

6

There had been flurries of snow all day, so light at times it was like flour falling on the face. The cold was intense and the blanket of the sky lying low over the town caused passers-by to repeat to anyone and everyone, 'Dark days afore Christmas without a doubt, this.'

Dick came running into the garage, crying, 'Do you think it's going to lie, Dad? Will we be able to skate down the hill? Bob Tanner said they did last year. It was great, he said. What're you doing, Dad?'

'What do you think I'm doing? Use your eyes!'

'Well, I can't see you, Dad' – Dick laughed now – 'you're half under the car.'

'Well, what would I be under here for?'

'Mending something likely.'

Abel screwed himself along the floor from under the car and into a sitting position and, wiping the grease from his hands with some tow, he laughed at the boy as he said, 'What you excited about?'

'Don't know, Dad. Just Christmas comin' an' the snow. Where's Benny?'

'Where he always is, in the bicycle shed.'

'I'll go and pelt him with a snowball.'

'You'll be lucky; you won't get a spoonful off the yard, it isn't lying.'

'It is on top of the wall.'

As the boy turned and scampered from the garage Abel checked him. 'Just a minute, Dick,' he called, and when the boy paused he said warningly, 'Go careful, don't tease him.'

'I never tease him, Dad.'

'Well, if he's in one of his moods keep clear of him.'

'All right, Dad.'

Dick now ran towards the wall bordering part of the frontage facing the road and, reaching up, drew his hand along the flat uneven top. But when he had reached the end of it his hand had gathered only enough snow that would fill a tablespoon. Standing now in the shelter of the wall he gently pressed the light particles together, but try as he might they wouldn't form into a ball; and so, keeping his hands cupped, he ran down the yard again, past the garage, past the machine shop where Arthur Baines was working at a lathe, and into the bicycle shed.

The shed was long, all of thirty feet, and about fifteen feet wide. One side was taken up with bicycle stands, and with the exception of two, every stand held a bicycle because this wasn't the kind of weather that favoured the bicycle trade. Taking up one half of the other side of the shed was a long narrow bench on which was spread an assortment of tools, and above it, like a row of portraits, hung bicycle wheels. Beyond the bench the floor was clear, except for an old-fashioned round coke stove which besides giving off a pungent smell glowed more brightly than did the naked gas mantle in the bracket attached to the wall above where Benny Laton was sitting.

Benny Laton had all the appearance of a man. He was twenty-three years old; he was five foot ten in height with broad shoulders and a large head; but his arms and legs were thin. Sitting as he was now, he looked a normal man; it was when he walked or talked that the normality ended, for his walk was gangling and his talk was childish.

Dick came to a halt at his side, saying, 'Hello, Benny.'

'Aw, you. Back then?'

'Yes, it's been snowin'.'

'I know that . . . dafty.'

'Guess what I've got in me hands?' Dick held his closed palms up towards Benny's face. He was grinning mischievously.

'Won't.'

'Go on, guess.'

'Bird.'

'Bird? . . . No, snow.' As he said the word snow he opened his hands and threw what remained of the snow from his wet palms into Benny's face.

What happened next occurred so quickly that it froze Dick's ability to cry out. As Benny's arm flung him aside he stumbled backwards and only managed to stop himself from falling by gripping a bike stand; then he was walking backwards with Benny advancing on him and holding in his hand a twelve inch spanner, all the while talking incoherently.

It wasn't until Dick felt the heat from the stove that he was able to give voice to his fear, and he shouted, 'Don't Benny! Don't! I meant no harm. Don't, Benny!'

'You . . . you took her away. Yes, you did.'

'Don't Benny! I'll be burnt. I'll be burnt.'

'Yes, yes, you will be burnt, you'll go to hell.'

'*Dad! Dad!*'

When the fierce heat struck the back of his neck and he knew that if he put his hand behind him it would touch the red-hot stove he let out a high scream; then another and another.

Abel had been crossing the yard towards the kitchen with the intention of telling Hilda that this particular job was finished and he was going to take the car round to its owner when he heard the scream; and Hilda heard it too, for she was busy at the sink, and in the shadowy light of the gate lamp she had seen Abel making for the house.

Both she and Arthur Baines reached the entrance to the bicycle shed at the same moment and they stopped and stood transfixed watching Abel moving slowly up the middle of the shed. He was talking quietly, soothingly, saying, 'What is it, Benny? What's happened? Stay your hand a minute, Benny.' Then he stopped as Benny moved a step nearer to Dick, the spanner held over the boy's head now as he cried, 'You don't come near me, mister. You don't come near me. You're not me boss. He's taken her away. I told me mam he's taken her away.'

Hilda was now standing at Abel's side and her voice, too, was soft and soothing as she said, 'Benny! Benny! listen to me. You wouldn't hurt Dick, you like Dick.'

'No, I don't. No, I don't. He wants to sleep in the house. Me mam says that, me mam knows. Big fellow'll marry you, me mam says; set his cap for you she says; then young 'un sleeps in your house. Me mam knows, she knows what he's up to, the big 'un.'

There was complete silence in the shed for a matter of seconds, then Abel moved forward again. His voice no longer soft now, he cried, 'Put that spanner down!'

'No.' As he spoke, Benny gripped Dick by the shoulder and as he did so the boy slumped in his grasp and, overcome by the heat and fear, he fainted.

It was at this point that Abel sprang forward, but as he went to grapple with Benny, the demented young fellow brought the spanner down with such force across his forearm that they all, with the exception of Dick, heard the bone crack.

The fact that he had at last hit someone seemed to take all the fury out of Benny and he stood now, the spanner hanging limp in his hand, looking to where Abel stood doubled up in agony. And when Arthur Baines took the spanner from him he made no protest, except to turn towards Hilda where she was lifting Dick from the floor and whimper, 'You used to like me. Best worker, you said, best worker you had, you said. Boss Maxwell liked me, he did.

Mam says things not the same since tramp came. Tramps, that's all they were, tramps. I'll tell me mam.'

'Shut up!' Hilda's voice was pitched on a scream and the young fellow shut up, and as he stood with quivering lips looking at her, she said to Arthur Baines, 'Get him home, Arthur, will you? Tell his mother what has happened and tell her I want to see her.'

'Will I give Abel a hand inside first and take the boy in?'

'No, no.' It was Abel speaking now, his voice slow and thick. 'I'm all right. We'll see to the boy; only get him' – he closed his eyes and jerked his head sidewards – 'get him out of here.'

Arthur took hold of Benny's arm and led him towards the door and the young fellow went quietly, until he reached the opening. Here pulling Arthur to a halt, he said, 'Want me coat.' But after getting his coat and putting it on, he still seemed reluctant to go and as Arthur went to pull him through the doorway he turned about and shouted, 'Tramp! Road tramp. Lookin' for soft spot. Me mam knows.'

It was as if Hilda hadn't heard what Benny had said, for she busied herself in gathering Dick into her arms; but Abel stood with his head bowed, his eyes closed. He felt no pain in his arm now, his whole left side seemed to have gone quite numb, but he was experiencing an emotion that was new and strange to him. Perhaps he imagined it was like that which men experienced before going into battle.

Something they feared but something inevitable, something they knew they had to go through with, and he knew in this moment that he had reached a turning point in his life and that before this night was out he would have taken another road.

He had been to the hospital and his arm had been set. Dick was in bed and asleep in one of the spare rooms upstairs; and now he was himself sitting before the fire drinking hot cocoa and waiting for her to speak.

He had returned from the hospital at half past eight, it was now ten o'clock and she hadn't spoken more than half a dozen sentences to him during that time. However, she had been very solicitous, cutting up a meal which she insisted on his eating, making him sit in the big leather chair, Mr Maxwell's chair, and placing cushions to support his slinged arm.

When she took the seat opposite him and sat looking at him straight in the face he knew he would have to say one of two words, either of which would alter his life, the one to direct him towards the road again, the other to security, but security at what a risk.

'Abel.'

'Yes, Hilda?'

'Things have come to a head, haven't they?'

'In what way?' God! why had he to stall like this; he knew what his answer was going to be, so why dither?

He felt embarrassed and ashamed when of a sudden she flung her head to the side and her young plump body writhed as if she were endeavouring to cut loose from bonds.

When she became still she again looked at him straight in the face as she said, 'Don't play blind, Abel. You know as well as I do how things stand. Do . . . do you want me to humble myself . . . bare my soul before you have spoken? Yet I know you'll never speak, never say it, just because of our position. Oh Abel!'

She had sprung so quickly from the chair to kneel by his side that he was startled, and when he openly cringed as her body knocked against his bent arm she cried contritely, 'Oh Abel, I'm sorry, I'm sorry, have I hurt you?'

'No, no; it's all right.'

'Oh, Abel.' She was staring up into his face, her lips trembling, her eyes moist; and now he put his free hand on to her hair and, stroking it back from her brow, he said, 'I . . . I know what must be said but, as you put it, I could never have brought myself to say it. Even now . . . well, I . . . I don't know . . .'

She knelt back on her hunkers and her face looked small and pitiful now as she whispered, 'I . . . I thought you liked me.'

'Oh, I do, I do.' His reply was quick and rang with truth; indeed there was no need to lie about his feelings for her, he did like her, he liked her very much, but he had no real desire for her, not like he'd had for . . . His mind closed down on the name that was no longer Alice as she said softly, 'I love you, Abel, I think I've loved you from the first moment you stepped through that door. I . . . I had to take a pull at myself when Mr Maxwell was alive but . . . but after he'd gone and I thought you were fancying our Florrie, oh I nearly went mad. I did, I did, Abel.' She moved her head slowly from side to side; then her two hands gripping his fingers, she pulled herself close to him and, her face against his shoulder, her eyes directed downwards to where his chest showed in the gap of his open-necked shirt, she whispered, 'I . . . I must tell you that . . . that I've never really been married . . .'

'What! But I thought—' His tone brought her head up and, her voice holding a slightly shocked note, she said, 'Oh, yes, yes, Mr Maxwell and I were married in that sense, in church, it was all done proper, but . . . but what I meant was he . . . he looked upon me more as a daughter and . . . well, I couldn't bear the thought of him as anything else. It . . . it was all arranged before the ceremony . . . well, that there would be nothing like that . . . you know what I mean.'

He looked at her mouth which was now forming a tight prim button, and he had the desire to laugh. He couldn't take it in, that she had shared the bed upstairs with that man and yet remained intact. What kind of flesh had he been made of? He wasn't all that old. And what kind of flesh was she made of? Yet there was one thing certain to him now, she wanted to be married, and not only in name, the desire was emanating from her like heat; it was in the pressure of her hands and the closeness of her body, and openly in the depth of her eyes.

The urge to laugh left him and for a while pity

took its place. He began to wonder if she would now accept the benefits of marriage without the ceremony. If that could be brought about he'd have no further need for worry.

He took his arm from around her shoulders and again he stroked her hair back from her brow, but he did not look into her eyes as he said, 'It must have been pretty tough for you, and I can understand just how you felt, so . . . well, if it's all the same to you, we . . . well, we can come together . . . be happy without the usual palaver, for after all . . .'

Her movement away from him was as quick as a few minutes before it had been towards him. She stood now gazing at him, one hand pressed across the corner of her mouth pushing it out of shape; her eyes wide, her small frame bristling, her feet planted firmly apart, she poured her indignation over him. 'What are you suggesting? I'm not like that! You think because our Florrie's loose that I'm the same. Oh yes, you do. Same family, no difference you think. She does what she does for money and what she can get and because I told you about Mr Maxwell you think the same of me, I married him for what I could get. Oh yes, you do. Yes, you do.' She wagged her head at him.

He rose to his feet but didn't move towards her and he said quietly, 'Listen! Listen, Hilda,' he said. 'I just thought you might prefer it this way. Everybody around here knows I was taken in off the road, what do you think they'll say when they know I'm aiming to marry you? Taking advantage, they'll say. Oh yes, they will.' He jerked his head towards her as if she had denied his statement. 'I made the suggestion . . . well, with the idea of bringing you comfort without embarrassing you.'

He watched as, like an injection, each word of his relaxed her, and when she sat down on the chair, her head and shoulders drooping, he looked towards her hands where one thumb was passing swiftly backwards and forwards over the front of her fingers. It was as if she were feeling the texture of some material, giving herself its name by touch alone. He had observed this habit of hers before, it spoke of nerves.

He went forward now and gripped one of her hands, and as he pressed it tightly against his waist he felt a deep sense of compassion for her; but there was no ingredient of what he thought of as love in it. He would have felt the same for some animal that had caught itself in a trap, or someone who was inflicting self torture upon himself; and that's what she had done, and was doing.

His compassion for her did not lessen when she whispered without looking at him, 'I could have nothing but marriage, Abel. I . . . I couldn't act loose, no matter how I felt.'

'I understand. It' – he swallowed deeply and now had to force out the words that spelt yes – 'it'll be as you wish.'

'Oh, Abel, Abel.' She was on her feet now, her arms about him, and when he gave a slight groan she cried, 'Oh, I'm sorry, I'm sorry, and you in pain.' She took one arm away from his neck and eased her body to the side; then she lifted her face upwards and when he bent his head and put his lips to hers her eyes were tightly closed, and his own body registered the shiver that passed through her.

When after a moment she stepped back from him, her face was bright, her eyes shining and her voice husky as, looking him up and down, she said, 'You're so big and so gentle. I've never imagined anyone so gentle as you, Abel.'

'You don't really know me.' He gave a small laugh and a shake of his head.

Swinging round like an excited girl now, she cried, 'Oh the plans I've got. I've lain in bed at night and thought what we'll do with the business, because I know you like the business. You do, don't you?' She turned towards him again and he said quietly, 'I'd be hard to please if I didn't.'

'We could extend if we could get Esther Burrows to sell that field of hers, and she will have to sooner or later because her money's running out. And we could sell petrol; I've thought a lot about that. There's plenty of places for pumps in the front.'

He had sat down again and now he watched her flinging the tablecloth over the table prior to setting the table ready for tomorrow's breakfast, talking all the while and all about the business, until she stopped and as if she were throwing off the businesswoman and returning to the girl again, she said, 'Do you think I could be married in white, Abel? I'd love to walk up the aisle this time in white. I wore just an ordinary costume . . . What is it?'

She moved slowly towards him where he had

risen from the chair, his face wearing a stiff blank look. His voice, too, held a note of firmness she had not heard before, at least not during this evening as he said, 'I won't be married in church, Hilda.'

She was aghast, and showed it in her face, her voice, and even in her outstretched hands. 'Not in church? But where?'

'The registry office.'

'*Oh no! No!*' She shook her head wildly. 'Never! Marriage in a registry office? There's . . . there's no holiness or anything good about it.'

'It's the same as a church ceremony.'

'It isn't. It isn't. Abel, I'm surprised at you. And what will the vicar say? He won't allow it. We've been church people for years. I've . . . I've always gone to him for advice, and Mr Maxwell was a sidesman, we met there. The vicar knew about our . . . well, I mean he knew about our marriage state and everything. He'd . . . he'd never stand for it.'

'Then I'm sorry, Hilda; but I won't be married in a church, a church of any kind.'

The flatness of his voice, the note of determination in it that brooked no softening told her immediately that the only way she could get this man was to marry him in a registry office.

When he made towards the door, saying, 'I'll go across now. Think about it, there's no rush,' she stared at him for a moment before asking, 'Will you be able to manage?'

He nodded and gave her a quiet smile as he answered, 'Yes, I'll manage all right. Good night, Hilda. Don't worry; there's been no harm done. If

. . . if you can't see your way to meet me in this . . . well, things could go on as they have been. We'll talk again in the morning. Good night.'

The look on her face checked his movement and when of a sudden she ran towards him and held up her face to his he knew there was no need to wait until the morning for an answer, it was given.

He sat in a straight-backed chair. The boy stood in front of his knees; his face was white and pinched looking, and fear was reflected in his eyes and his lips trembled as he said, 'Am I gona get wrong, Dad?'

'No, no.'

'I only threw some snow at him, Dad. It was only a little bit and it didn't hurt him and . . .'

'I know. I know.' Abel drew the boy closer, and now Dick put his hand tentatively on the sling as he asked, 'Does it hurt bad, Dad?'

'No, I don't feel anything now, just a slight numbness. But listen, I want to talk to you, and seriously.'

He stared down into his son's face; he wetted his lips preparatory to speaking; then clenched his teeth as if to form a barrier to check the words that must be spoken.

With a slight movement of his head to the side, he said softly, 'Listen. You know what I've been telling you about thinking of your mother as being dead?'

He waited. 'Well, don't you remember?' His tone was harsh now.

'Oh yes, Dad, yes.' Dick nodded at him; then his chin jerking upwards, he repeated loudly, 'Yes, yes, Dad.'

'Well, that's all right then. But even so we both know don't we, that she was alive and well when we left Hastings?'

'Yes, Dad.'

'And for all we know she's still alive?'

'Yes, Dad.'

'Now listen carefully. When a man has a wife and she's still alive he can't marry another woman. You understand?'

Dick blinked, looked to the side, then looked back at his father before saying firmly, 'Yes, Dad.'

'Well now, say that this man goes and marries another woman while his wife is still alive, it's a sort of . . . well, a sort of sin and he can be put in prison for it because a man is not allowed to have two wives. You understand?'

Again there was a pause before the boy said, 'Yes . . . yes, Dad.'

Abel now gripped the boy's shoulder and bending down further still until his face was on a level with and close to his son's, he said, 'Mrs Maxwell wants me to marry her. You understand? She wants me to marry her. If I don't, then things will become very strained; in fact we will have to leave here, and I'd have to look for work elsewhere.' He paused here. 'You know what happened when I attempted to look for work before, don't you?'

The boy's eyes were wide; the fear had been replaced by a look of deep perplexity. He did not say as he usually did, 'Yes, Dad,' but remained quiet, his young mind trying to take in the enormity of the situation his father was placing before him. His thoughts were ranging wildly around the danger of sin which would lead to prison, the feeling was akin to that which he experienced at the matinee on a Saturday afternoon when he saw the cowboys and Indians fighting and the bad man at last being shot or taken off to prison by the sheriff. But it was only bad men that went to prison, yet his father had said that if he took two wives he could go to prison. Then startlingly his mind presented him with a picture of a baby. He didn't reason why this should be, except that Georgie Armstrong's sister who was married three months ago had just had a baby and Georgie had had a fight at school with a bigger boy about it. Georgie was eleven and he knew all about babies. He said you could have one or you could have five, they were just like his rabbits, only they took a little longer to come, three months for each one he said and that the doctor had come and pulled the baby out of his sister's belly button . . .

'Are you listening?' Abel shook him roughly by the shoulder. 'It's all up to you. Do you realise that?'

'What is, Dad?'

'Boy, am I talking to myself? What have I been saying?'

'About not lettin' on about mam.'

'Well then, you must remember to forget, so to speak, that your mother is alive, because once I've married Hil . . . Mrs Maxwell and anyone finds out that I have another wife they'll send me to prison. I wouldn't need to have to worry about findin' another job. *Now do you understand? . . .* Tell me you understand that you must never mention your mother to anybody.'

'Yes, Dad.'

There followed a long pause while they stared at each other, then Abel said, 'You've made friends at school. This pal of yours, Georgie Armstrong. He'll tell you things and he'll expect you to tell him things back, but if you don't want any harm to come to me you must never confide in him, I mean . . . well, tell him secrets, like about things that happened when we lived in Hastings.'

'I won't, Dad. I won't.'

Again they stared at each other; then the boy said quietly, 'What'd happen, Dad, if . . . if me mam came and found us?'

Abel opened his mouth wide and gulped at the air. Then rising to his feet, he put his arm around his son and pulled him tightly against his side as he said, 'Don't worry about that. I don't think there's any likelihood of her finding us, I put her off the scent about us coming North before I left. Anyroad, should she come this way she'll go straight to yon side of the river and we are well inland here; people hereabouts are apt to keep to their own neck of the woods; some of them in North Shields haven't been this side of the river in their lives. No, don't worry about that, son, that's the least of my worries. The only thing I'm worrying about, and I'll go on worrying about, is if you should let it slip.'

The boy moved from his side and stood solemn-faced looking up at him now as he said slowly, 'I won't let it slip, Dad, never, 'cos I like it here.'

Perhaps it was a trick of the light coming through the small window but it seemed to Abel at that moment that his son changed. He saw him stepping prematurely out of childhood burdened with a secret that would grow heavier with the years and awareness, and he wondered how that awareness when it came would affect their relationship: would the boy's blind love for him perish in the open light of revelation? The fall of a god was always harder than that of a mere man, and he knew that in a way he appeared as a god to his son, he was someone who could do no wrong, someone who knew all the answers.

He turned and walked to the window and stood looking down into the yard, asking himself now if it was worth the risk. But before he could give himself an answer his attention was taken up by a car swinging into the yard, and when out of it stepped Florrie his whole body stiffened. He watched her hurry towards the kitchen door and when it closed behind her he looked at his watch. Half past eight. She was likely on her way to open her shop, but what did she want here? He hadn't set eyes on her for weeks now, not since the night her gentleman friend had unexpectedly reappeared. He stopped himself from going downstairs, this wasn't the time to come face to face with Florrie.

He didn't move from the window when he spoke to Dick, saying, 'Get yourself off to school.'

'Must . . . must I go the day, Dad?'

'Yes, you'll be better there.' He still kept his eyes focused down on the yard while the boy gathered up his school bag and put on his coat and cap, and when he stood behind him, saying, 'I'm off then, Dad,' he turned about and putting his hand on his son's cheek, said gently, 'You'll be all right.' He did not add, 'Remember what I said,' because he felt there was no need; the less said about it from now on the better.

When the boy was crossing the yard towards the gate the kitchen door opened and Florrie reappeared, with Hilda behind her. Hilda was putting her coat on and as she made for the staircase he drew back from the window and waited until her voice called, 'Abel! Abel!'

Slowly he went down the stairs and she greeted him with a flow of words. 'Dad was knocked down last night, he's in hospital. Do you think you can manage? Leave everything to Arthur, I mean the work; just keep your eye on things.'

Before he had time to reassure her she was exclaiming, 'Oh me bag! I've come out without me bag,' and turning from him, she dashed back into the house, while he walked slowly across to where Florrie was standing by the car. After a moment during which they stood looking at each other, he said, 'I'm sorry about your father.'

'Oh, he'll survive. But just in case, I thought she should know . . . By the way, she's told me the happy news.'

He continued to stare at her waiting for her to

add, 'Congratulations,' but what she said was, 'I wish you all you wish yourself,' and to this he answered, 'I'm afraid that's too tall an order ever to come true.'

The next minute Hilda was by his side. 'There now,' she said, 'I'm ready,' and as Florrie went round the bonnet to the far door of the car Hilda lifted her face up to his, and after a moment's hesitation he bent down and kissed her on the cheek.

There was a loud revving up and the car started and went out through the wide opening as if setting off for a race, leaving him standing in the middle of the yard.

Never before, not even when Alice went, had he experienced this feeling of aloneness that was in him now, for it was bordering on desolation, desolation of both mind and spirit.

PART THREE

The First Incident 1938

1

'Molly, may I come in?'

The young woman turned from the sink, looked towards the door where the boy in the school blazer was standing, and she said, 'Why, of course. What's the matter with you? You don't usually ask, what's the matter with you?'

As he stepped into the room he looked around the kitchen and in a whisper now he muttered, 'Your mother?'

'Oh, she isn't down today, she rarely comes down at the weekends.'

'Oh aye, yes.' He nodded at her.

She was now standing in front of him and, bending forward, she asked softly, 'What's the matter, are you ill?'

'Well' – he turned his head to the side – 'I've . . . I've been sick, and it . . . it went down my sleeve. Look, it's on the front of my blazer, and Aunt Hilda'll go mad if she sees it. Could . . . could I sponge it down?'

'What made you sick?' She was still bent down towards him. 'You been stuffing?'

'No.' He shook his head before saying sheepishly, 'Smokin'.'

'Smoking!' The word came out on a giggle; then their glances meeting, they both started to laugh further but checked themselves immediately with their hands over their mouths.

'Here, take your coat off,' she said, swinging him round and pulling the blazer from him. 'What were you smoking, tabs?'

'No . . . a pipe.'

'A *what*!' Again she was gurgling. 'Where on earth did you get a pipe?'

'Georgie. Georgie Armstrong. He'd got these old pipes of his father's and we were in the hut at the bottom of the garden. He was all right, he knew how to smoke, and I would have been all right an' all, I think, if it hadn't been for his mother.'

'She caught you?'

'I say she did. She . . . she came from nowhere.' He pressed his lips together to prevent himself from laughing again, then went on. 'She didn't say a word, but she lifted him up by the collar, and he still had the pipe in his mouth! She got a hold of me next and . . . and—' He now leaned over the kitchen table and, putting his elbows on it, dropped his face on to his hands in an effort to suppress his mirth.

'Go on, tell me,' Molly hissed at him.

Straightening up, he turned to her and ended, 'She . . . she put her foot in me backside and I went sprawling through the door on to me hands and knees. It was then I was sick and . . . and when I picked meself up I saw her tearing up the garden with Georgie, and his feet were hardly touching the ground. The funny part about it was she hadn't spoken a word.'

The laughter was getting a hold of them again, they looked into each other's face until, in an effort to smother his guffawing, he fell against her, and when his arms went about her she remained utterly still for a moment; then she held his shaking body to her and let her own laughter mingle with his.

Even when his laughter subsided he didn't move away from her, not until a voice coming from above seemed to cleave them apart like a knife.

'Molly! Molly!'

Molly went to the door that led into the hall and from there she called, 'Yes?'

'What's going on down there?'

'Nothing, Mother.'

'Come up here.'

'I'm seeing to the dinner; I'll be up in a minute.' She turned now and closed the door none too gently, then coming back into the kitchen, she said, 'I'd better press your coat, you can't put it on wet.'

'Oh, it'll be all right.' He was whispering again.

She took no heed of him, but brought out the ironing board from a cupboard, together with an iron, switched it on, then smoothed the blazer out while waiting for the iron to heat.

Dick sat looking at her, at the girl who had been his friend for years but who, during the last year or so, had somehow slipped away from him while becoming a young woman.

He watched her wet her finger on her tongue and apply it to the iron; then happening to look at him she paused and said, 'You're miles away again. What are you thinking about?'

'I . . . I wasn't miles away, I was thinking about you.'

'Oh.'

'It's just struck me that you're very like Aunt Florrie.'

'Oh now! Now!' She made a soft deriding noise. 'Your Aunt Florrie isn't only the smartest dressed woman in the town she's the best looking too, if I'm any judge.'

'Well . . . well, I wasn't meaning your face, I . . . I was meaning your figure like.'

'Oh thank you. Thank you.'

'Aw, I didn't mean it that way. You're all right.'

'Up to here you mean?' She held the back of her hand under her chin.

And yes, that's what he did mean 'cos she didn't look a bit like Aunt Florrie. Her black hair was as straight as a die and all other young women's hair seemed to be frizzy or wavy. And she hadn't any colour in her face; sallow, he supposed, was the word for her skin. But she had nice eyes; they were long-shaped with heavy lids. He remembered his dad once remarking about her eyes and saying they were beautiful, and his Aunt Hilda had added it was a pity the rest of her face didn't come up to them, which he thought wasn't very nice. But then his Aunt Hilda often said things that weren't very nice; more so of late. Faintly he could remember a time when she had, so to speak, been all over him. Still, she was all right, was Aunt Hilda; and she was a good cook.

To make up for his apparent tactlessness he now said, 'Dad once said you had lovely eyes.'

'Did he?'

'Yes.'

'But there, your dad is a very kind man.'

'Yes, I suppose he is.' He nodded at her and she made that little sound in her throat again; then whipping up the blazer from the ironing board, she threw it towards him, saying, 'Get it on. And the next time you want to smoke, try a tab.'

'I don't think I'll try anything again.'

As he buttoned up his blazer he went towards the door, saying, 'Ta, Molly. That's saved me a wigging. Ta-rah.'

'Ta-rah.' She placed a hand between his shoulder blades and pushed him through the door, and he turned and laughed at her before scampering along by the side of the house, then across the meadow and through the broken fence boundary, round by the garden outhouses, through the narrow cut between the garage and the bicycle shed, and so into the yard.

Arthur was at the petrol pump seeing to a customer. This recalled to his mind that it was Arthur's Saturday on, which meant that his dad would be free. The thought gave a lift to his spirits and he dashed up the yard towards the kitchen door, but slowed down to a walk before reaching it.

He opened the door and stepped quietly into the

familiar brightness, then looked towards the dinner table in surprise. He had fully expected to see his dad and Aunt Hilda sitting there and had been prepared for her demanding, 'Where have you been till this time?' However, he had no sooner closed the kitchen door behind him than he was given evidence of where his father and step-mother were, and the tone of their voices brought a slump to his shoulders and his chin drooping towards his chest. They were at it again, at least his Aunt Hilda was at it again. It didn't take much to set her going.

He tiptoed towards the far door and cocked his head to the side. His father was saying, 'I got more when I was a hand. And why can't it be a joint account, I'm supposed to be a partner, aren't I? Partner? Huh!'

'There's money there if you want it; I've never kept you short.'

'What are you talking about, money if I want it? You have every penny docketed that comes into this place. You attend to those books there as you do to your Bible.'

'Abel! Now I'm warning you.'

'Well, you can stop warning me and come to an arrangement, a fair arrangement . . . My name was to go up on the board, wasn't it? What happened to that? I've doubled the business in the yard in the last five years but to all intents and purposes I might as well still be the hand; in fact, to you I'm still the hand, aren't I?'

'Don't be ridiculous! I've given you everything you've asked for.'

'What did you say, Hilda, you've given me everything I've asked for?'

'I'm not going to stand here wasting my time talking to you.'

As Dick prepared to jump back his father's voice checked him as it did Hilda's, and in his mind's eye he knew that his dad had hold of her. Then his voice came deep and angry sounding. 'What have you ever really given me, Hilda? A new suit a year, rigged the boy out for school, four square meals a day. Oh, I'll grant you that. And yet that too has a selfish side because you like nothing better than stuffin' your face . . . No, you don't! You'll just stay and listen; for once you'll listen to me.'

This was followed by a silence in which Dick drew in a deep breath, then endeavoured to hold it in case he should cough. But when his father spoke again it was about something different, something personal, which embarrassed him, so much so that what he heard quickened his breathing and brought out a sweat on the back of his neck. He shut his mind to the first spate of words, then found his eyes widening and his ears seeming to stretch to take in the flood of words his father was pouring out, words he knew that were connected with . . . that other thing, the thing that Georgie Armstrong knew all about, the thing that he said happened between his mother and father. That's what his Dad was talking about now . . .

'So far and no further. You didn't like it, did you? Came as a shock to you, is what you said. You were made for old Maxwell. God! what a pity he had to go. He supplied all you needed, didn't he, nursed you, cuddled you, petted you; and with him there was no ripening, was there? All he needed was a little girl at night and a business-woman during the day, and you fitted his picture perfectly. Well, I'm no Mr Maxwell. I don't want any little girl to play with, nor do I want a boss woman over me during the day, I want a fair deal. I've put a lot of hard work into your business – *your* business, do you hear? – because you wouldn't let me start one of my own. That was in the plans to begin with. Oh yes, but it was soon put aside, wasn't it? I had to have nothing of my own. I had to depend upon you, hadn't I? I was still the fellow from the road. Oh yes, I was. Shake your head as much as you like, Hilda. I was still the fellow from the road and I still am, isn't that so? I catch you looking at me sometimes as if you're wondering why you took me on.'

Dick now turned his chin tightly into his shoulder as he heard a scuffling; then Hilda's voice came from the room yelling, 'Yes! You're right in part, but I didn't think at the time what I was taking on. You've made me think about it since though, because you act deep. I know no more about you now than on the day we were married. As for me not giving you anything, what have you given me, I ask you? You accuse Mr Maxwell of treating me as a little girl. Well, things might have been different if you had treated me with a little of his gentleness instead of always wanting to satisfy your lust. You should have married someone like our Florrie, she could have satisfied all your needs.

Oh yes, she would have satisfied all your needs.'

There was a short silence before his father's voice came to him again; and now his eyebrows moved up even further as he listened to him saying quite quietly and firmly, 'Yes, I should have, you're right there, Hilda, except it wasn't someone like Florrie I should have married, it should have been Florrie herself.'

'You beast! You cruel, cruel beast! You know what I feel about our Florrie, yet you could say that to me.'

'You brought it up, not me. Anyway, I've had about enough of this. I'll say now what I came in to say. I'm going to take five pounds each week out of that till, at least five pounds. I'll work out the profits and take a percentage. I think that's only fair for the twelve-hour day I put in. And now I'm going out and I don't know what time I'll be back . . . or if I'll be back. Aye, or if I'll be back.'

From the sanctuary of the scullery now, Dick saw his father enter the kitchen, then stop as Hilda's voice cried, 'You can't, I mean you've got to get back for tea, Mr Gilmore's coming. You know he is.'

'Well, Hilda' – his father had turned about and was apparently facing her – 'you can tell Mr Gilmore from me that he can go to hell, now and on all future visits . . . Do you know something, Hilda? He's the one you should have married. But, of course, his wife was alive at the time. What a pity she didn't go about the same time as Mr Maxwell because you would have made a wonderful pair.

And he's still got you in mind, do you know that, Hilda?'

'You're wicked. That's what you are, Abel Gray, you're wicked.'

As the kitchen door closed on his father Dick stepped back further into the scullery, but he didn't attempt to open the back door and make his escape because that door had a habit of creaking, and there in the kitchen now was Hilda. She was standing near the table, her face held tightly between her hands; then she disappeared from his view and he heard a slight thud, followed by a gasping cry and the sound of weeping.

After a moment during which he stood gnawing on his thumbnail while looking from one side of the scullery to the other, he moved slowly into the kitchen. Hilda was lying halfway over the kitchen table. Her head was resting on her forearms but, in unison with the rest of her body, it was rocking from one side to the other. She looked like someone trying to throw off a great pain and the sight upset him. He couldn't have explained why, but he knew that, over this present issue, he was more in sympathy with her than his father. He had already forgotten the substance of the issue, he only knew that somehow he was on her side in this.

'Aunt Hilda.' He put his hand gently on her shoulder and she started and seemed to roll on to her side. Now with one elbow on the table she rested her head in her hand while her eyes rained tears and her mouth opened and shut as if she were finding it difficult to breathe.

'Don't cry. Don't cry like that, Aunt Hilda. Come on.' He caught hold of her shoulders and pulled her upright. 'Come on, come on, sit up; I'll . . . I'll make you a cup of tea.'

She allowed herself to be led to a chair and there, looking up at him, she gulped, 'Oh, Dickie!' When she caught hold of his hands he expected her to say, 'How long have you been in?' but what she said was, 'Your father doesn't love me, he doesn't care anything for me. He doesn't. He doesn't.'

When she fell against him he put his arms about her and brought her head to his breast and for the second time in a half-hour, in less than half an hour he found himself being embraced by a woman, and returning the embrace.

It was strange but he realised that this was the first time that Hilda had really held him close to her. She had put her arms around his shoulders, she had kissed him good night on the cheek, but she had never held him like this. He found he liked the feeling. As his laughter had come easy to him with Molly, so now words of comfort seemed to flow from him. He didn't know exactly what he was saying or why he was saying it, but he was telling her that she was mistaken and that his dad thought the world of her, and that people said all kinds of things when they were angry. He had even reminded her of a sermon Mr Gilmore had preached one Sunday not so long ago about the sin of temper and of hurting people you love.

When she pressed him gently from her she was no longer crying and she looked into his face and said quietly, 'You're a good boy, Dickie. You're a very good boy. I've . . . I've been harsh with you at times but it's just because . . . well, I've . . . been so unhappy.'

She was about to cry again but with an effort stopped herself and, getting to her feet, she went to the sink and turned on the cold tap before holding her face sideways under it, then slowly dried herself on the roller towel, after which she looked out of the kitchen window, and her voice low, she said to him, 'Your dad's just gone into the garage. Go to him, will you, and . . . and stay with him? Wherever he goes this afternoon, stay with him.'

'Aye. All right, yes, yes, I'll . . . I'll do that. And don't worry, it'll be all right.'

As he opened the door to go out, she said, 'I forgot, you usually go to the matinee on a Saturday.'

'Oh' – he jerked his chin up – 'I wasn't going anyway; I've seen it.'

He ran down the yard now towards the garage and met his father just coming out, buttoning up his overcoat. He didn't stop in his walk but went towards the road. Dick kept pace with him, but neither of them spoke until they were on the pavement and hidden from the house by the high wall; and then Abel stopped and said, 'I've got some business to do.'

'Can't I come along, Dad.'

'No. Anyway, you generally go to the matinee the day.'

Again the boy said, 'I've seen it.'

'Well, go and watch the cricket then; they're playing on the bottom field.'

'Dad, let me go along of you.'

'No, I've told you, haven't I! I might end up going tramping over the hills and you've got no love for tramping, have you?'

'I wouldn't mind today, Dad.'

They stood staring at each for a moment until Dick said, 'She was crying, Dad, badly.'

Abel turned his head to the side and drew his bottom lip between his teeth for a moment, then he said, 'Well, if she's crying she needs someone to look after her, so go back and keep an eye on her.'

'But she . . .'

'She what?'

'It doesn't matter.'

Again they looked at each other; then Abel stalked away down the road and Dick turned back into the yard. But he didn't go towards the kitchen, yet he knew she had seen him for she was standing looking out of the window.

Arthur Baine's time for leaving on a Saturday was half past six and he was just about to close the garage when the car turned into the yard. It was a black high-body Rover and as the driver, a man in his early fifties, alighted he let out a long breath as if he had been walking instead of riding, and what he said was, 'Oh, glad I found you. You know, this is the first garage I've come across in miles; you'd think they'd never heard of the motor-car here.'

'We're just about to close, sir; what can I do for you?'

'Well, a number of things I should say. I'm nearly out of petrol, water, and oil; and then there's this brake' – he pointed to the lever near the driving seat – 'it's sticking. Had a job to get it to work coming down one of your hills. And my goodness they are hills, I've never seen so many. Well now, can you fix me up?'

'I can supply you with the petrol, oil, and water but if there's anything wrong with the brake, anything serious . . . well, I'm . . . I'm just off.'

'Oh! Do your best, have a look at it.'

The short thick-set man walked to the middle of the yard and was looking towards the door opening in the side of the garage when the young boy came out, and he said to him cheerily, 'Hello there, young man.'

'Hello, sir.'

'Nice big yard you have here.'

'Yes, it is a big yard.'

The man now moved round in a slow circle and he said, 'I wonder if it would be possible to have a glass of water?'

'Oh yes, yes, sir. If you'll come up to the kitchen I'll get you one.'

'Good. Thank you.'

Dick preceded the short talkative customer up to the kitchen door and, opening it, he called, 'Aunt Hilda, this gentleman would like a drink of water.'

Hilda, on hearing the kitchen door open, had come quickly from out of the sitting-room, and she paused for a moment, a look of disappointment on her face, then said, 'Oh yes, yes, by all means.'

Quickly Dick filled a glass with water and handed it to the man, who drained it at one go before handing the glass back to Dick and saying, 'Thank you very much.'

Smiling at Hilda, he said, 'There's nothing to beat God's wine when you're thirsty, although at other times we don't value it.' Then he asked, 'By the way, is there a good hotel in the town?'

'Well, we're just on the outskirts here but if you go right into Fellburn there's The Bull and also The Forestry . . . The Forestry is a very comfortable place I understand.'

'Thank you. Well now I must be on my way, that is if your man has been able to fix my brake.'

As the man turned and looked towards where Arthur Baines was lying half in and half out of the car, Abel came through the opening and walked slowly into the yard. He merely glanced towards the car and his gaze just flicked over the group at the kitchen door. It was his intention to go straight to one of the old rooms above the garage which he now used as a workroom, but a voice high with surprise halted him.

'Well I never! there couldn't possibly be two of you.'

Abel turned and looked towards the man hurrying towards him and for a moment his throat felt completely dry, yet at the same time he re-assured himself there was nothing to fear, it was only the doctor, the mad woman's cousin.

'Mr Gray, isn't it?'

'Yes.'

'Well! well! it's a small world. I never thought to run into you again. How are you? But need I ask? You look very prosperous. And . . . and' – he half swung round – 'don't tell me.' Then he put his hand to his brow and struck it twice, saying, 'Of course. Of course. He hasn't altered that much, he hasn't even grown all that much. Your boy.' He looked to where Dick was moving towards him with Hilda just a few yards behind; then he turned towards Abel again, a question in his eyes, and Abel swallowed deeply before inclining his head towards Hilda and saying, 'My . . . my wife.'

'Well, I never! How do you do, Mrs Gray?' He now walked towards Hilda, his hand outstretched, and when she took it he shook her hand up and down, saying, 'I'm very pleased to meet you. And you know, I've often thought of your husband.' He glanced back towards Abel. 'We met under the most odd circumstances. By the way' – he leant towards her, a broad grin on his face – 'you didn't have to chain him up to get him, did you?'

Hilda's eyes narrowed in perplexity.

'Not like Tilly did?'

Seeing her expression, he said, 'Oh, he's never told you about Tilly? Well, well' – he again looked towards Abel – 'he should have; you would have had a laugh.' Then turning to her once more, he went on, 'Tilly was my cousin. Not quite with it up here' – he tapped his forehead – 'but she took a fancy to your big fellow there, so much so that she chained him up to the byres to try to keep him. It was a very scary business, wasn't it, young man?' He looked towards Dick now, but Dick, his memory recalling in flashes the scene in the barn, merely nodded his head.

'It's all right, sir' – Arthur Baines had joined them – 'the brake had got jammed. I've fixed it.'

'Oh thanks, thanks. Well, well. Now I must be off and get settled in a hotel. Your wife's told me there's two good ones in the town.' He looked from one to the other, then back to Abel, saying on a laugh. 'You know, it's a pity you didn't stick with her, I mean Tilly. She died three months later, she would have left you the lot. But there it is, I came in for it. Perhaps it was just as well, eh? It ensured my early retirement and I'm now able to jaunt where and when I will. But it's been nice seeing you again; as I said, I've often thought of you. By! you were scared that day; you thought you had killed her, and for a moment I thought you had an' all. Well, goodbye again. Goodbye, young sir,' he said, putting his hand on Dick's head; then turning to Hilda, he again held out his hand, saying, 'I'm very pleased to have met you and I am glad to see he's picked himself a fine-looking little wife.'

The three of them stood and watched him getting into the car; they watched until he had turned it around, and when he waved to them they all perfunctorily answered his salute.

As Abel walked away towards the door that led to the workroom Dick made to follow him, but was stopped by Hilda touching his sleeve, and he turned obediently with her and went into the house. But no sooner was the kitchen door closed behind them than she confronted him, and with her head moving backwards and forwards in an action of disbelief she asked him, 'Was all that true?'

He nodded dumbly at her.

'You mean there was a woman who . . . who chained him up? . . . Was . . . was he living with her?' As her question ended on a high note he put in quickly, 'No, no; we had just stopped and asked for a night's shelter in the barn. And this woman – she . . . she looked crazy right from the start – she . . . she said that—' He looked downwards now and the words wouldn't come until she shook him roughly by the shoulders, 'Well! what did she say?'

'She said God had sent him to help her.'

Recognising the reason for his reluctance in making this statement she said quietly, 'Go on.'

'He . . . he worked all day cleaning out the pigs and clearing the yard, and it was pouring. That night . . . he said he was going the next day and when she brought his supper – she only brought food for one, she didn't recognise me.'

'What do you mean, she didn't recognise you?'

'She wouldn't allow me any food. I . . . I don't think she liked children. Anyway, she must have drugged the cocoa because when he woke up he was chained with an iron hoop around his ankle, and another round one wrist.'

'Oh dear God!' She put her hand to her face.

'And when I woke up I was dopey, but I found

an iron bar and I gave it to him, and when she brought his breakfast in he lunged at her. It caught her on the side of her arm and broke it, but when she fell she hit her head on the stones.'

He suddenly put his hand tightly across his mouth and the next minute he found himself sitting in the chair and her holding his brow.

'Are you going to be sick?'

'No, no; I just felt sort of faint.'

After a moment she said, 'Go on then,' and he looked up at her now and said slowly, 'That's all really, except that I sometimes dream about it. It's like a nightmare; I dream I'm fumbling among her clothes for the keys. Dad must have thought she could die because I remember we went into the village and we saw him, the doctor. He turned out to be her cousin and he took us back with him. Dad didn't want to go, I remember, nor me, I was scared stiff. But he was kind, the doctor . . .'

'You're sure you don't want to be sick?'

'No.'

A moment or so later Hilda said, 'Here, drink this tea then,' and as he drank the tea she stood watching him; and then she said quietly but without bitterness, 'You're a pair, aren't you, for keeping secrets. What else hasn't he told me?'

When the cup jerked in the saucer she had to grab it to stop it from falling while he spluttered, 'Nothing, nothing else, nothing.'

'It's all right. It's all right, don't agitate yourself. Look, sit there and have your tea, I'll be back in a minute.' She stroked his hair from his brow and smiled at him before she turned and went out and across the yard in the direction of the work-room. But he didn't start his tea, he went into the scullery and now he really was sick.

PART FOUR

The Second Incident 1941

1

'Where you going?'

'You know fine well where I'm going, I'm going fire-watching.'

'Huh! fire-watching. Tell me, are you the only one that does fire-watching in this part of the town? This must be the fourth time you've gone fire-watching this week.'

Esther Burrows screwed up her white peevish face, turned on to her side in the bed and added, 'Fire-watching in that? Why have a good frock on to go fire-watching? Now, who do you think you're hoodwinking? You're off out, aren't you, with some man or other? Or is it your little boy from next door? You should be ashamed of yourself . . . a child like that! I know what's going on and I'm going to . . .'

'What are you going to do?'

'I'm . . . I'm going to put a stop to it. I'm going to have her over here and tell her, or better still his father, and tell them that he's never out of my kitchen. A boy still at school! You should be right down ashamed of your . . .'

'Shut up!'

'What! how dare you speak to me like that? It's coming . . .'

'Yes, I dare; and it is coming to something, and it's long overdue.'

The tall young woman was leaning over the bottom rail of the bed, her arms spread wide gripping the rails, and the indignation that flooded her shook the whole bedstead as she cried, 'I've had enough! Do you hear? I've had enough. Now I'm going to give you an option. For the future you'll leave me alone and let me lead some sort of a life of my own. I've waited on you hand and foot for years, the only freedom I've had has been during this last year when I was called upon to do part-time work. And you even tried to stop that, didn't you? You had to be looked after, hadn't you? Do you know what you are?' She leant still further over the rails. 'You're nothing but a selfish bitch of a woman, you're a parasite, and you're a scheming crafty one into the bargain. Oh . . . go on, hold your heart and have another one of your attacks but let me tell you before you decide to put on your act that you'll lie there until morning because I'm not going to stay in to see to you. And I'll tell you something else while I'm on, I'm carting no more jugs of hot water up those stairs for you. If you are able to get downstairs to the shelter, then you are able to come down to the bathroom. All these years I've trapesed up and down these stairs, washed you, dried you, powdered you. Oh Mother!' She ground out the word, then shook her head before going on, 'You wore my father out mentally and physically; well, it's not too late to save myself, and so now I'm giving you an ultimatum. You allow me my liberty, the liberty I'm entitled to, or else I'll walk out . . . Oh yes, I will. You've rubbed it into me for years that I couldn't earn my living except by doing menial housework, you've held this house and your money dangling in front of my nose like a carrot; well, I've never liked carrots of any sort and I've found out that I can earn my living other than by being a slave to an ungrateful, selfish individual. So there now, you've had it.'

She loosened her grip on the rail, straightened her back, then walked towards the door; and there she turned and said, 'No, I'm not going fire-watching. If you want to know the truth I'm going to a dance . . . *a dance*. And I'm going with a man, a soldier. He's only a common private but he's a man.'

As she pulled open the door her mother drew herself up from her pillows, crying now, 'What . . . what if there's a raid?'

'Pray as you always do.'

As she banged the bedroom door closed the whole house seemed to vibrate, not so much with the sound from the door but with the trembling of her body. Every nerve seemed to be jangling.

At the top of the stairs she gripped hold of the balustrade and, bringing her head down on to the back of her hands, she muttered, 'Oh my God! My God!' How had she dared to say all that? But more so, from where had she got the courage to say it? For years it had been brewing in her: her mother's incessant demands, her pettiness, her selfishness had fermented in her until now it had burst from her like bad wine . . . But she shouldn't have spoken to her like that . . . But wait. No! She straightened herself. What she had done, what she had said had long been overdue, and she wasn't going to ruin the effect of her bid for freedom by snivelling feelings of guilt and remorse.

She went quickly down the stairs now, but she was still shaking when she took her coat from the hall wardrobe. After putting it on and tying a head scarf under her chin, she leaned forward and peered at herself in the hall mirror. Although the light was bad the outlines of her face looked sharp. Her cheek bones seemed to be pressing against the skin, emphasising the sallowness of it. Even anger, apparently, couldn't bring a rosy glow to her face. Her eyes looked big and dark . . . and fierce. Well, she felt fierce.

She now made a quick circuit of the ground floor adjusting the window blackouts; and lastly, before opening the front door she pulled back the heavy curtain covering it, readjusting it before stepping outside; then, having locked the door, she put the key behind the foot scraper. Two minutes later she was walking quickly through the garage yard and towards the kitchen door.

Just before she reached it, it opened and Dick greeted her with, 'You're late; I was coming for you.'

'Oh.' She made an impatient movement with her head, then went past him into the kitchen and when she saw Hilda standing with her coat and hat on she said quickly, 'I'm sorry . . . I'm sorry I've kept you waiting.'

'Oh, that's all right; it hardly ever gets started before eight anyway. The lads make sure they're there then because of the refreshments.' Hilda smiled; then her face straightening, she asked, 'What's the matter? Something wrong?'

Molly now bowed her head as she said, 'I've . . . I've had words.'

'Not before time. Of course it all depends upon what you said.'

They all turned and looked towards Abel who was sitting in the armchair before the fire and Molly said quietly, 'I've . . . I've made a stand but I think I've said too much.'

'Well, she's asked for it, I'll have to say that. Whatever you've said to your mother she's asked for it.'

Looking at Hilda now, Molly nodded and replied, 'I suppose so. But oh I did go on.' She gave a little embarrassed laugh. 'By the way I'm going to a dance with a soldier. He's only a private. I think the private bit shocked her more than anything else I said.'

They were all laughing now, Abel the loudest of all, and he rose from his chair as he said, 'You could get a soldier any day in the week, Molly; and not just a private. I'm surprised at the army, navy, and air force, I thought they had more about them. Well, not the navy, I suppose, as we don't see many of them in this quarter, but the other ones must have their eyes closed.'

'Oh! Mr Gray.' She turned her head to the side in a derisive movement which made him cry, 'I'm not joking. What's the matter with you! Don't you ever look in the glass?'

'Well, I think if we're going to get there we'd better be making a move . . . And stop jerking your shoulder like that, Dick. I keep telling you.' Hilda's voice cut in sharply as she made for the door and Dick, ignoring her remark, looked at Molly and said on a high laugh, 'In five and a half months' time I'll be in air force blue, and in six months' time I bet I'll have stripes. I might even have me wings. Then I'll come flying to your front door.'

'Why the front?' Molly's tone was flat. 'You've always used the back.'

Again there was laughter; then Abel, pushing Dick out of the kitchen, said, 'Get yourself away!' and as the three of them went down the yard he called, 'Be ready mind at half past ten because I'm on duty at eleven.'

Dick's voice came back airily, crying, 'You'll be lucky,' and Molly answered, 'We will. We will'; but Hilda made no reply, there was no need because he knew she'd be standing ready with her hat and coat on; her part in the evening's entertainment, that of helping with the refreshments, would be over. She had been to the church hop almost every Saturday night for the last two years and she never danced. She was thirty-six years old and she had never danced. Why? Did she consider that sinful an' all? The next row they had he'd put it to her.

He chuckled to himself as he sat down, stretched

his long legs out to the fender, put his hands behind his head, and lay back in the leather chair. Funny, when he came to think of it, they hadn't had words for well over a year now, well, almost eighteen months. It was the night he had got drunk, and by! he was drunk. He moved uneasily in the chair and closed his mind to the reason for his getting drunk, then let out a long drawn breath and relaxed.

He liked Saturday nights when he had the house to himself. It was the only time he got the chance to be alone in it and a chance to think; and Dick had given him food for thought the night. The lad was determined to join up, having his own ideas about the rights and wrongs of killing his fellow men. Only last week he had said to him, 'This is a big war, Dad; you either eat or are eaten.' His words sounded like a quote, and at the same time he was placing the last war in the category of a scrimmage. As were so many other youths, the boy was looking forward to joining up as if it were the preliminary to a world cruise, so what would be his reaction if he were found to be unfit to take the world cruise?

Abel pulled himself up straight in the chair and held his hands out towards the fire. It wouldn't be because of his height, height made no difference to a pilot or an air gunner, but that jerking shoulder and that too ready, too high laugh, alternating with the long far away silences, was something that no-one had faced up to yet, least of all himself. The lad was a bundle of nerves. But it didn't need a psychiatrist to point out the cause of the trouble, at least not to him.

It was about a quarter past ten when Abel drove out of the yard in the repair van. Hilda didn't mind walking to the church hall in the blackout but she always refused to walk back late at night and, as she said, encounter drunken sots.

The church hall, which was quite a large one, was used daily as a rest and refreshment room for the armed forces; and the Saturday night hops held there were patronised not only by those who could dance without the stimulation of intoxicating drink but by non-teetotallers too because 'the eats' were invariably good and plentiful. This abundancy in these very stringent times was rumoured to be the result of a friendship between the quarter-master at the adjoining barracks and a certain lady member of the church. Of course this was only a rumour. Some said it was the miracle of the loaves and fishes over again. And who was going to question such a miracle in these days? Not even the other lady members of the church committee, not when the miracle provided them with pats of butter, quarter pounds of cheese, and dried fruit now and again; and as long as the miracle in the form of Quarter-master Dickinson didn't get posted the Dorset Street restroom would continue to be popular.

Abel stood now just within the doorway of the hall and looked to where lines of linked couples were doing the Lambeth Walk to the accompaniment of the blaring quartet.

At the far end of the room he saw Hilda standing talking to the Reverend Gilmore. He often wondered if she made for him or he for her, for on most Saturday nights he would see them standing together chatting. She was already dressed for the road and he could detect a look of impatience on her face as she waited for the dance to finish, because Dick and Molly were still stepping it out at the end of a line. Dick had one arm around Molly's waist and the other around a young woman in uniform. He was evidently enjoying himself, as was Molly. He was glad Molly was having a good time because that lass was living in a cage. He wished she were a little younger or Dick a little older, or Dick a little taller and she a little shorter. Still, what was four years difference? Not as noticeable really as the three inches between them. It was a pity the lad had never seemed to sprout up; and there certainly wasn't much hope that he would now.

The music stopped, and the line of dancers to which Dick and Molly were attached was only a few feet away from him when as though with a final fling Dick, his arm still about the two girls, swung them round so that the three of them stopped in front of him, all laughing.

'Enjoyed yourselves?'

Abel looked towards Molly as he spoke. Her face still wide with laughter, she answered, 'Oh yes! It's been a grand night.'

Abel now looked at Dick, who had released the young woman and was laughing loudly; then his attention was drawn to the young woman herself, she was looking full at him, she had stopped laughing but her mouth was still wide open even while her eyes were narrowing; then as if she had just made a discovery – which she had – she thrust out her arm, her finger pointing, and said, 'I know you. Of course, I know you.'

Abel's face became straight and he said quietly, 'You do? Then you've got one over me.'

'Don't you remember me? Not at all?' Her voice was high.

'No, I'm afraid I don't.' As he spoke he was aware that Hilda had joined the group and that the Reverend Gilmore was at her side.

'The boat, on the river.' The young woman was now standing close to Abel looking into his face, her own bright with discovery. 'I'm Daphne. You remember? Mother and the boat. And . . . and don't tell me' – she turned now towards Dick – 'you must be . . . Why yes! Do you know I felt that we had met before; something —' She shook her head. 'Well I never! After all these years.'

Dick's face too was straight now, and his shoulder began to jerk. His mind was groping at the memory of the young girl; he couldn't place her with this well-built young woman.

Abel was conscious that Hilda's eyes were boring into him like screwdrivers, yet he hadn't looked towards her; nor did he now when he said, 'How is your mother?'

'Oh.' The young woman gave a high laugh. 'Oh, she eventually hooked a man; but as I remember she took some time to get over you. I also recall that she turned the boat round and cut our holiday short the morning you left. What you doing now? You live hereabouts.' It wasn't a question but a statement, and he nodded his head once; then turning and looking at Hilda for the first time he said, 'This is my wife.'

'Oh. Oh, pleased to meet you.' The girl held out her hand, but it was decidedly seconds before Hilda raised hers towards it. Nor did she make any comment whatever when the young woman said, 'We'll have to get together and have a chat, and about this husband of yours . . . You know, he could have been my stepfather.' She dropped the hand; then looking fully at Abel, she said, 'Pity you weren't,' then quickly turned again to Hilda and added, 'No offence meant.' No-one spoke, and so lamely she said, 'Well, I'll be seeing you some time. I . . . I often drop in here; just stationed down the road. Be seeing you some time, eh?' She was speaking to the four of them now and she took two steps backwards before turning about and crossing the now empty floor towards the refreshment counter.

'I'll get my things.' Molly's voice was small, and when she moved away from the group Dick followed her.

The Reverend Gilmore, face solemn now, turned to Hilda and in a voice in which he might have intoned a sermon from the pulpit he said 'Good night, my dear, and thank you once more for your kind help. I don't know what we would do without you.'

It might have appeared that Hilda was too full for words because she made no reply whatever, she merely inclined her head towards the vicar, then went quickly to the door, pulled back the blackout and pushed through into the blackness of the porch, and there she stood waiting.

It was only seconds later when Abel joined her and immediately she swung her dimmed torch up into his face and demanded, 'What was all that about?'

'Just what you heard.' His voice sounded slightly weary.

'Well, by the sound of it, what I heard indicated that you were having a carry-on with a woman on a boat.'

'I was having no carry-on with a woman on a boat. She offered to give the boy and me a lift in return for my help.'

'Well, and did you help her?'

'Yes; yes, I helped her. I got the boat through a lock, I swilled the decks, I did what a crew man usually does. I was only three days on the boat altogether.'

'Really!' She drew the word out. 'Then all I can say, you must have been a fast worker.'

'No; she was. And now for the rest of the story.' His voice low, he turned and hissed at her, 'She wanted me to marry her. And she wasn't the only one who was in the marrying mood around that time, was she, eh? Was she, Hilda?'

Before she could make any retort to this the door behind them opened and two people emerged, and the man, swinging his torch, said, 'Oh, hello there. It's you Mrs Gray. Good night. It's been a good one, hasn't it?'

She made a sound in her throat and the man hesitated before stepping out from the shelter of the porch and, his voice now low, saying, 'I was very sorry to hear of your sister's trouble. Hard lines him catching it like that. This war! Oh, this war! . . . Good night.'

There was silence for a moment during which Abel screwed up his face in perplexity; then he was holding her by the arm. Gripping it tightly, he swung her towards him and brought his face down to hers and, unseeing, he stared into it and demanded, 'What did he mean, your sister's man catching it like that?'

When she didn't answer he shook her and said, 'Do you mean to say that something's happened to Peter Ford and you've never let on?'

The door behind them opened again and Dick and Molly came out.

Abel, still holding Hilda's arm, led her towards the van. The torches flashed dully and they all took their seats in the van without exchanging a word . . .

In the garage yard Molly said, 'Good night, Mrs Gray. Good night, Mr Gray,' and they both answered flatly, 'Good night, Molly.' But Dick said nothing. Turning, he walked with Molly out of the yard, along the road, and towards her front door.

Back in the yard, Abel had put the van away and having closed the garage doors he stood for a moment hesitating, then looked at his watch. The illuminated pointer said five to eleven. He hesitated again only a moment now before hurrying towards the kitchen. Hilda wasn't there. He went into the hall where he found her standing in front of the mirror stroking her hair down, and without any preamble he said, 'I'm asking you again, what happened to Peter Ford?'

Now she rounded on him, her body bristling with temper. 'He went down with his boat three weeks ago, if you want to know. And why didn't I tell you? Well, you've got your answer tonight: that girl remembering your carrying-on with her mother on the boat; and then that other woman who was supposed to chain you up. You're woman mad. That's what you are, you're woman mad.'

For a moment he stared at her open-mouthed, then he shook his head and his voice was strangely quiet as he replied, 'And you know what you are, Hilda? You're a woman with a distorted mind, an insanely jealous, distorted mind; and you've never made anybody happy, me least of all. And you're jealous of your sister because she's the —' He seemed to be searching for a word. His eyes blinked, his mouth worked, and then he brought out, 'The antithesis of you. Yes, yes, yes' – he bounced his head three times, his voice loud now – 'she is the opposite in all ways from you; she's a woman who loves and is loved in return, and if she's had twenty men she'd still be purer in mind than you are.'

'Oh! Oh!' Her mouth was quivering, her eyes were full of tears, and now she cried brokenly. 'You see . . . you see, you give yourself away. There's another answer to why I didn't tell you, because you would have been round there like a shot.'

'Yes, you're right; and I'm going round there like

a shot this minute. Now just sit and worry about that, and pray. Oh yes pray, pray that nothing happens between us.'

When she closed her eyes tightly he swung round from her and went through the kitchen and out through the door, banging it behind him.

It was only five minutes' walk to the post. He went through the schoolyard and into the school and to the room used as a duty room for the wardens. There were four men in the room; one was writing at a desk, one was making tea, the other two were sitting talking. Each looked up and said, 'Hello there, Abel' and he answered 'Hello'; then going to the desk he looked down at Henry Blythe, the potter, and said, 'Do you think you could spare me a half-hour, Henry, I've just heard that my sister-in-law's man's been drowned and I'd like to slip along?'

'Yes, yes, Abel, of course, there's nothing much doing tonight, at least I hope not.' He grinned. 'Anyway, if the siren goes you can always scoot back. Is it very far?'

'No, not five minutes' walk away.'

'All right. Take your time, there's nothing spoiling, you'd just be taking calls the night anyway. By the way, you've never been along for the last fortnight or so; nothing for the kiln?'

'Yes, I've got one or two bits but I'm working more on some of those little ducks. The owner of the hardware shop in Cable Street says he can sell as many as I can do but he doesn't seem to want anything else but ducks.'

They both laughed. 'Well, perhaps he's got something there because they look lifelike, real. If you made them bigger you could sell them as decoys.'

'So long.' Abel nodded from one to the other of the men and went out; then he almost ran from the school to Brampton Hill.

What if she was in bed? No, no, she wouldn't be in bed; just after eleven, more likely she was out. He hurried up the drive and round the side towards the garden flat, but he stopped before he reached the french windows. He should have gone through the hall and rung the bell, he might frighten her if he knocked on the window. He couldn't see a vestige of light. Perhaps she was in bed after all. Or again, perhaps she had a very good blackout.

He walked slowly towards the window and when he heard the faint sound of music he drew in a sharp breath. The wireless was going. His hand went slowly out and tapped on the pane.

He waited, but there was no response to his knock. Again he tapped, a little louder this time; and now he knew it had been heard because the music stopped.

'Who's there?'

'It's me, Abel.'

There was silence, the blackout didn't move aside, the door didn't open, and so after a moment he said, 'It's me, Florrie, Abel.'

There was another pause, and now he saw the curtain lift and a hand come round and turn the key in the doors, and when one door was pulled open he squeezed in between it and the curtain. Then he was in the room and standing close beside her as she pushed the blackout into place again.

It was all of eighteen months since he had last seen her. It was shortly after the war had begun. They had met in the street and she had said jauntily, 'How goes it?' and he had answered, 'Not too bad. How goes it with you?' And to this she had replied, 'It goes very well. I was married last week.'

He hadn't spoken but just looked at her, and she had laughed as she said, 'Don't look so surprised, it happens. You should know that.' And he had answered stupidly to this, 'Yes, yes, I should know that.' Then he had added, 'As you once said to me, I can only wish you everything that you wish yourself.'

When she remained silent staring at him he had added still further, 'And I hope that is happiness.'

'Oh, I'll be happy. Never fear, I'll be happy. I am. I am.' She had lifted her thin shoulders, then had said, 'Well, so long, Abel. Happy days.' And she had gone from him and left him standing staring after her . . .

She had changed; she looked ill. She had always been thin but now she looked nothing but skin and bone. Softly he said, 'You're not well.'

'Oh, I'm right enough.' She turned from him and as she walked towards the fire she said over her shoulder, 'What's brought you, and at this time of the night?'

He didn't move from where he was as he said, 'I just learned, not half an hour ago, about . . . well, about your husband.'

Now she was looking fully at him across the room. 'You didn't know?'

'No.'

'But . . . but our Hilda did.'

'Yes, so I learned tonight.'

'My God! Our Hilda.' She shook her head. 'Sometimes I think she's not human, and yet . . .'

She watched him coming towards her. When he reached her he put out both his hands and took hers, and softly he said, 'I'm sorry, Florrie, I really am. From what I heard I understand he . . . he was a good fellow.'

She withdrew her hand from his and sat down on the couch, and she bent down and buttoned the bottom button of her dressing-gown, saying as she did so, 'Yes, yes, he was a good fellow, kind, none better.'

He asked now quietly, 'Was it in convoy?'

'Yes.' She nodded. 'Only out two days. He . . . he was sure they'd never catch him, I mean his ship. He had made about ten trips and had always been lucky.' She now looked up at him and said, 'I . . . I wondered, when you didn't turn up.'

He swallowed and shook his head, then said, 'I wouldn't have known even yet but . . . but someone said to her tonight . . .at the church dance – I'd gone to pick them up – that it was a pity about . . . about your man.'

She sighed deeply, moved her head a little, then muttered, 'She's a strange creature. She came round immediately after I phoned up . . . and she said she was sorry. She came again the second week, but I've never seen her since. And . . . and she never asked me round . . . I wouldn't go without being asked, you know that, but . . . but' – she shrugged her shoulders – 'I thought . . . well, I thought she would have told you.'

'She's jealous of you, in all ways she's jealous of you, she's got to be pitied.'

'Dear! dear!' Again she shook her head. 'I've given her no reason to be jealous of me, have I?' When she raised her eyes to his he looked back into them and said, 'No. No.'

'Oh dear God!' She now fell back against the couch and, covering her face with her two hands, began to sob.

Immediately he was near her and, his arms going about her, he turned her head into his shoulder, and as her crying mounted he stroked her hair, saying, 'There, there, let it out, it'll do you good.'

When at last her sobbing eased she pulled herself away from his embrace and leant back against the couch again, and after drying her face she looked at him and muttered, 'Thanks.'

He made no reply, just moved his head while he continued to stare at her.

Then she said, 'I feel so awful, Abel.'

'You're bound to; it'll take time.'

'Aw —' She closed her eyes for a moment before saying 'Not that kind of awful; I mean mean, small . . .'

'Huh! you could never be either of those two, Florrie.'

'Couldn't I?' She twisted herself a little towards

him and again she wiped her face; and then she said, 'You spend yourself, you give all your best to the rotters, and to the decent ones you behave like dirt, and he was a decent one . . . Peter. He was the kindest fellow I ever met.'

'Well, I am sure you were kind to him in turn.'

Slowly she shook her head and there was a shy note to her voice now as she said, 'Not really. You see he . . . well, he loved me, he really, really loved me and . . . and it made no difference when he knew that I didn't love him. I liked him, I liked him a lot, but that is not loving. He said he loved me so much it would be impossible for some of it not to rub off on me, and he was quite willing to wait a lifetime. He was a fellow who didn't have a lot to say, he wasn't very articulate, you know what I mean, but when he did get going, well, he had a way of putting things that some people would have called poetry.' She paused and looked towards the fire, then said sadly, 'He was sure that he was lucky, he was sure that he was going to come through all this. He . . . he had our life planned out for years ahead.' She now closed her eyes tightly, bowed her head, and swallowed deeply before muttering, 'The last thing he said to me before he left was that he wouldn't die before he heard me say four words . . . four words' – her voice was a mere whisper now – 'I love you, Peter.'

She was crying again but quietly, and he did not touch her or speak to her, for he was experiencing within himself again the great want, the deep aloneness, added to which he was finding himself jealous of a dead man.

She was still crying quietly as she went on, 'He wouldn't let me come to the bus that last night, he . . . he wanted to remember me in this room, but he was no sooner out of the door than I had the urge to run after him and say those very words. It didn't seem to matter about them not really being true, the only thing I wanted in that moment was to send him away happy. But I hesitated too long. When I got to the gate he had already jumped on the bus. But when I yelled he turned and saw me. He didn't wave, it was as if he was standing stock still, sort of suspended in the air outside the bus. It was a weird experience.'

When she shivered he looked towards the fire and seeing it low he rose and using the tongs from the coal scuttle he put some coal on to it. He did it as if he were used to doing it every day of his life. As he replaced the tongs he turned to her and said, 'Can I get you a drink, something hot?'

'I . . . I would like a cup of tea. But you'll never find the things, I'll see to it.'

He put his hand towards her without touching her. 'Sit where you are,' he said, 'I'm used to finding things.'

It was ten minutes later when he returned to the room carrying two cups of tea and as he handed one to her, he said 'There's a spoonful of sugar in the saucer.' Then he asked her, 'Have you been to work?'

'Oh yes. Oh' – she moved her head slowly from shoulder to shoulder – 'I can't stay in, I'd go mad. Yet just a couple of months back I was for giving it up. I'm losing interest in it; you can't get decent clothes now.'

After sipping at the tea she turned to him and asked in a polite conversational tone, 'And how have you been? I haven't seen you for some time.'

'Oh, jogging along, same old pattern. But like you, business is pretty flat except for the bikes. But then I do part time at the factory an' all now.'

After a moment he looked at his watch, then said, 'I'm afraid I'll have to be going, Florrie, I'm on duty.'

'Oh. Oh, I'm sorry.' She moved to the front of the couch. 'I didn't mean to keep you.'

'Nonsense. Don't talk rot. Look, I'll pop along tomorrow. What time will you be in?'

'I'm in most nights after six. But Hilda . . . I wouldn't want to . . .'

'It's all right.' He nodded at her. 'I'll be along tomorrow night. Now get yourself to bed . . . Don't get up.'

'I've got to see to the blackout.'

At the heavily curtained french windows they stood looking at each other and she said quietly, 'Thank you, Abel; it's helped a lot.'

He said nothing but turned quickly from her and went out.

When he reached the end of the drive he stopped for a moment before going into the street and he muttered to himself, 'He wouldn't die before he heard her say "I love you, Peter."'

Would he himself live long enough to hear her say, 'I love you, Abel?'

God Almighty! Wasn't his life complex enough already? He should say it was. At times, and more so of late, he had the desire to straighten it out by walking out; but then he would remember he had walked out once before, and what had he walked into? Yet in this moment he knew that if he could make Florrie say the words to him that she hadn't said to her husband, and mean them, then he wouldn't hesitate to add another twisted strand to his life. But with one difference, not before he had come clean to her.

2

'What are you going to do about that boy?'

Abel always knew Hilda was furious when she referred to Dick as your son, or that boy, but he also knew that her fury had no connection whatever with Dick.

'What do you expect me to do?'

'Get him to a doctor. He's just a jangle of nerves; he's beginning to stammer now.'

'It's mere excitement because he's got to go before the board next week.'

'You know that they'll never take him in that state.'

'Yes, I know; but he's got to find that out for himself.' He rounded on her now, his voice low and harsh. 'He's determined he's not going to be like me, a conscientious objector, he's going to show that he's for this war, so let him go and try.'

Hilda stared at him, and her voice seemingly calm, she said, 'You know something, you don't seem to care what happens to him. His nerves have got worse over the past two years and you should have done something about it. Why wouldn't you let me take him to the doctor and to see a psychiatrist when I told you it was my belief that he was worrying over something?'

He turned from her and picked up his overcoat from a chair, and as he put it on he said, 'Boys go through this phase.'

'Not without a reason they don't. Mr Gilmore . . .' She stopped abruptly even before he shot round on her, saying, 'I don't want to hear any more of Mr Gilmore's advice! You tell Mr Gilmore that when I want his help I'll come and ask for it, and by God! that'll be some days ahead.'

He fastened the buttons on his coat now as if he were testing the strength of the thread with which they were sewn on; then snatching his trilby hat from the chair, he started towards the kitchen door; and he had opened it before she said, 'Where you going?'

He turned his head and stared at her before he answered, 'It's Sunday, me half day, isn't it? I can go where I like; I'm free on me half day.'

Her face was working now, her lips trembling as she cried at him, 'Don't tell me you're going tramping and it coming down heavens hard.'

'I never said anything about going tramping.'

'Oh you! You!' Her lips pressed themselves tightly together after the words and then sprang wide as she cried, 'I know where you're off to.'

'Well, why ask the road you know then?'

'You're a disgrace! That's what you are, you and her, you're shameful.'

He now stepped quickly back into the kitchen and closed the door; and standing stiffly, he looked down on her as he said, 'Put your hat and coat on and come along with me. She's your sister, she's lonely, she needs someone.'

'Lo . . . nely!' The words, broken up, trembled out of her mouth as if it were bouncing over rocks. 'Her! who's had every man in the town, an' some. And then her husband not dead five minutes.'

'Her husband's been dead six months, and after your two secret visits to her you've never looked in on her since. If it wasn't for her father and me she'd have nobody.'

'Oh my—' she just stopped herself from saying 'God!' by clapping her hand over her mouth and turning her head away. But swiftly she looked back at him again, glaring at him now and crying, 'You know what you are, Abel Gray? You're a thankless beast, a godforsaken thankless beast. I've done everything for you and that boy since you came in that yard all those years gone, and what have you given me in return?'

His brows were in a deep furrow, his eyes half closed. 'What have I given you in return? Only twelve to fourteen hours every day except an occasional Saturday and me Sunday afternoon. Apart from that I've tried to give you love, but you wouldn't have any of it.'

'Love!' Her upper lip curled away from her teeth. 'You call that love. The very thought of it makes me sick.'

'Yes, it would.' He nodded at her, his voice and mien quiet now. 'Yes, I've realised that for a long time now, Hilda, you're the kind of woman, you're the kind of female that would be sickened by that kind of love because there's so little woman in you.

You wouldn't understand that, but, you know, there are females and women, and males and men.'

She took two steps back from him, now, her head shaking, her voice trembling as she said, 'You think you're clever, don't you? You can talk round things, you can make black seem white, but you can't make a prostitute into a good woman, or into a good female, and that's what she is. And you in your way are as bad. Yes you are. All those women, that woman on the boat, and the woman who was supposed to chain you up. Now I'm telling you, and I mean this, I'm not putting up with any more of it. You'll put a stop to it or else . . .'

He stared at her for a moment and, his voice still quiet, he turned from her saying, 'Well, just as you decide, Hilda, just as you decide.'

When the door closed on him she covered her face with her hands, then stumbled towards it and leant against it, and she moaned aloud, asking all the while, Why? why . . . ?

Walking with his head bent against the driving rain, Abel, too, was asking himself why? why? Why must he be so cruel to her? And he realised he was cruel. Yes, it was true, she had given him everything she could since he had entered that yard all those years ago. All but the one thing, the main thing, because that was so distasteful to her. But did the fault lie with himself? his lack of understanding what it had been like for her to be married to an old man, who apparently had insisted on the union being based on virginal lines? God! when he came to think of it, that would be enough to twist any young lass, send her headlong to hell wanting it, or fearing it as she did.

Where would it end?

Well, he could end it tomorrow by telling her the truth. No! No! He couldn't see anything making him go that far because strange as it seemed he knew that she loved him, she really did love him. She loved him as deeply in her own way as he loved Florrie, and because of that at times he could feel compassion for her.

His love for Florrie was burning him up – it was torture to be with her, and it was torture not to be with her – but things were coming to a head. Yet before they did he'd have to talk to her, tell her the truth.

He was wet through by the time he knocked on the french windows and when she opened them to him she exclaimed on a laugh. 'You look like a drowned rat, an outsize one.'

'I feel like one. It isn't only raining, it's sleeting.'

'Give them here; I'll hang them in the kitchen.' She was helping him off with his coat. 'I'll just make some tea . . . I've been baking.'

'Good, good. What do I smell?' He sniffed.

'Apple tart, scones, made with liquid paraffin, have your pick . . . No, you can't!' She flapped her hand at him. 'The apple tart's too hot to cut.'

As she disappeared into the kitchen he went towards the fire and bending down, he rubbed the palms of his hands together. Presently he turned about and stood with his back to the blaze. He felt more at home in this room than in any place he could ever remember. He supposed it was because it looked like her, elegant, warm, colourful.

Colourful?

She was coming back into the room now carrying a tray and as he went forward and took it from her he knew he wasn't linking colour to her skin, for her face was white and drawn. How old was she now? Forty-one. There were times when she didn't look thirty but one of those wasn't today.

'You're not feelin' well?'

'Oh, I'm all right, in one way that is.' She was pouring out the tea now and she paused as she said, 'I've had the hump for days. I don't know.' She moved her head slowly. 'It doesn't seem any use going on, nothing to look forward to. I've . . . I've even lost my interest in men.' She laughed a high almost hysterical laugh now and pushed him with the flat of her hand almost upsetting the cup of tea he had just picked up, and still laughing she cried, 'I'm sorry! I'm sorry!' Then her manner sobering again, she drank from her cup, in between times saying rather sadly, 'Hardly a week used to go by before but I'd have an invitation of one kind or another, and now the only ones I seem to get are nudges in the dark from the uniformed lads. I must be losing me touch.'

'Never! Not you.'

'Oh, I forgot.' She laughed derisively. 'I did have an invitation last week. It was funny really. He came into the shop, he said he'd seen me for the last two or three days from Middleton's, you know the boarding-house across the way. He was just passing through, he said . . . His business? Oh, he couldn't tell me, it was a sort of secret, and he offered to spend a secret night with me. Brazen as brass he was. He seemed surprised when I showed him out of the shop.'

She put her cup down on the table, then crossed her legs and leant her elbow on the arm of the couch as she said slowly, 'You know, Abel, once upon a time I would have laughed at that, it would have given me a giggle, but . . . but it didn't this time, instead it made me feel awful, cheap, low. You know what?' She turned her head slowly and looked towards him. 'When he had gone I thought of our Hilda and I asked meself if she was right after all, did I look a tart?'

'Stop it! Don't be ridiculous.' His voice was harsh. 'You look as much of a tart as I look a pansy boy.'

'Oh, Abel.' She was laughing in a jerky fashion but more naturally. 'Some pansy boy, you!'

'Well, you're as near to a tart as that. Take it from me. That fellow sounds the kind of bloke who would have tried it on with Hilda at a pinch.'

As they stared at each other they both bit on their bottom lips. Then their laughter was joined; loud, raw, they rocked with it. Perhaps it was the rocking that brought her into his arms but once she was there he held her tightly pressed against him, and a great heat swept through his veins as he realised that her arms were around him too and holding him as close as he was holding her.

When their laughter ebbed away they looked at each other, their faces wet but straight now; still enfolded they leant against the couch and no word passed between them. The seconds ticked away and formed minutes and not until after what seemed to be an eternity did he whisper, 'Aw, Florrie.'

And she answered simply, 'Abel.'

'It's been a long, long time, Florrie.'

'A long, long time, Abel.'

'How long have you known that . . . that I've felt this way about you?'

'I don't know. I only know how long I've felt this way about you.'

'Aw, Florrie. Really? Really?'

'Yes really, Abel. Remember that night in this room when . . . when we were getting on so well and he walked in, Charles. That seemed to finish it. Well, he had come to bid me a final goodbye, he was leaving for America with his family. But even then it was too late, you had taken my advice with regard to Hilda.'

The mention of Hilda's name pierced his mind and cast a shadow on the joy of the moment, and now, taking his arms from about her, he caught hold of her hands and, looking into her face, he said, 'I've got to tell you something. It's a long story, it's the story of my life, Florrie, but before I do it I'm going to say this to you: I've only ever loved one other woman in me life and then it was only for a very, very short period. It seems to me now at times that it never happened, and in this life I've only ever known you. And I'll tell you this, I've loved you, Florrie; and, yes, I've wanted you from the minute

I saw you. And it's got worse with the years. I thought, when you married, that was that, but no it wasn't. Still I'm not saying I'm happy about your Peter going. But he's gone, and so now I can say to you, I love you, Florrie, I love you with all my heart. Here I am, on forty-eight, soon kicking fifty, the fires in me should have died down a bit by this time but I seem to have been stoking them up all these years just for this moment. But no more for now; I've got to tell you something, Florrie, something that's going to come as a bit of a shock to you.'

He let go of her hand and moved slightly away from her as he said, 'Some years ago I broke the law and as yet I haven't been called upon to pay the penalty, but somehow I feel that time is running out for me; more so of late, I don't know why. Anyway, let me start at the beginning.'

So he started at the beginning. He told her of his young ideals, of how he met Lena, and the weariness of his life with her until he met Alice. After telling of the way Alice died he paused for a long moment; then he said, 'After that I had to go because even with my pacifist leanings I didn't trust myself, not after I hit her. Once, just for a moment, I had the desire to finish her off. It was after I found out she had written to the husband and the result of it. It was then I knew I had to get away from her, for both our sakes.'

He now went on to tell her the little episode of the boat and of how only a few months ago the young girl had recognised him; but it wasn't until he came to the story of Miss Matilda and of changing his name that Florrie moved, and here she put her hand to her mouth and shook her head in disbelief.

Then he ended, 'I hadn't really a choice, staying put in that comfortable house with a job . . . The important thing was I'd been offered a home for the boy. I can honestly say that he was my first consideration then. If I'd been on my own, well, I would have been up and off long before that. Strangely, the longer the boy stayed in that house the greater aversion he had to walking; even today he won't walk a step if he can ride. I'm . . . I'm not making excuses, Florrie' – he nodded his head at her – 'I'm just trying to explain the situation I was in. And, of course, there was you. Oh yes, there was you. I knew that if anything made me leave there I should lose sight of you.' He sighed now, then ended, 'So I went through a form of marriage with Hilda. The only thing I stuck out for was the registry office. It didn't seem so illegal somehow.'

She sat now staring wide-eyed at him.

'You're shocked?'

'No. No, I'm not shocked, but I'm amazed, and . . . and in an odd way I'm more sorry now for our Hilda because, being the sort she is, this will finish her if she ever finds out.'

He was silent for a moment during which he rested his head on the back of the couch. Then nodding as if to himself, he said, 'I don't know. I've asked myself time and again how it would affect her if it came to light and somehow I can't see her going to pieces, because you know, Florrie, there's a band of steel running through that little frame of hers.'

She said nothing for a moment, then asked, 'Have you deliberately prevented her from having a child?'

'Yes.'

'Do you think that was right?'

'It was better than bringing a bastard into the world. Now that fact would have killed her.'

'But she's always wanted a child. The only time we ever exchanged confidences she told me that she wanted children.'

'Then why did she go and marry a man like Maxwell? As for wanting children, she certainly doesn't hold with what . . .'

She broke in, saying, 'Yes, yes, you've a point there. I suppose she wanted so much, and if it was a toss up, it was better to have Three Newton Road and be childless than have Bog's End and babies so to speak. But, oh Abel, I hope she never finds out, not only for her sake but for yours. You . . . you could go to prison.'

'Oh, I've thought of that, oh yes; yet sometimes I think it would be preferable to the life I'm leading because then the burden would be off my back . . . and Dick's.'

'Dick's?'

'Yes.'

'Oh, of course, he . . . he must have known.'

'Oh, he knew all right. And can you imagine the pressure I had to put on him in order to make him forget that his mother was still alive. I feel very bad about this at times because it's now he's paying the price.'

'In what way?'

'He's a bundle of nerves; he's got a twitch to his shoulder, and he's even stammering now. He thinks he'll get into the air force, but they won't look at him, not in his state; and he'll blame me. I catch him looking at me at times now as if he were trying to make out what kind of fellow I really am. But then I think he has already made up his mind about me.'

'But I remember he doted on you. I can recall Hilda being irritated by him always following you about. She said it was "Yes, Dad. No, Dad," from morn till night.'

'That may have been so years ago but more recently his attitude has changed. I know he just can't understand how I can go on from day to day, and when he laughs too loudly or goes into dead silences, as he's doing more of late, I've had the urge to get him by the shoulders and bawl at him, "All right! All right! What am I to do? Go and give myself up? You can work for your living now, there's nothing to keep me here only . . ."'

'Yes, only . . .' She nodded her head slowly, and he repeated her words, 'Yes, only'; then added, 'Sometimes I'm so sorry for her, Florrie. When she's in one of her rare good moods and fussing over us I think, I'll tell her. I'll come clean, I'll tell her. She'll understand. And then as like as not she'll say something, mention someone, perhaps that damn parson, or turn her nose up in disgust about some trifling misdemeanour, and I know it would be no use.'

'Oh, Abel!' She was sitting on the edge of the couch, her hands joined on her knees, her body bent towards him, and she repeated, 'Oh, Abel!'

'You think me dreadful, a swine of the first water?'

Her head came up, 'Don't . . . be . . . silly.' The words were slow and spaced. Now she jerked her chin. 'The only thing I'm sorry for is you didn't tell me that night. But . . . but on the other hand I must say that the worst possible thing you could do to her would be to tell her now.'

He sighed. 'Aye, I know. But what's the alternative? Carry on like this for the rest of my life or until I'm found out?'

She did not give him a direct answer to this but what she said was, 'You owe her something. And what's more . . . well' – she looked downwards now – 'I know Hilda, she needs something, someone. I remember once when I was rowing with her. She was dishing out advice and telling me I should give up my way of life. She got on my nerves so much I said the only person she needed was God, and that she already had Him in the form of Mr Maxwell, and I hoped He satisfied her. I remember she went out crying, and I knew then there was a need in her and that it wasn't being filled by Mr Maxwell, or God.'

'Funny about God.' She glanced at him now. 'Peter believed in God. He didn't belong to any denomination but he firmly believed in God. He had a saying that he quoted now and again. It was

"All there is is God." I never fully understood it myself, but he did.'

There was silence between them, until he said softly, 'You know, Florrie, whether you believe it or not I think you loved him.'

She pondered on this for a moment, then nodded, 'Yes, perhaps I did. But there are all kinds of love.' Now she looked at him fully as she ended. 'But it wasn't the kind of love I'd felt for you over the years; and I'm sorry about this because he deserved to be loved.'

He didn't now come back with the trite remark 'And I don't?' because he knew that would evoke her immediate denial, and a denial might be too quick to ring true. He couldn't bear the thought that she might have a low opinion of him, and yet, even with her love for him, what did she really think of him because she was an astute woman, a woman of the world you could say? At best she would consider him weak. And giving the matter thought, she must consider him weak. And whenever he faced up to himself he, too, knew he was weak. Only in the more recent time had he allowed himself to think in this way, for in his young days he had been strong enough to stand by his opinions, and suffer for them. He had been strong enough to walk out on Lena; but now he knew that he wasn't strong enough to walk out on Hilda. If he had to leave it would be she who would give him his marching orders. Yet the thought of having to live the rest of his life with her while loving Florrie as he did was already creating a turmoil in his mind.

Then the turmoil was temporarily wafted away as Florrie's arms came about him and, laughing now into his face, she said in broad Tyneside, 'Eeh! Abel Gray, or Mason, or whoever you call yoursel', you're a bad lad. Do you know that? You're a bad lad. And if I had me way now you know what I'd do?'

He was returning her broad smile as he said, 'No,' and waited for her to change her tone and say softly, 'I'd love you,' because the words were written in her eyes. But what she said on a laugh was, 'I'd cook you a nice steak and kidney puddin'.'

When his hand came sharply across her buttocks she lay tightly against him and, her face hidden from him in his shoulder, she murmured soberly, 'Whenever you need me, Abel, I'll be here.'

'Oh, Florrie, Florrie, I need you every minute, all the time. Sometimes I've felt worn out, exhausted for the need of you.'

Her head still buried in his shoulder, they became quiet; then straining herself back from his embrace she rose from the couch and walked slowly towards the french windows and turned the key. When she looked at him again her gaze went straight into his and, holding out her hand, she waited to lead him towards the bedroom.

When had he ever felt like this? With Alice, no. He couldn't explain what he had felt like with Alice for he couldn't remember, but this, this he'd remember until the day he died. If he was never to go with her again, the glow, no, more than a glow, the radiance in which he had ascended to heights never dreamed of would remain deep in his memory for ever, and the fact that she, too, went along with him every pulsing moment of the way.

They hadn't spoken, not a word. It had been over for minutes now; still they hadn't spoken. But when at last she broke the silence her words startled him, 'I'm not too old to have a baby, am I?'

'What?'

'I said I'm not too old to have a baby. I want a baby, Abel. Oh, I want a baby so much. Somehow I thought it would have happened with Peter.' She turned on to her side now. 'You don't mind me mentioning him, do you?'

He, too, turned on to his side and he traced the outlines of her eyes with his forefinger, then came over the bridge of her nose to its tip, followed down to her lips, and traced their outline before he said, 'Nothing you could ever do or say, Florrie, could make me mind except if you were to tell me you didn't want to see me again. Do you know something?'

She made no movement but just stared into his face.

'I've heard people saying they felt so happy they could die, and I've always classed it as slush or tripe talk, but that expresses exactly how I feel at this moment. In fact I don't want to go on from here because every minute from now I'll be dropping back into reality.'

She now lifted her hands and cupped his cheeks and said softly, 'This is reality and it can go on as long as ever you wish.'

'That will be a long time, Florrie.'

'Not long enough for me, Abel . . . But about what I said, would you mind if I had a baby?'

'Not as long as it was mine. But . . . but have you thought about its name?'

'That wouldn't worry me, although it might worry it later. Huh! you never know. Yet I hope I'd be good to it, it wouldn't mind after all. And I'm sure it wouldn't mind when one day I'd let the cat out of the bag and tell it . . . him . . . her, that its Uncle Abel was its da'.' She laughed now, and when he said, 'I'll be an old man when it's in its teens,' her laughter took on a teasing gaiety and she finished, 'Whatever age you are you'll still be the same Casanova . . .'

'What!' His face became serious. 'You . . . You look upon me as a Casanova, Florrie?'

'Oh, I was just joking. But wait, aye, when I come to think of it you are you know, you are a bit of a Casanova. Look at all the women who have been in your life. Aye, look at them, and from your own telling.'

He stared at her, his face serious. All the women who had been in his life; Lena, and the loveless battling years he spent with her; Alice, that swift flash of tender passion that lighted his drab life, but for a flash of time only; then the incidents, first the boat, and then the barn, then Hilda. What did he know of women really? What pleasure had he had from women? In the last half-hour he knew the pleasure that he had missed in not loving and being loved by a woman like Florrie . . . or by Florrie herself, back down all the years. But then, would Florrie have been able to love him as she had done without her experience of men? If he had met her instead of Lena all those years ago would her loving have taken him to the heights then? She had once told him she had only known three men; now counting Peter it was four. They were really equal in the number of their experiences but far from equal in the quality of them.

He would be forty-eight shortly, what had he done with his life? Nothing. He had made no mark on anything or anyone. Yet the latter perhaps wasn't quite true. He had left a mark of hate on Lena, and another of jealousy on Hilda. What mark would he leave on Florrie? Just one of love he hoped until the day he died. But it was going to be a furtive love, love on the side, and as such it could go on for years and years. He didn't think he could stand that; he wanted to be with Florrie every minute of the night and day. He didn't want her only in bed, he wanted her face opposite him when he was eating, by his side when he was walking. He had first set eyes on her in 1932, nine years ago. He had been starved of her for nine years.

Suddenly he pulled her warm body tight close to him and as his lips pressed down on her mouth the tears sprang from his eyes, and when they wet her face she struggled from his embrace exclaiming, 'Oh! what is it, Abel? I didn't mean anything, I was just teasing you. Oh, my dear, don't cry like that. What have I said, what? I tell you . . .'

He shook his head and gulped in his throat,

saying now between gasps, 'That . . . that's got nothing to do with it, it's . . . it's just me, it's a weakness, I . . . I cry when I'm troubled, greatly troubled. But . . . but I hadn't thought it would affect me when I was happy, ecstatically happy.'

'Oh! Abel. Abel.' She now gathered him into her arms. 'You are so different. You're different from anybody I've ever known in all ways, and I've never known a man who cried, and I love you for it. I love you for it.'

PART FIVE

The Payment

1

'You know, when they turned me down, having waited nearly a year for my call up, I felt like jumping in the river, and it wasn't only because they wouldn't take me for the air force, but because they thought I didn't want to get into the air force, didn't want to get into the war at all. Eeh! I can hear meself going for that doctor now. I don't know where I got the nerve from but after being messed about for nearly three hours, and half of that time spent in a room by myself. You know something, Molly? I'm positive they had a way of watching me but it didn't strike me until after they turfed me out and said I'd be hearing from them. When it did I was in two minds whether to go back and wreck the bloomin' place, or, as I said, jump in the river.'

'You should have come for me and we could have jumped in together. I've often thought of doing it meself, but I'd like a hand to hold while I'm at it, just in case, you know, I decided to change me mind, then I could climb on top of my companion and clamber out.'

'Oh! Molly!' His head was resting on the palm of his hand, his elbows on the table, his shoulders shook with his laughter. Then his laughter stopped abruptly and he lifted his head and stared at her where she was at the sink washing up as she said, 'Have you ever wished anybody dead?'

'What! What makes you ask that?'

She turned her head towards him. 'Nothing; I just wondered. Have you ever wished anybody dead? What's the matter? What you blushing for?'

'Am I blushing? I didn't know I blushed. I'm not blushing, am I?'

'Well, you're pretty red.'

'Well, things you come out with would make anybody red.'

'Why should it? I just asked you a simple question, have you ever wished anybody dead? I was looking for a companion to me bad thoughts before we go into the river together.' She grinned at him.

'You wish somebody dead?'

'Yes, of course, else why should I ask you?'

He stared hard at her before saying quietly, 'Your mother?'

'Yes, me mother.' She turned round and stood with her back to the sink while she dried her hands on the tea towel; then she shook it out and said, 'It's wet, I'd better get another.' She was across the room and taking a fresh tea towel out of a drawer when he asked, 'You troubled about it?'

'Not any more' – she came and slipped into a chair opposite him – 'especially not since I've learned I'm not the only one.' She smiled at him, then added, 'But it isn't so bad now, only at odd times when she gets me goat. But years ago when I was fifteen, sixteen, seventeen, when other girls were out enjoying themselves, when I saw them going off to the pictures on a Saturday night with their lads, or walking past the gate on a Sunday arm in arm as they made their way into the country, oh then, boy! yes, I hardly drew a breath without thinking, I wish she was dead! Then I would spend half the night tossing and turning in nightmares riddled with guilt. I was always being put into prison, always lonely, and nearly always I woke up with her words ringing in my ears, "After all I've done for you." She still says that you know: "After all I've done for you." And what has she done for me? Made me into a bloomin' old maid . . . well, nearly.'

'Don't be daft. Old maid? Huh!'

'Who do you wish to murder?'

'Murder?' His eyebrows went up, stretching his skin around his eyes and bringing his lips apart.

'Well, tell me, who do you wish dead?'

He dropped his gaze from hers, nipped on his lip while his shoulder jerked twice, then he stammered, 'No . . . no . . . nobody in p . . . particular.'

'Nobody in particular? Do you wish everybody dead then?'

'No, no; don't take me literally. Well—' His head jerked from one side to the other in a sharp nervous movement and he gabbled now, 'Well, there was somebody. I . . . I thought if she was dead, well, it would straighten things out.'

'What things?'

'Oh, just something that happened.'

'To whom . . . you?'

'No. Well, what I mean . . . Aw' – he got to his feet – 'you know something, Molly? You're nosey.'

'Yes, I know I am. It's me only pastime. But I'm only nosey with people I like.' She rose quickly from the chair and went to the draining board and as she picked up a cup to dry it there spread over the town a great wail, and she closed her eyes quickly and said, 'Ah, not again! Three times in one week. Aw no.'

'You're going to get her downstairs?' Dick's voice had changed, there was a brisk note in it now and she said, 'Yes, I suppose so.'

'Shall I give you a hand?'

'Yes, you can, I'd be glad of it, but you'd better look out for squalls.'

'Well, if she goes for me I'll chuck her under the table.' He grinned. 'By the way, is it ready?'

'It's always ready; I keep the mattress permanently under there now. Come on.'

He followed her up the stairs and into the bedroom, there to see Mrs Burrows already sitting on the edge of the bed.

'You've taken you time.'

'The siren's hardly stopped, Mother.'

'That won't prevent them dropping the bombs, will it? . . . What do you want?' she glared at Dick now, and he answered lightly, 'Just came to give you a hand downstairs.'

'She can manage.'

'That's what you think; she makes herself manage.'

'Well! well!' Mrs Burrows was on her feet now,

supported by both of them, and she looked down on Dick as she said with cutting sarcasm, 'A little champion, aren't you? But, of course, if you're going to be of any real help to anybody you'll have to get a step-ladder, won't you?'

'*Mother!*'

'Yes, daughter?'

Molly said nothing to this but drew in a deep breath.

They were at the top of the stairs now and Mrs Burrows cautioned in a voice that no invalid should have been capable of using, 'Look what you're doing or you'll have me going down head first. We can't all go three abreast. Get on ahead you!' She almost pushed Dick off the top step with a sharp movement of her elbow and as he held out his arm to steady her he bowed his head and bit hard on his lip to quell the angry retort that had almost escaped him.

She was a devil of a woman. How did Molly put up with her! Wish her dead? If he had been in Molly's place he might have seen to it that she complied with the wish long before now. You couldn't believe that a woman could be so ungrateful, and to her own. It was hard to believe that there were people like her in the world, yet hadn't he found out early on that there certainly were. If he ever needed reminding the pain that he had now and again in his ear would conjure up another such as her . . . Yet no, his mother could never have been as bad as Mrs Burrows. And whereas Mrs Burrows had no cause for complaint against her daughter, his mother might just have had some cause for complaint. This thought had been niggling at him a lot lately and with his other suspicions it was breeding an anger in him.

'There you are. Careful.' He was helping Mrs Burrows down on to the mattress laid out under the table, but as his hands went to straighten her legs while Molly heaved her on to her pillows she smacked at them, saying, 'Take your hands off me.'

'Mother! you're being helped.'

'I want no help, not from that quarter.'

Molly now rose abruptly to her feet and, coming to the end of the table, she now pushed Dick out of the room, across the hall and into the kitchen. When she had closed the door he turned to her and said on a laugh, 'I can understand your death wish, but what's she got against me? I haven't set eyes on her now for months.'

Molly now went and adjusted the blackout over the kitchen window and from there she said, 'Nothing more than she's got against anyone else.'

He was silent for a moment, then said, 'Well, I'd better get in next door; but if Dad's in I'll come straight back and stay with you just in case there's any high jinks.'

She said nothing to this but went towards the back door and was about to pull the blackout curtain back when his words stayed her hand and she held her pose for a full minute before she turned and looked at him with her eyes wide and her mouth slightly open, and he repeated what he had said, 'I love you, Molly, I had to say it some time. I told meself when the siren went the other night, almost at the same time as the bomb dropped, that it might have been the finish of both of us and you'd never have known how I really feel about you, and so I made up me mind that the very next time it went I'd . . . I'd tell you, just in case I didn't get another chance. And . . . and you needn't come back with, "There's four years between us, not to mention the two inches and a bit," I know all that, it's been drummed into me for as long as I can remember. But the years and the inches don't make any difference to what's inside. I . . . I can't remember a time when I haven't loved you, Molly. But I . . . I don't want you to be troubled with what I've said, 'cos . . . 'cos I know what you think of me, just pally like.'

'O . . . h you! Dickie Gray, you fool.' Her lips were trembling, her head was bent towards him, and now her voice shook as she said, 'Why? Why do you think' – she made a quick movement with her thumb towards the kitchen door – 'she detests the sight of you, eh? It's . . . it's because . . . well, it's because she knows how I've felt about you ever since you first came into the yard. But I was that four years older, I was a big sister then, then I was a young woman and you were the schoolboy. Now I'm nearly the old maid' – there was a high treble note in her voice – 'and you're a young man, a good-looking attractive young . . .'

They were holding each other tightly, not speaking, not kissing, just holding tightly. When they drew slightly apart they looked at each other, then almost shyly they kissed, a soft closed-lipped kiss, almost like two children who were afraid of what they were about. That was until the querulous voice shattered them, crying, 'Molly! You Molly!'

'Damn!' But she laughed as she said it; then again they were kissing, hard and hungrily now, while the voice, louder, came at them, crying, 'Do you hear me? My back's breaking. Molly! Molly!'

As she pushed him from her, smiling into his face, she whispered, 'Come back. Come back as soon as you can.'

He stood for a moment, his short slim body straight and steady, his shoulders remained still, his lids were unblinking. He swallowed deeply and his Adam's apple bounced in his throat. He didn't speak but, thrusting out his hands, he grabbed hers and held them at each side of his face for a moment, then turned quickly and without paying the required attention to the blackout he pulled the curtain aside and went out . . .

Hilda was in the kitchen. As she turned from the fire a look of disappointment on her face she said, 'Where's your father?'

'I . . . I thought he'd be in, he was only on till nine o'clock.'

She sat down in the wooden chair and tapped her fingers on the arms a number of times before she said, as if to herself, 'He's likely had to stay on.'

'Why don't you come down into the shelter?'

'You know I don't like the shelter. I can't bear the confined space.'

'It's safer.'

She cast a sideward glance at him as she asked,

'How safe would it be if they dropped a bomb on the house?' Then she added, 'You go down if you like.'

'Me!' His voice was high. 'I don't want to go down there.'

When he came and sat opposite her she brought her glance to bear on him with a penetrating stare before she said, 'What's up with you, you look pleased with yourself? You . . . you haven't heard differently from the air force after all?'

'No, no.' He shook his head, and he felt a sense of added warmth as he realised that she was pleased he hadn't heard; then half shamefacedly he said, 'I . . . I think I'd better tell you, Aunt Hilda. I'm . . . I'm in love with Molly.'

'Huh!' She started to laugh, gently at first, then quite loudly. He'd never heard her laugh so freely for a long time; but slightly peeved, he said, 'You find it funny?'

'No, no, Dick; I don't find it funny that you should be in love with Molly, but I do find it funny that you should tell me something I've known for years. In fact, you've plastered it all over the place, you might as well have put it up on billboards.'

'Oh! Aunt Hilda, it hasn't been like that. I never . . .'

She now flapped her hand at him, still laughing as she said, 'Yes, you did. Has there been a day for years past when you haven't scampered over there on every possible occasion?'

'Yes, yes.' He was laughing himself now. 'But I thought . . . well, I thought you would think I was just being pally.'

'Pally my foot! Anyway, that's how you feel, what about her?'

He bit on his thumb nail twice before he said softly, 'I can't believe it, she feels the same way.'

'Well, I could have told you that an' all.'

'You don't object in any way?'

'Why should I?' Her voice was quiet, her face straight now. 'I'm glad, I'm glad for you. She's older than you I know, but that's what you need, Dick, someone older than you, steadier.'

'Yes, I suppose so.'

'Tell me' – she leant towards him now, her hands joined on her knee – 'I've wanted to ask you this for a long time. Is there, or has there been anything worrying you, I mean besides wondering about the air force and how Molly felt with regards to you. Have you had anything on your mind?'

His shoulder jerked, his lids blinked and he rose to his feet as he said, 'No, no, nothing, nothing important. Is there any milk left? I wouldn't mind a drink.'

'Dick' – her voice made him turn towards her again – 'I don't believe you. I believe you've got something on your mind, something worrying you that's caused these nerves. Now . . . now I've never mentioned her, your mother. I haven't probed, have I?'

Both shoulders jerked now, one after the other, then both together they almost cupped his head, and now she, too, rose to her feet, saying, 'It was your mother, wasn't it?'

The beads of sweat rolled from his brow and

down the sides of his cheeks as he muttered, 'Yes. Yes, in a way.'

'What did she do to make you like this?'

'Oh' – he looked downwards and shook his head from side to side – 'she was just bad-tempered and . . . and used to box my ears . . .'

. . . 'Oh my God!' They had sprung the distance between them and were clutching on to each other as the house shuddered.

She hadn't realised she had said 'Oh my God!' and she was saying it again when he cried, 'It's all right. It's all right.' Then he listened for a moment before adding, 'He's gone, over the town way I think, the anti-aircraft's coming from that direction.'

As he released his hold on her and went to make for the door, she shouted, 'No, no! don't go out yet, Dick, not yet.' Then putting her hand to her face, she said, 'There's another one!'

Again he said, 'It's all right; it must be in the town.'

'And another! Oh dear, dear, Lord!'

'Come on into the shelter.'

'No, no.' She shook her head wildly, then muttered, 'Abel. Where would he be?'

'He'll be in the post or thereabouts and that first one was t'other side of here and nowhere near the post, so don't worry. Look; sit down, I'll make you a drink.'

She allowed him to press her into a chair, and like a small girl she now sat with her hands joined in front of her knees, her body rocking slightly all the while.

He had just handed her the cup of tea when he heard his name being shouted and before he could get to the door Molly burst in. Banging it behind her, she stood with her back to it, one hand gripping her throat; and now both Hilda and he were holding her, asking at the same time, 'What is it? What's the matter? It didn't hit the house? It wasn't that near.'

'No, no.' She shook her head, swallowed deeply. 'It . . . it must have been the shock.'

'What must have been the shock?' Hilda was shaking her now.

Molly pulled herself away from the door and put her hand tightly over her mouth and held it there for a moment before she said, 'She's dead. It was after the bomb dropped. She . . . she cried out and sat up and bumped her head on the underside of the table. I . . . I thought it had knocked her out but . . . but she hasn't come round and —' She stopped and closed her eyes then said slowly, 'Her heart's not beating.'

'Come on; you could be mistaken, she's likely in shock and her pulse is weak. Come on.' As he went to open the door Hilda cried, 'Wait a moment. I'll leave a note for Abel to tell him where we are.'

Grabbing a pad off the dresser, she scribbled a few words on it and stuck it in front of the clock; then they were all running down the yard, along the road, and up the drive towards the house.

It was only minutes later when the three of them rose from their knees and Hilda, turning to Dick, said quietly, 'Go and find your father. Bring him as quickly as you can . . .'

As he ran through empty streets towards the school, only once was he hailed by a warden shouting, 'Do you want any help?'

'No, no, thanks I'm . . . I'm just going to the post, the Bower Road School one.'

He looked upwards as he ran. There was a glow in the sky towards the old town of Bog's End, and a brighter glow nearer still to the right of him.

There were two men on duty in the post room. He knew one of them, a Mr Blythe, and the man, putting down a telephone quickly said, 'You didn't catch it?' and he replied on a gasp, 'No, no, it's over Swanson Terrace way I think. I saw a blaze coming from there. But . . . but it shuddered us.' He looked round towards the other room. 'Is . . . is my father about?'

'No.'

'Has . . . has he gone over there?'

'I wouldn't know, Dick; he went off duty almost an hour ago.'

He remained quiet for a moment, then said, 'Oh. Oh, thanks.' As he went through the door, Mr Blythe called out to him, 'He's likely dropped in somewhere to have a pint; that's if he's been lucky enough to find a place with any.'

'Yes, yes.' He nodded back at the man.

Out in the schoolyard he stood still for a moment. The blaze towards Swanson Terrace seemed to be brighter, it was illuminating the sky, and away towards the docks he saw a long line of lights, dull from this distance but definitely fires. They had been trying for the docks for some nights now and likely tonight they'd found their target.

Where was his father? He walked quickly across the schoolyard now, but outside the gates he paused again looking first one way and then the other. Should he go back home and tell her that his father was off duty at the post but had gone to help the firefighters, or should he turn the other way and go down to his Aunt Florrie's?

Spurred now by a wave of feeling that was as near black anger as ever he had experienced, he was running towards Brampton Hill, his mind jabbering at him with every step he took. He had known for some time what was going on, he wasn't a fool. His father must think he was a fool. That day he had seen his father helping his Aunt Florrie out of the van and holding her hand before he would let her go through the gates and up the drive to her flat.

It was as his father had turned towards the van again that he had caught sight of him along the road and when they met he had said glibly, 'I saw your Aunt Florrie out shopping, I gave her a lift back.' He had only just stopped himself from saying, 'She must have dropped her basket or parcels some-where then.'

And his Sunday afternoon walks. His father no longer walked the fells. He had even seen him going towards them, then cutting down behind Wardle Drive. Now why should he do that?

When he reached the gates of No 46 he stood hanging on to them for a moment. Then he swung his torch on to the drive and began to run again, and he kept on running until he reached the house door. There he stopped. Bracing his shoulders, he buttoned his coat, smoothed back his hair, then went through the hall, along the corridor and to the door of the garden flat.

When a woman opened the door he stared at her for a moment thinking that it wasn't his Aunt Florrie, then when he recognised that it was, he put her changed condition down to the fact that she was standing under an electric light that was enveloped in a dark green shade. But when she said under her breath, 'Oh, Dick,' he went into the passage and she closed the door. He then saw the reason for the change in her. His Aunt Florrie had always been as thin as a rake, but the woman standing before him was fat, at least part of her was. His Aunt Florrie was pregnant, very pregnant. Quickly he turned his head away from her and looked towards the end of the passage, and there stood his father. He had his overcoat on and was apparently ready to leave. He came swiftly towards him now and when he spoke his voice was hard, 'What do you want here?'

'I could say the same to you.'

'Now! now! look here, boy.'

'Don't boy me.' Both his manner and his voice were aggressive. 'I'm no longer a boy. I stopped being a boy when I stopped saying, Yes, Dad, No, Dad. And that's some long time ago.'

'Please. Please.' Florrie had her arms spread out towards each of them as if to separate them and she pleaded now, 'Come in. Come in,' and she went ahead of them into the room. It was she who spoke first. 'Try to understand, Dick,' she said, 'about your father and me . . .' But turning his head to the side and flapping his hand at her, Dick cut her off, saying, 'I don't want to hear, Aunt Florrie. Anyway, I'm not the one you should be explaining things to.'

'Now look here . . .'

'Is that all you can say?' Even as he spoke Dick was amazed at his courage; then he added, 'Me Aunt Hilda sent me looking for you. Mrs Burrows died of shock when the bomb dropped. It dropped quite near. It could have hit us.' He now looked from one to the other, then said, 'It's a pity it didn't, isn't it, it would have solved your problems?'

As he turned towards the door to go out he knew that his Aunt Florrie was restraining his father. He went into the passageway again and had opened the door and was going across the hall when he heard his father say, 'Don't worry, it'll be all right.'

When his father caught up with him, they walked out together in silence, down the gravel drive and towards the gate, and there they almost bumped into a small figure and became entwined in leads, at the end of which were two dogs.

'Bugger me! Look where you're goin'.'

If Abel hadn't picked out the bristling figure of Mr Donnelly in the light of his torch, the voice itself would have told him who it was.

Mr Donnelly now silenced the yapping dogs with, 'Shut your traps, will ya!' Then turning his torch on to Abel and Dick, he said, 'Oh, it's you's, is it?'

'Anything wrong?'

To Abel's question Mr Donnelly now cried, 'Wrong? No! I've only lost me bloody house. The whole bloody street copped it, an' I would an' all only I wasn't there. They wanted to kip me down in the school with a lot of screeching women. I told them where to go.' His voice suddenly sinking to almost a whisper, he ended, 'Bugger me! T'was a shock to see the whole bloody lot gone. Anyway' – his voice lifted – 'Our Florrie'll put me up on the couch for the night.'

'There's always a room around our place if you're stuck, Fred.'

'Aye, well, thanks, we'll see; but let's get the night over, 'cos I'm a bit shook up.'

With no further words he left them, and after a moment they, too, walked on.

They had gone some distance along the road before Abel said, 'I want to talk to you.'

'I don't want to hear, me eyes have told me all I want to know the night.'

'Your eyes have told you nothing.' Abel had swung him round by the shoulders, and now they were peering at each other through the dark with Abel hissing at him, 'Who got me into this situation anyway in the first place? Think back, ask yourself. Do you think I would have trapped myself as I did if it hadn't been for you? It was done to keep you off the road.'

'You didn't lose anything by it as far as I can see. Me Aunt Hilda's been good to you.'

'Your Aunt Hilda hasn't been good to me;

you know nothing about it, boy.'

Dick now pulled himself away from Abel's grasp, saying, 'Don't keep calling me boy.'

'Well, don't act like one.'

'Oh, I suppose I could be called a man if I would countenance you having two wives and a mistress.'

'God Almighty!' There was such a desperate note in the words that Dick remained silent until Abel said further, 'I'm going to tell you something. I've loved your Aunt Florrie from the first moment I saw her and I've just learned lately she felt the same way about me.'

'What! with all the men she's had?'

The blow missed its aim and glanced off the side of his head; then Abel was holding him by the shoulders, almost hugging him to him, saying, 'Oh my God! what's happening to us? I'm sorry. I'm sorry.'

After a moment of stunned silence Dick thrust Abel from him and, his voice holding a broken note, he said, 'Don't you ever lift your hand to me again. If you do you'll get as much back, as big as you are. Now I'm telling you and . . . and I'm going to say it; you stand there and tell me you fell in love with her the first moment you saw her, well, all I can say is you quickly forgot Alice, the Alice who was so wonderful, the Alice that drove us out on to the road. Less than a year and the great romance was over.'

For a moment Abel did not answer and when he did it wasn't to retaliate, what he said now and quietly was, 'Yes, it appears like that. I grant you it appears like that, but it wasn't that way at all. You'll learn. Oh, you'll learn some day.' And with a definite plea in his voice now, he added, 'Can . . . can I ask you not to let on to Hilda? I mean to tell her, I've been meaning to tell her for a long time, but . . . but not at the moment.'

They walked on side by side, the silence heavy between them, and it wasn't until they were nearing the yard that Dick spoke, when, as if he were just continuing the conversation, he said, 'There'll be no time you can tell her when it will be easier, there'll be no way to soften the blow, you know that.'

'Yes, yes, I know that.'

'No matter how she goes on at times she cares for you . . . more fool her.'

Abel made no reply, he couldn't for at this moment he was suffering a hurt which until now he hadn't experienced. Of all the things that could happen to him in his life the last one he would have believed possible was the rejection of him by his son. The boy, the adoring boy, the boy who was no longer a boy but a young man . . . a man, a man who had acted like one tonight. In some corner of his mind there was pride in him that this flesh of his was making a stand against immorality. His own retaliation had been against the immorality of a nation, the immorality of killing, but his son's was a more common kind. He was making his stand against the immorality of sinning if you like, the sinning of one person against another, and when he dubbed it sin his son wouldn't be thinking of the social code but of the pains such immorality, such sin inflicts on another human being.

He had the urge to turn on him now and say, 'I'm going to tell her. Right now I'm going to tell her': but what would that mean? He would have to tell her not only that she wasn't his wife but that he was soon to be the father of her sister's child . . . God! No! No! The boy was right, he couldn't do it, for there was no way he could soften the blow; and she didn't deserve to be felled, as the truth would surely fell her.

2

'Look, dear.' Dick put his arm around Molly's shoulder. 'It would have happened some time, she had a bad heart. And you haven't a thing to blame yourself for. Good lord! after the way you've looked after her, and what you've put up with from her?'

Molly lifted her head from her hands and as she stared over the table towards the door that led into the hall she said, 'You remember what we were talking about last night?'

'Yes, yes, I remember, we were talking about wishing people dead. We could have talked about it last week, last year, and it wouldn't have affected you, but we just had to talk about it last night; and now you're going to enjoy having a guilt complex about it.'

'Enjoy!' She snapped round in her chair, and he stared down into her face as he said, nodding his head, 'Yes, that's what I said, enjoy.'

Molly made no reply as she looked back at him. Within the last twenty-four hours he seemed to have changed, he was a different person. Only once today had she seen any nervous movement in his shoulder. With an authority that she would have attributed only to his father he had handled the funeral arrangements, he had directed the men when they moved her mother to the mortuary, and now he was speaking to her as he had never spoken before, with a note of maturity in his voice.

As she stared at him a strange thought entered her head: she knew that he would never again laugh at his own shortness of stature, and that more likely he'd hit out if anybody mentioned it, even in a jocular way. He was right too about the guilt feelings, not that she was enjoying them, but that she was allowing herself to be plagued with them. It was stupid of her because she had nothing to blame herself for where her mother was concerned; she had been a hand-maiden to her since she could toddle. But one thing she was sure of in her mind, she wasn't going to say she should have loved her mother, for not even a saint could have stood the daily railings of a person like her mother. Even so, she wished . . . yes, she wished that they hadn't talked as they did last night, because after he had gone she had stood over there by the kitchen door and, looking across the hall, she had pictured the querulous creature lying under table and when the voice had come to her again, crying, 'Do you hear me, Molly?' she had thought how wonderful life would be without her. And now here she was without her, and wonder was far away, and she was sick with the feeling of guilt and remorse.

'Come on. Come! Aunt Hilda's holding dinner for us.' He smiled at her now. 'You know what she's like if she's got to wait for a meal. She likes her food, and she's beginning to show it for she's fatter. She's always nibbling. They say it's . . .'

He stopped himself from going further and adding, 'A sign of frustration, or to fill some need.' Recalling the open row that he'd had with his father last night, and his discovery of his Aunt Florrie's condition, it was more than ever clear to him now that there was an emptiness that needed filling in the woman who had been a mother to him for so long and that she could only attempt to assuage it by eating.

'Come on.' He had her by the hand and just as he went to open the door he turned and, taking her into his arms, he looked into her face as he said, 'Everything's going to be plain sailing for us two from now on; whatever happens to anybody else things are going to be right for you and me, understand?'

She looked into the so familiar face. It seemed to have added a number of years on to itself overnight, and she nodded her head but made no comment, but when he kissed her with a short hard kiss on the lips she thought wryly, Funny, how compensations are handed out. His Aunt Hilda would say, 'God works in a mysterious way his wonders to perform.' And she knew it was a wonder. Oh yes, it was nothing short of a wonder that Dick loved her. She had only to look in the glass to realise how great was the wonder. And the wonder was intensified by the knowledge that Dick considered the luck to be all on his side.

On the step he paused as he said, 'We'll cut across

the field. Your field, do you realise that? It's your field now.'

She glanced at him sideways as she said, 'I hope it'll soon be ours.'

'Aw, Molly!' He shook his head. 'I wasn't thinking along those lines.'

'I know you weren't but —' She leant her head towards him and smiled a small knowing smile as she said, 'I bet it hasn't escaped your Aunt Hilda's notice.'

'No, you're right, I bet it hasn't. But it's your land and you do what you like with it.'

'We'll see.'

They rounded the back of the outbuildings and came through the passage into the yard; then both stopped and glanced at each other as the sound of raised angry voices came from the kitchen.

After a moment of listening Dick said, 'That isn't Dad; come on . . . Look.' He stopped and pointed to where the two dogs were tied by a length of string to the drainpipe, and he said under his breath, 'Mr Donnelly.'

When they opened the kitchen door both Hilda and the old man looked sharply towards them; then almost instantly Mr Donnelly turned his verbal attack on Dick. Pointing at him but looking at Hilda, he cried, 'You could take them off the road, give shelter to any scum, but when it comes to your own . . .'

'Shut up!'

'Don't tell me to shut up, girl.'

As the old man staggered towards the table and

leant on it for support Dick realised that although his speech wasn't yet slurred nevertheless he had had a lot to drink. He was again yelling at his daughter, 'Don't tell me to shut up. You know what you are, you're an ungrateful sod. You always have been and—' He half turned and, addressing himself to Dick and Molly, he cried, 'All I was askin' was shelter, a room for few nights, an' what did she say, no, not in her house. I could 'ave the rat hole up above the garage, but only for few nights mind . . .'

'They're . . . they're very nice rooms, Mr Donnelly,' Dick now put in quietly. 'We . . . we lived in them; they were comfortable . . .'

'Don't tell me how long ya lived in 'em. I . . . I know how long ya lived in 'em, lad. An' she had them all done up fancy for ya. But what're they now, eh? Woodwork shop; least they were two years gone back when I climbed those stairs.'

'There's only one room a workshop, Mr Donnelly.'

'Well, t'other room ain't gettin' me, boy. If it's so good you . . . you go up there an' I'll take your bunk . . . Aye; aye. Now that's fair, isn't it?'

Before Dick could make any reply Hilda shouted, 'There's going to be no exchange of any kind. You're just doing this on purpose to . . . to upset me. You've got plenty of cronies down at your own end who'd give you shelter . . . And what about our Florrie?'

'Our Florrie?' He turned to her again. 'Our Florrie'd put me up like a shot if she could, but she's only got one bedroom, you've got four of 'em up 'bove.' He thumbed towards the ceiling. 'And anyroad she's hardly room for herself, and when her belly gets emptied next month or so she'll want all the room she can find. She put me up on the couch last night an' me dogs an' all, an' it was your man who said, "If ya want a bed come round, Fred." Didn't he?' he now appealed to Dick. 'You were there, weren't ya, on Florrie's drive when he said it?'

'What did you say? Where?' Hilda was walking slowly from the fireplace to the end of the table, but she didn't look at the old man, she looked towards Dick as she said to him, 'What's this? Were you at our Florrie's last night?'

He swallowed deeply. 'Just for a minute,' he said.

'Just for a minute?' she repeated. 'You went to the post to get your father if I remember, didn't you? If he was at the post how did he come to be at our Florrie's?'

'He . . . he had just called to see if she was all right.'

As she nodded at him the colour of her face changed, even her neck looked red; then turning her gaze on her father she demanded, 'What do you mean about . . .?' She hesitated and the old man cried at her, 'Go on, say it. Soil you mouth, lass, soil your mouth. I said when her belly empties an' the bairn comes.'

As Dick watched her hand clutch at the end of the table there arose in him a momentary hatred against the old man, but more so against his father. But the

300

latter feeling wasn't momentary, it was already there.

'You didn't know? Well, you wouldn't, would ya' – the old fellow was still yelling – 'you never look the side she's on. She's scum to you, but you're not fit to wipe her boots. Do you hear me? You're not fit to wipe her boots. An' she's done something that you couldn't manage, for all her age; aye, she has.'

'Get out! Get out this minute!' Her fingers began to claw along the edge of the table as if in search of something to grip, and then she was screaming at him, 'Get out! Do you hear me?' and it stressed the height of her feelings when she cried at him, 'God! I don't know, I don't know how I ever came to be connected with you. Out!' Her arm was outstretched, her finger pointing towards the door. But the old man didn't move; he had been leaning over the table supporting himself on his hands, but now slowly he straightened himself and seemed to take on inches and, strangely, both his voice and his mien appeared sober and there was a depth of deep fury in his tone as he said, 'Well now, lass, I'm gona relieve your mind by tellin' you somethin', aye, by tellin' you somethin'. An' it's this, you're not connected with me, do you hear? Eh, do you hear? What'll you say if I tell you you no more belong to me than those two there do.' He flung his arm to the side. 'You'll be relieved to know, lass, that you're a bastard. You were born a little bastard an' you've grown into a big bastard. Aye, by gum! if there was ever a true word spoken I've just said it.'

He paused and now he smiled, a rather terrible smile, as he said, 'You're losing your colour, lass. I'd sit down if I was you 'cos there's more to come.'

Hilda didn't sit down but she backed from the table as if from a reptile and when her heel touched the fender she stopped. Her lips apart, her eyes wide, she stared at him like an entranced hare as he now, in the same terrible tone, went on talking. He talked and he talked, giving her every sordid detail of his love life; and then there was almost the sound of tears in his voice when he said, 'I took you on as a sort of lost love, I devoted me life to you. Aye, I did, I devoted me life to you. Nothin' was too good for you, the others could go to hell but you must have, and you know, there's a thing called irony, and by! I've often thought an' all that God must have handed that out as a punishment to me 'cos the irony of it was you never took to me. Not from the time you could toddle you never took to me; you took to Annie. Oh aye, you took to Annie, but not to me. You got under me skin but I put up with it 'cos I saw your mother in everything you did. But now' – his voice rose sharply – 'I know that if I'd married her she would have likely been as big a bitch as you, 'cos you've got it from some place. On the other hand though you could have got it from him who did the trick on her. But only God knows who that was, likely one of many. Aye, lass, grope for support, I think you'd better sit down.'

'Leave her alone, Mr Donnelly.' Dick moved towards Hilda. 'And I think you'd better go.'

'Bugger me eyes! don't you start, young 'un, else I'll soon deal with you. I'll go when I'm ready, you hear me! I'll go when I'm ready.'

'Sit down. Come, sit down, Aunt Hilda.'

Hilda didn't sit down, what she did was to push Dick's hand aside; then gulping in her throat, she stretched her neck upwards two or three times before she spoke, and as she spoke she bent her belly forward in the direction of the old man and what she said was, 'Do you know something? Do you know something, *Mr Fred Donnelly?* That's the best news I've heard for years, it's the best news I've heard in me life.' Her voice was rising almost to a scream now. 'You think you've done me down, don't you, by spewing this at me? Well, you couldn't have done me a better service. Now I feel clean. Do you hear me? I feel clean because I know I'm not connected with you. Now again I say *get out. Get out of my house and I never want to set eyes on you again ever. Ever.*'

The old man remained standing. His jaw moving from side to side ground his teeth into audible sound. Then almost jumping round he made for the door, dragged it open, paused for a moment to unloosen the dogs, then went down the yard in a staggering run.

Dick stood and watched him for a moment before turning to Molly, who had stood mute through all this. He motioned to her to go to Hilda, who had now turned and was standing with her raised arms and hands pressed against the mantel-border, her head dropped forward in between them, and he whispered to her, 'I'll get Dad . . .'

Abel was at the far end of the garage working on a lathe and when Dick made frantic gestures to him to stop the machine he did so, then said, 'What's the matter?'

'Everything, I should say.' Dick's tone was the same as he had used last night on the walk back from Florrie's.

'What do you mean, everything?'

'Mr Donnelly's just been. He must have taken you at your word that there would be a room for him here. Well, Aunt Hilda seemed to have other ideas about having him in the house and she told him so. He was very drunk, at least he was when I first saw him but I think he's sobered up now. He . . . he made a disclosure which he imagined would floor her. Well apparently it didn't. But that might just be on the surface . . .'

Abel was wiping his hands on a piece of tow as he said, briskly, 'What disclosure? What did he say? Get on with it.'

'Oh, you needn't worry.' Dick's face was tight. 'He told her that Florrie was going to have a child but he didn't mention the man . . . he must have forgotten.'

'Now, now! lad, don't you start that again. What did he come to say?'

'Apparently he didn't come to say anything, he only wanted to stay here, but when she wouldn't have him he just told her that she doesn't belong to him. He told a long tale about a woman he loved, someone who married his brother, and after he was killed in the pit she went off and got herself pregnant with somebody else.'

When he saw Abel turn away and put his hand to his brow and say, 'Lord God above! not that,' he muttered, 'You knew about this?'

Abel let out a long shuddering breath as he said, 'I've known about it for a long time.'

'That . . . that she wasn't old Donnelly's daughter and . . . and not Florrie's sister?'

'Yes, yes.'

'How?'

'Oh, I overheard Florrie and him going at it one day, but I didn't know then what it was all about. It was only later that Florrie inadvertently let it out of the bag.'

'And you've kept quiet about it?'

Dick almost jumped as Abel rounded on him, crying now under his breath, 'What do you think I should have done? Told her that she didn't belong to them?'

'No, no.' Dick shook his head. 'I'm sorry. Lord!' He turned to the side and now pushed his fingers through his hair, saying, 'Everything coming at once.'

'Yes, everything coming at once.'

Looking at his father, his voice and manner somewhat mollified now, he said, 'She's in a state, she . . . she needs comfort, but . . . but not from me.'

Abel stood with his head bowed; then after a moment, he muttered, 'Go on in; I'll be there in a few minutes.'

'Dad.' It was the first time he had used that name

for many months, and as Abel looked up at him he said, 'As I said, she knows about Aunt Florrie, but . . . but if she brings it up you . . . you won't tell her the truth, will you? I don't think she could stand much more, not after today's do. It would likely turn her brain.'

Abel glanced away for a moment, then his voice dry and throaty, he said, 'Don't worry, I'm . . . I'm used to lying, I'm a dab hand at it.'

As Dick went slowly out of the garage Abel looked at the piece of tow which he was holding in his hand and he crushed it tight in his fist and for a moment he had a picture of himself in the barn straining against the iron shackles.

Slowly he opened his fist and let the tow drop from it; then he walked out of the garage and up towards the house, and as he went he hoped he wouldn't have to lie, that she would have already sensed the truth, and that as she had turfed out her father she would also do the same with him, for then his problem would be solved.

For the moment he had forgotten about the ceremony he had gone through with her in the registry office.

3

Not on that particular Saturday, nor on any day during the following six weeks did Hilda mention Florrie or her condition. She knew, without it being stated in words, who had fathered the forthcoming baby, but she realised that were she to bring it into the open, Abel would walk out on her. The disclosure would be like a licence allowing him to go free, and she couldn't bear the thought of life without him. Life with him was a pattern of taut questions and answers during the day, and the wide gulf in the bed at night.

At nights she would lie awake on her side listening to his deep, steady breathing, and she would still her crying in case it wakened him because should he awake and hear her he would make no movement towards her, which would only add to her humiliation. She longed for him to turn to her and to cuddle her and soothe her, but he had never reacted like that for years. The very last time he had turned to her, his gentle fondling and soothing had changed swiftly into what he termed loving and she had protested with as much energy as he was using, saying, 'I'm tired, I've had a hard day and . . . and I want none of that. You can't act like a human being for five minutes.'

That phrase, you can't act like a human being, had the same effect as that of the last nail in her coffin for now she knew she was literally dead to him as far as emotion went.

Slowly and terrifyingly she knew there was growing in her another being, a questioning being, an anti-religious being, an anti-Reverend Gilmore being. It was a woman who was asking wouldn't she have saved herself years of unhappiness if she had been able to look upon this act, which her mind told her was dirty, in a non-religious way. Or again, look upon it as the women in the Bible did? Mr Gilmore was always reading and quoting the women of the Bible, but when you got down to rock bottom what were they? A lot of Mary Magdalenes, a lot of whores. But were they any the worse for that? Christ hadn't thought so, so why had she felt that she had to be better than them?

More and more now she was blaming Mr Maxwell and the vicar for inveigling her into the association, the so-called marriage which had been no marriage. If she had been initiated into marriage from the start things might have been different. The other woman was asking her now, what she would do if Abel were to give her another chance? If one night he were to turn in the bed and take her into his arms, how would she respond? The self she had lived with so long turned its head away and said, 'I don't know.'

One consolation she was finding, and which remained a surprise, was the fact that Dick was on her side; and what was of equal surprise was the knowledge that there was an open rift between him and his father. The child had adored his father, the schoolboy had adored his father, the youth . . . the early youth had adored his father, but the young man had cut down on his adoration, and the man of nineteen certainly didn't adore his father, and she felt she knew the reason for it! Dick must have been aware of Abel's association with Florrie and had spoken boldly out against it. Perhaps at bottom this was the reason for his nerves. But no, this nervous business had been growing since he was sixteen.

At times she wondered what she would do without his support, and Molly's. Molly was a nice girl. They planned to marry next year. The sooner the better, she thought, because it was strange how attractive a plain girl could suddenly become to certain men when it became known that she now owned a big house and a good piece of land, not to mention a few thousand pounds.

Men were crafty, wily, out for the best chance; they'd jump at anything that offered a good set-up. Abel had jumped at a good home and business; he hadn't married her because he loved her, he had never loved her, she knew that now. She had known it from the beginning, but she had loved him . . . Yet could you love without the other thing? He had said you couldn't, it was all part of the whole. Aw, life was hell.

Eeh! she must stop thinking that way; she was using terms in her mind that would have brought her to her knees a few years ago. Twice this week she had brought out the exclamation My God! Only yesterday she had said 'Damn it!' when the milk boiled over the stove. She was changing, she knew she was changing and she was afraid, and sad, afraid both of the change in herself and sad that it was too late for it to have any effect on Abel.

Abel, too, had changed, at least towards her, during the past weeks. His manner had been softer, he was more considerate. He had stopped spending all his spare time, even part of his dinner time, up in the workshop whittling away at those animals of his. Twice recently she had come in from church meetings to find the tea-break cups washed up and the table set for the evening meal. She hadn't remarked on it because she feared she would have said, as her mother used to say, 'It's thin butter on your conscience . . .' Her mother . . . she wasn't going to go into that again because no matter what kind of face she had put on when that revelation had been thrown at her it had caused a wound inside her which was still wide open.

She stood now looking down the yard at the passing army trucks. The war was in its third year, it couldn't go on for ever. When it was over people would want cars, they'd want to get away on holidays, business could soar. But would it matter if it didn't? No, not if Abel wasn't with her.

What would he do when the baby was born? He wouldn't be able to keep it to himself then, he'd be bound to give himself away . . . and what then? Would she raise Cain and give him the chance to walk out? or would she humble herself and say

'Don't leave me, Abel. You can see to her and the child, only don't leave me?'

She turned from the window and went through the kitchen and into the hall and up the stairs to her bedroom, and there, sitting on the edge of the bed, she covered her face with her hands for a moment. But when her throat became tight with tears she rose quickly from the bed again, muttering to herself, 'Don't. Don't,' because she knew that if he came in and asked why she was crying there would bound to be a show-down.

She went and stood in front of the mirror and appraised herself. She was thirty-seven. She hadn't a line on her face or a grey hair on her head. She looked much younger than her years, and she could still be called pretty. But then there was her figure. She had put on pounds lately, and she couldn't afford to put on pounds, not with her height. If only she could stop eating. She moved nearer to the mirror and fingered her cheeks. She had a better skin than their Florrie. She shook her head impatiently: why couldn't she stop saying *their*. *Their Florrie*. She was no longer their Florrie or our Florrie as she herself was no longer our Hilda. Oh no, she was no longer our Hilda to either that horrible old devil or his daughter.

Yet, when she asked the question of the mirror her thoughts fell into the old idiom: Why do they all fall for our Florrie? What is she after all? She's got no looks to speak of, and no figure; a yard of pump water, that's what she looks like . . . so why?

The only answer she gave herself was '*Men*', and

on this she turned from the mirror and went from the room, her head moving from side to side as if in denial of the truth her mind was presenting to her with regard to the attractiveness of their Florrie.

Florrie's baby was born near midnight on a Thursday night but Abel didn't see it until twenty-four hours later, which meant he hadn't seen her for forty-eight hours altogether. She was in high spirits when he left her on the Wednesday afternoon. The child wasn't due for another week and she laughingly said she had never felt better in her life except that she had put on a little weight and she would have to see about getting it off.

He entered as usual by the garden door. After turning his key in it he had pushed it slightly open and slid in between it and the blackout, but as his hand went to pull the blackout aside it was stayed by the sound of a baby's cry, a young baby's cry. His mouth fell into a gape, his eyes widened, then he was round the curtain staring at Fred Donnelly coming out of the kitchen carrying a tray. It was the old man who spoke first and what he said was typical. 'Taken your bloody time, haven't you?' he said.

'Sh . . . e's had it?'

'Well what the hell do you think that is cryin'? Me whippets haven't been at it so you can't blame them.' He grinned from ear to ear at his joke.

'Is . . . is she all right?'

'Well, you're not likely to find out standin' there glued to the bloody spot, are you?'

Abel closed his eyes for a moment, smiled weakly, then hurried across the room and into the bedroom. But once inside he again became still and looked towards the bed where Florrie was sitting propped up with pillows, and to the side of her in a cot was the howling baby.

He gazed from one to the other and it was she, like her father, who had to stir him into movement, saying, 'Well, if you're coming in, come in; there's somebody wants to see you.'

Ignoring the child for a moment, he walked slowly up to the bed; then sitting on the edge, he leant towards her and gathered her into his arms. Presently, he drew himself away and, looking into her face, asked quietly, 'Are you all right?'

'Perfectly all right.' She cocked her chin upwards.

'When . . . when?'

'Near midnight last night.'

'But . . . but you were all right when I left you?'

'Yes, I was, but you weren't gone five minutes until I knew something was afoot, I phoned Mrs Kent and she came straightaway; then later on the doctor came. He said it was the quickest thing he had seen in years.'

'Was it bad, hard?'

'Well' – she sighed – 'I wouldn't want to go through it again this week.'

He laughed and dropped his head against her brow, and as he sat like this she said, 'You're not interested at all in what we've got?'

'Oh! Florrie. Florrie!' He rose quickly now from the bed and went round to the other side and stood over the cot looking down on the crinkled face, on the working lips and blinking eyelids and the head with a tuft of hair sticking up from the crown.

After a moment, lifting his eyes to her, he said, 'What is it?'

'It's a baby.' Her voice was low now and tinged with laughter; then she added softly, 'A girl.'

'A girl.' His smile widened. 'I'm glad. Oh yes, I'm glad. Are you?'

'Yes, of course. I wouldn't have minded either way, but I think I am . . . I am glad it's a girl.'

He came round the foot of the bed again and sat beside her, then said anxiously, 'How are you managing? You're going to see about Mrs Kent staying?'

'Don't worry, Mrs Kent's been. She's coming in every day; and Dad . . . well' – she nodded towards the bedroom door – 'he's been marvellous.' Of course he shocks everybody within earshot but nevertheless he's . . . he's been marvellous. Her face lost its smile now as she ended, 'I've been glad of him, Abel.'

'Yes yes, I suppose you have . . . I should have been here.'

'I'm glad you weren't.'

'You are? Why?'

'Well. Well, you would have stayed all night and there would have been questions. You know what I mean.'

'Oh! Florrie.' Again he was holding her, talking into her hair now. 'How am I going to stand it?'

'It will become a pattern. Don't worry, we'll work something out.'

Raising his head he looked at her steadily as he said, 'Don't you want me with you all the time?'

'Oh, don't be silly!' She bowed her chin on to her chest, then muttered, 'Don't make me say it. It was bad enough before but since that do with Dad and her . . . Abel!' – she now raised her head and looked at him – 'I couldn't live with myself if . . . if I knew she was going to be left alone, I mean altogether. To be deprived of her family and then of her husband, well, it's enough to send her round the bend. Aw, Abel' – she now put her arms tightly about him – 'I want you, I want you every minute of the day, but I know, I know meself and . . . and I couldn't be really happy if I took you completely away from her. I . . . I know I have you, every bit of you, so it's not hard for me to say "Don't leave her", although I know it's hard for you to stay. Anyway, leave things as they are for a time; you'll find it'll work out. Strange how things work out. Be happy, be happy with me in this moment because I've never been so happy and contented in my whole life. I'm so happy I'm beginning to fear that something will happen to shatter it. It's got nothing to do with you or me, I don't know what it is, I suppose it's just a natural fear that happiness brings, you become terrified of losing it. Anyway, don't worry; you'll see, everything will work out. You know, as I lay here today I thought how strange it is about all the little things that happen to make wishes come true, it's as if life is cut out to a pattern. And I think it is, I think our lives are cut out to a pattern from the beginning and that one day we'll be sewn together like that' – she took his hand and linked her fingers tightly in his – 'and nothing or no-one will be able to unpick us.'

4

It was the first batch of the miniature ducks he had taken to the shop in weeks. The hours he now spent nursing his daughter left him little spare time for his workshop, but during this past week he had gone at his whittling at a pace which suggested he had a time limit to get an order out. His earnest application to his woodwork craft was not solely created by the fact that he would from now on need to add money to his savings, although if there wasn't as yet any need to support the mother he was nevertheless determined from the start to be responsible for the expenses of his daughter. She, he had decided, was going to have the best that could be obtained, and black market prices were high, even where baby commodities were concerned. But his hurry sprang from some deep urge that kept pestering him to add to his capital, telling him he could do nothing without money.

So on this particular winter's day of alternate flurries of sleet or snow and hail he pushed open the door of Roger Lester's art shop. The term art had at one time encompassed a great many sidelines. Besides artists' materials, various pieces of china depicting scenes of Newcastle and Durham would have been on display, even Sunderland cut glass. But now Mr Lester sold whatever he could get his hands on and a number of empty shelves in the shop showed that he wasn't too successful; and therefore his welcome of Abel was warm and genuine. 'Hello, there,' he said. 'Am I glad to see you! Where've you been? I thought you must have got it in one of the raids. Ah. Ah' – he dug with his finger the flat box that Abel was carrying – 'come on let's see what you've got in here.'

'Not over much this time, I'm afraid, but I'm getting down to it again.'

The box on the counter and now opened, Mr Lester lifted the birds and animals one after the other from their nest of cotton wool. 'Ah, this is new. A blackbird.'

'No, a rook.'

'Well, there's not much difference, they're both black. And a swan. Nice, nice. But only two of them? Ah, the ducks.' He now picked up two of the small ducks and placed them in his palm, saying as he nodded his head, 'Of all the animals you do you can't beat these. You'd think that little fellow was trying to pick fleas off himself.' He traced the rounded neck back to the tail. 'Work of art this. I've always said it, haven't I, a work of art. You should have gone in for this in a big way instead of cars and bikes.'

'I might yet.'

'You'd be wise. Well, I can assure you these won't be on the shelf for long, but I shall keep some back for special customers. People can't get anything to make a decent present these days, they'd pay any price for them. Why, a funny thing happened not an hour gone. You know my Andy's little 'un, Stephen? Well, I gave him one of your last batch – it was this one, the duck preening it's feathers – and you know he carries it around everywhere; holds it in his fist as he goes to sleep his dad says. Well, there he was in the shop standing over there, not an hour ago as I said, and in comes this woman, out for a day I think because I've never seen her before, not round here, and she didn't speak our lingo either. She wanted some writing paper, and there was Stephen buzzing around the shop holding the duck out as if it were an aeroplane – you know how bairns do – and what does she do but she takes it from him and stares at it. And then she says to me, "Do you sell these?" and I said, "I do when I can get them." And then she says, "Do you make them?" and I laughed and said, "Me? No! no! I haven't got clever fingers like that." Then after a moment she asks, "Who makes them then?" and I said, "Oh, a man at the other end of the town." And at that she said, "Oh, is it a Mr —" I think she said, "Mason" and I said "No, his name's Gray." Then she turned the thing over in her hand and looked at it, and I am positively sure she would have pocketed it if Stephen hadn't said, "Give me me duck." She then wanted to know if you had a shop and I said no, you had a garage . . . What is it? What's the matter? . . . Here . . . you all right? Come and sit down, man. Here, sit down on the chair.'

'No, no.' Abel shook his head. 'What . . . what was she like, this woman?'

'Thinnish, in her forties I should say, decently put on, whitish face, small features you know, bit peevish looking I thought.'

'What . . . what time did you say she was here?'

'Oh, about an hour ago.'

Abel turned swiftly towards the door now and Mr Lester called, 'What about settling up?'

'I'll come back later.'

'All right, if it's all the same with you, all right.'

He was in the street now and only just stopped himself from running. God Almighty! Lena. After all these years, Lena. It couldn't be anyone else. Nobody would have recognised the duck like that. *Lena! What must he do? What could he do?*

He ran across the road now and jumped on a bus. His mind was racing, throwing questions at him, giving answers, answers without hope. He knew that it wouldn't take her two minutes to connect the name Gray with that of Mason. Oh Hilda. Hilda. If he had only told her. Now this revelation on top of all the rest would, as Florrie had said, surely turn her brain. She had been acting strangely of late too; he was positive she knew about the baby, and he couldn't understand why she wasn't bringing it into the open. But Florrie said she could; Florrie said that in her position she would be doing exactly the same because she wouldn't want to lose him, Oh! God. Lose him? If he could only lose himself.

Two stops before the house he jumped off the bus but remained standing on the edge of the pavement until the bus had receded far into the distance. He was feeling sick and not a little afraid. One thing he knew he couldn't hope for, that Lena's character had softened with the years. She would show him no mercy, she would glory in bringing him down.

The panic swirling in him made him sweat, it ran from his hair into his eyes, and as he stepped off the pavement a lorry driver tooted his horn sharply and, sticking his head out of the cab, shouted, 'Why don't you wait for a bomb, mate!'

Having reached the other side of the road he stood perfectly still for a full three minutes; then he squared his shoulders, jerked his chin upwards out of his collar, smoothed the pockets of his double-breasted greatcoat downwards as if pressing out the creases, and began to march, his step quickening as he neared the yard. He hurried up it, and into the kitchen, and came face to face with his wife . . .

Lena had hardly altered except that she seemed smaller; she was still thin, and there was no trace showing in her face of the girl he had married, but there was in every line of it the woman who had screamed abuse at him when he walked out of the cottage door almost twelve years ago.

'Hello, Abel.'

He couldn't associate her voice with a cat teasing a mouse before the kill, it was more like the composite baying of dogs before they tore the stag to shreds; and if ever there was a stag at bay he knew that he was in a like position now.

'She won't believe me.' Lena moved her thumb slowly over her shoulder towards where Hilda was sitting in the high-backed wooden chair staring at him as if she were paralysed in both speech and movement. 'She's hardly opened her mouth, she's been struck dumb. You're a bad lad, Abel, aren't you, going through a form of marriage with another woman when you already had one? By the way, where's me son? . . . What!' She gave a short sharp mirthless laugh now. 'Have you been struck dumb an' all? Oh, you're wondering how I found you out, are you? Well, you shouldn't have gone on making them little ducks; nobody could make little ducks like you. Well now, what are you going to do about me? Eh? Eh?'

When surprisingly he took a quick step forward towards her she seemed nonplussed but when, his voice holding a deep, firm ring, he said, 'What I'm going to do is this, I'm going to tell you to get out and do your worst. I walked out on you twelve years ago because I couldn't stand the sight of you any longer and I haven't changed,' she turned her head quickly and looked towards Hilda, then back to him, and she cried, 'By! you've got a bloody nerve. You walked out on me because you couldn't stand the sight of me, you say? You walked out on me? You did not, you scuttled from Hastings when the woman you were carrying on with was murdered by her husband. I've just told her that.' She thumbed again towards Hilda, but still Hilda made no move whatever. 'An' if you hadn't gone her brothers would have scuttled you, there would have been another murder done. You left me to escape the consequences of your whorin'.'

'Get out! Do you hear me? Get out! because I haven't changed much in twelve years and what I threatened to do that day I might just do now.'

When he took another step towards her she backed from him and towards the door and as she did so she cried, 'Oh, don't think you're going to get off as easy as that, Mr Abel Mason or Gray, you're going to do a stretch, an' I am going to do a jig the day they send you down. I'm goin' to stand up in court and tell them all that I've suffered through your neglect and for deprivin' me of my bairn all these years. I'm going straight from this very room to the polis station, so look out and don't try to run away again.'

'Get!' – his arm was stretched out, his finger pointing – 'and go to the polis; I'll be quite willing to do a long, long stretch not to set eyes on you again. Now go!' He reached beyond her and pulled open the door, and she stumbled backwards into the yard yelling, 'I'll see you get your deserts, by God! I will. I'll show you up from one end of the country to the other; I'll put you in all the papers.'

He banged the door on her voice, then stood with his back to it looking towards where Hilda still sat like an effigy incapable of either movement or speech.

Minutes passed before he walked slowly towards her; then dropping on his hunkers he reached out to take her hands, but when his fingers touched hers she drew them back as if she had received an electric shock. But still she didn't speak, only continued to stare at him as he began to talk to her softly, soothingly. 'Hilda. Hilda, listen to me. I know I've done wrong. It's been on my mind all these years; I've never really known a minute's peace. And believe me, I wouldn't have had this happen to you for all the world, I wouldn't. No matter how I've acted towards you I wouldn't have hurt you like this. I could have walked out any time over the years but I knew you didn't want me to, so I stayed on. Yet in my heart I knew it would come out some day. But . . . but not like this. I should have told you. Somehow though I felt it would be depriving you of something, a family, and you needed a family . . . Say something, Hilda, please. Please say something.'

She didn't say anything, but with a jerk of her body she moved the wooden chair back from him; then rising slowly but keeping her eyes on him, she walked round him, then backed towards the door and out of the room. When he heard her going upstairs she was still walking slowly, it was as if she were pausing on each step.

As he dropped into a chair by the kitchen table he realised he still had his coat and hat on, but he made no effort to take them off. What was he to do? Almost immediately it seemed, he was given the answer.

When he heard the thud he rushed into the hall to see a suitcase lying at the bottom of the stairs, then another one came tumbling down to join it. He stood staring at them for a moment; then as he went to pick them up there followed a spate of clothes, suits, shoes, shirts, ties, underwear, all tumbling down the stairs, some not reaching the bottom but getting caught up in the banisters until the whole staircase was littered with his clothes.

The scurry and flurry following so quickly on her numbness was startling, but he could make no protest, all he could do was to gather up the articles and press them into the cases. But when these were both full there was still enough to fill another two or more.

It was as he brought the last of his clothing from the stairs and added them in a heap on the kitchen table that Dick came in the back door. He had just come off his shift and was still in his overalls, his hands and face streaked with engine grease.

Before closing the door he stopped and stared at his father, but Abel merely glanced at him before going back into the hall and picking up the two suitcases.

'What's . . . what's happened?'

'Does it need any explanation?'

'But—' Dick looked in perplexity at the jumble of clothing on the table.

'Your mother's been.'

'No! Oh! Oh God!'

'Yes, oh God!'

Abel stopped stuffing the underwear into a shirt which he was using as a bag and said slowly, 'In one way I would say I was glad if it wasn't for the effect it's had on her.' He jerked his head towards the ceiling. 'Stay here with her and see to her, will you?'

Dick stared at him, making no response for a

moment; then he said, 'Me mam?' The word sounded strange to his ears. 'What . . . what is she like?'

'Can you remember the day we left?'

'Yes. Yes, sort of, vaguely.'

'Well, all I can say is she hasn't improved, she's a vixen.'

'What is she going to do about it?'

'Oh, see me along the line for a long stretch. She's promised me that.'

'Oh, dear God!'

Abel now put out his hand and gripped Dick's shoulder and, looking at him steadily, said, 'Don't worry. I knew I had it coming some time, and strangely, in a way it's a relief. I'll pay whatever price they decide. I'll have to, I'll have no other choice. Then I . . . I can be with Florrie.'

'What about . . . what about her?' It was Dick who now jerked his head towards the ceiling, and for answer Abel simply turned and pointed to the table, then to the suitcases standing on the floor. 'She wouldn't even listen,' he said; 'she wouldn't even speak. If she had gone for me I'd have felt better about it. I'm . . . I'm a bit worried about her so don't leave her, will you?'

'You going to Florrie's now?'

'Yes; where else?'

'What if me mam comes back?'

'I don't think you need worry about that, although she might want to see you. She talked about you as her child. Anyway, when you see her and hear her I think you'll understand fully why I walked out.'

'I do understand, I did then, but what I've never been able to understand is . . . well, your deceiving Aunt Hilda.'

Abel now bent forward towards Dick as he said, 'Your Aunt Hilda wanted to be deceived; I didn't ask her to marry me, she did the asking. I'll tell you now, I even offered to live with her. I would have preferred that. Oh yes, I would have preferred it that way, but with her religious outlook she would have none of it. I had to put up a fight not to be married in a church, it didn't seem so bad in a registry office.'

'I'm sorry, Dad.'

'I know you are, lad; but as long as it's all right between you and me things aren't too black. I may as well tell you, I've been upset lately the way things have gone.'

'Me too.'

'Look, I'll stack these things in the garage. I'll have to make a couple of journeys, but once I'm clear I think you'd better ring for Doctor Cole. You can tell him what's happened, he'll know how to treat her then.'

'All right . . . Dad.'

As Abel turned from the table, the bulging shirt in his arms, Dick, his stammer evident again, said, 'Wi . . . will . . . will they c . . . come and take you, I m . . . mean what happens in a case like this?'

'I don't know. I know as much about this end of the business as you do, but I'll soon find out, won't I?' He smiled wryly; then holding the bundle to one side, he put his free arm out and now pulled Dick towards him and pressed him tightly as he said, 'Don't worry about me, just stay here and see to things . . . and her.'

5

The detective inspector knocked on the door of the garden flat and Abel opened it to him.

'I am enquiring for a Mr Mason.'

'I'm he.'

'Oh. I'm Detective Inspector Davidson. Your son told me where I might find you.'

'Come in.'

The inspector came in and stood aside while Abel closed the door. He did it slowly, and as slowly he walked past the man and into the sitting-room, and there he motioned with his hand towards the couch where Florrie was sitting nursing the child, and he said, 'This is Mrs Ford.'

The inspector inclined his head forward and Florrie, now getting to her feet and laying the child in the corner of the couch, said in a low voice, 'Won't you sit down?'

'If you don't mind, I'd rather stand; this won't take long.' He now turned to Abel and said, 'You know why I've come?'

'Oh yes, I know why you've come.'

'A Mrs Mason has laid claim by showing as proof her marriage certificate that she is your wife, and also' – the inspector now cast his glance to the side before raising his eyes again and looking straight at Abel – 'we have confirmed with Somerset House that the certificate which she produced agrees with their records. These records also show that a man using the name of Abel Gray, by which I understand you are now known, did subsequently go through a form of marriage with a person of the name of Hilda Maxwell.'

The formal words and tone were in keeping with the inspector's appearance and after Abel had acknowledged his statement by one single movement of his head the man now said, 'I must caution you from now on you need not say anything, but anything you do say will be taken down and may be used in evidence at your trial.'

When Abel sighed the inspector said, 'I'd be obliged if you'd come to the station with me, sir, for questioning.'

Abel turned and looked at Florrie. Her face remained straight, only her eyes told him what she was feeling.

A few minutes later he was dressed for outside and he had opened the door leading into the hall; then pausing, he said, 'Just a minute, I forgot something,' and hurrying back into the sitting-room, quickly closing the door behind him, he went to Florrie and took her in his arms, and after kissing her hard and quickly on the lips he whispered, 'Don't worry. What's to be will be. Just remember, nothing can separate us in the long run.'

She made no answer, only gulped in her throat, then pressed his face tightly between her hands . . .

On the journey to the station the inspector surprisingly dropped his official manner and, almost like a friend, said, 'Have you a solicitor?'

'No.'

'Well, the quicker you get one the better.'

'Thanks, I'll do that.'

'Do you know anything about the proceedings you're going into?'

'No, not a thing.'

'Well then, if you had a solicitor with you he'd likely tell you to plead not guilty.'

Abel turned his head swiftly to him. 'But I am,' he said. 'I've committed bigamy. I'm guilty all right.'

'That's as may be, but if you plead guilty they can keep you inside tonight and then when you come up before the magistrates in the morning and you still hold your plea as guilty you can be kept in jail until your trial.'

'I won't be able to get bail?'

'Not if you plead guilty.'

'Huh!' Abel shook his head, then, on a wry smile, said, 'I'll get out until the trial if I say I'm not guilty?'

'That's the way it goes.'

. . . And that's the way it went. In the police station he went through much the same procedure as he had done in Florrie's sitting-room, only here the atmosphere was different, and it ended with him being bailed to appear before the magistrates the following morning.

He was visibly shaken when he walked down the

steps and into the street from the police station, and he stood for a moment thinking about a solicitor and where he would find one. He had never had need of a solicitor. Hilda had one, but he couldn't go to hers. Florrie had said there was a tall building off Cuthbert Street that housed solicitors and accountants. She, too, had no need of a solicitor in Fellburn, the business of her shop had been settled in Newcastle.

When a few minutes later he looked at the well-polished brass plates, he saw the name Thomas Gay and Co., Solicitors, Commissioners for Oaths, and underneath a list of four names headed by a John E. Roscommon. He looked at the other names. Well, it didn't matter which one, did it, they'd all likely know what to do.

He went into the building and up the stairs and through a glass door marked 'Thomas Gay & Co.' and to a glass-partitioned desk where a prim young woman looked at him and said, 'Well . . . yes?'

'I'd . . . I'd like to see Mr Roscommon please.'

'Have you an appointment?'

'No.'

'Well, let me see' – she turned to a book – 'how about Wednesday at three?'

He stared at her for a moment before saying slowly, 'I want to see him today.'

She stared back at him, her eyes widening. 'I'm afraid that's impossible. Mr Roscommon is fully engaged.'

'One of the others?'

'They're all engaged.' She moved her head slowly, then she bent forward as if speaking to a child and, peering up at him from under the partition, she said, 'You've got to make an appointment to see a solicitor.'

'Miss Wilton!'

The young woman turned to look at the old man who was addressing her. He beckoned her to one side and although Abel couldn't hear what he was saying he distinctly heard what she was saying. 'It isn't done,' she said; 'Mr Blackett would go on.'

Now Abel heard the old man say, and quite distinctly and firmly, 'Leave Mr Blackett to me' and to this the young lady answered with an indignant 'Eeh!'

Now the old man was looking through the partition at Abel and was saying, 'Your name, sir?'

'Gray . . . Mason . . . Abel Gray Mason.'

'Would you mind taking a seat, sir?'

'Thank you.'

Abel took a seat and he watched the old man disappear through a door and he was left staring at the partition and at Miss Wilton who was staring back at him in no friendly fashion. Under other circumstances he would have laughed at the expression on the young girl's face, but he doubted at this moment if he would ever laugh again.

It was almost five minutes later when the old man returned and, in the same polite manner, said, 'Will you come this way, sir?'

Abel knew that his exit was being closely

watched by Miss Wilton and as he went up a narrow corridor the old man said, 'The young lady is new to the work but she's right in one way, it is usual to make an appointment.'

'I realise that now but I'm . . . I'm badly in need of advice at the moment.'

'I understand that, sir. This way.'

They now crossed an open office where four typists, busily tapping away, raised their eyes for a second and glanced at him; then through another passageway; and now the old man was opening a door and ushering him into a sparsely furnished room.

'Mr Gray Mason, Mr Roscommon.'

The man sitting behind the desk rose slowly to his feet, but that hardly brought him up to Abel's shoulder. He didn't speak, he just motioned towards a chair and Abel, sitting down said, 'I . . . I'm sorry to barge in like this but . . . but time is precious, you see, I've got to appear in the magistrates court tomorrow morning and it's . . . it's all happened so quickly. I . . . I didn't realise . . . well, the procedure . . .'

The small broad man closed his eyes for a moment and said, 'All right, all right, Mr Mason. Now just settle back and start from the beginning. What's your case?'

On an outgoing breath Abel said, 'Bigamy.'

'Oh.' Mr Roscommon showed no surprise whatever. 'How many times?'

'Oh. Huh!' Abel smiled wryly. 'Only the once.'

'Only the once.' Mr Roscommon now began to

apply himself to his desk pushing papers here and there. Finally, he drew one towards him – it was blank – and again he said, 'Well now, start from the beginning.'

Abel started from the beginning. Twenty minutes later Mr Roscommon stopped making notes and asked the first question. 'Where's your wife living now . . . your legitimate wife?'

'I . . . I don't know.'

'You don't know? Oh. Well then, we'll have to find out, won't we?' He looked towards the clock and said aloud, 'Half past eleven. And that's not the only thing we'll have to find out before tomorrow morning.

'How has the woman . . . well, the one you've been living with as your wife taken this matter?'

'Very badly.'

'Is there any hope she'll stand by you?'

'No, none.'

'. . . And you pleaded not guilty?' He was tapping the writing on his pad now, and he went on, 'Yes, of course, else you wouldn't be here. Well now, as I see it, Mr Mason, the worst part of all this isn't the fact that you married another woman while you still had a wife, although that is what they'll have you on, but the reason why you left your wife in the first place, because looking at it from the judge's point of view, no matter how cruel or unhappy your mistress was with her husband she would likely be alive today if it wasn't for you. Well, need I say more?'

No, he needn't say more. And he had never

thought of Alice as his mistress. They didn't call them mistresses in the working class – his woman, or fancy bit was the name by which she would be known.

'Well now, your wife. She'll likely come on you for maintenance . . . You don't know, I suppose, how she's been living, I mean, has she been supporting herself?'

'I don't know.'

Mr Roscommon sighed. 'We've got a lot to go into.'

'What will happen after tomorrow morning, sir?'

'Oh, you'll go up before the magistrates.' He paused, then said, 'Let me see. What have I got on tomorrow morning? Shall I be able to go with you?' He pulled a book towards him, thumbed the pages, then said, 'H'm, h'm. Yes, yes, that's all right. It'll likely be early. Oh, well now' – he again looked at Abel – 'what will happen then? Well, you'll plead not guilty, and I'll ask for bail for you while the papers are being sent to the Director of Public Prosecutions, so you'll be out and about until the committal proceedings.'

'Is that the trial? And how long will I have to wait?'

'No, no, that isn't the trial, that's only . . . well, a sort of preparation. It'll take place in about three or four weeks' time. From there you'll be committed for trial at the assizes. Now where they'll be held remains to be seen, it'll be the nearest to the committal proceedings. It could be in either Newcastle or Durham.'

'Can you give me any idea what the usual penalty is for a case like this?'

'Oh.' Mr Roscommon pursed his lips in a soundless whistle. 'You could get anything up to seven years, but it all depends on who's on the bench and the prosecution. Oh yes, the prosecution. If the prosecution has a good barrister he can colour off-white to black, so it'll be up to us to get you one who can bring the black to off-white again. But don't look so down' – Mr Roscommon smiled for the first time – 'I've even known cases like this where the judge has dismissed the whole affair. It could happen if he's had trouble with his own wife.' He laughed a deep rolling chuckle now, but Abel didn't join him.

Mr Roscommon now lay back in his leather chair and rolled a pencil between his own hands as he asked, 'What is your wife like, good-looking? Appeal of any kind?'

'None whatever. To my mind she's a vixen and looks it.'

'Oh yes, yes.' Mr Roscommon nodded now. 'She would look a vixen to you because you're prejudiced, but you must remember, all men, and especially those in court, won't be seeing her through your eyes, it'll be what she sounds like that could sway the balance. Anyway' – Mr Roscommon rose suddenly to his feet – 'I've got a lot of work to do on this so I'll bid you goodbye until tomorrow morning.'

Abel was already at the door and when the small man held out his hand he took it, and as the solicitor shook it he said cheerily, 'There's one thing in your favour, there's a war on; people's views have changed, widened. The powers that be have more important things to deal with than family issues, and who knows the judge might think you're worth more to the country in the factory than in gaol. Part time, you said, and you run a cycle repair business as well?'

'Yes.'

'Ah well, funny thing to say, but this war has come as a god-send to many. Good day to you.'

'Good day.'

As in a daze, Abel threaded his way through the typing room, along the corridor, past the outer office where Miss Wilton's eyes seemed to be waiting for him, and down the stairs into the street.

There's a war on. He had forgotten for a moment there was a war on. He had forgotten that he had spent hours of the night helping to clear the debris of a house almost brick by brick so the joists wouldn't crush an old woman and her dog, both still alive in the basement of the house. He had forgotten that they had let him down through the cross beams that were supporting half an intact wall that tended any minute to collapse. He had forgotten that he'd had to prise the dog from the old woman's arms before he could lift her and push her upwards, all the while she crying for the dog. He had lifted the dog very gently, for its back legs were badly crushed, he didn't think it had long to survive. They had pulled him up through the hole only just in time, and when a few seconds later he had stood and watched the wall cave in he felt physically sick.

Of a sudden he again felt sick and very tired; and oh God! he had the desire to cry. He must get home, home to Florrie.

6

The house was quiet . . . dead. Dick was still asleep.
It was only half past five in the morning; the town
was not yet astir, but even when it was the house
would still appear dead.

She put the kettle on the gas ring and went about
the usual routine of brewing the first cup of tea, and
while it was brewing she pulled the damper out of
the fire, placed some pieces of coal gently on the top
of the still hot ashes and raked the fire, the dead ash
falling into the pan underneath the grate. Then
having poured herself out a cup of tea, she sat
down, not in the big wooden chair, she never sat in
that now, but on a kitchen chair near the table.

While sipping her tea she stared at the blackout
frame fixed over the kitchen window. Her
thoughts were jumping from one thing to another,
as they were in the habit of doing these days, always
avoiding the main issue. There hadn't been a raid
now for three weeks. It was a pity, because she
wished one would blow the place to smithereens,
with just her in it, because there was nothing more
to live for. Everybody in the world seemed to have
something to live for except her. Dick was always
trying to hide the fact that he had a lot to live for.

What would she have done without Dick these past weeks, and Molly too; they had both been wonderful. But it was Dick who had held her in the night when during that awful fortnight she'd had the bouts of screaming. But for him, they would have put her away, sent her for treatment was how they put it. At nights now, when she got all tensed up the only thing that made her take a pull at herself was the memory of those nights of alternate screaming and laughing. She didn't know which was the worse, her screams or her laughter. The doctor said it was shock. When it stopped, she had gone back into that strange silence and in it she spent hours, even days going over her life. At the end, her mind would always ask herself the same question: What had she had from her life? And the answer would be . . . nothing, because nobody had ever really loved her. She excluded from her thoughts her supposed father because he hadn't loved her, what he had done all the years while bringing her up was hug to himself the dream of the woman who was her mother. Yet she could still think it strange that a horrible little man like that could love with such intensity.

That was the word that had been missing from her own love, intensity. She had loved Abel, but not with intensity; at least not when she married him she hadn't, and not during all those fruitless years either; not until now. Dear God! not until now, for now the feeling she had for him was all consuming. She should be hating him. She did hate him, but all the while she wanted him, she needed him, she loved him, and with intensity now, and for the first time she knew that this feeling was real love and so different from anything else she had experienced in her life. She loved him in such a way that she'd be willing to live in the house with him even if he never came within a yard of her again, but what was more telling still she would gladly live with him on his own terms, the terms that he had laid down about loving.

She rose from the chair and, going to the fire, she put more coal on it; then poured herself out a second cup of tea and sat down again. Today was the day, likely his last day of freedom; surely his last day of freedom. What would they give him? Would what she had done shorten it in any way? She had asked Dick to take the letter to his solicitor. He had hesitated, asking, 'You're not going to make it harder for him, are you?' and all she answered to that was 'No; it should help.'

She knew she would have a struggle today to stop herself from going to the court in Newcastle, she longed to look on him just once more; but she couldn't bear the thought of seeing that woman again, or their Florrie . . . But if their Florrie was wise she'd keep away. This last statement reflected the old Hilda, the authoritative Hilda, the condemning Hilda. But there again, too, her feelings towards their Florrie had changed. During her screaming period she had seen herself springing on Florrie, bearing her to the ground and beating her until she lay still, after which she had taken hold of the child and thrown it – her mind had always shut down in the scene showing where the child landed. But now her mind seemed to have put a cocoon around Florrie, it was as if she no longer existed. She didn't even think any more: I'm glad she's been made to suffer, perhaps because she fully realised that Florrie's suffering would be short, compared with her own, only the length of time he would be away from her.

Her thinking ceased abruptly as Dick came into the kitchen, and she turned to him and said, 'You're up early.'

'Yes; I've been awake for some time, I heard you come down.'

'I've just made the tea.' As she went to rise from the table he said, 'It's all right I'll get it.'

When he had poured himself out a cup of tea he sat down at the other side of the table, but before raising the cup to his lips he looked across at her. Their eyes held; then he put out his hand towards her and she placed hers in it, and when he gripped it tightly she bowed her head and bit down hard on her lip, and he said gently, 'Try not to think about it. You can't do anything, none of us can do anything, it's out of our hands.'

7

Mr Justice Hazeldean looked over the courtroom. He wished he could keep his mind on the case in hand but his whole body seemed to be bursting with relief, he could even call it joy, so much so that only his long training prevented his face from slipping into a broad smile, it even prevented him from getting up and dashing home and putting his arms around his wife because she would still be crying with relief.

Yesterday they had been childless, they had been childless since they were informed their only son was missing, presumed dead. Now this very day, this very morning they had received news that he was a prisoner-of-war. He was wounded when his plane crashed and had been in hospital since. They didn't know the extent of his wounds, but he was alive.

He made his mind return to the case proceeding. Old Benbow was in good form this morning. He was doing his prosecution with passion; he hoped for the prisoner's sake that Collins was as good with his defence. This case wasn't plain sailing, however, it wasn't just bigamy; there was the reason why this man had left his wife in the first place. Nasty business that. And now the wife – she was a little thing, the kind that Margaret called snipey – Oh dear, dear. She had started quietly enough, mouse-like in fact, but now she was haranguing her husband, in spite of Mr Benbow's efforts to calm her down . . . What was her name? Mason. Mrs Mason. Well, she was showing her true colours. H'm. H'm. One could see why it would be some-what difficult to live with a little termagant like her . . . The defence was protesting. He conceded their protest. That bit was enlightening.

He now looked towards the prisoner in the dock. He certainly had a way with women, or so it seemed, did that big fellow. If what his legal wife had just tried to bring out was true, he was now living with his illegal wife's sister. Well, well! quite a list: a mistress, a wife, an illegal wife, another mistress. That is what was known, there might be a lot still unknown. He was indeed a fellow. Yet looking at him, one wouldn't put him in the category of a Don Juan. He was big, granted, and good-looking in a way, but he had a quiet air about him. Well dressed too. He could be taken for middle-class any day in the week, but he was a working man. He gave a little chuckle inside. He was indeed a working man, four or more women! He was indeed a working man, a hard working man.

He wished Benbow would get that woman off the stand, he couldn't tolerate the sound of her voice. She was now ranting about having to support herself all these years. Oh dear me, there was the defence popping up again. He gave a quick glance at his watch. How long would the case take? It was the last before lunch. Margaret was to meet him at the club. He would like to buy her something, something big. Well, it could be worked. Harrison had a friend who had a friend in the black market, jewellery department. He chuckled again. Why not? Why not indeed! This was an occasion to be celebrated. He'd see him before he left the court.

Ah! now this was interesting – he was brought back to the case again – Mr Collins was jumping into his client's defence from the deep end, reading a letter from the illegal wife. Well, well! so the prisoner hadn't wanted to marry her; he had apparently done everything in his power not to. Well, well! But he had proposed living with her. However, she had insisted on a ceremony. H'm. H'm. What a lot of trouble she would have saved everybody if she hadn't insisted on a ceremony. And now she had written that he had been a very good husband and a wonderful father to his son. H'm. H'm.

He looked at the prisoner again. The man had changed colour. A few minutes ago he was a pasty white, now you could almost say he was blushing. There was feeling there; somehow one could say that this fellow was perhaps more sinned against than sinning. He looked the kind of fellow women wanted to mother. They always wanted to mother the big 'uns. For himself, he found that generally most big chaps were wind and water. And yet what about Arthur? Arthur was big enough and there was no wind or water about Arthur; no, he was a doer was Arthur. How many raids had he led this last year? Well, his raiding days were over now. But he wasn't dead! No! he wasn't dead. He was alive and would soon be home. The end of the war was in sight; oh yes, well in sight . . . Oh! the fellow was on the stand now and had changed his plea to guilty. Well, well! But he seemed to have nothing to say for himself. Collins was working hard in his defence pointing out the other reasons why he left his legal wife. She was a nagging woman – oh he could believe that – lazy, and cruel to their son, the evidence of which was with the young man who now had a defective ear. Why did Collins use such terms as defective ear? In the language of today it almost sounded as if the ear had gone over to the enemy. He again chuckled to himself. Why couldn't Collins simply say his hearing was affected?

He was saying that the prisoner and his child had tramped the roads for several weeks and it was mainly because he, the prisoner, wanted to make a permanent home for his son that he had taken Mrs Maxwell's offer. Ah! Ah! The prisoner didn't seem to like that bit, and Collins wasn't going to give him the chance to speak at this stage. Dear, dear. He wished he would cut it short. Anyway, he knew what sentence he was going to give the fellow.

Oh! So the wife was asking for maintenance, was she, while living with her cousin in North Shields? Oh, there she was again popping up, yelling that she was his housekeeper. Would this man need a house-keeper in a two-roomed flat. She was a little bitch of a woman, and proving herself to be a liar. He had a good mind to let the fellow go free just to spite her; he couldn't stand snipes of women. In the prisoner's shoes, he, too, would have walked out on one like this. She had said she wouldn't divorce the man, well now, if what was being hinted at now were true, he could divorce her, couldn't he? Who was his solicitor? He looked down at his notes. John Roscommon. Ah well, Roscommon. He had his standards had Roscommon, he didn't make many mistakes, and he had chosen well in the defence, too. Collins had done a good job. He had shown that fellow had a case. And yes, in a way he was a brave man for it had taken courage of a sort to be a conscientious objector in the last war, for it had been the women one had to face then. Like savages they had been, out for blood, and in many cases did actually draw it.

But then there was still that business at the beginning. Murder was a nasty thing, no matter how it came about, and as that little snipe had said there would now have been another if the deceased's family hadn't been wiped out in a raid. But now for the summing up. He'd have to read the fellow the Riot Act, but he'd do it, as Margaret would say, in a low key.

Addressing the accused, he now began:

'I would say that all this has come about through you taking the line of least resistance. There are many men with nagging wives, many men who would like to walk out, but they have a sense of their responsibility, which they pledged to both church and state when they took part in a marriage ceremony . . . Then there was the reason for your leaving your wife. I am sure it has crossed your mind that that woman in question might have been alive today but for your association with her. You could argue whether she would have been happy; that is a debatable point, no-one can justify ending a life because of unhappiness. And now we come to bigamous marriage. It says something for you that the woman with whom you went through this form of marriage speaks well of you, in fact she would like to take the whole blame on herself, and she gives you credit for refusing to marry her in a church. I suppose in your own mind you imagined you were putting things straight, at least with the Deity . . .'

He stopped here and sent a warning glance around the court to still the tittering; then he resumed: 'It was also to your credit that you did in no way profit from your association with this woman. She was head of a small but profitable business when you became associated with her. This business, I understand, is still in her name and all you have received is a moderate weekly wage; if you had been a rogue instead of just a weak man, you would, I am sure, before now have made something more of this. You could have persuaded her, no doubt, to put the business in your name, and failing that, in joint names, but you did none of these things. The only way that I can see you have profited from this association is in providing a home for yourself and your son. In the meantime you seemed to have repaid this woman with affection and kindness, so much so that she wishes you nothing but well. I —' He now looked round the court as if he were searching for a face; then he let his eyes rest for a second on Lena before going on, 'I take it from the hearing that your legal wife has no wish to divorce you, in fact she seems determined not to give you your freedom, but that, on your own saying, you will never return to her, and on the evidence I have just heard it would seem that you may have grounds yourself for divorce. But that is another matter.' He knew he shouldn't have put that bit in, but oh, he didn't like that woman's face. He paused again, looked down at his notes, then raising his head, looked straight at Abel as he ended, 'I have no need to stress that there is a war on and your services would be better employed outside than inside a gaol, but nevertheless you have broken the law and you could be sent to gaol for seven years, but because I feel, as I have stated, that you are a weak man rather than a bad one I sentence you to nine months' imprisonment.'

What did the fellow say? his lips had moved. He imagined he had said 'Thank you sir', and with relief too. He was standing straight. Ah well, with good conduct he could be out in six months, and he was the kind of fellow who would behave himself.

Now to get to the club and Margaret and see her smile the first time in weeks. That fellow didn't know it, but if it hadn't been for the news about Arthur he might just have sent him down for seven years, war or no war.

Nine months. Florrie looked at her father and he, nodding at her, said, 'Aye, and he got off light. He was damn lucky. As the old fellow said, he could have got seven years. And that wife of his, if she'd had any say in it she would have put him away for thirty. God! there was a bitch of hell if ever there was one. No wonder he walked out on her. I would have murdered her. If she's like that now what was she like in the beginning. She got up the judge's back 'cos she kept interrupting. You could see. Aye, you could see.'

Nine months. Florrie pressed the child tightly to her before laying it down on the couch; then going to the fireplace she put her hands on the mantelpiece and leant her head against it, and from there she said, 'I know he forbade me to go, but do you think that he expected me to be there after all?'

'No; don't be so bloody soft, woman, you'd have only made things worse for him. What would it have looked like? He left his first wife for a woman, then goes and marries another, and now he's living with her sister and her sitting in the courtroom! Somebody would have twigged like that bitch of hell herself because she knew all about you, she brought it out.'

'She did?' She turned quickly from the fireplace.

'Oh aye; but the judge shut her up. I'm telling you, Abel was damn lucky this morning 'cos old Hazeldean isn't noted for short sentences. I tell you, when I saw who was on the bench I thought two years at least. Oh aye, I did.' He shook his head at her.

'But nine months!'

'He'll only do six of them, and what's six months after all. Come on, buck up. Look, I'll get you a drink.' As he went towards the cabinet she said softly to him, 'Dad,' and without turning round he said, 'Aye?'

'I know you've got a decent flat now but . . . but would you mind staying with me for the next week or two. I could make the couch up here for you and . . .'

'Don't go on. I've got it all worked out, I'm staying till he comes out.'

'Thanks, Dad.'

Having poured out the two whiskies he brought them to the couch and, handing her one, he said, 'Sit down; I want to tell you something.'

When she had seated herself, he said, 'Go on, have a sip of that,' and as she did so he said, 'You haven't got only to thank the judge for his leniency this mornin', if it hadn't been for her' – he jerked his head – 'things might have gone pretty black for 'im.'

'You mean . . . ?'

'I mean Hilda.'

Florrie moved to the edge of the couch before she asked, 'Was she there?'

'No. No, but she had sent a letter.'

'A letter?'

'Aye. The solicitor read it out. It said that she had practically forced him into the marriage and he had been good to her. She said that he had never done her out of a penny, and he could have, he could have grabbed the whole business and gone off. Or words to that effect. Anyway, I thought I was listening to a miracle, I couldn't believe it was our Hilda writing that letter. She must have changed.'

After a moment, Florrie said quietly, 'I'll owe her that an' all. I've . . . I've put her through an awful time. I feel guilty about it. All the time I feel guilty about it.'

'It was nobody's fault but her own. She pushed him into it, dragged him into it, an' by her own admittance. The judge said he was weak.'

'He's not weak!' Her tone was vehement. 'He's kind, too kind.'

'Well, have it your own way, but I would say he was soft, damn soft for not putting up a stand against her getting him into the registry office. Anyway, as I see it, she's got his sentence halved this mornin' 'cos he had nothing going for him until that letter was read out. An' why do prosecutors have more to say than them that are standing for the defence, eh? My God! you should have heard how that fellow went at him. It was as if Hitler was being tried. But you know, prosecution or defence, it's all a bloody game with them 'cos as I waited outside to give a nod to Abel there they were, the two of them, walking along together grinning like Cheshire cats, in fact I heard them laughing as they went through the door. Bugger me eyes! what chance has anybody got. I'd like to bet they have it all cut and dried afore they go into that place.' He swallowed the rest of the whisky and as he put the glass down on a table he moved his head slowly as he said, 'But I'm still surprised he only got nine months.'

Nine months; but he could be out in six. Even so, she could see the days stretching away, seven days a week, four weeks in a month. Twenty-four of them before she saw him again! No, it needn't be. She suddenly turned and lifted up the baby. She could go and see him. Of course. Of course. What was she thinking about? She could visit him. Last night they had talked about everything under the sun but not about the possibility of visiting him in prison. The last words he said to her this morning as he held her tightly were, 'Whatever happens, remember there's only you, there'll only ever be you.'

Oh! Abel. Abel.

'Come on, lass, come on. Enough of that now! There's the bairn to see to, an' life's got to be lived.' He gave a rumbling laugh before he added, 'As long as Hitler keeps his bloody bombs to hissel.'

8

The Reverend Gilmore took up his characteristic pose, that of joining his hands together at his waist and bending slightly forward, as he said, 'I must talk to you, Hilda; it's important, important to both of us. Shall we sit down?'

'I'd rather not, I'm . . . I'm busy.'

The vicar showed no undue surprise at her attitude towards him and he demonstrated this with his words as he said, 'I understand exactly how you're feeling, and what you have suffered these past months. No-one knows better than I do, or has felt more for you, but now I must speak plainly.' He straightened his body slightly before going on. 'You know I have been a friend to you for years, you have sought my advice and I've always given it to you honestly, but now I . . . well, I haven't come here to give you any advice, I've come here to ask you a question . . .'

'I wish you wouldn't, Mr Gilmore.'

'Why?'

'Just because I don't want to hear your question.'

'So you know what it is?'

'I've a pretty good idea.' As she turned from him, his hand shot out suddenly and caught at her arm and she became still; then moving her head slowly to the side she looked at him, and when he said, 'I'm offering you marriage, Hilda, honourable marriage,' she asked tersely, 'The same as you persuaded me to go through with Mr Maxwell?'

His chin went up, his body straightened, but he still retained his hold on her, and his voice changed now as he said quickly, 'You weren't exactly a young girl, you knew what to expect from that proposition.'

'I didn't, not really. No, I didn't, and I was a young girl, innocent.'

'Then you deceived me, Mr Maxwell, and yourself also; but . . . but now Hilda.' He made to draw her to him and he showed his astonishment when she snapped her arm from his grasp and, looking him straight in the face, said, 'Mr Gilmore, I wouldn't marry you if you were the last man on God's earth, and I don't thank you for the offer either. Looking back, you have caused more harm in my life than good, at least you have caused me to create more harm in it than good.'

'Hilda! Hilda! How dare you say such a thing.' He was genuinely shocked and showed it. 'You have changed. This disaster that has fallen upon you has changed your character entirely.'

'Well, if that's so I've got the disaster to thank for something positive. And look, as I said, I'm busy and . . . and I would like you to leave. And furthermore you needn't expect to see me in church again.'

The Reverend Gilmore was stunned into silence, but seeming to remember his vocation, he apparently forced himself to work at it now, saying slowly, 'Whatever you feel about me, Hilda, you mustn't take it out on God. It's not going to help you at all denying the Almighty.'

'I'm not denying the Almighty, I'm only telling you that I won't seek Him under your guidance again, I'll find my own way to God, at least I hope so.'

'I hope so too. Indeed I hope so.' His tone was like that of a schoolmaster who had lost a battle with a pupil; and he glared down on her for a moment before stalking from the room, and if the resounding clash echoing from the front door was anything to go by it proved that the vicar was more than a little put out.

Hilda sat down on the couch and, leaning her elbow on the arm, drooped her head on to the support of her hand as she asked herself how she had put up with that man's sanctimonious twaddle all these years. But to go for him as she had done proved without doubt the change in her. She couldn't recognise herself. There had been times of late when she was a little afraid of what was happening to her. Things that she would have condemned a year ago, and verbally to Abel, thereby arousing his quiet disdain or open angry comment, now didn't even attract her notice.

On nights when, afraid to stay in the house alone, she waited at the open gateway for Dick returning from his late shift, or from taking Molly to the pictures, and watched the uniformed men going by, their arms round girls, making for the outskirts and lonely lanes, she no longer thought: Scandalous! it should be put a stop to. A different one every night no doubt. She just let them pass without mental comment. Perhaps the sight of the entwined figures aroused somewhere in the hitherto shuttered depths of her a feeling akin to jealousy.

Last night while sitting wide-eyed, propped up against the pillows, she had asked herself, would she now willingly make Abel happy if she was given the chance, and her answer had been that it was a stupid question, because she would never get the chance. A woman like her never got a second chance, second chances were doled out to people like Florrie who weren't afraid to take them; to people who grabbed at life, and lived it, lived it as if each day was their first and last.

On the sound of three hoots of a car horn penetrating the house, she pulled herself up from the couch. The signal meant that Arthur was in need of help. That was another thing she hadn't realised, all the work that Abel had done in the yard. He had not only done the repairs to the odd car they got in, but repaired all the bikes, and that was a no mean feat when he had to literally make his own spare parts. He had also seen to the running of the business. She had imagined that she was running the whole show because she did the books, but during the past months she had learned differently. She had also learned that Arthur Baines didn't work for her as he had done for Abel; she was a woman, and as she heard him say, she didn't know a chassis from a bumper or a three-speed from an inner tube. She could have enlightened him on these points, but she knew that if she had words with him, he would walk out, men were scarce, even old men.

She was tired of the business, she was tired of everything. Perhaps when the war ended Dick would take the business over and she would retire . . . and do what? Go on coach tours, like the widows with money did before the war; go on a sea voyage hoping to find another man. No, she mustn't give up the business, and war or no war she must let Arthur Baines know she was still here. But oh, the effort.

As she opened the kitchen door she saw Dick hurrying up the yard. It was his day off from the factory and he had been out since eight o'clock this morning and now it was just on four. She never asked him where he went because most times when he went out without Molly she knew where he was bound for. Time and again she had wanted to ask him how Abel was taking things, but she couldn't bring herself to do it; and he never mentioned his father. With him leaving early this morning, she guessed where he was going.

She stepped back into the kitchen. Arthur Baines could get on with it whatever it was.

She waited for Dick's coming, and he smiled at her as he came into the room. As he took off his coat he said, 'Phew! I'm hot . . . You all right?'

'Yes.'

'Anything happened?'

'No. Oh well, I had a visit from Mr Gilmore.'

'Oh!'

'I . . . I don't think he'll be back again.'

'No?' Dick showed his surprise, and she shook her head and, her face unsmiling, she said, 'No; he made me an offer of marriage.'

'Oh Lord!'

'Yes, oh Lord!'

'I'm . . . I'm sorry. You refused him? You did, didn't you?'

'Yes.'

'He's got a nerve. At his age! he's near retirement I should say.'

'I think he's past it, he's only being kept on because of the war. Anyway, as I said, he won't be coming back again, and I won't be going to hear him.'

'You're not going to church any more?' Dick could not prevent his eyebrows from rising.

'Not his anyway; perhaps not any, it'll all depend how great the need is.'

Impulsively he caught hold of her hand, and when her head dropped on to her chest as she muttered, 'Oh Dick!' he put his arms around her and said, 'There now. There now.'

When she drew herself away from him she blinked her eyes and rubbed her hand over lips before asking, 'Have you had anything to eat?'

'No; I'm starving.'

'Well, hang on just a minute, I've got a casserole in the oven. I'll just slip down and see what Arthur wants, then I'll get you something.'

. . . By the time she returned he had set the table for both of them and she looked towards it, saying,

'Oh good!' then having heaped his plate with the food she put it before him.

He looked at it, then from it to her and said, 'What about you?'

'I'm not hungry.'

'You should eat.'

There was a vestige of a smile on her lips now as she said, 'At one time you were always telling me I was eating too much.'

'Yes, I know, but now you're eating too little, the flesh is dropping off you.'

'Well, that's all for the best, I'm getting a figure for the first time in me life.'

He took up his knife and fork, but dropping his hands to either side of his plate he looked down on the food as he said, 'I saw him today and from what I can gather he'll be out in a couple of weeks or so.'

He now raised his eyes to hers and she said quietly, 'I'm glad. Believe me' – she nodded her head – 'I'm glad. I won't begin to know any peace until he's free.'

'He asked after you.'

She stared at him for a full minute before she said, 'Don't be kind, Dick; I'd rather you didn't.'

He dropped the knife and fork on to the table and, bending forward, he said, 'I'm not being kind. I've never said this before, have I, and I've been to see him a number of times. I tell you he asked after you. What he said was just simple. "How's Hilda?" he said. I think he realises better than anybody that his stretch would have been two or three times the length it is if it hadn't been for that letter you wrote.'

She walked round the table, then went to the fire-place before she said, 'It . . . it was as little as I could do. I hadn't played fair by him no more than he had played fair by me. I . . . I never made him happy. You understand?' She turned her head to the side. 'I felt I owed him something. If . . . if I'd been sensible and not been so damned hidebound he might never had gone to our Florrie, even . . . even though I knew he was struck on her from the first.'

Dick stared across the table at the bowed head. It wasn't the first time she had said damn over the last months, nor used the term, my God! How she had changed. His dad wouldn't recognise her. What a pity it was all too late.

As he looked at her now he knew he felt for her as if she were his mother, his real mother; and she had been a mother to him for years. That other woman, that woman in the court that day, God above! if he had blamed his father before for Alice and the consequences of his association with Alice, the sight of his mother that day in the court lifted all blame from him. She was a little hell-cat, a mean-faced little hell-cat. He felt there was no part of her in him and he had actually prayed to God that when he and Molly married and they had bairns none of them would be a throw-back to their granny.

She had collared him in the street after the trial. He had avoided her earlier in the court corridors but when she stopped dead in front of him in the street and said, 'Well, we haven't grown much, have we?' he was back in the cottage and she was yelling at him: 'Well! where have you been? Pick this up!

Pick that up! Take that!' Every time he thought of it he was made aware of the slight deafness in his left ear. What she said next had inflamed him: 'Well, he's got his deserts at last.'

For answer, he had almost shouted at her, 'It's a pity you didn't get yours,' on which he had turned from her and she had yelled after him, 'Like father like son, thankless sods!'

The encounter had been brief, a matter of minutes but he hoped he'd never come face to face with her again.

He pushed the plate to one side, rose from his chair, and went round the table and, putting his hands on Hilda's shoulders, said, 'I want to say something to you I've never said before, and it's this. I . . . I look upon you as me mother. I always have done since I came to live in this house. I'm not going to call you Aunt Hilda any more, from now you're going to be me mam, because that's what you've been to me. And I want to thank you for all the care and attention you've given me over the years . . .'

'Aw Dick! Dick!' Her voice cracked, the tears sprang from her eyes; then, her mouth agape, there issued forth a long drawn out wail and he pulled her towards him and pressed her face tightly into his shoulder but crying roughly now, 'Stop it! Don't start that again. You're over all that. Now listen to me, stop it!'

When her crying didn't ease, he thrust her from him and taking her by the shoulders, actually shook her, even while he gulped in his own throat. 'Now

363

look,' he said, 'I've got a couple of hours before I'm due on duty an' I want to have a bath an' get changed, then go and see Molly, but I won't be able to do anything if you don't stop it. Now then! And that's another thing I want to say to you. Molly's on duty up Primrose Square way, and I'm at the school tonight. Now they've been shorthanded there for a week or more since Mrs Ratcliffe went down with flu, so what about you coming and taking over the phone, it'll be better than sitting here alone?'

'I . . . I couldn't.' She was drying her face now on the tea towel that she had grabbed from the rod, and she almost choked as he pulled her round to him again and said, 'Yes, you could. Look, I'm worried stiff when you're left here on your own, you won't go into the shelter . . . I never know what you're up to.'

'The raids have slackened, there hasn't been any for ages, likely won't be any more . . .'

'Oh, what about the doodle-bugs over the south coast. It could be our turn next. Look, I'm having no more arguments, you're coming so that's that. And now, if you don't mind, I'll have me clay cold dinner.' He stared at the table now and demanded, 'Where's me tea? And don't say I shouldn't drink tea with meat 'cos I've always drunk tea with meat.'

His rough strategy worked. She put the kettle on and began to busy herself around the kitchen, and as he looked at her his heart felt sore for her. She'd had a rotten deal. She had her faults, but who hadn't. And she hadn't deserved what she had got.

Of a sudden he thought if it wasn't for Florrie his dad would come back here and things would be different for both of them. But Florrie was deep in father's life, as firm and lasting as the concrete base of a bridge.

There were only ten minutes to go before he was relieved. He looked towards where Hilda was sitting in front of the stove. She looked tired. He smiled at her and nodded towards the clock, and then he looked to where Henry Blythe stood laughing with George Thompson as they pointed out to each other some of the children's crayon drawings tacked to the partition, and it was just as Henry Blythe said, 'I think that's supposed to be a Messerschmitt, he's made it the size of a matchstick, but he's made the Lancaster bomber almost a foot long,' that the siren screamed overhead. They all turned and stared at one another; then almost simultaneously they said the same words: 'Oh no! it's six weeks.' They were scrambling now for their tin hats and overcoats and Henry Blythe, turning to Hilda said, 'Do you think you can see to the phone?'

'Yes, but I . . . I won't be here by myself though, will I?'

He looked at her somewhat in surprise, then said, 'No, no; someone'll be along of you, although he might have to dash off for a while. It all depends on . . .'

Dick interrupted him, saying to Hilda, 'It's all right, don't worry. Just sit down there' – he led her round the desk – 'and if any calls come in write them

down. One of us must be here to run the errands.'
He smiled at her.

George Thompson now said, 'I'll go round the
building, Mary and Ronnie Biggs are on the north
side but Hannah Farrow is by herself on the road.'
He buttoned up his coat, adjusted his tin helmet,
then went out.

'Well, I might as well make another pot of tea.'
Henry Blythe took up the teapot and walked
towards the kitchen, and as he did so the sound of
the pop-pop of the anti-aircraft guns came to them.
Looking towards Hilda, Dick said, 'Don't worry.
Don't worry. They're at the far side of the town; in
fact, I think they're beyond it. It could be Gateshead
or Newcastle.'

When Dick next heard the sound of the anti-
aircraft guns he knew they weren't at a distance but
inside the town now. Bog's End way, which meant
the docks, but as yet there was no sound of any
explosion.

Minutes passed. Henry Blythe returned with the
enamel teapot full of tea and proceeded to fill
three mugs. It was just as he handed one across the
wooden table to Hilda that the whole school
building shook. By the time the next explosion
rocked them the three of them were crouched
under the Morrison shelter that was placed against
the wall of the classroom. The building shuddered
again with a third explosion, then a fourth.

There followed a silence, and in it they crawled
from the shelter and stood up.

When the phone rang it was Henry Blythe who

leant over the table and picked it up, and he nodded three or four times before putting it down. Turning to Dick, he said, 'Bottom of Brampton Hill got it bad. They must have got wind of the factory but they missed that. It seems a number of the big houses are levelled. They want help, all they can get. I'll go down and take the others with me. You'll be all right here, Dick, you'll carry on . . .'

'Mr Blythe, if . . . if you don't mind I'd rather go. You see . . . well' – he glanced towards Hilda and found her staring wide-eyed at him – 'I . . . I have an aunt down there, lives in number forty-six, I'd just like to make sure, if it's all right with you.'

'Oh, it's all right with me, get yourself off. Only tell the others.'

. . . Long before he came to the top of the hill he was running in the glow of flames, and when he came to the brow and looked downwards his stomach seemed to turn over inside its casing. They had said the bottom of Brampton Hill. It might be towards the bottom but the houses that were blazing were just past the middle and forty-six was just past the middle.

Further down the hill he had to thread his way around fire engines, over hose pipes and through milling men; and then he came to where the gate had been, and he looked towards the blaze at one end of the house, then to the enormous heap of tangled wood, brick and mortar at the other. He now ran to where they were guiding people into ambulances and his voice sounded high and cracked as he asked one uniformed man after another: 'Forty-six. Are these out of forty-six?' and got such answers as, 'Where's forty-six? There's about six of them down.'

Pushing, he now made his way up what had been the drive. In the glow from the fire he could see that one end wall of the big house was still standing and, as if floating in the air, a part of the third storey. It had likely been the attic and was held by a section of roof, which in turn was being held by the remaining wall.

The noise and confusion, the smell of burning, the mingled cries of people who were still able to cry, whirled around him, making him sick and dizzy.

'Look, catch hold of this!' The end of a large timber was thrust into his arms and without any protest he backed with it while two other men pulled it gently from a pile of rubble. When it had been laid on the ground he hurried forward and said, 'The . . . the garden flat.'

'What?' The man turned a face to him that looked as if it had been freshly powdered.

'The garden flat. There was a garden flat.'

'Everything's flat, chum, you can see for yersel'.'

'The people, the people inside.'

'Look' – the man rounded on him – ' we don't know who was inside or how many; we'll be lucky if we find out by mornin'. Now if you want to make yourself useful get at them stones and move them gently.'

He didn't do as he was bidden and start moving the stones, but he scrambled over the strewn debris and round what he thought was the corner of the house and to where the garden flat had been. There was no sign of it, at least above ground. What was here was a huge hole. There were men round it. Pulling at the sleeve of one, he stammered, 'Ha . . . ha . . . have you got anybody out?'

'Not yet. There was a shelter underneath, there was bound to be somebody in it.'

'There . . . there was someone in the flat above an' all, my aunt and her child and . . . and her father.'

'Oh!' The man was shouting now. 'There were two adults and a bairn here, this is a relative.' The man turned to him again. 'You sure they were in?'

'They . . . they were bound to be, the baby's young. She . . . she doesn't go out at nights.'

'Well, all I can say, lad, it's a pity she didn't go out this night in particular; can't see anybody standing a chance down there. Still, we'll have a go now we've got something sure to go on.'

When the man started giving directions Dick said, 'I'll . . . I'll help. I must see—' he couldn't finish and say, 'if they're dead or alive'; as the man said there was little hope.

'Well, gently does it. Straddle that beam if you can.' He swung an arc light from a standing support towards the hole. 'You're about the lightest of us, ease yourself along it. Go careful because it's at a steep angle, but once you feel it give, stop.'

Dick threw his leg over the beam, then cautiously hitched himself forward. The sweat was raining from his face as he glanced downwards into the

tangled debris of wood, brick, and, what now made
him want to retch, recognisable pieces of Florrie's
furniture. She had loved her furniture. Oh Florrie!
Florrie! Oh Dad! Dad!

He was brought sharply from his moaning
thought by the man shouting, 'It's steady then?' and
after a moment he called back. 'Yes, quite steady.
It . . . it seems fixed tight.' He pointed to where the
beam disappeared into a mass of stones.

The man's voice came to him again, shouting,
'Well and good, we'll take it from there.'

And so they took it from there. He became lost
in time. He was aware, yet unaware, that his back
was breaking, his arms were snapping, his throat
was choked with dust, his clothes were torn and
covered with lime. For how long he and the other
members of the team were in the hole at a stretch
he had no idea. He only knew that they lifted blocks
of stone that would in ordinary times have denied
any combined human effort; that they passed pieces
of furniture from one to the other, those pieces that
couldn't be pulled up were put in a sling, or were
roped.

It was some time in the early dawn when a fresh
set of men took over and he was hauled up from the
hole, which was now much deeper than when he
had first dropped into it. It was as he sat on a pile
of rubble that he became aware of Hilda and Molly.
Molly was carrying mugs of tea from a Salvation
Army canteen trolley, but whatever Hilda had been
doing she had stopped and was now standing
staring at him, and he, because of his exhaustion,

said no word to her but dropped his head into his hands.

It was Molly who brought his head up as she pressed a mug of tea into his hand. He had just finished drinking it when a shout came from the hole; 'Someone here.'

He pulled himself quickly to his feet; then the three of them moved forward. He could not see what was happening down below until the men on the rim of the hole moved aside and a form was laid gently on the rubble. It was that of a woman, but not the one that was in their minds.

'There's a number here in the corner, some alive I think.'

They were now pushed back, and all they could do was to wait.

As each figure was hauled up from the shelter they looked down on it. A few were groaning, the majority would never groan again.

They all now seemed to lose count of time until a distant voice yelled, 'God! I think there's a bairn here. Aye, aye; yes, there is.' At this Dick pressed forward and lowered himself once more down into the mangled depths. As he went to scramble over the head of Florrie's couch that was sticking end up a man gripped his arm and said, 'Steady! Wait on. Steady.'

'The bairn, is it alive?'

'Aye, yes, I should say so, we heard it whimpering. But it's fast under a woman; she must be lying over the cot.'

Dick threw his lower lip tightly between his teeth;

then he said quietly, 'Let me give a hand, she's . . . she's a relative.'

'We'll all give a hand, mate, but slowly does it. Don't go too close. Help to move this stuff here so as to make the way clear for her when they get to her. She's fast held across her back from what I can see, but it's just her arm caught in the front.'

Dick looked in the direction in which the man was pointing, but all he could make out at first was bits of twisted wood that could be remains of anything. Then he saw the broken bedhead over which was draped a narrow strip of velvet curtain. He knew it was velvet and he knew it was red; Florrie had them hanging both in the bedroom and her sitting-room . . . And then he saw the form, at least the humped back. He couldn't see the legs, and from the top of the hump an arm protruded; the head and the other arm were lost behind a jagged slab of plaster.

Quickly and silently they worked now, passing the debris from one hand to another. Once he stopped and muttered, 'It hasn't cried again,' and the man said simply, 'No.'

When they managed to dislodge the piece of plaster that was covering her head, it also exposed part of the cot over which she was lying, and at that moment the cry came again from the baby. They stopped all activity for a moment to listen to the loud, natural, hungry cry.

'Careful, careful. Easy, easy.'

These words were said over and over again; then they were changed to, 'There you are then. There you are then,' and at this point he saw that one of the men had eased the child from under Florrie's contorted body. He didn't pass it to the man next to him, but came stumbling over the rubble with it, saying, 'There doesn't seem to be a scratch on it, its face is hardly dirty. And that's a healthy yell, isn't it?' Then he stopped as Dick said, 'I'll take it, it's . . . it's my niece.' He could have said, 'my sister', but that would have complicated matters.

Yet when the man put the child into his arms he knew he couldn't get out of the hole with it, he knew he'd have to pass it on. But now lifting his head, he shouted as he held out the child to further waiting arms, 'Give it to my . . . my mother. She's up there waiting.'

Hilda and Molly were standing some way back from the hole now but they heard clearly each word that Dick had yelled, and they glanced at each other. Then Hilda drooped her head forward and looked towards the ground; but only for a moment before she took four slow steps to where the men were standing waiting. When the dust-laden bundle appeared over the rim of the hole as it passed from one set of arms to another, she stared at it, her body stiff, her arms by her sides, until there was a movement from a Red Cross uniformed figure beside her; then her arms almost shot out and child was in them, Florrie's child, Abel's child.

'All right, missis?'

She moved her head once.

'You'll see to her? There'll be a doctor at the dressing-station wagon if you want him.'

Again she moved her head.

Molly was at her side now, and Hilda turned to her and went to speak, but no sound came from her throat. She coughed and swallowed deeply before bringing out in a cracked voice, 'I'll . . . I'll have to get her home and . . . and cleaned up. Will you stay and see what's happened to . . . to our Florrie?'

'Yes, yes, I'll do that. Can you manage?'

Hilda merely nodded as she moved away, her head bent over the baby.

Molly watched her for a moment; then she turned swiftly back towards the hole again, there to see a man carrying a medical bag being lowered down into it. Her voice a whisper, she asked the man next to her, 'Is she . . . is she alive . . . the mother?'

'I don't know, lass, but somebody down there is, they've just called for a doctor. This one they're bringing up now though doesn't look as if there's any life left in him.'

Molly now looked down on the thin crumpled figure they were laying out on the stones. Although the face was covered with lime she immediately recognised Mr Donnelly and she thought, Poor soul! Poor soul!

She didn't know how many times she repeated these words during the next half-hour, or was it an hour, until she found Dick standing by her side. She hadn't noticed when he came up, all her attention had been on the makeshift stretcher to which one of the victims was strapped. When Dick stumbled away, she went by his side holding on to his arm, and she was surprised when his steps took them over the tangle of pipes running from the fire engines, past the row of army lorries, and towards the still standing wall that separated the garden from the street. Here, pulling himself gently from her hold, he leant his face against the stone and began to cry. Molly said no word as she turned him from the wall and into her arms, until he straightened up and, drying his face, said, 'I'm sorry.'

'Don't be silly . . . Is . . . is she dead?'

'No.' He shook his head. 'Perhaps it would be better if she were. The doctor had to take one arm off and her foot is crushed, and her back's got it worst of all I think.'

'Poor, poor, Florrie.' Molly's voice was breaking now.

'Yes, poor, poor Florrie.' He did not add, 'And poor, poor Dad.'

There was a jinx on his father, he seemed fated never to be happy. He would be torn to shreds by this latest blow of fate, blaming himself for not being with her. If he had loved her before he would love her more now . . . if she lived. And she must live, at least until he came out, otherwise . . . well . . . His mind refused to take him further.

9

The child lay gurgling in its new cot. She kept the
cot mostly in the kitchen where she could keep
looking at the child. She wanted to keep looking at
it; she sat for hours looking at it, whether it was
awake or asleep. She kept telling herself not to do
this, she kept telling herself that she only had it for
a short time, she kept telling herself that Abel would
be out any day now and he would take the child . . .
But where would he take it? He had nowhere to
take it to. She was going to tell Dick today to tell
him that she would look after it until he got settled,
and she knew that that would take some time
because wherever he went it would have to be a
place where a wheel-chair could be taken in. And
another thing, Florrie wouldn't be out of hospital
for weeks, months, so she could have the child with
her all that time . . . That's if he agreed to let her
stay. But what was the alternative? He could put
her in the care of a council home. No, no; she
wouldn't stand that. She'd even go to him herself.

Turning from placing a kettle on the stove, she
went to the cot and, bending over it, she smiled and
chuckled down into the laughing face, saying,
'There now. There now. You're either laughing or

you're crying, and either means you want to be lifted up, doesn't it? Doesn't it?'

Having given herself the usual excuse to hold the child, she was about to take it from the cot when she heard Dick's familiar quick step coming up the yard, and she straightened herself and went back to the sink. She was scouring it out when he opened the door.

Any faint semblance of the boy that might have remained up till a week ago was gone, so also had the stammer and the twitch to his shoulder, which in a lesser form had persisted even after the court case. Stark reality had replaced the subconscious fears.

He didn't speak, but going to the cot he looked down on the child. Then he took off his coat and threw it over the back of the chair before walking towards the fire. After staring down at it for a moment, he said, 'I couldn't tell him.'

She turned sharply towards him now, saying, 'You should have; he's got to be told some time.'

Slowly sitting down in the wooden armchair, he said, 'I daren't risk it, not in that place. He might have gone berserk and tried to escape, and it's only another week or so. He . . . he couldn't understand why she hadn't come. I told him she'd had a bad dose of flu. By the way' – he turned his head towards her – 'I . . . I called at the hospital on my way back. She would like to see you.'

'What!' Her hand went to her throat. 'She said that?'

'Yes.'

She, too, now sat down.

'You'll go?'

She moved her head slowly from side to side while looking down towards the floor. 'I . . . I don't know; I don't think I could face her.'

'You shouldn't hold anything against her now.'

'Oh, I don't. I don't.' Her head was up and shaking now. 'It's just that . . . well —' She rose from the chair, her fingers twisting each other as if her intent was to wring them off. Then with her back to him, she muttered, 'I've wished her ill, I . . . I don't think I could face her.'

He came and put his arm around her shoulder; then on a small laugh, he said, 'Join the gang.'

'What?' She turned her head up quickly towards him as he said, 'Molly went through purgatory because she had wished her mother dead. For years and years I wished my mother dead so that Dad wouldn't have to go through what he is going through now. Retaliation is a natural feeling, we all experience it. You go and see her. She needs someone, someone belonging to her.'

'No, that's silly. We don't belong, you know that.'

'Yes, you do; you were brought up belonging. Birth has nothing to do with it, it's the early years you spend together I think that matter. Why do I feel about you the way I do and not about the woman who bore me? Come on.' He squeezed her to him for a moment. 'We'll go along together tonight; Molly will look after the bairn. But now' – he released his hold on her and pushed her gently

378

away from him – 'I'd consider it a favour if I was offered a cup of tea.'

This gentle bullying of her about his food and drink was the only tactic he seemed able to use in an effort to divert her, but she didn't smile at him, she merely bowed her head and went towards the stove and took the kettle off and mashed a pot of tea.

The nurse had opened the ward doors and the horde of visitors had swarmed in, scattering to this side and that as if driven by a powerful wind, but Hilda still stood in the corridor. Her body stiff, her throat tight, she looked pleadingly at Dick now as she said, 'You go in first, go on, please. I'd rather see her on my own . . . Just sort of prepare her.'

He shook his head for a moment, then turned away, and she remained standing where she was, waiting. But when she saw him returning in a matter of minutes her eyes widened and she shook her head slowly in protest against a sudden thought, but he reassured her, smiling and saying, 'It's all right, she's just been moved into a side ward, number two.' He turned and pointed. 'That's it.'

'Is she worse?'

'I don't know. Just stay put.'

She stayed put for five minutes this time and when the door opened and he came out unsmiling now, he said to her, 'She's got to go down again to the operating theatre, in the morning.'

'It's bad?'

'Well, she doesn't look any different, but . . . but

I think there's something gone wrong with . . . with her spine. Go on.' He pushed her gently. 'She's waiting for you.'

She moved towards the door, she went through it, she was in the room, then she was standing looking at the stranger lying flat in the narrow bed. Oh my God! my God! she couldn't move either backwards or forwards until the voice, the known voice, said, 'Hello, Hilda.'

She had to force her legs towards the bed, and then she was looking down on to the face that she had been jealous of all her remembered life.

'How are you?' It wasn't her asking the question but Florrie. What could you say to that? She moved her head, and when the tears rolled down her cheeks Florrie said, 'Now, now. Look.'

'I'm . . . I'm sorry.' The words were the most sincere Hilda had ever spoken in her life, and in answer to them Florrie said, 'It's me who should be saying I'm sorry, Hilda. You've . . . you've gone through so much, and . . . and I've added to it. It's been on my mind. Yes, I'm the one that should say, "I'm sorry".'

Hilda closed her eyes for a second and when she opened them she found herself staring down on to the one hand that lay limp on the top of the bed cover. Then her eyes travelled to the cage covering the bottom of the bed and in her imagination she saw the mangled foot. She'd had lovely feet, lovely legs; she had always envied her her legs, long, slim, springing legs. Her own had always been short and thick. But hers were still whole. Oh God! God! why had this to happen? She wouldn't have wished this on the devil himself. And at this moment she felt that she was the cause of it all. It had all come about through her thinking.

'How is Lucy?'

'She's . . . she's fine. Oh yes, she's fine.'

'I'm glad you've got her, Hilda. Hilda . . . sit down a minute.'

She drew the chair up to the bed and sat down, her hands tight gripped in her lap, and she stared at Florrie, whose head was now turned towards her on the pillow, and as she waited for her to speak she thought, 'There's nothing recognisable about her except her eyes; and they were like saucers, full of pain.

'Will you listen to me for a moment, Hilda?'

'Yes, yes, anything, Florrie.'

'We've . . . we've got to speak of him . . . Abel, he'll . . . he'll be out shortly. Dick hasn't told him, so he's going to get a shock. And . . . and he'll have nowhere to go. Would you . . . would you take him back, Hilda?'

Hilda screwed up her eyes tight for a moment and, her head bowed deeply on her chest and her voice merely a muttering whimper, she said, 'He wouldn't come back to me, Florrie, it's the last thing on God's earth he would do. He'd never come back.'

'You don't know, Hilda. He'll . . . he'll want to be where the child is.'

'He'll . . . he'll likely get a place and take it with him.'

'Well, he's got to find a place first. In any case he'll have to work, and the child will need looking after. He'll . . . he'll leave her with you, I'm sure he will for the time being. He . . . he owes you that at least. That's if you'll look after her. You don't mind looking after her?'

Almost by an involuntary action Hilda's head jerked upwards as she said, 'Oh no! Florrie, no. I want to look after her. She's a lovely bairn.'

'Thanks, Hilda. I . . . I don't deserve it.'

'Oh, be quiet.' Hilda's head was hanging again until Florrie said, 'They say I'm going to be all right, but . . . but I don't believe them, because I . . . I can't move my back or my legs. But even if I get through, what kind of a life lies ahead? A wheel-chair at best.' She turned her face away now and the muscles of her throat contracted before she added, 'And then that would mean a sort of bungalow. In any case I'm going to be a handicap, and no man, no matter how good he is, would want to be saddled with such a handicap.'

'He will.'

Florrie brought her face round again and looked at Hilda. Their eyes held tightly for a moment until Florrie, closing hers, brought out on a note of pain. 'Oh Hilda! Hilda! I'm sorry. I'm sorry.' When her mouth opened wide and the tears gushed from her eyes and down her nose and a high moan escaped her, Hilda got to her feet and, bending over her, whispered, 'It's all right. It's all right. Don't you worry about me; it's yourself you've got to think about, and you'll be all right. He'll see to you, he'll never leave you. I know him, I know him. That much at any rate, I know him. It's always been you right from the beginning and I don't mind now, I don't Florrie, believe me. I . . . I just want you to get better. I'll . . . I'll look after the child until you're fit. And don't worry about him, he'll . . .'

At this point the door opened and a nurse entered and her 'Tut! tut! tut!' brought Hilda upright. But when the nurse said, 'You'd better go now,' she gripped hold of Florrie's hand and looking down into her swimming eyes, she muttered chokingly, 'Don't worry. Don't worry about a thing; it'll all pan out.'

As she left the bed she couldn't see Florrie, she could only hear her gasping cries, and she had to grope for the ward door, and when she stumbled into the corridor she almost fell against Dick and her muttering became incoherent.

When the nurse came out of the room she looked at them both and said stiffly, 'No more visiting tonight!' and Dick said flatly, 'Come on, it's no use hanging around. I'll come over in the morning and try to find out what's going on.'

He said no more and they walked in silence back to the house. The twilight was deepening, but she didn't say as at one time she would have done, 'Look, put a move on I want to get in before it's dark, there's the blackouts to see to.' Instead she walked slowly, her head bent slightly forward, her eyes directed towards the pavement; and they must have been halfway home before she said quietly,

'She wants me to take Abel back when he comes out, but I couldn't, could I?'

It was a question and he turned his head sharply towards her and stared at her for some time before he said, 'No! Oh! no.'

She looked at him now as she said, 'That's what I told her; because it's the last thing he would do, isn't it, come back?'

And now he said, 'Yes. Yes, he would never do that. It would be . . . well —' he moved his head in small jerks as if searching for a word and then came out with 'an imposition'. Then he added, 'Knowing Dad, no, he would never do that.'

'No; I told her.' She was looking ahead now and she repeated, 'He'd never do that.' Then she added almost in a whisper to herself, 'It's the last thing he'd do.'

10

The door opened and as Abel stepped out into the world again Dick hurried towards him, and he held out his hand as if he had only just been introduced to the man before him.

Abel did not immediately take Dick's hand, but when he did it wasn't to shake it, just to grip it tightly. And then he turned and gazed about him. Following this, he looked again at Dick and now he smiled, a broad smile, then asked eagerly, 'How's Florrie, is she better? I . . . I thought she would have written this last week.'

For answer Dick turned and started to walk up the street, saying quietly, 'Dad, I've something to tell you, but let's go in and have a drink. There's a pub up here, we may be lucky . . .'

When he was pulled sharply round to face his father, he gulped in his throat because the stud of his collar had jerked against his Adam's apple.

'What's wrong? Something wrong with Florrie?'

'She's . . . she's not well, Dad.'

'How not well? You said she had the flu, is it pneumonia?'

'No, no, nothing like that. Look.' He glanced about him at the people walking past, then said,

'Look, let's go in some place. Come on, it's not two minutes away.'

He had to tug on Abel's arm now to get him to move and he knew that his father had his eyes on him all the time. He led the way into the saloon bar which was empty; then going to a table in the far corner, he sat down, and when his father was sitting opposite him he looked into the tense waiting face and said, 'There was an air raid, Dad.'

He watched Abel's hand move up the side of his face and press it tightly there before he said, 'Yes?'

'She . . . she was hurt.'

'Badly?' The question was brief and sounded ordinary.

'Yes, yes, rather badly.'

Abel now leant back in the chair and, closing his eyes tightly, said, 'Let's have it, no more shilly-shallying.'

So Dick let him have it, but haltingly and through a mutter. He said, 'She's lost an arm and' – he couldn't go on for a moment, but drooped his head further and his voice was scarcely audible as he finished – 'her spine's broken.'

It was a good minute before he raised his head again and looked at his father. Abel was sitting quite still, staring straight at him but certainly not seeing him. When he did speak it was to ask a quiet question. 'She'll live?'

'Yes. Oh yes.'

'And the child . . . it went?'

'Oh no, no.' Dick now watched his father's

eyelids blink a number of times before he said, 'She's alive?'

'Yes, simply because Florrie . . . well, she lay over the cot, there wasn't a scratch on her.'

'Great God!' He shook his head, then said slowly and with some bitterness, 'She'd have been better off if she hadn't?'

'No, no, she wouldn't, Dad, she would have gone with her father, I feel sure of that.'

'Fred . . . he got it?'

'Yes.'

Abel sighed a deep, slow sigh; then almost springing up from the chair he said, 'What are we sitting here for? Come on.'

Dick didn't move. 'I've given the order, Dad. Just stay put for a minute, we'll have this drink and then we'll go. Anyway, the bus isn't due for another fifteen minutes. Come on, sit down.'

Abel sat down, and after a moment, while he held his head in his hand, he looked across at Dick and asked quietly, 'What's the matter with me, lad? Can you tell me what's the matter with me? I put the finger of disaster on everybody I touch.'

Dick made no reply, because it seemed to be true. Alice, his mother, Hilda, and now Florrie.

He now watched Abel rise quickly from the table, and he could do nothing but follow him, and as they walked towards the bus stop with no words between them now, he thought, He's never asked where the bairn is.

*   *   *

The nurse said, 'It isn't visiting time.'

'I know that but I want to see her.'

'I've told you it isn't visiting . . .'

'Get me hold of whoever's in charge, will you?'

The nurse stared at the tall, gaunt man for a moment, then turned away and went in search of the sister; and as he waited Abel looked to where Dick was standing at the far end of the corridor.

When the sister appeared she said, 'It isn't visiting hours.'

'I would like to see Mrs Ford.'

'What relation are you to her?'

'None at the moment but she's going to be my wife.'

The sister didn't raise her eyebrows but her eyes narrowed as she said, 'Your name is?'

'Mason. Abel Mason.'

'Ah yes.' The bits and pieces were dropping together in her mind to form a picture. This was the fellow she had heard about, father of the child and a bigamist into the bargain. He must have just come out. Well! well! She moved her lips in and out as she seemed to consider. She looked first at the nurse, then towards the door with number two written on it, and abruptly now she said, 'Five minutes, no longer.'

His expression didn't alter, he didn't say, 'Thanks', but he turned towards the door at which her finger was pointing and then went quickly to it and opened it.

For a moment he couldn't see her because she was lying flat and was hidden by the cage at the bottom of the bed, but when he did look down on her his heart seemed to freeze within its own cage and he held his breath for so long that he could have imagined he was drowning. She had her eyes closed, she seemed unaware of any presence in the room, perhaps she thought it was a nurse pottering. He looked quickly about him, then pulled a chair towards her and, sitting down on it, he slowly stretched his hand across the bed and picked up the one that was lying on the coverlet. At this she opened her eyes, and the start she gave caused him to say rapidly, 'There now. There now. Quiet. Quiet. It's only me.'

'Abel . . . Oh Abel!' Her hand, jerking within his, pulled itself free and moved up to his face, then over the back of his head.

When his mouth fell on hers it betrayed no vestige of his hunger; even while it lingered the fierceness and longing that was in him did not rise. When once more they looked at each other she said again, 'Oh Abel!' Her eyes were blurred with tears but his were dry, bone dry, with a hard dryness that pricked and stung like sand under his lids.

'You're going to be all right?'

'Yes, yes.' She nodded.

He now closed his eyes and bowed his head as he muttered thickly, 'If only I'd been there.'

She smiled now, then with the shadow of her old self she said, 'There would have been a pair of us then and' – she now patted his cheek – 'Sister would never have let us have the beds in the same room.'

He gave her no answering smile but said, 'I'll have you out of here in no time.'

She didn't say, 'Yes, yes,' but what she said was, 'Give me a hankie, I want to dry my eyes.'

He dried them for her; but when he went to take her hand from her face she caught it and held it to her mouth for a moment, and then she said, 'I love you, Abel.'

The sand was stinging and burning his eyeballs; there was an implement as sharp as a knife grinding between his ribs, it was striving to reach his heart and tear it open. He had never laughed at the idea of people dying with a broken heart, perhaps the subconscious memory of Alice had caused him to accept this as a fact, but this pain that was in him now was so unbearable he felt that death would be preferable.

She said now, 'Have you seen Lucy?' and when he shook his head she murmured, 'Hilda's been so good. Always remember that, she's been so good.'

'What!' The name and the implication at this point brought him out of himself for a moment and he said again, 'What!'

'She's got Lucy.'

'Hilda?'

'Yes.'

He shook his head in disbelief.

'She's been to see me.'

Again he said, 'Hilda?' but got no further for the door opened at this point and the nurse appearing said, 'You'll have to leave. There's visiting tonight at seven.'

He got slowly to his feet and, bending down, once more put his lips to hers; but he said nothing more, he just looked at her, he looked deeply into her eyes and she read there the things that he could only say in the night.

When he reached the end of the corridor Dick was waiting for him. 'Is there a cloakroom around here?'

Dick pointed, saying, 'Yes, at the end of the corridor, turn right.' He walked with his father towards it, but did not follow him inside because he was thinking, He wants to cry. But when, five minutes later, his father appeared his eyes were dry. There were no signs of tears in them, and he thought that was strange for he usually cried when he was deeply moved. Had those months in prison hardened him? As they walked out of the hospital he stared at his father's profile, and the only answer he could give himself was, He's changed.

'What kind of a room is it?' asked Hilda.

He turned away towards the fireplace and hesitated before he said, 'Not much. It's clean though. He says it'll do for the present; it's better than the digs.'

'Whereabouts is it?'

He hesitated again, longer this time before answering, 'It's in Bartwell Place.'

'Bartwell Place?' Her voice was high. 'That's in Bog's End!'

'Well' – he turned towards her – 'it's the most convenient spot for him, it's halfway between the factory and the hospital.'

'How much is he paying for it?'

Dick was forced to smile here and she cried at him now, 'Well, there's no disgrace in being practical.'

'No, no, there's not, Mam.' He had fallen into the habit of calling her mam with an ease which was in a way a surprise to both of them, because she now accepted it as if it were her right, in fact she acted towards him now more as a mother would, not watching her every word in case he, too, would leave her.

'Well, what is he paying for it?'

'He didn't tell me and I didn't ask.'

'He'll have to have something different from that if he's to get her out.'

'He knows that and he's on the look-out for some place.'

'How . . . how soon do you think she'll be able to come out?' She was at the cupboard and her question was low, muttered as if she were speaking to someone inside it.

When he made no reply she turned to him and said, 'I was talking to you, I asked you . . .'

'Yes, I know you did, and I can't give you an answer.'

'Why?' She came towards him and they stood with the table between them looking at each other; then he said, 'I . . . I have me doubts as to whether she'll ever come out. It seems she's in a bad way. I was talking to one of the nurses.'

'You never said.'

'No, I know. But we should have surmised something, she's been down to theatre three times lately.'

After a moment she turned from the table and

went towards the crib and she looked down on the sleeping child as she asked softly, 'Does . . . does he ever speak of her?'

Again she had to turn to him and wait for an answer and when it came it was brief and he said, 'No.'

Dick now watched her bend over the child and adjust the blanket under its chin, and he realised that in a way she must be suffering as much as either Florrie or his father, because if his father did manage to get a bungalow and Florrie ever came out she would naturally want the child, and his father being who he was would see that she had her, and also someone there to help look after her. On the other hand, if Florrie died the child was all he would have left, and still being who he was, he would take it because although he hadn't mentioned it, it didn't mean that he didn't think about it. He had seen him holding his daughter, and when he held her he was holding the mother. Poor Hilda. Although he knew that she was grateful for his presence in the house, and for Molly's company too, it was the child that was bringing her comfort now, and as long as she could keep her it would go on doing so. But once it was taken from her she would be lost again.

Automatically he now went towards the wireless to switch on the news, and as he did so he thought there was so much tragedy in this house that it made him forget the greater tragedy of the war. It was strange but the war seemed to be of no consequence to him now. He didn't even think of the air force any more, what he thought about was the lack of happiness in those close to him. When you got down to rock bottom it was the personal issues that mattered. The woman with a broken back, the man who had never known happiness, and her standing across the kitchen there, the wife who had never really known what it was to be a wife.

He had said to Molly that they would be happy, in spite of all the emotional turmoil around them they would be happy; but what he had learned over these past weeks was that people were entwined one with the other, and that you couldn't isolate yourself from them and say, 'I am going to be happy', because their emotions penetrated you and cast a shadow over your happiness, they tinged your love with sadness and fear until you were being forced to believe that sadness and fear were part of love. He didn't want to see love like that, not his and Molly's love. He didn't want his life to be like his father's.

11

She had said to Dick, 'I'd like to see our Florrie, again;' and to this he had answered, 'The only clear time is a Wednesday afternoon because he's there every evening and Saturday and Sunday afternoon too.'

She had said, 'I'll go tomorrow then,' and so here she stood, holding in one hand a basket containing a box of home-made cakes and her month's ration of sweets, and in the other a bunch of flowers, and she was staring with stretching eyes and open mouth at the empty bed. It was stripped right down to the mattress.

When she dashed into the corridor she almost overbalanced two visitors approaching the ward, and now running towards the duty room she went straight in and gasped, 'Mrs Ford! Mrs Ford, where is she? Have they moved her?'

'Eeh! I know nothing about it.' A woman turned from the sink where she was washing dishes. 'You'll have to see the nurse or sister. Go to the office.'

She was in the corridor again; then she stopped and darted back into the kitchen. 'Where's the office?'

The woman looked at her as if she were mental

and said, 'Right afore you, in that door there where it says office.'

She turned about again and the next minute she was knocking on the door marked office. It was some seconds before it was opened by a nurse, and she gabbled at her, 'Mrs . . . Mrs Ford, where is she? Have . . . have they moved her?'

The nurse, holding the door-handle, looked back over her shoulder towards the sister seated behind the desk, and she, rising to her feet, came forward, saying, 'Come in. Please take a seat.'

When she took a seat the sister said, 'I'm very sorry but Mrs Ford died this morning. You should have got word, and a message was sent to the man who comes to visit her, but there was no reply, he must be out at work. Anyway, a note was left for him.'

She's dead! Florrie.

When she sprang up from the seat the sister took her arm, saying, 'Sit quiet for a moment,' but Hilda, shaking her off, muttered, 'No! no! I've got to get back and . . . and tell Dick; he's got to go and find his . . . his father.'

The nurse and sister looked at each other.

Hilda now went towards the door, then stopped and turning she asked flatly, 'Where've they put her?'

'In the mortuary.' The sister didn't add, 'Of course', but her tone implied the words.

'Oh! Oh!'

She ran along the corridor, out of the hospital, round by the bed that had once held flowers but was now showing the stripped stalks of brussels sprouts, and into the street.

There she hesitated and looked first one way and then the other before she turned in the direction of home, running one minute, walking the next, talking to herself all the way. Dick wouldn't be finished till five, but she could go to the factory and perhaps he could get off an hour earlier and go and meet his father and tell him, break it to him. That's what she would do, she would go to the factory. But she'd have to go home first and leave these things. The bairn would be all right with Molly. It was a good job she was on the night shift. Yes, yes. She was still gabbling to herself like someone demented.

As she went up the yard a man said, 'You not doing business any more, I've been waiting round here half an hour for me bike?'

'Oh, I'm sorry. Turnbull, isn't it?'

'Yes.'

'Just wait a minute.' She opened the kitchen door, threw the flowers and the basket on the table, picked up a bunch of keys from a nail, flung out of the kitchen again, locking the door behind her; then opening the garage door she again said, 'Turnbull?'

'Yes.'

'Here . . . here it is.'

'It's taken some time,' said the man; 'it's been here over a fortnight.'

She turned on him now angrily. 'Well, you know yourself we can't get labour, nor bits. You're lucky my son works in his spare time doing them.'

'He gets paid for it, doesn't he?'

She wheeled the bike forward and thrust it at him and when he said, 'What's the cost?' she ran into the office, looked up a narrow ledger and shouted towards him, 'Twelve and six,' and at this he shouted back at her. 'God! I could have got a secondhand one for that.'

She almost pushed him and the bike out of the garage; then having locked it she was running once more. It was a good fifteen minutes' walk to the munitions factory but she covered it in less than ten, and after making enquiries at the gate the porter, looking up a ledger, said, 'Gray, Dick Gray. Aye, number four shop. Along the end there.' He pointed . . .

Five minutes later she was walking out of the gate with Dick and he was saying, 'I knew it was coming, I knew it would happen, but not as quick as this.' She looked at his grease-smeared profile as she said, 'Do you . . . do you think he knew?'

'Yes, he was bound to. There's been a change in her these last two weeks but I knew he kept hoping. But he wouldn't expect it to be so sudden.'

When they came to the crossroads and their ways lay in different directions she confronted him squarely and quietly. She said, 'Stay with him as long as he needs you, I'll . . . I'll be all right. If . . . if I want company there's Molly. He'll have to see to the funeral and things, he'll . . . he'll need help.'

He looked at her steadily for a moment, then bending forward, he kissed her on the cheek before turning quickly away.

As she walked blindly homewards she kept repeating to herself, 'Oh! Florrie, Florrie!' and each time she spoke the name it was a plea for forgiveness. Since they were young she had slandered her, and since Abel had come into her life her jealousy had bred hate in her; and now she was gone, and it was too late to say to her, 'I'm sorry for all the things I said about you.'

When she reached the kitchen she sat down at the table without taking her hat and coat off, and laying her head on her arms she cried, and as she cried she talked to the woman who for years she had thought of as her sister, she talked to her as she had never talked to her in her life; and finally, before raising her head from the table she beseeched her, 'Please, Florrie, let me bring up your child. Let me keep her. Please. Please.'

12

Dick couldn't understand his father. That night he had met him outside the gates of the works. Although his very presence he knew must have conveyed to him why he was there, and he had given him the news as gently as possible, Abel had just stared at him, then walked on in the direction of Bog's End. Once, he had stopped and put his hand out against a lamp-post; his arm extended to its full length, he had stood supporting himself while he looked down at his feet; then had walked on again.

Inside the dingy room, Dick had expected him to give way but all he had done was to sit down and stare towards the gas ring that stood on the bare table next to the shallow sink. When he had said to him, 'Will I make you a cup of tea?' he answered by a shake of the head.

Not until he had mentioned the funeral did his father speak. 'The funeral will have to be arranged,' he said, and Abel answered, 'I'll see to that.'

After Abel had left the room to go to the outside toilet and when, twenty minutes later, had not returned, Dick had opened the back door to see a strange man standing in the yard. He was leaning against the doorway to the upstairs rooms, and he looked towards Dick while nodding towards the lavatory as he said, 'That bugger's takin' his time.'

When his father came out a few minutes later he passed the man without looking at him, and when he entered the room he said to Dick, 'You go home now; I'll be all right.'

'I'm not going to leave you like this.'

Abel had then turned and looked at him as if he were seeing him for the first time that night, and he said quietly, 'I'm going to be like this for a long time, lad, a long, long time, so you go home.'

Dick swallowed deeply. 'I'll go back and get a wash and change,' he said, 'but I'll be along later.'

'I might be out.'

'I'll be along anyway . . .'

Abel hadn't been out when he returned that night, nor the following four nights preceding the funeral . . .

The sun was shining and the frost glistened on the grass. Beside the minister and the grave-digger, the only people present at the graveside were his father, Hilda, and himself.

As the coffin was lowered into the earth, Dick took Hilda's arm and turned her away. Her face was red and swollen and the tears were running quietly down her cheeks. When they reached the chapel she said to him, 'I'll go.'

'He'll likely want a word with you.'

She shook her head vigorously now, saying, 'Oh no! No!'

'Wait nevertheless.'

When, at last, Abel left the graveside Hilda

watched him approach. It was the first time they had come face to face since the day she had thrown him out of the house. He stood before her now looking down on her, and he said quietly, 'Thanks, Hilda.'

What could she say? If she had thought of anything the words would have stuck in her throat. She just made a movement with her head.

'I'll . . . I'll take the child as soon as I get a fresh place.'

Now she actually started and, staring up at him, her words coming in a gabble, she said, 'It's all right. It's all right. As long as you like, I mean I'll look after her for as long as you like. Dick here' – she flapped her hand to the side – 'he can bring her to see you whenever you want and . . . and you can take her out and things, whenever you like.' Again her hand was flapping towards Dick. 'Dick will fetch her. I mean, he'll bring her to you.'

Abel nodded at her, saying, 'Thanks. Thanks, Hilda. It's very good of you. I appreciate what you're doing. I . . . I know it isn't easy.'

'Oh.' She shook her head in an emphatic denial of what he was saying, but when he went on, 'I'll . . . pay for her keep,' she almost cried at him in her old manner, 'Oh no! Please, please, don't. Spare me that, please.'

'Oh. Oh, I'm sorry. Well, just as you like . . . just as you say. But . . . but I'm grateful.' He stared at her for a moment longer; then turning slowly, he looked down the path to where the grave-diggers were still busy covering up his love, burying his love . . . No, not burying his love, he'd never be able to bury his love. He didn't want it to be buried, he wanted to suffer it to the end of his life, he wanted to hold the pain to him in the knowledge that it had been born of a rare thing, the thing that had taken years to hatch, but which when it had sprung into life had brought him happiness that could only be explained by the word ecstasy. Such happiness nearly always died in pain; all the great loves in history had been like this, they had all died in agony. But no matter what the payment, he wouldn't have forgone a moment of it. There was one thing that was surprising to him about Florrie's going, he had never cried over her; he had the strange feeling that at the present time his emotions would, if he were to cry, flow out in blood not water.

But Hilda was saying goodbye. He turned to her again, saying politely, 'Thank you. Thank you, Hilda.' Then he watched her walk away, and part of him marvelled at the change in her, there seemed to be no bitterness in her now. Florrie's death must have expunged it. Yet even before Florrie died Hilda was looking after the child. That must have taken some doing to take the child, his child, Florrie's child, into her home, into the God-protected home, in which sin was frowned upon. Oh no, no, he mustn't get back into that way of thinking. She was changed, something about her had changed radically. They were all changed. His son was changed.

He turned towards Dick now. His son was a man, and he was a good man. He would always be a good man, that was if there was not too much of himself in him, for then that would surely lead him into disaster. But on the other hand far better he inherited too much of himself than too much of his mother. This thought reminded him of the letter he had received only that morning. It was from his solicitor telling him that the divorce proceedings had begun.

He turned away towards the gates of the cemetery and as he went his mind said, 'I can marry Florrie now. I can marry Florrie now.' He stopped and gave a quick shake of his head and, looking at Dick, he said, 'Will you come back along of me?'

'Yes, of course. Where else do you think I'd go.'

13

For the next nine months they worked to a pattern. Either Dick or Molly would push the pram on a Saturday afternoon and a Sunday afternoon to Bartwell Place, and there they would leave the child with Abel.

That he enjoyed having her Dick was certain, for she was now walking and chatting in her own way. But he never took her outside the door. What he was also certain about was that Hilda didn't know a minute's peace until the child was returned home. He knew that her fear was that one day Abel would say, 'I've found a decent place and . . . a housekeeper.'

That word had been mentioned between them when discussing the child, but only once, and it was he who brought it up. What he had said was, 'He's looking for a place but as I told him he won't be able to manage without a housekeeper, because she's a handful now.'

She had turned on him with a shadow of her old temper crying, 'A housekeeper! The child looked after by a housekeeper! Oh, I know what house-keepers are, I've seen some of them.'

He almost read her thoughts. If her idea of a

housekeeper looked after the child, it would be with one aim in view: to hook the father.

He knew the very night that Hilda made up her mind about what she was going to do. It was when he and Molly and she were sitting before the fire and Molly said, 'We're going to be married next Easter, Aunt Hilda.' Hilda had looked from one to the other and replied softly, 'I'm glad, although' – she turned her eyes on to Dick – 'I'll miss me man about the house.'

'Huh!' He had punched his doubled up fist towards her. 'You'll hardly notice the difference, I'm in and out of both places all the time now, sometimes I feel I'm on a diabolo.' Then he had added, 'I intend to go on working at the factory when the war's finished, Mam, they're going to be needing spare parts for planes for some time yet.' He had given a hick of a laugh, then said soberly, 'I think you should make up your mind to get somebody permanently in the yard. As Molly's just said, we can see the end of the war and that can mean cars again and people mad for them, it could mean big business. Young Stephen's all right with bikes, but that's all . . .'

'Stephen isn't all right with bikes, he's fumble-fisted, he does more harm than good. And that's not the only thing' – she had jerked her chin upwards – 'I'm going to get rid of him as soon as I can, I'm telling you. He's as bad as Arthur Baines.'

It was the following day she said, 'How is he?'

He had just returned from carrying the child down to Abel's. He always carried her now if

406

possible, he hated pushing the pram. To her question he had answered, 'Oh, much as usual'; then taking the cup of tea she offered him, he placed it on the table and, sitting down on a wooden chair, he put his elbows on the arms of it and leant his body forward and almost groaned as he said, 'I always want to cry when I see him. That room, there would be more comfort in the workhouse. And he doesn't go out.'

'Is . . . is he drinking?'

'Drinking?' He turned his glance towards her. 'No, no; I shouldn't think so, I think he's saving every penny. I don't even think he eats properly, he's skin and bone, and . . . and he looks so lost. He can't go on like this.' He stared up into her face and repeated, 'He can't, something will happen to him. I'm . . . I'm surprised he hasn't tried to do something before now. I think he would have if it hadn't been for the bairn.'

She now seated herself by the side of the table and she traced her finger along the edge as she said, 'What is he saving for?'

'Oh, I don't know, except to set up a house somewhere.'

'And take Lucy?'

It was a long pause before he replied, 'Yes, I should say that's his idea. He's . . . he's very fond of her, he always waits for her coming.'

She was still tracing her finger along the table edge as she said slowly, 'I'll die, Dick, if he takes the child from me.'

'Oh! Mam.' He didn't move towards her, he just

stared at her, and for once he could find nothing to say in the way of comfort.

'She's all I've got. She's altered my life, I . . . I seem to see things differently now. I . . . I couldn't bear it if I lost her.' Her fingers stopped moving; she turned and looked at him, as if waiting for an answer to the solution of the problem, and when he gave it he knew he was only voicing something that was already in her own mind, and had been for some long time. 'The only way you could really keep her,' he said, 'would be to have him back,' and this she confirmed by saying softly, 'Yes, I know,' then added, 'but would he come back? That's the point, would he come back?'

'His divorce will be through shortly,' he said, only to be taken by surprise when she sprang up and shouted, 'I wasn't waiting for that. He could have come any time, I wasn't waiting for that.'

As he looked at her open-mouthed, he realised how greatly she had changed. This wasn't the Aunt Hilda speaking, Aunt Hilda could never have existed. He said now in an off-hand tone, 'What do you propose to do about it?'

'You'll see tomorrow.' She moved her head in small terse nods and said again, 'You'll see tomorrow.'

He was standing in the yard holding the pram, shaking it up and down assisted by Lucy who was gripping the sides and chattering unintelligibly but loudly as she did when she was happy, and what made her happy was bouncing the pram.

But he swung quickly around when Hilda came through the kitchen door, and he was still staring towards her as she turned her back on him to lock it.

'Well, what are you looking at?'

'Nothing.' He pushed the pram handle towards her, then walked a little behind her as she marched out of the yard.

She was made up. It was the first time he had seen her with lipstick on. He was sure she had rouge on too. And she was wearing her best coat, and he hadn't seen that hat before. Well! well! one could die from the shocks one got, but he hoped, oh, he hoped to God that there were no shocks awaiting her, that the charge she was about to make this afternoon would win her battle and bring her some happiness, eventually that is, and in doing so also bring peace to his father.

When twenty minutes later he knocked on the door and his father opened it he knew a moment of apprehension because he couldn't translate the look on his father's face as he stared at Hilda with the child in her arms.

It was Hilda herself who broke the spell. Her voice brisk yet quiet, she said, 'May I come in?'

'Oh yes, yes.' He pulled the door wide, then looked towards Dick who was saying, 'Shall I leave the pram out here today?'

'No, no; fetch it in, it wouldn't last two minutes out there.'

In the room they now stood looking at one another until Abel said, 'Oh. Oh, sit down.' He pulled a chair forward, but before Hilda took a seat she held out the child towards him, and when he took her into his arms he gazed at her for a moment and, her hand gripping his chin, she made a noise. 'She's saying, "Da-da",' he said.

Dick laughed. 'She's been saying it continually since yesterday,' he said.

'Oh,' Abel smiled at his daughter, who had Florrie's eyes and Florrie's mouth. When he kissed her on the cheek it brought the quick response of her arms around his neck and self-consciously, he again looked at Hilda. 'She . . . She's in fine fettle,' he said.

'Well, she's about the only one that is that I can see.'

'What! Oh, me? Oh, I'm all right.'

'Huh!'

Dick looked at his father's puzzled expression. The battle had begun and he wasn't ready for it. Would he surrender or would he stand out against her? Well, it remained to be seen how strong the enemy was; and the enemy was now on her feet.

Hilda had risen from the chair as abruptly as she had sat down, and now she was walking slowly around the room. The sight of it really appalled her and her surveying of it was definitely embarrassing Abel for he now said, 'I . . . I won't be here much longer, I've got a place in view.'

'Have you?' She was nodding at him. 'Well, by the look of you I don't think you will survive long enough to enjoy it.'

Again Abel turned his gaze towards Dick looking

for an answer, but all he got from this quarter was a slight raising of the eyebrows and an almost imperceptible movement of the head which said, 'Well, I know nothing about it.'

'Sit down, Abel.' She was standing in front of him, and he hitched the child from one arm to the other; then pulling the only other chair in the room forward, he sat down. Now their faces were almost on a level, and when she spoke her voice was firm but quiet as she said, 'Now don't interrupt me until I finish. You can't go on living in this mucky den any longer, it'll be the end of you. I've come to take you back home . . . *Don't. Don't. Don't.*' She put up her hand in the manner of a policeman directing traffic, then went on, 'I've said let me have me say. I . . . I don't want anything from you because you've got nothing to give, I know that, I've faced up to that, but I . . . I want to keep the child. And what's more I need a man about the place. Dick's going to be married shortly and I'll be there on me own, and I've got a fellow there now who's neither use nor ornament, and he's doing me out of money every day. You'll be doing me a favour if you come back. And I'm going to say it although I shouldn't, you owe me a favour, and this is the way you can repay it; so if you want to pay your debts get your few things packed and let's get out of this because it isn't fit for a pig to live in.'

He didn't move and the child was strangely still in his arms. They were both looking at her, the child at the woman who had become its mother, and he at the woman who had once thought she was his wife.

He, like Dick, noted with amazement that she was wearing make-up; he noticed, too, that she was no longer podgy; but what was most evident was the change within her. She was asking him to come back, she was offering him cleanliness, warmth, and good food . . . and comfort. The comfort of her? The first three he wanted, but would he ever again be able to take comfort from her . . . or any other woman for that matter? The question was a blank in his mind. He lowered his head and looked down at the worn oilcloth that he had not so long ago scrubbed on his hands and knees; then raising his head slowly, he looked at her and said, 'I'm still a married man, Hilda.'

'I'm well aware of that.'

He could have almost laughed. He said now, 'You've got your name to think about, there'll be talk. You can't stand up to that vicar about a thing like this.'

'I've already dealt with the vicar.'

Now he actually did want to laugh; and yet, no, he didn't, the feeling that was rife in him wasn't actually touching on laughter. But it wasn't touching on tears either. Oh no, no, he'd never cry again, now or ever.

His head was drooping once more when her voice checked it as she turned from him; saying briskly to Dick, 'Get your father's things together and let's be gone.'

As if he was fourteen, fifteen, or sixteen, scampering to do her bidding, Dick almost ran to the rickety cupboard and pulled a suitcase down from it, and having put it on the bed he opened the lid and began packing his father's few possessions. He did not turn towards them as he heard her voice saying quietly, 'Give her here,' but he knew she had taken the child and had put it in the pram and it was she who opened the door and pushed it into the street and there stood waiting.

His father was standing over by the door leading into the backyard and he said softly, 'Dick,' and as he approached him Dick could see that he was hardly capable of speech, and when the words tumbled out in a mutter, 'I don't know. It isn't right. I'm . . . I'm ashamed,' Dick gripped him by both arms and even attempted to shake him as he said, 'It's for the best. We all want you, and she needs you. And as she said, you owe her something. Don't forget that, Dad, you owe her something . . . you owe her a lot . . .'

A few minutes later they were all in the street and, like a family out for a Saturday afternoon walk, Hilda went on ahead pushing the pram while the father and son walked behind.

It wasn't until they entered the yard that Dick realised how deeply affected his father was. His face was devoid of colour, his cheekbones were pressing white through the skin, his eyes looked sunken in his head, and as he walked up towards the kitchen door he looked first to one side then to the other. His gaze remained longest on the window above the garage and his thoughts must have gone to the room that had afforded them shelter when they first came into this yard.

'There now. There now. Stop your yelling and I'll give you your tea in a minute. Here, you take her, Dick, and don't let her down on the floor yet, she's got her good things on.'

Dick paused with the child in his arms and he looked at Hilda with admiration. It was as if they really had just returned from a Saturday afternoon's outing. Then he looked towards his father. He wasn't sitting in the big wooden armchair near the fire but at the corner of the table. He was still wearing his overcoat and holding his trilby on his knee.

When Hilda said quietly, 'Give me your coat here,' he did not rise from the chair, nor did he look at her. Something was happening inside him, something had burst in his bowels like burning white lava. It was rising, spilling forth its fire through his ribs and up through his gullet. He yelled at it, screamed at it, 'No! no! Never! Not again! Never!' He could bear this, this humiliation, he could bear everything as long as he remained closed within himself, as long as he could withstand human kindness. As long as he could imprison his emotions nothing could touch him, but he was losing his power. The strength was flowing from him. He couldn't combat the force of this burning flood; he went down before it.

When the release came through his eyes, his nose and lastly his mouth, he gave a great cry and, burying his face in his hands, he rocked himself as a woman might in agony.

For a matter of seconds Hilda stood and watched him; then, putting her arms about him, she pressed his head into her breasts and, her own voice thick and choked, she comforted him, saying, 'It's all right. It's all right, you're home. It's all over. There now. There now. Come on, dear, come on.' She couldn't remember when she had called him dear, yet she called his child dear all the time.

When his hands left his face and went around her hips she did not delude herself for she knew that the action was to be compared to that of a child seeking comfort and protection.

She looked through her blurred streaming eyes to where Dick was still standing holding the child and she knew now that she had two children to care for, one to bring up into womanhood and the other she hoped to lead into peace. She did not ask that it should be into love; yet life could be long and she could but hope . . .

Dick stood, the child held close to him, and looked at his father. It seemed to him at this moment that he only ever saw the real man in his father when he was crying. His face was wet but he knew he would never cry like his father cried because he'd never be half the man he was. This man who had done nothing with his life except impinge it on four women had, he felt, in him something naturally big; perhaps it would show itself in the years ahead if only in bringing some happiness to the woman he had wronged and who was now savouring a certain joy from his agony.

THE END

A SELECTION OF OTHER CATHERINE COOKSON TITLES AVAILABLE FROM CORGI BOOKS

THE PRICES SHOWN BELOW WERE CORRECT AT THE TIME OF GOING TO PRESS. HOWEVER TRANSWORLD PUBLISHERS RESERVE THE RIGHT TO SHOW NEW RETAIL PRICES ON COVERS WHICH MAY DIFFER FROM THOSE PREVIOUSLY ADVERTISED IN THE TEXT OR ELSEWHERE.

All Transworld titles are available by post from:

Book Service By Post, P.O. Box 29, Douglas, Isle of Man IM99 1BQ

Credit cards accepted. Please telephone 01624 675137, fax 01624 670923, Internet http://www.bookpost.co.uk or e-mail: bookshop@enterprise.net for details.

Free postage and packing in the UK. Overseas customers allow £1 per book (paperbacks) and £3 per book (hardbacks).